PRAISE FOR *WATCH ME DISAPPEAR*

"Having already proven herself master of the page-turner with her two previous novels, [Janelle] Brown succeeds in crafting a narrative that is compulsively readable—it goes down like candy—but she also creates an empathetic portrait of a father and daughter flailing after the loss of the magnetic center that held their family of three together, all the while offering insight into the darker sides of motherhood and a failing marriage." —*Los Angeles Review of Books*

"*Watch Me Disappear* is a surprising and compelling read. Like the best novels, it takes the reader somewhere she wouldn't otherwise allow herself to go. . . . It's strongest in the places that matter most: in the believability of its characters and the irresistibility of its plot." —*Chicago Tribune*

"[Daughter] Olive's insights feel fresh and real. And, once disclosed, the reason for [her mother] Billie's disappearance is particularly satisfying."
—*The New York Times Book Review*

"A smoldering summer read with depth and insight."
—*New York*

"Janelle Brown's third family drama delivers an incisive and emotional view of how grief and recovery from loss can seep into each aspect of a person's life. . . . Brown imbues realism in each character, whose complicated emotions fuel the suspenseful story." —Associated Press

"*Watch Me Disappear* manages to be a thrill ride for mystery fans as well as a meditation on the gap between who people really are and who we want them to be." —*Harper's Bazaar*

"Like a darker, meatier *Where'd You Go, Bernadette,* Brown's latest explores the messy inner life of a mother just starting to feel invisible to her own family. This brilliantly layered novel is full of twists and turns, tender and biting and vibrant. Readers who can't get enough of the 'Girl'-type suspense trend will be more than satisfied with this tautly paced domestic drama." —*Booklist* (starred review)

"Brown's novel is more than just a page-turning suspense story. It's a gripping family drama that focuses on the choices we make and the ties that bind us to the ones we love." —*Publishers Weekly*

"Clever and compelling, this ricocheting tale reveals that, even in the closest families, how little we know of the ones we love, and how our own secrets are often the hardest to bear, can cost us dearly in the end."
—Lisa Gardner

"A riveting, seductive read . . . Brown has written a novel that provokes thought even as her story twists and turns. I loved it." —Sara Gruen

"Be careful: Once you start Janelle Brown's expertly crafted and wonderfully mysterious novel, you won't be able to stop." —Edan Lepucki

"Tantalizing and twisty, *Watch Me Disappear* is both a spider's web of a novel and a moving exploration of the deeper mysteries of marriage and family. You won't be able to put it down, but you won't forget it either." —Megan Abbott

"The plot is gripping enough: A woman's disappearance leaves her daughter and husband in a limbo that moves rapidly into true mystery, with ever-widening gaps between acceptance and doubt, memory and history, truth and lies—all very slippery and treacherous and thrilling. But the real magic of *Watch Me Disappear* is Brown's gift for evoking familial love in all its mad permutations—and the more intensely for the high stakes of what has been taken, and what is yet to be found. This is a story you simply don't want to end—but then, lord, what an ending!"

—Tim Johnston

"I devoured *Watch Me Disappear* in one sitting. In this poignant and captivating story of a missing woman and the family she left behind, Brown deftly peels away the layers of a loving marriage to reveal a haunting mystery and a devastating truth: that no matter how much you love someone, you can never truly know them." —Laura McHugh

"There's the family coping with loss and its attendant questions. There's the Manic Pixie Dream Girl who's revealed to be darker and possibly more dangerous than believed. There's the supernatural quality of Olive's visions (is there a medical explanation, and does it matter?). There's the natural shifting that happens in a family when children turn into teenagers, and there's the ode on perfect Berkeley motherhood. It's because the author deftly incorporates all these themes into one building mystery, however, that the book is so page-turning. Readers are likely to be unsure of which outcome would be most satisfying until the very end. Moody but restrained, this is a familiar tale that sets out to upend itself—and succeeds."

—*Kirkus Reviews*

BY JANELLE BROWN

All We Ever Wanted Was Everything

This Is Where We Live

Watch Me Disappear

Pretty Things

WATCH ME
DISAPPEAR

A Novel

JANELLE BROWN

 Ballantine Books · New York

Watch Me Disappear is a work of fiction. Names, characters,
places, and incidents are the products of the author's imagination
or are used fictitiously. Any resemblance to actual events, locales,
or persons, living or dead, is entirely coincidental.

2020 Ballantine Books Mass Market Edition

Published in the United States by Ballantine Books,
an imprint of Random House, a division of
Penguin Random House LLC, New York.

BALLANTINE and the HOUSE colophon are registered trademarks of
Penguin Random House LLC.

Originally published in hardcover in the United States
by Random House, an imprint of Random House, a division of
Penguin Random House LLC, in 2017.

Grateful acknowledgment is made to Riverhead,
an imprint of Penguin Publishing Group, a division of
Penguin Random House LLC, for permission to reprint
"Gott spricht zu jedem . . . / God speaks to each of us . . ."
from *Rilke's Book of Hours* by Rainer Maria Rilke, translated
by Anita Barrows and Joanna Macy, translation copyright © 1996
by Anita Barrows and Joanna Macy. Reprinted by permission of
Riverhead, an imprint of Penguin Publishing Group, a division of
Penguin Random House LLC. All rights reserved.

ISBN 978-0-593-16028-2
Ebook ISBN 978-0-8129-8947-2

Cover design: Scott Biel
Cover images: © Mark Owen/Trevillion Images (woman);
Martin Ruegner/Digital Vision/Getty Images

Printed in the United States of America

randomhousebooks.com

2 4 6 8 9 7 5 3 1

Ballantine Books mass market edition: August 2020

To Auden & Theo

WATCH ME DISAPPEAR

PROLOGUE

IT'S A GOOD DAY, or maybe even a great one, although it will be impossible to know for sure later. By that point they'll already have burnished their memories of this afternoon, polished them to a jewel-like gleam. One of the last days they spent together as a family before Billie died: Of course Jonathan and Olive are going to feel sentimental about it. Of course they will see only what they want to see.

Still, Jonathan will think, on the spectrum of all their days together, ranging from *that time the whole family got food poisoning at Spenger's Fish Grotto* to *the day Olive was born,* this one certainly ranks closer to the top.

It is, for one thing, a clear sunny day, which is no small piece of luck when you're on a Northern California beach in October. The sand is actually warm between their toes, instead of dank and gritty; but the air also has the crisp autumnal bite that makes you want to wrap yourself in something soft. No one acts crabby, or restless, or bored. Billie has packed some particularly delicious sandwiches—pesto chicken for the adults, hummus for Olive (who has recently gone vegetarian)—and they wash these down with tepid cocoa from a thermos.

After they eat their lunch, Billie and Jonathan sit on the beach while Olive goes down to the water's edge and mucks about barefoot in the surf. There's a tree-sized piece of driftwood that's been deposited near the crest of the tide line, and Jonathan sits with his back braced against this. He's brought printouts of a half-dozen *Decode* features that urgently require his attention, but the whole point of the day was family time, to compensate for all those days and nights vacuumed up by his job. Besides, how can he focus on narrative coherence and Oxford commas when the tide is low and the surf is high?

Billie uses Jonathan's bent legs as her chair, her long hair draping down his thighs. She studies the surfers bobbing out at the break as she scoops up sand and lets it trickle through splayed fingers, absently picking out rocks and twigs. Jonathan reaches out and takes a strand of her hair, one of the silver threads that are starting to lace through the dark brown. He rubs it gently between his fingertips, testing its texture, testing the temperature of his wife.

"What are you, a monkey?" Billie says. She's built a tower of smooth stones, and she examines it, then flattens it again.

"Still hungry. Looking for snacks," he says. He looks up to see Olive at the edge of the water, studying them from a distance. He waves at his daughter, and she arcs her own arm back in a half-moon of acknowledgment. She looks happy, but sometimes it's hard to tell: Her down-turning mouth frowns even as it smiles, contradicting itself. A wave washes up the sand, licking at her bare toes, and she dances away from it.

Billie follows his gaze. "How is she going to manage?"

He releases her hair. "What do you mean?"

"In life. The world is tough on soft things. She's going to need to grow a thicker skin or she's going to spend her whole life being too afraid to try anything."

Jonathan studies his daughter, silhouetted by the crashing sea. She's spied something beneath her feet—a shell or a hermit crab or a piece of trash—and her brow furrows as she leans down and picks it up to examine it. He feels a flash of empathy for her, the bookish child he used to be in silent communion with the child she is. "She's just sensitive. That's normal for fifteen."

"I was *bold* at that age," Billie says crisply.

"You were not the typical kid," Jonathan says. Billie laughs at this and tips her head backward over Jonathan's knees to smile at him. There's sand speckling her cheekbones, stuck in the delicate lines around her eyes, and he gently wipes it away. "Anyway, Olive is tougher than you're giving her credit for."

She lifts her head and examines their daughter in the distance. "OK. Good."

"If you're so worried, talk to her," he adds.

"I tried when I took her hiking last month. Didn't go well." She sits upright and leans forward and away from him, running a hand through the tangle of her hair. "She used to soak up every word I uttered like it was gospel. She doesn't do that anymore." Jonathan notes the edge of pained querulousness in her voice.

"Oh, please. She still worships you," he says. "She's just a teenager, she's individuating. Keep trying, she'll come around soon. And it's good for her to know you care." As Jonathan watches Billie, he thinks that the person it *really* would be good for is his wife, who perhaps needs to feel needed by their daughter again. You don't realize how much you'll miss the asphyxiating intimacy of early parenthood until you can finally breathe again.

"Always the optimist, my Jonathan." She says this as she's looking out to sea, her words swallowed up by the pounding surf, so that for a moment he's not sure he's heard her right.

He blinks, a flush of gratitude. "Billie? I still think—"

But she cuts him off, her words cooling quickly: "I can tell by your tone of voice where you're going, and *don't*. Just don't. I don't want to talk about it."

Down at the other end of the beach, the group of surfers has emerged from the sea, and they strip their wetsuits back like banana peels, bare flesh emerging from black neoprene. The boys jostle up against the girls, crowding their space, grabbing at their towels while the girls pretend to be indignant. Billie carefully wipes the sand from her hands as she stares at the surfers, the muscles in her back going taut under the thin cotton of her T-shirt. Jonathan wonders if she's seeing a former version of herself in the girls, in their loose-limbed freedom, in the way they demand that the entire beach notice them. He remembers that Billie—the girl he fell in love with sixteen years earlier, and honestly, not *so* much changed—and he reaches out to massage the tenseness away, but she shrugs him off.

They sit there like that for a while, silently watching the surfers collect their towels and then disappear in the opposite direction. Once they're out of sight, Billie's shoulders go slack. She stretches, lets out a muffled sound that's a cross between a sigh and a groan. "You know, I might do a backpacking trip one of these weekends soon. Maybe up the Pacific Crest Trail."

"Again? With Rita?"

"No, by myself." She gives a little laugh. "You know, just me alone with my thoughts."

"Sounds nice. But is that such a good idea?" he says, hiding a small hiccup of anxiety: *Alone with what thoughts?*

Billie ignores this and stands up, crumpling the waxed paper from her sandwich with efficient finality. She beckons to Olive, who walks toward her mother with her hands full of some algae-covered flotsam that she's plucked from the sea. "If we're going to see those butterflies before it gets too late, we should head up," Billie announces. She turns and jogs up the dunes without checking to see if her husband and child are following her.

The monarch preserve is crowded, but not with butterflies. The arrival of the annual migration was announced in the local news earlier that week, and apparently Billie wasn't the only one to flag the story, because the tourists are out in force. Olive trails after her parents as they wander up and down the wooden walkways, craning her neck to scan the trees. The occasional butterfly flutters by overhead, an orange fleck backlit by the sun. The place is loud with the squeals of kids and shouting parents, unlike the reverent, hushed temple to nature that Olive had imagined. She dodges a woman now, followed by another, all of them busily Instagramming any old insect that flits by, as their children lunge at the butterflies with sticky hands. Alarmed, Olive wants to shout: Don't they know that if they touch the butterflies' wings, they'll die? Did no one teach them to Leave No Trace? She looks around at the overflowing trash cans, the parents wielding aerosol sunscreens, and worries that this is why there aren't more butterflies here today. Or is it global warming, pesticides? So many potential reasons why the monarch population is declining precipitously; she should really get her mother to plant milkweed in the garden.

Her mother disappears for a while, wandering off without warning, as she sometimes does. But as Olive turns back along the path, she hears Billie calling her name. Olive follows the sound of her mother's voice and finds her lying on her back in a little hidden corner of the wooden walkway. She has her hands crossed over her belly, the collar of her fleece zip-up spread underneath her head as a pillow.

Olive lies down beside her mother on the sun-warmed wood. She follows Billie's finger to where she is pointing. There, directly above them, the eucalyptus trees are pulsing. Hundreds of monarch butterflies are clinging to the branches, their wings moving in syncopation. The leaves droop under their weight, swinging heavily in the breeze.

Olive's breath stops in her throat, something huge and beautiful aching within her.

"Why do you think they come here?" her mom asks in a low voice. "Of all the places in the world they could go, they come here, to this *zoo*, every winter. Couldn't they find a secret place, somewhere they could be more alone? Or do you think they want to be here, where people are? That they instinctually want to be seen?"

Olive considers this. "I think it's dew hydration and wind protection. There's a sign at the entrance. That's what butterflies need most, and they get it from the eucalyptus and the fog off the ocean."

Billie flaps her hand as if thrusting this explanation aside. "There are lots of other places with eucalyptus up and down the coast that they could choose. They come back here, to this *one place*, despite the hordes." She is quiet for a minute, watching the butterflies clustering above them, as thick as barnacles on the eucalyptus leaves. "All that glory. And the worst part of it is, no one here really appreciates what they've been allowed to see. Instead they take this precious thing and just fuck it up."

There is an odd, angry hitch in Billie's words. Olive turns her head to look at her mom. Billie has her eyes closed tight, but a tear has escaped from one corner and is slowly working its way down toward her earlobe. "Mom?" Olive says, alarmed. "I'm sure the butterflies are OK here. It's a sanctuary, right? So *someone's* watching out for them."

"I know." Billie's eyes are still closed, but she turns to rest her face in Olive's hair before turning back to gaze up at the butterflies. Olive hears footsteps on the boardwalk, and then her dad is lying down next to her. He reaches across Olive for her mom's hand. They lie there like that for a while, Olive's parents' hands clasped over her body, silent. It feels like they are breathing in time with the pulsing of the butterflies and the swaying of the trees. In the distance, Olive can hear the waves crashing against the rocks.

Finally, a pack of schoolchildren comes thundering along the walkway, and the butterflies lift in unison and fly off in search of a safer branch. As the three of them also rise, Billie dries her face with the back of her sleeve, and Jonathan snaps a family selfie for posterity (their last family photo, and it's not a good one, Billie's face blurry as she tries to avoid getting her picture taken; and Jonathan squinting from the sun; only Olive in clear focus), and then they head back down the path toward their car.

As they drive back home—Billie nodding off in the front seat, Olive absorbed by her iPhone in the back—Jonathan thinks about his wife's tears and smiles. He assumes that Billie, like him, was touched by the grace of that moment: the fragile butterflies triggering an exquisite consciousness of the miracle of existence, of the growing girl lying between them, of the stretch of days stringing out behind them. Of the days that he believes are still ahead.

1

OLIVE IS CROSSING from the Sunshine Wing to the Redwood Wing, on her way to her third-period English class, when her dead mother appears for the first time. Weaving through the eddies of girls, twenty-six pounds of textbooks tugging at her shoulder, the blue skirt of her uniform clinging stubbornly to her thighs, Olive suddenly feels as if she might faint. She assumes at first that she is just overheating. Claremont Prep is housed in a rambling nineteenth-century Craftsman mansion that has been neglected in the name of "authenticity"—the knobs to the classrooms are all original cut crystal and spin uselessly when you turn them, and the windows don't actually open because they've been lacquered over too many times, and Olive often has to take cold showers after badminton practice because the boiler can't keep up with the demand of twelve girls simultaneously shaving their legs—and on rainy days, like this one, the overworked furnace fills the hallways with a moist fug of girl-scented heat.

Olive stops and presses her hand against the cool glass of a display case to stabilize herself. She digs in her backpack for a bottle of water and closes her eyes. She feels as if she is standing at the center of a turntable, the hallway whipping around her in dizzying circles. She catches an acrid whiff, as if something is burning.

When she opens her eyes again, she is somewhere else entirely. Or, rather, she is still in the main hall of Claremont Prep—she senses the thrum of bodies swinging past, the drumming of the rain against the stained-glass clerestory windows—but somehow she is also somewhere else entirely. A beach, to be exact.

The beach isn't really there, *of course it's not*, and yet . . . there it is: the overcast sky, the pebbly sand, the dunes lashed with sea grass, waves that are dark and hungry. She can almost feel her Converse sneakers shifting in the sand, the salty air sticking to her skin. This alternate world seems to exist as an overlay draped across her surroundings: Through the waves Olive is dimly aware of two other junior girls—Ming and Tracy—hanging up posters for the Fall Frolic; and just behind the ragged dunes is a line of lockers; and somewhere inside that thrashing surf is the double-doored entrance of the Redwood Wing. It is as if the two worlds exist simultaneously, each overlapping the other, a kind of waking dream.

She blinks. It doesn't go away.

The time they gave her nitrous at the dentist's of-

fice: That's how she feels now, her brain opaque, diffuse, as if someone has reset its dial at half speed. Time seems to have stopped, or at least slowed. She senses her body tipping backward, the backpack full of books losing the battle against gravity. The third-period bell is ringing somewhere faintly in the distance.

That's when she sees her mother.

Billie stands a few yards away, right where the sea meets the sand, the water slapping at her bare toes. It is as if she's been standing there the whole time and Olive has only just grown aware of her.

Her mother's hair is long and loose, the brown giving way to silver at the part. It flies in a wild halo around her face. She is wearing a gauzy white dress that whips around her bare legs as the wind blows off the sea, its hem dark with ocean spray. Her mom was never a wearer of dresses (she tended toward performance fleece), so this strikes Olive as slightly weird (*as if nothing else happening here is weird?*), but still. It's *her. Mom.* Olive feels the word swell up inside her, painfully filling her lungs until it stops her breath entirely.

"Olive!"

Despite her diaphanous appearance, Billie's voice isn't at all spectral; it's strong and clear, as if right inside Olive's brain, and loud enough to drown out the frothy shrieks of the girls down the hall. Olive opens her own mouth and gasps out the only word that she can muster: *"Mom?"*

"Olive," Billie says, her voice lower now, almost chiding. "I miss you. Why aren't you looking?"

"Looking for what?" She's hallucinating, isn't

she? She isn't *really* talking to her dead mom. She closes her eyes and opens them again.

Her mom is still there, looking amused. She smiles, revealing deep grooves in her sun-etched face, and she outstretches her hand as if to take Olive's own. "Olive," she says with a note of disappointment in her voice. "You aren't trying hard enough."

There's a burning sensation in Olive's chest that's making it hard to breathe. "I'm trying as hard as I can, Mom," Olive whispers, tears welling up in her eyes, but the weird thing is that she doesn't feel sad, not at all. She feels almost . . . transcendent, as if she's *thisclose* to getting the answer to some vital question that will make everything clear.

And then it comes to her, the answer she's waiting for. It floods her with a giddy rush: *Mom isn't dead.*

Olive lurches forward with the force of this epiphany. Where did it come from? She takes a step toward her mother, and then another as her mother's figure starts to fade and recede before her; and then she starts to run, although it feels like she is running through wet cement. She feels the backpack slip off her shoulder and slam to the floor behind her. She understands that she needs to grab her mother's outstretched hand, and that if she can somehow seize it, she will be able to drag her mother through that translucent overlay and back to her, back into Olive's world, back to . . .

Wham. She runs straight into the wall.

Olive is momentarily blinded with pain—a goose egg will later rise on the spot where forehead connected with plaster—and when she can finally see again, her mother is gone.

The world comes collapsing back in around her: the rank locker smell of dirty gym clothes and spoiling bananas, the squeak of rubber soles on waxed oak, and the thrilled faces of the three gaping freshmen who have gathered around her, so close that she can feel the heat of their gummy breath.

"OhmyGodareyouOK," says one freshman, an unfortunately pimpled blonde whom Olive has never spoken with before (Holly? Haley?). She leans in as if to touch the lump on Olive's forehead, and Olive flinches.

"I'm fine, thanks for the concern, really, but it's no big deal," Olive says, smiling apologetically as she backs away. She clocks her backpack on the ground a few feet away and sidles toward it. Ming and Tracy, still on ladders at the end of the hall, have stopped what they are doing and are watching with overt fascination the tableau playing out before them. She waves at them. Tracy waves back with a silly little finger-wiggle, but Ming just stares at Olive, her brow puckering behind the severe curtain of her black bangs.

Meanwhile the three freshmen are following closely behind Olive, not ready to give up rubbernecking quite yet. "You just ran straight into the wall," Haley/Holly says accusatorily. "It was kind of crazytown."

Olive reaches down and grabs her backpack. Its weight in her hand grounds her, and she swings it over her shoulder, then tugs her skirt straight. The presence of the girls makes it hard to hang on to the answer that she just had in her grasp, and she desperately wants to escape so she can think all this over, figure it out. "Honestly, it's nothing," she says. The girls continue to peck around her, unsatisfied. *Oh, please let me be alone,* she thinks. "Just," and her voice drops as if letting them in on a secret, "I'm a little hungover. You know?"

"Ohhhhh," the girls say in low knowing voices that fail to conceal their utter unknowingness. Not that Olive knows much, either—she's been hungover exactly once in her life, after a sleepover at Natalie's house during which she polished off half of a leftover bottle of Christmas crème de menthe. But one thing she's learned during her five-year career at Claremont Prep is that underclass girls believe there are secrets to a better life that will someday be unlocked, like the upper levels of a videogame, once they are able to drive a car or procure alcohol or get their braces off. She wishes she could tell these girls that things get easier, but in her experience they don't. Not really. (With the possible exception of being able to drive yourself: That *is* pretty great.) You just discover that there are even bigger, more complicated problems that you have to solve.

In any case, with this small untruth, Olive is at last able to untangle herself. She continues to walk in the direction of the Redwood Wing, aware that the girls are whispering behind her. (She hears just a snippet: *You know, the girl with the dead mom . . .*) And then, as the warning bell rings, she turns abruptly and exits to the courtyard.

The October air is sharp and wet against her face. She stands under the eaves, the rain splattering the rubber shells of her Converses, and tries to focus. *Mom isn't dead.* She allows herself this thought again, gingerly, as if she's metering out a particularly tasty piece of chocolate cake. The storm rushes through the oak trees, sending a shiver across them, and Olive realizes that she's trembling.

She finds herself thinking about her mother's books. Years earlier, when Olive was in seventh grade, Billie had given her a dog-eared collection of Lois Duncan novels that she'd found at a yard sale. "These were my favorite books when I was your age," Billie told Olive, dropping them on her desk. "My parents didn't allow me this kind of stuff—my dad was a preacher, he called them *devil books,* he wanted me reading the Bible instead—but I'd hide them under my bed anyway and read at night with a flashlight." She spread the books out, examining them with a faint smile.

"I'm supposed to be reading *The Adventures of Huckleberry Finn,*" Olive had said, secretly skeptical of the mass-market covers and broken-down spines.

Billie wrinkled her nose. "That racist old saw? I'll tell you what happens: Tom finds the gold, and the widow adopts Huck," she said. "Now. Read these. They'll never give you these kinds of books in school, even though *this* is the stuff that's really fun. God, junior high is so dull and confining. Don't let them box you in with those dreary assigned-reading lists."

Olive was thrilled by this—her mother, openly defying authority—and so, that night, she began flipping through the first pages of *Down a Dark Hall.* It turned out to be a story about a boarding school called Blackwood where telepathic kids are forced into servitude by an evil headmistress, Madame Duret, who uses them to channel the spirits of famous dead artists. Immediately, despite herself, Olive was hooked:

> She did not sleep well at Blackwood. She dreamed. She knew that she dreamed, for when she woke in the mornings the feeling of the dreams still clung to the edges of her mind, and yet in most cases she could not remember what they had been.

I know that feeling, Olive had thought. She often woke up in a state of vague panic, sensing that something had happened in the dark over which she had no jurisdiction. She would lie there with her heart pounding, terrified and awed by this sense that there was something bigger than she was, something that was just out of her grasp, something she needed to understand to make everything settle properly into place.

She finished *Down a Dark Hall* before she went to sleep that night, then demolished the rest of the pile by the end of the month: the book about the girl who can astral project, the book about the girl who can read minds, the book about the girl who has visions about people halfway across the world. There *was* something freeing about all the possibility contained in these books, of transformation just over the horizon. Secret worlds unfurled before her, inviting her in. *What if?* she would ask herself with a delicious shudder. *What if it's all true?*

What if? She stands there in the Claremont Prep courtyard now with her eyes closed, the rain soaking through her shoes as she thinks of phantoms, and visions, and possibility. Her mind keeps settling back in the same place: *What if Mom is still alive, somewhere, and she has reached out to let me know?*

Rationally speaking, it isn't *completely* beyond reason, given the circumstances of Billie's death.

For the last year, ever since the accident, Olive has felt like she's been in a constant state of waiting: waiting for Billie to walk through the door, waiting for her cellphone display to light up with the word MOM, waiting for her mother's voice to waft up the stairs calling her down for dinner. It's as if her mom is always just offstage, about to enter, but keeps missing her cue. Maybe Olive has felt that way for a reason: Maybe, deep in some part of her brain that no one really understands, she has secretly known that her mom isn't actually gone.

She thinks of her mother's outstretched hand. *Why aren't you looking?* And it's obvious, suddenly, what she meant: *Why aren't you looking for me?*

"Olive." A voice yanks her back to the present. Her eyes fly open to see Mrs. Santiago, the school counselor, standing in front of her, her stout body swathed in voluminous layers of earth-tone knit-wear. "Don't you have English with Mr. Heron right now?"

"I needed a little fresh air," Olive says. "I was just about to go in."

Mrs. Santiago scrutinizes Olive's face. "Do you need to visit the school nurse?" She twists her lips, and her brown eyes grow soft as—Olive can see it coming a mile away, she has seen it a thousand times in the last year, this well-intentioned but exhausting concern that, honestly, often feels more about *them* than *her*—she reaches out and grips Olive's upper arm. "Or do you need to talk, hmm? I know it's almost the anniversary of your mother's . . . Well. It's very normal to be having emotional feelings right about now."

Feelings. Yes, she has one. Olive smiles, a grin so wide that Mrs. Santiago's hand slides off and hangs with quizzical surprise in midair. "I'm fine," she says. "Thanks for your concern, Mrs. Santiago. But honestly, I feel great."

And she does. She feels *great* as she heaves the backpack up and cradles its bulk in her arms, thrusting the courtyard door open with her shoulder. She glances at the hall clock—five minutes past ten—and begins to run, and that feels amazing, too, light and free. Behind her, Mrs. Santiago is watching her with bafflement and in most likelihood making a mental note to get Olive back in for a psychiatric evaluation, but Olive doesn't care.

My mom isn't dead after all. This conviction grows, pulsing through Olive as she runs through the Redwood Wing, past the glass case prominently displaying her science fair model of a vertical-axis wind turbine; past her own locker, smelling faintly of the dried lavender sachets she keeps there because they remind her of her mother's shampoo; past the administration offices where she once spent endless hours dutifully filling in "grief worksheets" with Mrs. Santiago, which didn't make her feel better at all. But now—*now* she feels great.

Why aren't you looking for me? You aren't trying hard enough. She realizes now that she has been summoned. By her mother. Who supposedly died a year ago. Summoned—where? To do what? It makes no sense at all, and yet somehow it seems so very clear. She thinks of that line in the book that she read all those years ago—*the feeling of the dreams still clinging to the edges of her mind*—and for the first time, she thinks she knows what it is she's been dreaming of.

By the time she swings herself down into her seat—*Waiting for Godot* flung open on the desk before her, Mr. Heron winking at her from the front of the classroom as he taps the face of his Apple watch with a finger—Olive is certain. Her mother is still alive out there, somewhere, and Olive needs to try harder, much harder, to find her.

WHERE THE MOUNTAIN MEETS THE SKY

My Life with Billie Flanagan

———

BY JONATHAN FLANAGAN

I read, not long ago, about a psychologist who claimed that he'd made two strangers fall in love in his research lab: All it took was thirty-six probing questions and four minutes of staring into each other's eyes. This could work for just about any potential couple, the doctor wrote. "Love," as he'd manifested it, was not an unfathomable mystery—not some cryptic brew of chemical attraction and compatible personalities and a shared passion for cowboy poetry or Russian opera; not kismet, luck, or fate—but a simple matter of openness to intimacy. Take two people with a mutual willingness to connect, convince them to expose their innermost thoughts, and presto: true love.

There's part of me—the pragmatic left-brain part, honed by journalism school and nearly two decades at a news publication—that appreciates the logic in this. With seven billion people on the planet, it would make sense that instead of one true love you would have a multitude of potential connections in search of reciprocity. But the other part of me—the part that loved one woman and one woman only my entire adult life—finds this "love quiz" notion depressingly clinical. It sounds like rats in a cage, learning to press the proper combination of buttons to receive their food pellets, and that can't be right.

Because there *was* something magical about my immediate connection with Billie. From the very first moment, that soggy evening when she burst through the closing doors of the rush-hour J Church streetcar, rain flying off her, and plopped herself into the last available seat, which had just opened up next to me. Like a kite, sailing through a storm right to me.

She turned to me, water trickling down her face, and she said something that I couldn't quite hear over the Smashing Pumpkins song blasting from my Discman. Later, Billie would tell me that she'd simply commented about the weather, but as I fumbled with my headphones I could have sworn that she'd said *There you are*. As if she'd known all along that we would find each other there, on that crowded Muni car. The floating, wistful chords in my ears, the steam coming off her skin: Who was I to argue with this luminous girl with the fairy-like pixie haircut, laughing as she wrung the rain from her dripping clothes? She had somehow sucked all the light from the bus and drawn it into herself.

So I echoed her words, thrilling to them—*Here I am*— and she smiled back at me, her entire face brightening with delight. That was it for me. There was no need to ask her about her "most treasured memory" (question 17) or to make "three true 'we' statements" (question 25): I knew that our life together had begun.

Six weeks later, we were engaged. Looking back at those weeks, I remember them the way a drug addict probably recalls a bender: as a giddy blur, time that seemed to disappear into a single throb of annihilating emotion, chased by a dim awareness that I was dancing on a precipice.

Billie was beautiful, with the kind of unforgettable face you see in old movies—a study in dark and light, pale skin and black eyes, an elfin chin and freckled cheekbones—and she was also an aspiring artist, which of course thrilled me. Four years older than me, she possessed a worldliness that I aspired to. But what I loved most about Billie was her capacity for joy, her fearless abandon. Sure, I liked indie rock and often drank too much—who in San Francisco didn't back then?—but Billie introduced me to Ecstasy, and skinny-dipping in Lake Merced, and driving around on rented motor scooters at night, taking photographs. I never knew what to expect with her. She destabilized me.

By the time I met Billie on that bus, I had managed to make myself a minor name in the fish tank of San Francisco's incipient tech journalism scene. As a junior writer at *Decode* magazine, I would stand around at parties on South of Market rooftops, my hoodie pulled up against the fog, and make proclamations like "There's no real freedom until all information is free" and "The true democracy of the digital revolution spells the end of traditional power structures." And when I sat down in front of my computer and wrote these things down, they got published and read by hundreds of thousands of people, and that somehow made them true. I was twenty-six years old in the new millennium and the whole world was changing and I was at the very forefront of it.

And yet, with all the thrilling things happening around me, Billie was the only part of it that really took my breath away. I'd spent my career that far writing about what the world was like, but she'd actually been out there *living* in it:

She'd lived through an abusive childhood with tyrannical, religious parents; lived through running away her senior year of high school; lived through an itinerant radical phase in the Pacific Northwest with a drug-dealer boyfriend, a period she referred to as her Lost Years. Her diminutive Tenderloin apartment was hung with artifacts from her years of world travel: Indian saris, Balinese carvings, Turkish pottery. She even had the scars, emotional and physical, to prove just how much she'd lived: the faint holes in her eyebrows and nose from old piercings, the blurred flesh on her calves where her regrettable tattoos had been lasered off, the way her gaze went someplace far away when she talked about her childhood.

Six weeks after we met, Billie took me for a midnight picnic on a secret rocky peak above the Castro where the view was, she promised, "tremendous." There we sat, collars turned up against the freezing wind, drinking cheap Chianti straight from the bottle and looking out at the endless stream of taillights passing through the city below us.

"Look at all those people," I remember her saying. "Like locusts. Eating and drinking and shopping and going about their business without a bigger thought in their heads. Just plowing down anything that gets in their way without realizing what they are doing to the planet." She cocked a finger at a yellow Hummer barreling down Market Street and pulled an invisible trigger.

I loved this: the righteous activist, passionately opinionated. "Sure. But think of the flip side of that," I said. "Think about what a miracle it is that we're all working in concert with one another. Every day humans get a fresh chance to decide whether we're going to destroy each other or build a better world, and you know what? For the most part, we do the latter."

She laughed. "You really believe your own propaganda." But she turned to study my face. "Seriously, you're so upbeat. I love that about you. I can't decide if you're the smartest person in the room or the most naïve. I hope we all get to live in your world." She reached out and slipped her hand into the pocket of my hoodie, sliding a cold palm into mine. Her voice grew thick. "I guess I've seen things that you haven't. It's made me pessimistic. Growing up with my parents telling me I was going to go to hell, and then all those years with Sidney, who took me into some bad places . . . it changes you, you know? You never trust people after that."

I gripped her palm, warming it with my own. I'd had a painful childhood, too—my sister, Jenny, died in front of me, a swimming pool accident, when I was eight—but it was full of love. Billie couldn't claim the same. When we were together I felt this imbalance acutely, as if I needed to make some transfer of the abundance that life had gifted me. When she lay quiet in my arms I could feel her racing heart, sense something broken underneath her tough shell. It pained me to know that she'd been damaged by people who hadn't loved her enough. How could I possibly fix that?

"You trust *me*, don't you?" I asked.

She turned to look at me. "I do," she said thoughtfully.

"Then let's get married," I heard myself saying.

She stared at me with surprise, as if suddenly seeing me for the first time. "You're insane. We just met," she said, shaking her head, but I could see by the fire in her eyes that she was secretly pleased.

It was insane. And yet in Billie, I felt like I'd found a missing part of myself, someone whose bold life complemented my own intellectual bravado. If this was what love was—the feeling of giddy expansion mixed with raw vulnerability, the sense that someone finally understood the texture of my heart—I knew I would be crazy not to seize it.

"I mean it," I said. "I love you. I want to make you happy. Let me take care of you."

She laughed and squeezed my hand so tightly that it hurt. "I thought I'd been taking care of myself since I was a teenager."

"Everybody needs someone to take care of them," I replied. "Whether they know it or not."

She looked at me for a long time. "You're right." She leaned in and kissed me hard. "OK. Let's do it. I love you. Let's get married."

And so we did, two near-strangers jumping off a cliff together. For sixteen years, I tried my hardest to live up to that promise: to watch out for her, be her safe harbor. We made a beautiful life together, raised a beloved child, and built a nice home, at which point I must have forgotten my vigilance.

Because in the end, I didn't manage to keep her safe at all.

2

THE CLAREMONT MOMS are circling. They flutter around Jonathan, a flock of predatory birds in lululemon and boyfriend jeans; hair freed from ponytail elastics in order to swing flatteringly around faces, shoulders thrown back in order to lift chests up to pre-breast-feeding heights. They hold voluble debates about tutoring schedules and real estate prices and the senior snow trip, only a few feet away from where Jonathan stands in the parking lot, their bodies angled *just so* in an invitation for him to join the conversation.

He sips his coffee and leans against the door of his Prius, pretending not to notice. He's grown used to this over the last eleven months, being the sole single dad at pickup, though he's still not quite sure what to do with the attention, just as he wasn't quite sure how to handle the flood of mom-cooked lasagnas and cookies last winter after Billie died. He is unclear whether he is an object of curiosity, pity, or desire (perhaps some combination of all three?), so he mostly smiles politely and studies his cellphone as if he has critical emails to return (he doesn't). With every breath thinking, *Too soon, too soon, too soon*.

He doesn't have to be here, submitting to their attentions—there are buses and carpools, Olive is perfectly capable of getting herself home—but Claremont pickup has come to be his favorite part of the day. He would never say that there's been an *upside* to Billie's death, but if anything positive has come from the last year, it's this: He has time now, so much time, for Olive. If only Olive actually wanted to spend that time with him. It is a bitter irony, he thinks, that he spent the first fifteen years of his daughter's life—years in which Olive *wanted* to cuddle and go for fro-yo and play endless games of gin rummy—working seventy-hour weeks; and only now that he's quit his job and settled into the loose (and, let's admit it, somewhat lonely) schedule of a full-time memoirist, his daughter has apparently lost interest in being his buddy. She disappears into her bedroom the minute she gets home; any free non-homework hours are spent with her best friend, Natalie.

But at least they have this: twenty minutes in the car together every day. Forty-five if he can convince her to stop at the Cheese Board for a pletzel on the way home.

A willowy brunette drifts in Jonathan's direction: Katrina, the real estate agent mother of Olive's friend Tracy, a recent divorcée with a penchant for alarmingly translucent shirts. "Hey, *you*," she says, slipping an arm around him and squeezing him right in the ticklish place where his waistline hits the top of his pants. "Where have you been?"

"I've been here, actually." He points at the asphalt under his sneakers. "Every day."

Katrina purses her lips into an ovoid of approval. "What's this I hear about you writing a book about Billie? A memoir kind of thing?"

"Yes," he says. She stares at him, waiting, until he realizes he's supposed to elaborate. "It came out of the speech that I gave at her memorial last year, maybe you remember, about how we met on the J Church in San Francisco." Someone took a video of the speech and put it up on Facebook and it went viral. Half a million views. He wasn't initially aware of this fact—having not posted the video himself (he still hasn't figured out which of the four hundred memorial attendees did it) and being too distraught to pay any attention to Facebook in the months after Billie died—until an agent called him and suggested he turn it into a book. "It could be a memoir about your marriage to this modern supermom icon, and how your love was torn apart by tragedy," the agent, Jeff Freels, told him. "Like a modern retelling of *Love Story,* but true."

At first Jonathan was appalled by the idea. He was already weary of the media frenzy around his wife's death, and this struck him as a kind of macabre profiteering, peddling Billie to strangers with an insatiable appetite for catastrophe. Besides, their relationship *wasn't* some kind of perfect idyllic romance; things had been rocky at times, as in any marriage. But as time passed and the local news swiftly moved on to someone else's misfortunes, the reality of life as a widowed father set in and the idea of a book started to feel less objectionable. In fact, it seemed to solve a lot of problems in one go. It would give him a reason to finally quit that all-consuming job at *Decode,* just like Billie had always encouraged him to, and spend more time with his daughter. Instead of blunting himself flat with bourbon every night, he would have a constructive outlet for all his pain. Plus, the book would ultimately be for Olive, a tribute to her singular mother, and what was so bad about that? Why *not* paint a loving portrait of her mother that she would cherish forever?

It was a risky move, throwing away a lifetime of stability, but it was one that Billie would have approved of. He called the agent back: "OK, I'll do it." By February, he'd emptied his desk at *Decode* and settled into the life of a full-time writer.

"Oh! I remember your speech! It had me in tears," Katrina breathes. "It's just wonderful that you're writing about Billie. If you want, I could share some of my own stories about her, how extraordinary she was, how *inspiring.*" Her hands drift up toward her eyes as if she feels tears coming on, although Jonathan faintly recalls that Katrina and Billie stopped hanging out some years before her death. "God, this must have been such a difficult year for you."

Difficult. The word is inadequate to his experience, and for a moment he feels a million miles away from this woman, unable to understand how she could pick one so trivializing, so mundane. Learning how to speak Chinese is *difficult*. Winning a Pulitzer Prize is *difficult*. Losing the love of your life in an inexplicable act of carelessness, listening to your daughter sobbing herself to sleep every night, wondering if your wife's skeleton is still rotting at the bottom of a ravine somewhere: That isn't *difficult*. It's the fucking end of the world.

"We're surviving," he says.

Katrina leans in close enough that he can see mascara flakes in her lashes. "Time heals all wounds." He nods soberly, as if this is the very first time he's heard this infuriating platitude. "Listen, why don't you and Olive come over for dinner next weekend with Tracy and me? I'm sure it's been a while since you two had a home-cooked meal."

This is not at all the case; not only has he proved himself a passable cook, but their refrigerator is constantly brimming with food from Billie's best friend, Harmony, who just happens to be a professional caterer. "What a nice offer. I'll check my schedule and get back to you," he says, compulsively twisting the platinum wedding band he still wears. He edges away from Katrina and toward the school's stairs, as if in anticipation of the bell.

This proves to be the wrong choice, though, as Vice Principal Gillespie has just materialized in the doorway of the school. She positions herself on the top of the stairs, coolly surveying the parents assembled below, rail-thin and hawkish in her tweedy skirt suit and pumps. Jonathan quickly backs away, but it's too late: She's spotted him.

"Jonathan!" Her voice is just a little too loud; he

can sense the other parents turning to watch her descend the stairs toward him. "Got a minute?"

He showily lifts his forearm in an instinctive wristwatch-examining move, a clear farce, since he has neither watch nor anywhere to go until Olive is released by the bell. When that fails to slow Gillespie's approach, he attempts diversion: "Is something wrong with Olive?" he asks as she comes closer.

"Olive? No, she's her usual ray-of-sunshine self," Gillespie says. "But you said there would be a check on my desk this week and . . ." She lets the accusation linger there.

"Ah, right. Well, the funds are still tied up." He makes a face that is intended to express his frustration at the powerful forces that have unexpectedly detained his money. "If you can give me a little more time?"

Gillespie's brow draws together, her beaky face going suddenly sincere. "Look, Jonathan. I really wish you'd talked to me about this before the school year started, and we could have put you on a payment plan. But we're three months past the tuition due date, and I've already given you every concession I can. We can revisit this in the spring semester, but for now . . ."

"Just a few more weeks," he says. "I'll see if I can move some money around."

This is a lie, since there is no money that can currently be moved around, let alone $26,720 worth of it; just a series of moving legal deadlines and promised checks that will arrive at some too-distant point in the future. Tuition for private school was never painless, but when he had a senior editor's salary at *Decode* and a wife who also contributed a part-time income, it was low-grade pain, like a toothache or a mild hernia. Now the pain level is more like attempting to remove your spleen without any anesthesia.

Lately, during his nocturnal anxiety attacks, he's begun to wonder if the most reasonable solution to this problem would be to simply pull Olive out of private school and put her in Berkeley High. Billie was never keen on private anyway; Jonathan, with his own Stanford University education in mind, was the one who'd pushed for it, eventually convincing Billie that Olive would go overlooked in an enormous public school. Maybe that was a mistake, but now, five years in, Olive is solidly a Claremont Girl. How can he take that away from her when she's already lost so much? Claremont is Olive's entire life.

Plus, there's a solution just on the horizon. If he's patient a little while longer—or, rather, if he can convince Gillespie to be patient—it should all sort itself out. In the meantime, what is the school going to do, kick out the girl whose mom just died?

Fortunately, at that moment the bell rings, and the Claremont Girls begin spilling out of the front doors of the school, an onslaught of braces and blue plaid. The parents snap to attention, cutting off conversations mid-syllable, and move in unison to cull their offspring from the seething hormonal herd.

Olive is one of the last students out of the doors, as usual, wading stunned into the light, her cell-phone already in hand. Jonathan waves at her and she glances around to see who's watching, then lifts a covert hand in greeting.

"What's up, buttercup?" he says as she approaches.
She rolls her eyes. "Don't be weird, Dad."

He takes in his daughter as they make their way
to the car. She's accessorized her school uniform
with a pair of striped leggings and a hoodie that
used to belong to Billie. Blue smudges of exhaustion
darken the pale skin below her eyes. That skin is her
mother's, along with the wide-set eyes and the hair,
but the rest of Olive's looks, including the broad
brow and the squared jaw, belong to Jonathan. She
is not conventionally beautiful, his daughter, not
like her mother—where Billie was delicate and
spare, Olive has round edges and skin like rising
dough, and Olive is awkward inside her body, unlike
her graceful, athletic mother—but there's something
about her face, something gentle and open, that
makes people take a second look.

He notices a lump on her forehead, centered exactly above her left eyebrow.

"What's that?" he asks, pointing.

Olive reaches up to touch it. "I bumped into a
wall," she says. She offers him a tentative smile,
which strikes him as a strange response to a head
injury.

Jonathan leans closer to examine it. The lump is
turning green and purple around the edges. "Ouch.
Isn't the school nurse supposed to call home for
something like that?"

"It's a *bump*, Dad. Not an open head wound."

"Still. Should we go get you an ice pack? Some
Tylenol? A Hello Kitty Band-Aid?"

Olive makes a face. "Medical marijuana?"

"I think you'll survive," Jonathan says as they

climb into the Prius and pull out into the long line of traffic exiting the parking lot.

"Pot's supposed to be better than over-the-counter painkillers, Dad," she says, and he can't quite tell if she's being serious. "'Cause, you know, *organic*."

"Don't make me have to start worrying about you," he quips. He doesn't; not about these sorts of things, at least. Sometimes, though, he wishes he did have to worry. Surely it wouldn't be that bad for her to have an illicit beer or two, to go to parties; to stop worrying about the big picture so much and be just a *tiny* bit reckless? It's not that Olive doesn't have any friends—there's Natalie, of course—but when her light is on at one A.M., Jonathan knows that it's because she's got her nose stuck in a novel, or is sitting at her laptop fretting about some grisly news story she read on the Internet, not because she's gossiping on Snapchat.

She has no obvious interest in boys yet, either, and yes, she's at an all-girls school without much male contact, but still, it concerns him. He wonders if she's concealing that part of herself from him, or if this is just another aspect of normal teen life that her mother's death has stolen from her. If she's too sad for first love.

They drive in comfortable silence through the streets of Berkeley, past the bike shops and Indian restaurants and boutiques selling practical footwear. The morning's storm has passed, but dark clouds loom ominously overhead; the road is slick with oily puddles. A few blocks from home, Olive speaks up.

"Dad, I was thinking," she begins. "Maybe I can drive myself to school now that I've got my license?"

"What, you don't like me picking you up?"

"I like that *you* like it, Dad," she says, giving him a sweet smile. (Jesus: His daughter, placating him like he was an oversensitive child; when did *that* start happening?)

He frowns. "Is this your way of telling me that I'm smothering you?"

She looks out the window. "It just makes more sense, you know? We've got Mom's car just sitting there, wasting valuable resources. Plus, it'll give you more time to write."

"Sure, if that's what will make you happy," he says, his heart quietly breaking. He doesn't get it; Billie *always* picked Olive up, and as far as he knew, Olive never objected. Is this something to do with him, or is it just the inevitable detachment that comes with turning sixteen? He'd try to dig deeper on the subject with her, but every time he attempts anything beyond their basic conversational fallbacks—*What movie do you want to watch / What time is your Green Team meeting over / Would you like fries with that?*—he seems to hit a wall. It never used to be this hard with her; he always thought they had a pretty good relationship, even if Billie did tend to overshadow him for Olive's attention. But now, no matter what he does, he can't quite seem to step into the hole that Billie left. He's not sure if the ghost of her mother is in the way, or if he is guilty of parenting misdemeanors of which he was never apprised.

"It will, thanks for understanding." She peers intently at a new vegan café where two hipsters with hillbilly beards and trucker hats eat rice bowls in the window. Something in her face looks pensive. Jonathan turns down into their neighborhood, driving past a line of shaggy Craftsman houses with their redwood shingles swollen with rain, their gardens tangled and loamy.

As they park in front of their house, he can see two pumpkins in a shadowy corner of their porch, huddling against each other for warmth. Jonathan brought them home from the grocery store a week earlier, thinking that he would carve them with Olive, but she ended up staying at Natalie's house until late, and then the pumpkins were forgotten; so they now sit there on the porch, rain-splattered, unadorned. Looking at them, he has a sudden memory of his wife sitting at the newspaper-covered kitchen table, oblivious to the pumpkin pulp on her face, applying a stencil with a fine-point Sharpie. Their house usually had the best pumpkins on the block—perplexed owls, luminescent spiderwebs, pointillist skulls, designed by Billie and carved (with decidedly less skill) by Jonathan and Olive—at least until day three, at which point the delicate gourds would sprout mold and melt into putrid glue on the front porch. Billie was always more interested in the making than the cleaning up.

"Is that Harmony?" Olive asks abruptly as they are unloading jackets and soggy umbrellas from the backseat of the Prius.

Approaching from the opposite direction, with precision timing, is Harmony's Kia. She pulls crookedly to a stop and climbs out of the car, laden with two canvas bags. She hoists these high, smiling.

"Bounty from last night's catering job," she calls from across the street. "I hope you like Little Gems, because I've got a lot of them."

"I like gems of all sizes," Jonathan calls back. "I'll take semiprecious stones, too, if that's on offer."

"She means *salad,* Dad," Olive says under her breath. "It's like miniature romaine."

"I know," he says. "Ha ha?"

But Harmony has thrown her head back and is laughing as if this is the funniest joke she's ever heard. His wife's old friend is one of those women who embody the word *abundance:* She is lush and pink and always slightly damp from exertion, like a milkmaid in a Vermeer painting. Her blond hair is pinned up in messy braids that frame her face; her Dansko chef's clogs clatter on the asphalt as she ferries groceries across the street to them.

She gives Jonathan a moist kiss on his cheek and envelops Olive in an embrace, but Olive quickly wriggles free and races up the path and into the house. Harmony turns back to Jonathan with raised eyebrows, and he shrugs.

"Sorry," he says. "She's in a little bit of a mood."

"Well, she's allowed to be. It's the anniversary coming up soon, right?" He nods as Harmony leans toward him, her wide blue eyes narrowing. "And you? How are you holding up?"

"*You* know. Sometimes it feels like the fog that's surrounded Olive and me is finally lifting; like maybe we're halfway back to normalcy. And then I'll sit down to work on the book, and the next thing you know, I'm at the bottom of a bottle of bourbon with snot pouring down my face." He stops, the words snagging in his throat.

Harmony's face twitches with emotion, her eyes going moist, but she says nothing. He's learned to appreciate this about her: the way she refuses to overshadow his sadness with her own. "There's a meditation for mindful grief that I find helpful, if you'd like me to share it with you. And you know I'm just a phone call away if you need to talk."

"I already have you on speed dial." As nearly everyone else has fallen away this year—the well-meaning acquaintances losing interest, the friends abruptly busy with their own minor life dramas—Harmony is one of the few who's stuck around. Billie's death was the first time Jonathan really felt the absence of extended family. His own parents are infirm and halfway across the country, and Billie's were estranged long ago; and the only sibling either of them could claim—Jonathan's sister, Jenny—died decades earlier. Instead, Harmony stepped in and took over the caretaking that a parent or sister otherwise might, from monitoring their house and fending off the TV cameras when Billie first went missing up in the mountains, to planning the memorial when Jonathan proved emotionally incapable.

He's indebted to her for this, and for her uncanny ability to show up at the exact moment when he seems to need it the most, with a coffee or a farmers' market box. With Harmony, he can be himself, because she *gets* it: She lost Billie, too. If he's driven her crazy with his endless talking about Billie— tirelessly circling his grief, his worries about Olive, this fresh void in his life feeling more like a wall around which he has to learn to navigate—she's never once shown it.

"Dinner Monday?" she asks. "I'll cook for you guys."

"Amazing," he says, just as his phone starts ringing in the pocket of his jeans. He pulls it out and reads the display: JEAN BURSCH. "Sorry, I have to take this. My lawyer."

Harmony's eyebrows shoot upward. "Good luck," she whispers. He watches her saunter back across the street toward the car, her hips swaying as she walks. He turns away, suddenly uncomfortable.

When he answers his phone, Jean's voice is coated with a shiny shell of optimism.

"Good news! We've made progress! Our court date is confirmed for November first. Conceivably we could have all this wrapped up by the holidays."

Jonathan walks slowly toward the house, taking this in. Sodden worms are expiring on the front path, refugees from the earlier downpour. The plane trees sway as a gust of wind passes through, releasing a fine spray of rainwater across the top of his jacket.

"November first," he repeats. He watches a mother walking by pushing a stroller, a baby's watery face peering anxiously out from beneath a plastic rain cover. "I can't believe this process has taken a whole year."

"We're lucky. It could have dragged on much, much longer. The hoops you have to jump through for missing-presumed-dead cases are not your usual hoops."

Missing, presumed dead. This phrase drives him

insane, the way it insists on inserting doubt where there is none. The facts are simple: Billie went backpacking by herself along the Pacific Crest Trail in Desolation Wilderness. She never came back down the mountain. No one was sure exactly what had happened, but the official verdict was that Billie had probably gone off-trail (this would have been so very *Billie* of her) and fallen into a ravine, hurt herself, and couldn't hike out. Or maybe she was attacked by a wild animal, or just got lost and died of hunger and thirst.

Even now, a year later, Jonathan is plagued by the question of how long it had taken his wife to die. What if she had lain there for days, somewhere under the ponderosa pines, hurt and helpless, hearing the search helicopters overhead but incapable of summoning them? He lies awake at night, imagining the horror of it all: Her waning hope that someone might find her, wherever she was, before it was too late. The dawning awareness that death was approaching as she measured out drops of water and the last crumbs of her granola bars. Then nothing but her fading breath and the scuttling of pikas and yellow-bellied marmots across the granite slopes. It's unbearable to think about. Instead, he prays that death was instantaneous: that she fell, broke her neck, and didn't have to suffer such a lonely ending.

For the first day or two after Billie failed to return from her hike, Jonathan had clung to the hope that she'd just decided to take a little more time to herself. Everything considered, it wasn't entirely out of the question. There had always been that loner streak in her; she could be haphazard, unpredictable. He could still remember the time, years earlier, when she'd vanished for a weekend with no explanation, leaving Jonathan trying to explain to Olive that Mommy was tired, she'd gone on a vacation by herself. "I just needed some space to breathe," Billie had said when she came back, as if that explained everything; and he'd pointed out patiently that the space was fine, but the lack of communication was not. Maybe she'd forgotten that lesson.

But the days passed, long past the point when she would have run out of food and water. Meanwhile, Billie's Subaru remained parked at the trailhead, her credit cards lay dormant, the wireless company couldn't trace any phone activity. Wall-to-wall local TV and online news coverage failed to turn up anyone who'd seen her, other than a pair of backpackers who'd briefly chatted with her on the trail. After a week, a search-and-rescue volunteer found Billie's shattered cellphone at the bottom of a steep cascade of barren rock near Pyramid Peak, fourteen miles off the Pacific Crest Trail. Even then, Jonathan believed that she might be alive nearby, surviving on nuts and berries.

But she wasn't. The authorities searched for nine days before giving up: nine days of sitting with Olive in a freezing, featureless room in the ranger headquarters, Jonathan knowing that Billie had been missing far too long but still grasping at some tiny speck of hope. Sleeping under scratchy wool blankets across three folding chairs; drinking coffee with powdered creamer out of Styrofoam cups; his arm going numb from where he kept it clenched around Olive's shoulders. On the last night, it snowed. The next morning, the head ranger came in and offered Olive a box of doughnuts as if sugar might cushion the blow, and Jonathan got to watch his daughter's face collapse inward as this weather-battered man uttered the words *We're calling off the search*. The understanding hit him like a fist in the gut a half second later, choking him wordless.

For a month or two, Jonathan continued to clutch at other straws, including the awful possibility that Billie could have been abducted. But that theory was put to rest when her hiking boot was found half submerged in a riverbed in mid-December, and the authorities explained to him that there was no plausible way she could have been dragged, shoeless, from so deep in the wilderness without anyone noticing. (More likely, they said, she had taken off her boot because of an injury, and it had been washed downstream in the current.) The other option—that she was murdered somewhere out there—was too horrible to even contemplate.

In the meantime, there was no body to cling to, nothing to bury or to burn or to cry over. Maybe that's why Jonathan writes about Billie now, and why he continues to hang on to the objects she left behind, things that prove she once existed. The drawer stuffed with jogging bras that still smell faintly of her deodorant. The running shoes on the front porch, muddy soles fissured and dry. The Tana French mystery by her side of the bed, with a bookmark placed halfway through as if Billie might have the opportunity to find out what happens in the end. Probably he should sort through all of his wife's stuff, but he can't quite bear to do it.

Billie's body: Its absence has left him with an emotional, legal, and financial mess to unravel, the court having refused to issue a death certificate until Billie's death is "verified" by "diligent search or inquiry." Jonathan wouldn't have predicted that a death certificate would be that important, but it is. All year long, he's felt like he's existed in a state of limbo, waiting for some mysterious Powers That Be to acknowledge the validity of his grief. Not that a death certificate will make Billie any more or less gone than she already is, but he can't shake his hope that this one piece of paper might give him some sense of conclusiveness that has been eluding him.

And then there's the vexing fact that the lack of a death certificate also means no probate, which has led to a total tax mess and (most distressingly) prevented a life insurance payout—the latter being a rather substantial quarter-million-dollar sum that would, let's be honest, really help right about now. He is running, worryingly, on fumes. Although his agent ultimately sold *Where the Mountain Meets the Sky: My Life with Billie Flanagan* for an advance that seemed rather astonishing—more than his annual salary, even after eighteen years at *Decode*—what he didn't anticipate was that this money would be trickling out in depressingly small quantities over the course of three years. The initial payment he received last spring vanished long before Labor Day.

Making matters even worse, he discovered not long after Billie's memorial that their finances were in a shockingly bad state. Billie had served as the family accountant, and somehow she had failed to alert him that they were grazing the bottom of their savings account. Probably this shouldn't have come as a surprise—Bay Area life had grown radically more expensive, while their own incomes had not risen commensurately. Still. For the last few months, he's been slowly and painfully chipping away at his 401(k) just to cover his mortgage and health insurance premiums; anything deemed not quite as urgent (say, tuition bills) has slipped to the wayside.

But here they are, finally, close to a resolution. All those months of meetings and depositions and affidavits are ending in this, a court hearing in which they will once and for all "prove" that Billie is dead, and receive a death certificate. *Prove.* He jokes about it with his friend Marcus sometimes—"I'm trapped in a Kafka novel"—but in his lowest moments, the cruelty of it all makes him want to scream. Such a phenomenal pointless *suck* of time and money and emotional energy at the exact moment when you have zero to spare.

"So, just one last hoop we need to jump through before the court date," Jean is saying on the other end of the line. "We need to put notices in several national newspapers, notifying Billie that we're looking for her."

He kicks at a slick of dead leaves on the porch, pushing them into a soggy pile to attend to later. "Let me make sure I'm understanding this correctly. We're supposed to put messages in a newspaper for a dead woman to read?"

"Try not to think about it too much," Jean says.

He laughs despite himself. "Even if Billie *were* alive, she wouldn't be reading classified ads. A *news-*

paper classified? Do they even still exist? Has no one in the court system heard of Craigslist?"

"You can look it up, if you like." Her voice is apologetic. "Code 12406(b)(1). Diligent search and inquiry. It specifically says newspapers. Anyway, in the ad, you'll want to ask if anyone knows about her whereabouts. Something along the lines of"—she pauses—" 'If you have any information about the whereabouts of Sybilla "Billie" Flanagan'—what was her maiden name again?"

"Thrace. But she never used it. She was estranged from her parents, hadn't spoken to them since high school."

"That's right. Well, we'll put the name in there anyway, just to cover our bases. And then 'please contact' with the phone number of the police. You know what? I'll write it up for you so you don't have to deal with it at all."

Jonathan looks up and realizes that a parking enforcement officer has pulled up behind his Prius and is issuing a ticket: He forgot that it was street sweeping day on this side of the street. He gestures frantically, but the attendant ignores him as he sticks the ticket under the windshield wiper and drives off. That's fifty dollars that he can't really spare. On top of the five hundred dollars an hour that this conversation is costing him, not to mention the bill he's going to get for the time it will take Jean to place those ads.

"You still there?" Jean asks.

"Yeah," he says. "You know what? I can call in those classifieds myself. Just tell me what I need to do."

———

Inside the house, it's quiet and gloomy. Their house is—like most on the block—a shingled Berkeley Craftsman, splintery and dark, jammed with original period detail but permanently drafty. It's been raining all week, the heating system working overtime, and the close air smells of wet towels and scorched dust. Jonathan switches on a lamp, so that the thin glow of its LED bulb illuminates the entry and living room. Catsby, Olive's latest stray—a dyspeptic calico with one gnawed-off ear—comes running, sees that it's Jonathan, and turns away, uninterested.

There are heaps of discarded clothes by the front door; tumbleweeds of cat hair drifting along the hall; a curdled whiff from the recycling that needs to be taken out. Billie wasn't a meticulous housekeeper—she let things go a little too long; surfaces would be neat and clean, but move anything aside and you'd see a film of dust, dirty laundry on the floor of the closet—but now that Jonathan is in charge, things have truly gone downhill. How did his wife manage to keep on top of the endless Sisyphean nature of homemaking? He marvels at how invisible she used to make it look, how uncomplaining she was. It's not that he never did a load of laundry or washed the dishes or swept the floor; he contributed the best he could. But he never grasped the scope of all the things that magically appeared—a fridge full of food, vacation itineraries, doctor's appointments, new upholstery on the couch, regulation uniforms for Olive—until he was responsible for all of it himself.

He maneuvers through the house, picking up the most obviously offending messes, stopping, as he often does, to glance at the easel that sits in the prime spot on the back sunporch. It has Billie's last unfinished painting on it: a landscape of some ocean vista, the horizon sketched in pencil, her palette of blue paints dried to a crust. The stool before it remains positioned *just so* to catch the last lingering rays of the sun. Sometimes, when Jonathan is not at all sober, he'll stumble out to stare at the painting and just marvel at the pitiful symbolism of it all.

He heads to the kitchen and deposits the bags of salad on the counter, then starts to dig in the refrigerator in search of something to go with it. He retrieves a slightly limp zucchini from the crisper and examines it, putting a pot of water on to boil.

Olive materializes in the kitchen behind him, drifting toward a bowl of overripe bananas with a frown. "You really need to go grocery shopping, Dad," she says. "There's nothing to eat."

"There's Little Gem salad," he says. "Rather a lot of it."

"We're out of toilet paper, too. Unless you intended that as an environmental-consciousness measure? In which case, yay, but *ew*." She grabs a banana and heads for the door.

He tries to think of something to say that might stop her departure. "I just had an update from the lawyer," he blurts.

She stops and turns around, the half-peeled banana hanging limply from her fist. "Sorry, what?"

"The lawyer," he says. "She says we finally have a court date. Early November."

A curious expression crosses Olive's face, her brow furrowing as she takes this in. "After that," Olive says slowly, "Mom is officially dead? But legally speaking, as of now she's not dead *yet*?"

"That's the idea."

"I get it."

He stops chopping the zucchini to look at Olive. "Does that upset you? Should we talk about this some more?"

Olive leans on the kitchen counter, pushing aside a pile of mail, mostly athletic catalogs that haven't yet noticed that Billie no longer needs ultralight hoodies and dry-weave leggings and Gore-Tex-lined hiking pants. With one hand, Olive gingerly traces the lump on her forehead. "Dad. Remember when you once told me about the importance of journalists keeping an open mind? Of—objectivity?"

"No, I don't, but yes, that's true." He notices a strange smile flickering around the corners of his daughter's mouth, and an ominous premonition spiders up the back of his neck. Something is going on. "OK. Lay it on me."

"I don't think Mom's dead," Olive blurts. And then, reading the confusion and dismay on Jonathan's face, she continues in a rush, "Just listen to me. I know this is going to sound crazy, but I *saw* her."

For a split second, something in Jonathan's chest seizes. *Is it possible?* Then he reaches across the kitchen and gently tugs at Olive's hand, holding it in his own. It lies in his palm, heartbreakingly small and yielding. "*Olive.* I see her all the time, too. Any time I pass someone on the street with hair like hers,

I do a double take. Women who walk like her, or are wearing hiking gear, or have her profile. Every single time, there's a second when I'm convinced that it's really her. But it never is."

Olive tries to pull her hand away. "No, Dad, that's not what I meant. Listen. I saw her, but I didn't *see* her in person, exactly. More like a . . . *vision?* Dad, don't look at me like that. Seriously. OK? I had this whole conversation with Mom this morning. She just appeared on this beach, wearing a dress. . . ."

Jonathan grips her hand tighter. *What is this?* He can hear a fire alarm going off somewhere in the distance; or maybe that's just the ringing of his own incipient panic. "I'm confused. You were at the beach today?"

"*No,* Dad." She wrestles her hand free. "I was at school, and I started feeling strange, and then . . . It's hard to put into words. But essentially I looked up and I was on a beach, and Mom was there with me and she told me that she wanted me to come find her."

"Come find her," Jonathan echoes softly, trying to digest this.

Olive's face is radiant, pinkly glowing. She leans in toward him as if sharing a secret, strands of brown hair flying loose from her ponytail. "Yes! See? She was alive. She *is* alive."

Jonathan feels his precarious edifice collapsing around him, what little hard-won recovery he's managed dissolving like a castle made of sand. What is going on? Is this some belated emotional fallout from Billie's death? Should he get Olive to a therapist? Or, Christ—what if it's a brain tumor? He is silent for a minute as he grasps for the most rational response. "Oh, Olive," he says softly. "I know it's hard to give up hope. It took me a long, long time to accept that she was gone, that we weren't ever going to find her. What you experienced, it sounds like some kind of hallucination—"

She interrupts. "Dad, you said you'd be objective."

"There's objectivity and then there's reason. I mean, you're talking about the *supernatural,* Olive. Which—" He's unsure how to finish this thought. Instead, he tries to grasp at the fragment of logic he was following before. "There was something in *The New Yorker* a while back—an Oliver Sacks piece, I think?—about hallucinations caused by grief, I could look it up. . . ."

Olive shakes her head. "Dad, I *talked* to her."

The look on her face is a needle in his heart. "It may *feel* like you did, but the more probable explanation is that something is going on with your subconscious. You know, it's the anniversary coming up, and with all the legal weirdness and formalities, you're probably feeling emotional. I know I am. Your brain can play tricks on you."

"My mind wasn't playing tricks. It was incredibly clear," Olive says. She has backed up against the cabinets, her cheeks flaring bright red, but for some reason it's the calm certainty in her voice that stops Jonathan: as if his daughter is already beyond reach, a committed acolyte of some strange new religion. "Look, Dad. Open your mind, OK? It's *possible* she's still alive, right? They never found her body.

That's why they won't issue a death certificate! They think there's a chance she could have survived."

"That's just the standard legal process." There's a sour pang in his stomach, the discordant clash of a half-dozen conflicting emotions. "They do that for any case where there's no body, as a matter of procedure. It doesn't mean that anyone believes that she could still be alive out there. Not anymore."

"*I* believe it." Olive plants a palm in the center of her chest. "Dad. She told me to *look* for her."

Jonathan is suddenly furious. "*Stop it,* Olive. This isn't healthy. Your mother is gone. *Dead,*" he snaps before he can stop himself. Immediately, he is stricken with remorse. He puts his hand to the hair at his temples and tugs on it, hard enough that it makes his eyes water. "Look, I'm sorry—" he begins.

But it's too late, Olive has already shut down. "I shouldn't have said anything," she mutters to the floor.

"No, I'm glad you did," Jonathan says, not feeling glad at all. "I'm just trying to figure out what to say."

"*GOD,* Dad, don't you get it?" Olive throws up her hands. "It's not about *saying* anything. It's about *doing* something. I want to do something real for once. Can't you open your mind just this one time? Mom would have tried to look for *you.*"

"Hey—" he begins, taken aback. But Olive is already marching out of the room, her stride stiff and off-balance. Jonathan looks down at the pile of half-chopped zucchini in front of him and realizes that he's cut his thumb. Blood seeps from a cut by his fingernail. He sticks the finger in his mouth and sucks at it, its coppery tang making him queasy. He thinks of Olive's words—*She just appeared on this beach, wearing a dress*—and a familiar memory bubbles up: his wedding, seventeen years earlier, a hastily assembled celebration with a handful of be-mused friends, his parents perplexed and out of place. They'd been married on a beach right outside Big Sur, on a misty day that was cold and dreamlike. A few glasses of champagne into the reception, Billie had run into the sea, pulling him in with her. Her filmy wedding dress dragging with seawater, his loafers full of sand: He could still remember the transcendence of being so happy he didn't give a damn that the water was freezing, didn't care that he wasn't going to get the deposit back on his tux, didn't care about anything but Billie's slippery hand clinging to his as if he alone were responsible for keeping her afloat.

Billie had loved it out there by the ocean, the windblown cypress and the fog that stung your eyes with salt and the cliffs clawed away by the ravaging waves. He used to feel like there was something of the sea hidden inside her, something wild and un-fathomable.

Dammit, Billie, he thinks, *you left me alone with a troubled teenage girl. How am I supposed to do this by myself?*

3

SUNLIGHT, VICTORIOUS, HAS FINALLY broken through the afternoon cloud cover, and it illuminates great square patches of the Berkeley public library, alternately warming and blinding the patrons. The towering window wall of the reading room, over two stories high, has turned the library into a greenhouse, causing its occupants to shed their fall layers. Sweatshirts and hats and jackets lie in flaccid heaps across tables, chairs, the lower-lying bookshelves.

At the other end of the table, where Olive sits making lists in a spiral notebook, a homeless man leafs through a Stephen King novel; from five chairs away, Olive can pick up the scent of unwashed hair and dried sweat and something vaguely fecal. She feels sorry for him and wishes she had her leftover sandwich from lunch to offer, but she's already tossed it in the trash. Wait—is that presumptuous of her? Maybe he's not hungry at all. Maybe he needs different things: a shower, a job program, better healthcare. Or maybe he's chosen this life for himself, and her assumption is just an assertion of her bourgeois privilege. She read an opinion piece about this last week on *The Huffington Post*.

As if he can read her thoughts, the man glances up and catches her looking at him. She offers him a smile, but he just stares back with watery eyes. Olive tucks her head under her arm and continues to write, in small neat letters:

1. If Mom is indeed alive and
2. She has not called to tell us that she is alive
3. Then she must be

She hesitates for a minute and then quickly writes:

a. In trouble
b. Suffering from amnesia
c. Stuck somewhere where there is no phone or Internet? (Still in Desolation Wilderness?)
d. Angry at us

She stops again, considering this last point. If her mom is angry with her, why did she ask her to come find her? *Olive, I miss you:* She said that, didn't she? Yes. Olive scratches out the word *us* and replaces it:

d. Angry at *Dad*?

She thinks about this. She remembers the way her father used to grab at her mother and draw her into his lap. Her mother would curl up there like a cat, and her dad would rest his nose in her mom's hair and leave it there, as if trying to breathe her in. It was *awkward*—middle-aged people weren't supposed to act like that—but secretly, Olive loved it.

But they hadn't done much of that in the past few years. Instead, her dad kept getting more and more consumed with his job, and her mom was always off running marathons or biking the coast or hiking mountains, spending whole weekends by herself or with her friend Rita. In that last year, Olive sometimes heard her parents fight, hoarse whispers that were indecipherable through the bedroom door.

Though it was upsetting, it didn't seem like a *crisis*. But maybe Olive had missed something pivotal. Had something awful happened between them that made her mom feel the need to run away?

This kind of thinking—the *why* and the *how*—makes her brain hurt. She turns the page of her notebook and starts again.

1. Places Mom could be:
   a. On a beach

And then she stops. She might as well have written *on Planet Earth*. California has 840 miles of coastline. The beach she saw could have been Stinson Beach, which is, strictly speaking, the coastal beach closest to Olive's home. It could have been a random beach on the Monterey Peninsula, which is where they tended to go to the beach most. It could have been *any* beach: Pescadero, Mendocino, Moonstone, Gualala, Malibu, who knows?

And this is assuming her mom is even in California.

Olive tries to remember more details about what the beach looked like—something about it tugs at her, something familiar—but by this point, a full twenty-nine hours after her vision, what remains is mostly a collection of filmy impressions, a tingling glow of hope, a memory of the expression on her mom's face. Except for her mother's message: *That* has lodged, stonelike, in her chest. *You aren't trying hard enough.* She can't shake this feeling, no matter how incredulous her father was. What she doesn't get: How can he stand doing nothing if there's even a fraction of a chance that Billie is alive?

But what, exactly, would *something* be? She can't figure out a course of action, let alone put a finger on what, precisely, happened to her the day before. If it *was* a vision of some sort, does that mean she'll have more? More detailed ones, with clearer information? Is it possible to trigger them herself instead of waiting to be summoned?

She pushes aside her notebook and looks at the pile of books that she's collected from a dusty shelf at the back of the stacks, filed under 133.9 M817-1, SPIRITUALISM PARAPSYCHOLOGY. *A Skeptic's Guide to Parapsychology; Margins of Reality: The Role of Consciousness in the Physical World; Connections: Visionary Encounters with Your Beloved; Frontiers of the Soul: Exploring Psychic Evolution.* They seem legitimate enough, except for the last one, a yellowing paperback whose cover, with its hallucinatory sunset and cheesy font, is a little *too* wacko. She shoves it to the bottom of the pile and picks up *A Skeptic's Introduction to Parapsychology*. She flips to the introduction and starts to read. *Have you ever experienced a phenomenon that you could not explain? Something that made you question the very nature of your reality? Have you ever seen or known or understood something unknowable, something that caused you to ask yourself,* Am I psychic?

Am *I psychic*? She lets the possibility of it wash over her. She's always felt herself to be unexceptional. Not the prettiest or the smartest or the wildest girl in her class; neither a natural born leader nor a strong athlete. It felt like there was a big hollow *zero* at her center. She would soak up her mother's stories about her own Lost Years—the decade during which Billie, a teenage runaway, had roamed around the Pacific Northwest and then traveled the world, hanging out with artists and activists and drug dealers—and would sense that she was failing her mother in some way. "Anyway, you don't want to do what I did," Billie would say, abruptly cutting herself off, but somehow Olive knew that she meant the exact opposite.

Not that her mom was so radical anymore—she was the very *image* of normalcy, with her zippered fleeces and her suburban-mom ponytail, carrying chia-seed muffins to the Claremont Girls fundraising committee meetings, designing logos for online pet stores. Still, at the end of Olive's freshman year, when she brought home her latest A's-and-B's report card, Billie had stared at it a long time, as if she couldn't quite understand it. Then she pushed the paper away with the tip of her pinkie and leaned in to murmur in Olive's ear. "*Anyone* can follow the rules. Find your own thing. Don't just do what everyone expects you to do. Remember: You have the right to become whoever you want to be. Don't worry about what other people might think . . . because you will be *exceptional*, Olive. But you have to be willing to try."

What does that mean? Olive had thought at the time. She still wonders: Who *does* she want to become? And how would that be unexpected? The hot impulses she sometimes feels are too nebulous and fleeting to pin down to action. So what else is there? Well, she's a feminist . . . along with the entire student body of Claremont. She tends to read novels when she is supposed to be studying, but that isn't exactly *unexpected* or *exceptional*. The abandoned animals that she rescues? When she tried to make that her *thing* by volunteering at a local animal shelter, it ended badly: She couldn't bear to arrive every week only to discover that the dogs she'd snuggled with the previous week had since been put down. So she quit.

Looking back now, she feels like the most interesting thing she's done with her life was to start the Green Team at her school, and yeah, she's pretty proud of what they've done, the carbon-footprint reduction program and the tree plantings and all that. But even *that* doesn't seem remotely radical enough; it's barely significant at all compared to the shit her mom used to pull when she was young— tying herself to trees and lying in front of bulldozers. In the year since her mother's death, Olive has felt acutely conscious of her uselessness: just one puny human among billions.

But to be *psychic*—*that* would be something. Something amazing. Something beyond-bonkers special.

Why not? she thinks. *Why not me? Maybe* this *is what I'm meant to be.*

She scans the rest of *A Skeptic's Guide*—which is basically an argument in favor of the existence of paranormal phenomena—and then puts it aside in search of something with more useful advice. She picks up *Connections,* a fat hardback whose bold neon-hued font reminds her of the self-help books that they sell in piles at Costco.

The Greek oracles, or psychomanteums, *were able to travel to distant places by looking deep into mirrors and entering a hypnagogic state,* Olive reads. *The same technique can be used to visit the spirits of your loved ones virtually anytime you want. The ancient art of mirror-gazing is a proven method for bridging the natural and psychic realms, available to anyone who has the patience and discipline to train his or her mind.*

This is more like it. *Connections* recommends that Olive fast for twenty-four hours and then sit before a mirror at twilight in a darkened room and try to conjure up her mom's essence. *Mirror-gazing is most likely to happen in moments of relaxation, which will ease the transition into an altered state of awareness. Have photographs and personal items of your loved one around you, in order to imprint them on your mind. You'll know you've entered an alter-*

nate state of consciousness when the tips of your fingers begin to tingle.

It feels kind of silly, taking psychic instructions from a book—the exact opposite of yesterday's spontaneous, ecstatic encounter—but what other option does she have? Olive closes her eyes and concentrates very hard on the tips of her fingers to see if it works. A square patch of sun has shifted, and she can feel it warming her face, the back of her eyelids flaring pink.

After a while, she can sense the rhythm of her blood hurtling through the veins in her thumbs, but she doesn't *see* her mother. Not in the way she did yesterday. Instead, a memory flickers across the backs of her lids: Her mom in the backyard in a winter rainstorm, soaked, as she stands with her chin lifted to the sky and her eyes closed. Turning to see Olive watching from the back porch, and shouting over the thundering of the rain, *Come on out. It's just a little water.* Her mother's skin whipped pink with the cold, her arms sweeping grandly at Olive, who, with an electric tingle, steps out into the downpour to join her.

"Olive?"

She opens her eyes and sees Natalie standing on the other side of the reading table, a stack of sociology books in her arms. Olive's pulse quickens. "Hey, *you*," she says back, keeping her voice low.

In the last year, Olive has watched a lot of her friends just kind of . . . fade away. Not that she was ever going to win popularity contests before, but she had a decent enough social life, mostly with other Green Team girls like Ming and Tracy, who also got worked up about things like reforestation and fracking. And then, with a stroke, she became Poor Olive Whose Mom Died in a Tragic Accident, an unfathomable new identity, and her friends didn't really know what to do with her anymore. She tried expressly *not* talking about it, so as not to bum people out—*Oh, I'm fine, but how are you doing?* she'd quickly say when people asked—but it was there anyway, a yoke of tragedy hanging around her neck, and people were probably worried that if they got too close, they'd have to help carry it. Because now Ming and Tracy and the other girls stay a safe distance away. They'll tag her on Instagram, or invite her to group social events, even sit with her at lunch, but never actually call, or make plans one on one, never something that would require them to think about, you know, *death*. Olive can't really blame them.

It doesn't matter, though, because she has Natalie. And that's all she needs.

Natalie is dark-haired and floppy and adorable, someone you want to grab and nuzzle, like a puppy, except that she's also edgy and funny and unfiltered, which is why Olive can't get enough of her. She's the school Debate Club champ and is likely to be the class valedictorian, an achievement that boggles Olive's mind and that Natalie doesn't seem to care about at all. "As long as I get into a college that's on the other side of the country from my parents, I'm happy," she once told Olive.

Natalie's dad is a lawyer who speaks in monosyllables, and her mom is a lawyer who screams, and it's obvious that the only reason the divorce papers haven't been drawn up yet is because they are waiting for Natalie to graduate. Her family is rich, like a lot of the kids Olive goes to school with. Not mansion-rich—not in Berkeley—but the kind of rich where they spend vacations in France and drive German cars and live in houses where everything is new and imported from Scandinavia.

Today Natalie's frizzy curls have sprung free from her headband and she's untied her regulation Claremont tie (a short, stubby, peach-colored thing; Claremont Girls hate that tie, in all its limp-dicked androgyny) so that it hangs slackly on either side of her neck. Her blazer, which she's decorated with a collection of feminist lapel pins (WELL-BEHAVED WOMEN SELDOM MAKE HISTORY), is wadded up and dangling perilously from the straps of her backpack.

Natalie plops down in the chair opposite Olive, casting a glance at the homeless man at the other end of the table. She twitches her nose, then delicately drapes a hand across it to mask the smell. "What's up? You OK?" Natalie's voice is far too brassy for the library, and a woman at the next table turns and hisses at them.

"Yeah. Why?" Olive glances discreetly down at her pile of books, their covers a glaring advertisement for her dalliance with the supernatural.

"You're sitting here with your eyes closed, looking kind of *clinical*." Natalie tilts her head, noticing the books on the table. She spins them around to examine the titles. "*WTF*, Olive. *Exploring Psychic Evolution*? Who's assigning you this stuff? Turnbull? This looks way more interesting than *my* sociology reading list."

Olive pulls the book back, her face getting hot. "It's not an assignment."

Natalie laughs. "So, what, you're psychic or something?" She looks up and sees Olive's expression. "Oh. *Oh!* Seriously? You're kidding, right? Where's this coming from?"

Olive hesitates for what feels like a minute but is probably only seconds. Then she lowers her voice to a whisper: "If I tell you that I spoke to my mom yesterday, will you say that I'm nuts?"

Natalie stares at her for a long time; and just when Olive is convinced that this was a mistake and she's about to become the social pariah of Claremont Prep, even more than she already is— *crazytown!*—Natalie leans in. "You know, my grandma used to swear that she could talk with my dead grandpa." She speaks in an excited whisper. "She said she'd wake up in bed in the middle of the night and hear him snoring right next to her. And sometimes, when I used to visit her house? I swear things would move around when we weren't in the room. Little things, like spoons and mail."

Natalie looks at Olive, big brown eyes unblinking, smiling as if she's just offered a gift. Olive, grateful, resists the urge to reach out and grab Natalie's hand, to squeeze her friend's soft fingers between her own. "I had a vision of my mom while I was walking to class yesterday," she says. "Right in the middle of the Sunshine Wing."

Natalie's eyebrows shoot up a half inch. "You saw her ghost?"

Olive leans in. "Here's the thing—I'm pretty sure that my mom *wasn't* a ghost." She can feel herself getting swept away again, by the exhilaration of that moment. "She spoke to me really clearly—she told me she missed me and that I should look for her." Olive fingers the cover of *A Skeptic's Guide to Parapsychology*. "Natalie—I think she's *alive*."

Natalie's necktie has snaked down from around her neck; it coils on the table, forgotten. "Alive. OK." Something flickers across her face—something loose and sad, like pity—but it passes. She leans back and looks up at the ceiling of the library as if absorbed by something she's just spotted there. "*Wow*. That's intense."

"You believe me?"

Natalie's eyes drop and they skip across Olive's face, measuring. She sits there spinning *Connections* in a slow circle with the tip of her finger. "They never found your mom's body, right?" She seems to arrive at a decision, and an odd sound comes out of her mouth, half gasp and half laugh. "Wouldn't that be *amazing*? Oh, Olive! You saw her? You actually *talked* to her?"

Olive nods, at a loss for words.

Natalie wrinkles her nose. "But—if she's alive, where is she?"

"Yeah," Olive says. "That's what I need to figure out. Also why we haven't heard from her in the last year."

Natalie sits back in her chair, tugging absently at the end of her ponytail. "Maybe someone abducted her when she was hiking," she offers. Then, registering the distress on Olive's face: "Or maybe she just has amnesia?"

Olive glances down at her notebook. "That's on

my list. But it sounds like something out of a cheesy soap opera."

"Transient global amnesia. That's what it was called." Natalie gives the ponytail a yank and holds it there, thinking. Her voice grows more determined. "We talked about it in our psych section, remember? It happens with head injuries. You can't remember anything for more than a minute. Like that old movie."

Olive tries to imagine how her mom might have managed to lose her mind and stumble out of Desolation Wilderness unseen. Still, it's the option she likes the most. "But if she has amnesia, how does she know to contact *me*?" she wonders.

Natalie shrugs. "Maybe it's subliminal or something. You're tapping into her subconscious thoughts? Some kind of, I don't know, telepathic bond?"

Olive likes this, an invisible cord connecting her with her mother. "I'll buy that. Big question is, how do I find her?"

"Do you think she's up in the forest? Surviving on rainwater and berries?"

Olive thinks about this. She can recall in vivid detail the photos of Desolation Wilderness that she downloaded off the Internet last year, a folder full of hiker candids and nature photography that she studied, wondering where in all that forbidding vastness her mom might be. Trying to pinpoint exactly which ravine was the one where they found her mother's lost hiking boot, buried in the muck. She shakes her head. "By this point, either someone would have found her or she would have figured her way out, right? Anyway, I saw her on a beach." She thinks. "I couldn't tell which one, though. Pacific Ocean, probably, judging by what the water looked like."

Natalie's hands slide down to rest on the table, her body growing still as she relaxes into the idea. "What was her favorite beach? I remember reading that people with amnesia subconsciously gravitate toward places that meant something to them. You could start by going there, bring her photo with you and ask around in case someone's seen her."

Olive thinks about this. "I don't know my mom's favorite beach. She went to a lot of them."

"Maybe ask your dad?"

Olive shakes her head. "I tried to tell him about seeing Mom. He told me I was just hallucinating."

Natalie rolls her eyes as her phone begins to bleat in her backpack. A half-dozen heads turn to stare at them. Natalie makes her *Who, me?* innocent face back at them, then stands up, winding her tie around her fist. "That's my mom, she's waiting for me in the car outside." She stops, looking at Olive. "You're doing OK? You're not freaking out about this?"

Olive nods, standing. "I'm fine," she says, and it's true: With Natalie standing there across from her, she feels like it's all making more sense. "I just wish I knew what to do."

"I can help. Just let me know how," Natalie says. Abruptly, she leans over the table and gives Olive a hug. They stand there like that for a minute, the wooden table biting into the tops of their legs, their reaching arms awkwardly pressing against their necks. Olive can feel Natalie's warm breath on her skin, and it sets off goose bumps.

Natalie pulls back first. "Text if you think of anything, OK?" she chirps. She heads for the exit, humping her stack of books in the crook of her arm.

Olive checks the time on her cellphone. At the end of her table, the homeless man has fallen asleep with his head on folded arms; a rivulet of drool pools on the pages of his book. Olive locates a granola bar at the bottom of her backpack and slides it over toward him, leaving it within reach of his yellowed fingernails, then starts to gather her things.

At home, Olive sits at her desk for a long time, staring uncomprehendingly at her German homework but mostly thinking about her mom. In her lap, Catsby-the-cat purrs, while above her head, Gizmo—a one-legged parakeet Olive found in the garden last spring—rattles her birdcage bell, working valiantly to taunt the cat. Downstairs, Olive's father is banging around the kitchen, most likely overcompensating for her mom's death by making some unnecessarily elaborate dinner.

She knows that her father wants her to keep him company while he cooks; the weird hungry look he gets on his face whenever she walks into the kitchen makes her feel like the shittiest daughter on the face of the earth. But she never really knows what to say to him anymore; it's like there's a giant Mom-shaped vortex in the room just sucking up all the air. Plus, he isn't at ease around her, the way Mom was: He tries too hard. He wants it too much. He cracks silly jokes to make her laugh, probably because when she smiles, he can reassure himself that she's actually not *too* sad. But she is sad. She feels like she's failing him every time she opens her mouth, so it's easier to stay up here in her room and hope that he figures out how to be happy by himself.

She stares blankly at her homework, unable to focus. It's barely six o'clock and already pitch-black out, the clouds damping all light; when she tries to look out the window to the street, all she can see is her own reflection. A face as bland and unmemorable as instant oatmeal, a body that falls straight from neck to thigh with no sign of a waist. She knows she's not supposed to care so much that she's not beautiful, like her mother—there are so many more important things to worry about, like Ebola and ocean acidification levels—but she can't help herself.

She turns to the Rainer Maria Rilke poem she's supposed to be memorizing:

> Lass dir Alles geschehn: Schönheit und
>   Schrecken.
> Man muss nur gehn: Kein Gefühl ist das
>   fernste.
> Lass dich von mir nicht trennen.

"Olive?" She hears her dad calling up the stairs. In her lap, Catsby hisses, the hair along his back lifting. He stabs Olive through her sweatpants with bared claws, and she yelps, jumping up. As she does, she abruptly feels so faint that she has to grip the arm of her desk chair and sit back down again. It's as if the house is dropping out from below her, tipping her off-balance, and she's in danger of flying right off the surface of the planet. That strange smell again—something burning. She looks back up at the window to orient herself and has just enough time to think *Oh my God* as she recognizes her mother's form mirrored back at her.

Billie stands a few feet behind Olive's chair. She looks just as she did yesterday—same hair, same dress, same bemused expression. Olive sits motionless, battling excitement and nausea, afraid that if she turns around to see whether her mother is really standing behind her, the moment will pass. Instead, she stares at her mother's reflection in the window, transfixed by the familiar way Billie is holding her elbow with one cupped hand, the way her hair blows around her ears, the clench of her thigh muscles outlined underneath the white dress.

This is *real*, she thinks happily, only now realizing that she's been half worried that she imagined the whole thing. She stares at her mom and waits for her to speak.

But Billie says nothing. She smiles, puts a hand on her hip, cocks an eyebrow. As they look at each other, time grows elastic, stretching and contracting. Olive tries to take in a detail that might help her pinpoint a location—is her mom standing on the beach, and is it one that Olive recognizes?—but the reflection is too indistinct to see clearly. Still, she can sense a vast open space and a night sky shot through with stars, an implausible number of stars.

"So, are you going to stop staring and get off your duff?" Billie suddenly asks in a voice so loud it makes Olive jump. "You keep sitting there and the world will pass you by."

"Sorry, Mom," Olive says. "You have to help me. Where are you?"

Billie gives an impatient shake of her head, as if waiting for Olive to figure it out herself. The air seems to dance around her head, a soft flurry of tiny wings flickering through the dark. Are those moths?

"Just tell me—" Olive says, more urgently, right as her father opens the door to her bedroom. For one disorienting second, it feels as if all three of them are there in the room, like old times. In that fleeting moment, Olive feels the best she's felt all year.

"Dad, look," she blurts, leaping up; but by the time she spins fully around, there is no one standing behind her chair at all. Just her father with an oven mitt on one hand and a small square of paper in the other. She turns back to the window, but her mother has vanished from view. All she can see is the barren oak tree in their front yard shaking in the wind, its battered branches illuminated by the neighbor's motion-detector light.

Her father follows her gaze back out the window. "Yeah, I should trim that tree before it ends up in our living room," he says. He turns back, registering Olive's odd expression. "Hey. You feeling all right?" He is overly solicitous, smiling a little too hard, and Olive can tell that he's feeling guilty about their argument the previous night. "All that German poetry giving you weltschmerz?"

For a second, she debates telling him. But what's the point? He clearly didn't see her mom, and Olive isn't interested in a rehash of their previous conversation. *"Es geht mir gut,"* she says instead.

"*Das ist gut.*" He grins, and the lines in his face deepen, and Olive can glimpse why the Claremont Moms always get so self-conscious when he shows up at school. The square jaw that looks so awkward on *her* makes him look strong and capable, and he's got thick sandy hair that's shaggy enough to make him look vaguely cool for a dad, and his deep-set gray eyes are framed by long, dark lashes. Olive doesn't have those lashes. This is patently unfair.

Her father is talking. "Look, I want to go back to what you said last night." Before Olive can interject, he shoves the scrap of paper he's holding into her hand. It's a business card: MEREDITH ALBRIGHT, FAMILY THERAPIST. "I think maybe it would help you to talk about your mom with someone. And this woman, she's supposedly a really terrific therapist." He pauses. "Harmony recommended her."

"Harmony?" Olive repeats her name, aghast. "You told her what I said?"

Harmony always seems to be around these days, puttering around the kitchen or cutting flowers in the garden or hanging out with Dad in their living room, as if she's slid into the spot that Olive's mother only recently vacated. It was nice at first to have her mom's friend there helping out; plus, Harmony was good at lifting Olive's dad out of that heavy blankness that hung over him in the months after Mom died. He didn't drink as much when Harmony was around. But it's been a year now, and her dad is doing a lot better—especially since he began writing the memoir—so she's ready for Harmony to start having her own life again rather than invading theirs.

Her father looks taken aback by her reaction. "I

just told her that it seemed like you were still struggling with your mom's death."

Olive can't help herself. "Mom's *not* dead. I told
you I saw her."

Her father flinches. "Look, just hear me out.
Maybe you did see your mother, maybe you didn't.
Either way, it can't hurt to go talk to a professional
about it, can it?"

*Why do adults think that every problem can be
fixed by sending you to talk to a more qualified
adult?* Olive thinks. It's like a game of hot potato:
Whenever you have an idea or emotion that doesn't
fit comfortably into the box that the world has built
for you, everyone goes into a frenzy trying to find an
expert who can convince you to climb back inside.
Olive is tired of therapists, of career counselors and
school nurses, with their pointless worksheets and
probing questions that accomplish exactly nothing.

*You keep sitting there and the world will pass
you by.*

But then she looks back up at her dad, noticing
his hopeful expression. His eyes are ringed with
puffy circles of fatigue, as if the day has drained
him. She wishes she could share with him the light-
ness inside her, her belief that things are about to
change for the better. She *isn't* crazytown. She is
clearheaded and calm, as if she's about to walk into
a classroom and ace a midterm for which she is 100
percent prepared.

Dad may not believe me now, she thinks, *but he
will when I find Mom.*

"Whatever," she says. "Sure. Fine. *Warum nicht?*"

"Great," he says, brightening. "Thanks, Bean.

I'm glad." He slides his arm around her shoulder and gives her upper arm a playful nip with the oven mitt.

"Yeah, but Dad," she says. "For the record. You don't need to worry about me."

Her father laughs. "It's just my nature," he says as he starts to back out of her bedroom. "Dinner's almost ready. Fettuccine Alfredo."

"I'll be down in a minute." Olive flips off her lamp and grabs her German reader to mark her place. Then she stops, scanning the translation of the Rilke poem:

Let everything happen to you: beauty and
    terror.
Just keep going. No feeling is final.
Don't let yourself lose me.

I won't lose you, Mom, she thinks. She seizes on the image of her mom's face flickering in the dark. And then she knows: *Not moths. Butterflies.*

She fishes her phone out of her backpack and types up a quick text to Natalie. *Offer 4 help still good? Let's go 2 beach this Sat. I have an idea where Mom might be.*

The answer comes back two seconds later. *Pick me up at 10.*

Olive deletes the messages from her iPhone history, to be on the safe side, before going downstairs to join her father.

WHERE THE MOUNTAIN MEETS THE SKY

My Life with Billie Flanagan

BY JONATHAN FLANAGAN

In the early years of her life, Olive was her mother's shadow, one fist always clutching at the fabric of Billie's pants as she went about the day. She bumped around in Billie's wake, undeterred by flour in her hair and water splashed in her face and bruises on her toes. I sometimes wondered if this would eventually drive Billie crazy, but if anything, she seemed to encourage it.

Often I'd wake up in the middle of the night and discover that Billie was missing from our bed. If I tiptoed down the hall and stood outside the door to Olive's room I would hear the two of them whispering to each other in the dark. When Billie slipped back between our sheets I would roll over to her and ask, "What does she tell you?" "Oh, girl talk," Billie would murmur. Sometimes I'd peek in on Olive, too, but whenever I crouched by the side of her bed, watching her chest rise and fall, she never woke up.

Instead of enrolling Olive in preschool, Billie took her on

nature walks in Strawberry Canyon; to pick through the tide pools in Pescadero; to hear free concerts in Stern Grove. When neighborhood moms came over to our house and complained about the grind of parenthood—the endless diapers, the whining and the tantrums, the broken sleep—Billie would glance over at Olive, quietly looking at picture books in the corner, and demur. The day when we finally walked Olive over to the local kindergarten, I saw Billie staring at the asphalt yard, the molded-plastic play structure, with a look on her face of pure rage.

I was jealous of their relationship but also happy to see Billie so lit up by motherhood. I'd think of my own mother, worn down after the death of my sister—sweet but defeated; supportive but incapable of really understanding me—and feel thankful that my daughter had something better, something more intimate and vivid.

I was also relieved that Olive had one parent who was constantly present. As I'd risen up the ranks at *Decode,* the technology revolution that I'd insisted was going to make everyone's life easier had ended up making mine harder. Work spilled into all the previously empty spaces of my life: emails late at night, phone pinging with text messages during meals, round-the-clock deadlines as *Decode* morphed from a weekly magazine to a wholesale "media company" with hourly updates. I'd somehow enabled a twenty-four-hour rat race in which I could never step off the track. I consoled myself that at least my salary was freeing up Billie, even if all she seemed to want to do with that freedom was focus it on Olive.

One day I got a call at work from the front desk of Olive's school, wondering if Olive was feeling better. Apparently, Olive had some kind of terrible virus, had missed kindergarten for three days; they'd been trying to get in touch with

Billie, but she wasn't answering the phone. I hung up, perplexed—hadn't Olive been sitting there at the breakfast table just that morning, smiling happily in her rainbow jammies as she ate her oatmeal?

I bailed out of work and headed home. When I walked through the front door, I discovered our house transformed into a Moroccan den. Billie had draped the living room in velvet fabric, blocking out the light from the windows. The furniture was pushed to the walls. There were candles burning on the mantels and on the precarious arms of the sofa, whose cushions were scattered across the floor and repurposed as lounge pillows. Olive and Billie lay there, picture books scattered among the ruins of a picnic. Still in their pajamas at two in the afternoon.

Seeing me, Olive froze, her guilty conscience written across her face; but Billie began to laugh. "Olive, we are so *busted*." She waved me down into their den, and I tucked myself into the tiny space beside them. Books slid under my rear: Greek goddesses, the Brothers Grimm, Hans Christian Andersen.

"So, what's going on here?" I asked.

Olive looked at her mother and then me. "We're doing math this week, and Ms. Chang made me cry, so Mommy said I don't have to go to school if I don't want to."

Billie wrapped a protective arm around Olive. "Olive came up with her own method for doing subtraction, and the teacher told her she wasn't allowed to do it that way. What the fuck. They're trying to zap every bit of creativity right out of her." She squeezed our daughter against her chest. "We're not sending her back there."

I struggled to absorb this. "But why didn't you tell me?"

"The last thing you need is more stress. I thought I'd tell you once I'd figured out the solution." She looked down at

Olive, smoothed the fuzzy part of her hair. "Besides, I needed some time with my baby. I missed her."

Olive smiled up at me, smelling like animal crackers and orange juice. "Mommy says that sometimes it's important to have a secret," she said.

I remember raising an eyebrow at Billie and seeing her look back at me, wide-eyed: *Who, me?* Then she unfolded herself, standing up so that the drapes caressed her dark hair, as if they, too, couldn't help but want to touch her. Looming above us, the candles flickering across her face, she looked giant, heroic. "Isn't it, though?" she said. "When Olive looks back at her childhood, what will she remember? All those identical days in the classroom or the few days we played hooky together?"

Billie was right, of course. Although Olive was enrolled in a new school by the following Monday, that stolen week remains one of her most vivid childhood memories: "The time Mom pretended to homeschool me by feeding me cookies in a fort in the living room."

Other people didn't get this about our marriage. When I told my parents what Billie had done, they reacted as if the fact that she didn't confer with me on every single child-rearing decision was something to be worried about. But I understood the opposite: that magic was an essential part of what made Billie such a good mom, magic that was antithetical to the conventional and mundane. Yes, Billie sometimes went rogue, but I also never received the kind of desperate accusatory phone calls I often overheard at the office— "When are you coming home? The baby is crying, we need milk, you're late." Billie had rejected this corrosive side of parenthood, the part where two people bicker over territorial lines in the sand. She trusted that everything would all work itself out, that we would all find each other in the end. And we always did.

Later that night, after Olive had been tucked in bed, Billie and I went back to her Moroccan den and drank a bottle of wine and had sex by candlelight. Afterward, she poked at a velvet curtain, sending the shadows shimmering across it. "I always wanted a secret hideout when I was a kid," she said. "Once I built one in my bedroom, and you know what my father did when he found it? He knocked it to the ground and then took me down to the basement and shut me inside. Said that an honest person wouldn't need to keep secrets, and besides there are no secrets from God, I couldn't hide from His judgment, and that I should think about *that* while I said my prayers."

She laughed, a sharp ironic bark. "When I was twelve, I found his porn stash hidden under the porch. It was all *Barely Legal* kind of stuff, cheerleaders and girls in bobby socks. So much for no secrets, right?" She paused, remembering. "A few years after *that* was when he got caught feeling up my best friend."

"Jesus, Billie. I'm so sorry."

She glanced over at me, shaking her head. "No. I don't want you feeling sorry for me. I don't feel sorry for myself. I made sure that didn't define me."

So I quietly held her in my arms, wondering how she'd managed to spin magic out of that mess, to be such a terrific parent when she'd had such bad ones. Perhaps we were not doomed to echo our parents after all; perhaps we truly had the ability to write our own life stories, to change the endings if we wanted to. Together, the two of us could build something entirely new.

With Billie, I felt the freedom in this possibility.

4

JONATHAN SITS ON THE floor of Billie's bedroom closet, sorting through sixteen years of his wife's existence. Stacks of musty sweaters and grass-stained running shoes; socks missing their mates, holes at the heels; silk scarves received as Christmas gifts from Jonathan's mother and rarely worn. Bowls full of unidentified buttons, a dusty stack of old *Outside* magazines, a box stuffed full of Olive's grade school artwork.

A growing line of shopping bags stands sentry outside the closet, scrawled with Sharpie instructions: SAVE—DISCARD—DONATE—GIVE TO OLIVE.

He's already tackled the vanity and the overflowing master bathroom drawers. Billie's hairbrush, woven with dark threads: into the trash. The oxycodone she was prescribed after a biking accident but never took: put aside for recycling. Her jewelry box, filled with tangled chains: give to Olive. Congealing bottles of expensive hand lotion, yellowing packets of holiday novelty tissues, four different kinds of sport sunscreen. Flotsam of little importance—just *stuff*—and yet together it somehow added up to a human being, each worn-out sandal or solitary earring a moment, a decision, a reflection of taste and opinion.

And this *stuff*—it's everywhere. In every room, every drawer, every countertop. Even the freezer: Just last week, Harmony unearthed a Ziploc of frostbitten scones labeled in Billie's handwriting: CRANBERRY-LEMON. Harmony was about to throw it in the trash when she noticed the panicked look on Jonathan's face. She silently put it back where she'd found it.

He knew—he's *known*—that the refusal to purge was a kind of magical thinking: as if Billie might walk back in the door and be furious to discover that he'd donated her clothes to the Salvation Army. He's treated Billie's possessions like totems, keeping the possibility of her alive; keeping her fresh in his mind. No *wonder Olive's attempting to hallucinate her mother back into existence,* he thinks. *Billie's the only piece missing here: Olive's just completing the puzzle.*

This morning when he woke up, he decided it was finally time. Olive's mental health was clearly at stake. They were heading into rocky waters again, with the anniversary coming up; he needed to do everything he could to help Olive through that, even if it meant confronting the task he'd spent an entire year avoiding. Jonathan had waited until Olive left for the day—he'd allowed her to take the Subaru into the city with Natalie for cryptically described teen girl entertainments (museums, shopping, sugar consumption) with the promise that she'd check in via text—before yanking open the freezer and retrieving the bag of frostbitten scones. He tossed these in the trash and replaced the lid with a click of gut-wrenching finality.

Then he went upstairs to Billie's closet, opened the doors, and inhaled its familiar smell. It no longer smelled quite so much like *her;* mostly, it smelled like dust and old sneakers.

Three hours and eleven garbage bags later, Jonathan feels—well, not *good,* exactly, but a whole lot better than he'd anticipated. *This is necessary for both of you,* he chastises himself as he tosses a pile of old T-shirts in a bag (pausing to press a lingering finger against a familiar turmeric-colored stain and recall, *Lamb curry*). *Part of the process. We need to start moving forward.*

(And yet doesn't he know firsthand, because of Jenny, that that's not how it works? That grief isn't something you can walk away from after a finite amount of time, but is something that washes you along, tumbling you in and out with the tides?)

He climbs on the stepladder to check the top shelf, where he discovers one last dusty shoe box, shoved toward the back. He pulls this out, sits cross-legged on the closet floor, and opens it. Inside are a handful of childhood photographs and a stack of yellowed sketchbooks.

He starts with the photographs first. He has seen them before, but it's been years. There's a Sears portrait of Billie as a toddler, stuffed into a frilly white dress, her mouth curling down into the start of a wail; and a photograph of her parents posed stiff as flagpoles in front of a rusting station wagon. They look like they've stepped out of 1952, even though the picture was surely taken in the late seventies, their faces gray and grim. Behind them, a dust-stricken Central Valley farmhouse, a tire swing shaded by an orchard of almond trees.

He turns the photos over to examine the backs, but they aren't labeled. *How sad,* he thinks. *The only remaining pictures of Billie's family, exiled to a forgotten shoe box.* Then again, Billie wasn't one to romanticize her unhappy childhood. She'd run away from home—some tiny rural hamlet outside Bakersfield—during her last year of high school, not long after her father got caught molesting her friend. She never spoke to her parents again. Not even a birth announcement when Olive was born. "Why would I want to do *that*?" she said when Jonathan made the suggestion, and he could have sworn he saw the hair on her neck stand up. It reminded him of a dog with raised hackles. "They get what they deserve. They have no right to enjoy my life now."

He stares at the picture of her parents, trying to imagine his wife springing from the loins of these two unpleasant strangers. And yet there's something of Billie in her mother's face, coarser and faded but with the same firm set to her chin. Maybe Billie's mother would have been beautiful, too, if she'd lived a different life.

He puts these aside and lifts the cover of one of the notebooks. Inside are sketches—pencil renderings of his own face, captured back in his twenties. In one of them, Jonathan gazes directly at the artist, his lips parted as if he's about to speak, his eyes squinting slightly as if looking into a bright light. He stares at it, remembering the way Billie used to sketch him all the time when they first met. Later, it was all landscapes.

He's about to put this in the GIVE TO OLIVE pile when he notices a photograph stuck to the back of the sketchbook. He carefully peels it off and examines it. It's a Polaroid of Billie that he's never seen before, probably taken around age twenty or twenty-one, during her Lost Years. She's almost unrecognizable: The girl he'd meet years later as a brunette with a pixie cut here has long bleached-blond tangles. There's a stud in the tender flesh of her nose, a ring in her eyebrow. She's wearing wire-rimmed glasses instead of the contacts she'd later upgrade to, and she gazes through them directly at the camera, as if staring it down.

Behind her, his arm wrapped possessively around her neck, is a young man with eyes as black and inscrutable as a crow's, peering out from a face otherwise obscured by wild curly hair and several weeks' worth of stubble. He grins smugly at the camera. Jonathan turns the photo over and reads the writing on the back: *Sidney, 1992.*

He flips the photo back over to study it more closely. Sidney was Billie's boyfriend during her Lost Years, a former philosophy major turned anarchist-activist drug dealer. They'd met not long after Billie had run away from home; together, they moved around the Pacific Northwest for years, until Sidney was finally arrested with a stash of drugs—pot? or acid? Jonathan can't remember—in the trunk of his car. It was his third strike. He got twenty years.

"Oh God, Sidney" was the way Billie always referred to him. As in, "Oh God, Sidney. I can't believe I stayed with him for so long." Still, whenever she talked about him, she got a hot look on her face, as if she secretly relished the brazen things they'd done together: "You want to hear about stupid, try chaining yourself to an old-growth redwood while high on three tabs of acid with a half-dozen bulldozers full of angry loggers coming straight at you. Yeah, Sidney did that. He got three weeks in jail for that stunt. Right intentions, wrong execution, and of course I was left to clean up his mess."

Billie fled the Pacific Northwest right after Sidney was arrested for the last time, "scared straight," as she put it. She traveled the world for several years before heading to San Francisco in the late nineties in order to take advantage of the dot-com boom. By the time Jonathan met her on the J Church streetcar just after the end of the millennium, she was finishing a graphic design degree at the Academy of Art, learning HTML, and utterly broke.

He turns the photo in his hands, thinking. He knows nothing about Sidney, really, not even his last name. They met only once, and briefly, at Billie's memorial service—the man had come out of nowhere, probably lured out from the rock he was living under by the press reports about Billie's death. He gripped Jonathan's hand and muttered a string of unfinished thoughts—"Sorry, that woman, Jesus"—and then disappeared again as Jonathan reeled, astonished by his presence. He left an impression of stubble and flannel and stringy unkempt hair, and a sharp smell, something itchy and intense oozing from his pores.

Jonathan later regretted not talking more to him that day, because Sidney had always been the mystery at the center of Billie's Lost Years, the character Jonathan least understood. Not because Billie failed to talk about him but because Jonathan could never quite wrap his head around the archetype. Jonathan hadn't exactly encountered a lot of convicted criminals in his life—they didn't hang around Stanford, or the Berkeley Bowl, or the cubicles of *Decode* magazine—so Sidney felt more mythical than real, like a character from a fairy tale: the Bad News Boyfriend. Up until the memorial, Jonathan didn't even know what Sidney looked like: Billie had lost all her photos from those years when her backpack was stolen while she was traveling in India.

Or so she said, he realizes now. Because apparently there was this one photo, which she had kept hidden away. He studies it, wondering—why? It's not like they kept in touch: The one time Sidney wrote to her from jail a few years back, she burned the letter without even reading it.

Probably she just wanted to put that period of her life firmly behind her, he thinks now. She never did seem particularly nostalgic about her past, not even in the early days of their relationship, when he was plying her for stories. Instead, both Lost Years Billie *and* Art Student Billie were swiftly supplanted by Berkeley Mom Billie, who emerged when Olive was born a year after they married. *That* had taken Jonathan by surprise. This new Billie spent her days ferrying Olive from playdates to Mommy and Me music, baking from-scratch cupcakes, and hosting kids' birthday parties at Fairyland. Baby-Wearing Club charter member, room mom, PTA secretary, silent-auction chair: It was as if motherhood had been a role she was determined to conquer. He sometimes suspected that Billie was attempting to rewrite her own dysfunctional childhood through her relationship with their daughter. How else to explain why someone with such a fiercely independent edge would pivot into a life of such domesticity?

Billie's artistic ambitions also seemed to fizzle, not long after her first solo show failed to sell out. She settled into part-time freelance Web design work, mostly designing logos and banner ads for dot-coms. On the weekends, she sometimes pulled out her paints, but whenever he encouraged her to make a real go of her art, she recoiled. "And what? End up being one of those artists whose work hangs forgotten on the walls of the local Brew Ha Ha, getting splattered with latte foam? I'd rather paint only for myself."

Had he failed to give her something she needed to thrive? He couldn't quite tell, and whenever he raised the subject with her, she insisted she was perfectly happy with the way things were. "Why, you don't think motherhood is a valid life choice?" she finally snapped; and she was right. His doubt was unfair. If she didn't express any regret about the life she'd left behind—the oils going dry, the travel backpack sold in a yard sale, the tribal tattoos long ago zapped away—who was he to fixate on it?

After a while, he almost forgot about Lost Years

Billie. So it was a shock, five years back, when they bumped into Harmony up on College Avenue one afternoon. They'd taken Olive out for ice cream and were walking back home with their melting cones when, from behind them, a woman's voice had tentatively called out: "Sparrow? Is that you?"

Billie froze for a second. One hand jerked reflexively up in the air, and a wild expression crossed her face; for a heart-stopping moment, it was as if he was looking at the untamed girl she once was, someone capable of things that he couldn't quite wrap his head around. She turned. "Oh my God. *Harmony.*"

Jonathan turned to see a pretty blond woman in a batik sundress, all soft and fluttery, rushing toward them. "Sparrow?" he muttered to his wife.

Billie kept her eyes focused on the woman in her path. "It was my nickname way back when. Don't laugh." A smile spread itself across her face as the woman ran into her arms. She murmured into the woman's hair, her mint-chip cone dripping green goo on her friend's shoulder. "Harmony. My God. What are you doing here?"

Harmony pulled back and gestured at a man who was coolly sauntering up behind her, in a vintage three-piece suit despite the heat. Jonathan, in flip-flops and stained shorts, grimaced in awkward acknowledgment. "We just moved here from Austin. Sean got a job as an associate professor in the MFA program at Mills. He's a poet!" The boyfriend gave an ironic little smile, his eyes twitching toward Billie's snug T-shirt, but she seemed too absorbed in her long-lost friend to notice.

"I can't believe it. All these years." Billie glanced

over at Jonathan and then smiled at Olive, who was staring at her mother as if she were a stranger. "Harmony and I knew each other up in Oregon."

"We used to—" Harmony hesitated and glanced at Billie, as if searching for the right shorthand.

"Go to protests together," Billie finished.

Harmony dimpled. "We met at a sit-in, right? The dam that was endangering the wild salmon?"

"It was spotted owls," Billie corrected her a little sharply.

"That's right!" Harmony leaned down toward Olive, who was soaking all this in with her mouth slightly agape. "I was in my first year at U of O, fresh in from the suburbs, and your mom was this gorgeous independent rebel type from California, and oh my God, I just idolized her. She was always the most confident person in the room."

Billie laughed, and Jonathan noticed a slightly manic edge to her hilarity. "She still is," Jonathan quipped, but neither of the women seemed to register his presence. They circled each other, gripping each other's arms a little too tightly.

In the years that ensued, it sometimes felt like the two women had never let go. Every time he walked into the kitchen, there they were, deep into a bottle of wine and whispering to each other, glancing up at him with an enigmatic expression. Harmony seemed to wake up something inside Billie, something he'd never seen in her when she hung out with her revolving group of kombucha-drinking Berkeley mom friends.

On the surface, Billie and Harmony didn't seem to have terribly much in common. Harmony was a personal chef/caterer, although this was just the most recent iteration of an otherwise haphazard career that also included soy-candle-making, food blogging, and kundalini yoga instruction; she was in and out of relationships and had lived in seven cities over the last decade. She was pliable and nurturing in all the places where Billie was spiky and opinionated, and sometimes Jonathan was surprised that Billie had chosen her as her friend. Then again, it was difficult *not* to like Harmony, the way she slid into their lives like a warm fuzzy blanket, dispensing hugs and foot massages and freshly baked cookies. Billie seemed to regard Harmony as the little sister she'd never had: fondly, committedly, but not without exasperation.

He looks back down at the photographs and the sketchbook, at the pencil strokes in Billie's familiar hand, stricken with a sickening feeling of lost time. He sets the sketchbook in the box and pushes it toward the growing GIVE TO OLIVE pile. He puts aside Billie's childhood photographs to frame. The snapshot of Sidney and Billie he shoves into the pocket of his sweatshirt, not sure what to do with it.

He opens another shoe box, this one less dusty, and finds Billie's collection of marathon finisher medals. He stirs them around with his hand, cheap ribbons and clattering aluminum, and then fishes one out. San Francisco Half Marathon, 2012.

Billie's late-in-life obsession with outdoor sports started with boot camp. She won a gift certificate at a Claremont Girls fall fundraiser and went to the first class out of idle curiosity. She came home enthralled with her teacher, Rita, a platinum-haired cancer survivor with a tattoo of lucky dice above her mastectomy scars. *Rita* was brash, gutter-mouthed, unapologetic. *Rita* had brushed up against her own mortality and survived. *Rita* was fearless and did whatever she wanted.

Rita talked Billie into trail running, then half marathons, then mountain biking, which led, inevitably, to hiking and mountain climbing. Billie latched on to her new hobby the way she often did with new interests: obsessively, as if determined to master it. Jonathan didn't mind, not at first. It was good that Billie had something to challenge her, especially now that their daughter was pulling away into the self-reliance of puberty. Plus, something of Lost Years Billie had reawakened in her with the return of Harmony; it turned out that the environmentalist who willingly camped out in a giant redwood tree for months at a time hadn't been entirely extinguished. Maybe Billie had lost interest in the activism of those years—driving the long way around Earth Day protests, shunning the local Sierra Club chapter—but she still had nature in her heart.

In the last year of Billie's life, the outdoor adventure trips started devouring entire weekends, jaunts with Rita that took her all over the West Coast, leaving Jonathan and Olive behind. Jonathan didn't particularly like this—not the days-long abandonment, not the somewhat dangerous nature of the activities—but it wasn't his place to object. She needed something for herself, especially considering the hours that *Decode* was demanding now that he was senior management; it wasn't fair that she had to hold up the rest of their lives single-handedly. So he said nothing when she packed up her backpack and headed off to the mountains, not even to point out that maybe it wasn't wise to go hiking alone.

The things you regret in retrospect.

Jonathan shoves the medals back in the box and blows his nose. He stands and examines a pile of hiking gear heaped in a basket in the corner of the closet. Picking up a pair of climbing gloves, he turns them in his hands, remembering his wife heading off at the break of dawn for a weekend climb up Mount Shasta with Rita. The sideways light of a summer sunrise; Jonathan groggy from a late night at work, conscious and present only out of a sense of needing to see her off. Her profile to him as she jammed energy bars and freeze-dried meals into her backpack, which smelled like the factory in which it was made. Her spandex-clad rear end flexing as she stretched, the swish of the nylon of her shell, her twin braids swinging under her baseball cap. A map spread out on the counter, trails marked in red.

He grips the gloves in his fist. What to do with this stuff? Some of it is barely used. And it's not as if Olive has ever shown any interest in mountain climbing.

But Rita climbs, it occurs to him. He experiences a quick pang of nostalgia for Billie's quirky friend. They'd never spoken after the memorial service, although Rita had sent a giant tropical orchid plant that Jonathan promptly killed with neglect. He hadn't even thanked her, finding it far beyond his capabilities at the time to acknowledge the countless condolence bouquets that were ghoulishly dying all over his home.

I should call her up and give her the hiking gear, he thinks. He looks at the gloves and then the mountains of Billie's belongings, the dresser drawers and bedside tables that he has yet to tackle. *I'll finish up later,* he decides. And then he fishes his cellphone out of his pocket and pecks his way down the contact list in search of Rita's phone number.

Rita hasn't changed much in the year since Jonathan last saw her. Her cropped hair is still a blond so platinum that it looks almost white, sprayed aggressively in place, and she wears neon-pink trainers with her skull-print hoodie and camouflage jogging pants. Her skin is unnaturally tan for this overcast Northern California morning.

"Jonathan," she says, sitting across from him. "It's really great to see you. You're OK? Olive's OK?"

They've met at a café not far from Rita's house in Oakland, not one of those new on-trend pour-over coffee places but an old-school diner that Rita recommended, where the coffee costs a buck and tastes like burnt peanuts. Their waitress is old and Slavic and appears to be talking to herself as she swipes at their table with a rag that smells like sour milk. Through the window, Jonathan can see an underfunded public school across the street, kids playing on a playground pieced together from old pipes and discarded tires. So much concrete, so hard on knees and elbows and developing brains. Sometimes he wonders if he's spending a fortune on Olive's fancy private school purely so that when she falls, she lands on grass.

Rita has ordered a plate of scrambled eggs with fruit. He watches as she takes the syrup pitcher off the counter and drowns her meal. She catches him staring and shrugs apologetically. "I hate eggs. This is the only way I can gag them down. But I've got an Iron Girl race in three weeks, so I have to load up on protein." She makes a face at her fork. "Let me tell you, the second I cross that finish line, I'm going to face-plant into a pile of doughnuts."

"See, I've got the face-plant part down, but not the triathlon part." He points at his plate, with its puddle of burger grease and mountain of under-cooked fries.

"Oh, stop it, you're torturing me." Rita smiles. "Honestly, you look good, considering. Have you lost weight?"

"It's the bereavement diet," he says. "I wouldn't recommend it to your clients."

Rita stares at him for a second, then throws her head back and laughs. "You should try boxing. It's great for venting aggression."

"Aggression? I'm the least aggressive person I know. Ask anyone." He eats another fry, smiling.

She studies him. "*Everyone's* aggressive. You should see me in the morning before I have my coffee. My kids clear out of the room the second I walk in it." She wipes off the food clinging to her lips. "Anyway. I'm guessing that you didn't summon me on a Saturday because you wanted fitness tips?"

Jonathan pushes a canvas bag across the table. "I'm finally clearing out Billie's closet, and I came across some things that I thought you might like.

Some equipment you might be able to use. A few mementos—hiking maps, that kind of thing."

Rita touches his hand with her fingertips and squeezes her eyes shut. Her face sparkles with some kind of glittery eye shadow that has fallen down from her eyelids to dust the top of her cheeks.

Jonathan continues, "And I also wanted to thank you for all the things you did for her while she was alive." He swallows, his throat gone dry. "I think she enjoyed the way you kept her on her toes. No one else really did that."

"Billie always liked to be surprised." Rita smiles, remembering. "I wish we'd been able to spend more time together."

"More?" He pokes at his burger. "You saw her more than *we* did that last year. All those weekend trips you took."

Rita gives him a sharp look. Her fork stops halfway to her mouth, syrup slowly dripping down to the paper place mat. "What weekend trips?"

"The hiking trip to Mount Shasta? The marathon in Mendocino . . . that weekend when you went backpacking in Yosemite . . ." He trails off as he registers the confusion on Rita's face, and a single horrible thought flies into his mind: *Oh shit*.

Rita carefully puts down her fork. "I'm not quite sure what you're talking about. We didn't go to Mount Shasta together. Or Yosemite. I *do* remember doing a half marathon with her a few months before she died. But that was local, in San Jose. We didn't have to do an overnight trip for it."

A fleeting hope passes through him: Maybe he's mixed up the trips or is remembering wrong. After all, it's been a while. But dread starts to build as he fumbles in his pocket for his phone and puts it on the table, stabbing at the buttons with fingers that have gone numb. "Let me show you—all of those trips were in our shared calendar." He pages back a year and then spins the phone toward her. "See? Here. And here. Shasta? Yosemite?"

Rita leans over to examine the calendar, but she's already shaking her head. "Truth is, that last year, she was bailing out on me a lot. We'd make plans and then she'd cancel them at the last minute. I know we *talked* about hiking up Mount Shasta, but believe me, it never happened." She lifts her eyes and registers his distress, recoiling. "Oh shit. Me and my big mouth. I'm sorry."

"No need to be sorry, it's not your fault." He can barely get the words out as his growing horror slowly squeezes his vocal cords shut. It just doesn't make sense. He tries to recalculate the facts, making them add up to something other than what they do, but he keeps landing back at the same unbearable conclusion. *Billie was lying.*

Rita blinks across the table at him, her eggs forgotten. "I figured she was just burning out. She'd been going so strong. All that running and hiking and biking . . . it can take a real toll on your body. Sometimes it's good to just take a break." She sucks in her upper lip and chews on it. "So I assumed that was what was going on."

Jonathan shakes his head, his thoughts spinning in frantic circles. If Billie wasn't with Rita, where was she? He looks down at his meal as if answers might be found in the congealing meat. When he looks up again, he can read in Rita's eyes what she's thinking, because it's the same thing he is: *Billie was having an affair.* Why else would she lie about where she was?

It's impossible. Sure, they had their issues, after all those years of marriage (and he has a sudden little bump of guilt, remembering one particular lapse of judgment), but he never would have failed to notice a marital rift *that* big. Or would he? Because, judging by the missing weekends, he was clearly too blind to notice *something.* So what else did he miss? *Christ.* He mentally runs through every behavioral tic of Billie's last year on earth, her restlessness all of a sudden interpretable in a whole different light. If it was an affair, with whom? That divorced dad, Zack Something, on the fundraising committee at Claremont Prep—he was always standing a little too close to her, maybe something was going on there? Or one of those fit backpackery types, someone she might have met on a hike or at a race. A Cal student seeking Mrs. Robinson. A dot-com billionaire. Who knows.

The smell of bacon from his burger is nauseating; he slides his plate over to the next booth and then stares blankly at his hands spread-eagled on the table before him. They seem large, clumsy, useless.

"Maybe she was going on those trips but just doing it alone and not telling anyone. She did that sometimes, right? I mean, that's how she died, hiking alone . . ." Rita says. She's looking more stricken by the minute, as if all this is her fault.

"Maybe that's it," he hears himself saying, as if by convincing Rita that this is true, he might convince himself. But he remembers it too clearly for there to be a mistake. He remembers Billie returning from her Mount Shasta weekend, sunburned and sticky. He remembers her dropping her backpack on the kitchen floor, downing a glass of water, and looking directly at him. "I beat Rita to the summit," she said, and smiled. "We made a bet, so she had to carry my tent back down the mountain."

If Rita didn't carry Billie's tent back down the mountain, who did? Was there ever a mountain at all?

Back at home, Jonathan goes straight to the bedroom. He kneels on all fours and scrabbles around underneath his bed, casting aside dust bunnies. There it is, deep under the mattress where he shoved it a month after Billie's death. Jonathan pulls it out carefully: a tote bag in tourmaline-blue leather, his gift to Billie on her fortieth birthday.

Inside this, protected by a neoprene sleeve, her laptop.

He climbs up on the bed and sits there, his back braced against the headboard, weighing the laptop's titanium heft in his hands. His pulse races way too fast, making rational thought difficult. He thinks of his neat little love story in a thousand pieces on the floor. *Where the Mountain Meets the Sky,* 210 pages (so far) of connubial bliss with a tragic ending: Could he really have overlooked a major plot point in the third act?

"This is a bad idea," he whispers. Even if his wife *was* having an affair, what would it help him to know about it now? Why ruin his tender memories of her? (A more practical whisper: *How will* this *fit in your memoir?*)

He plugs the computer in and powers it up, waiting for it to groan back to life.

The keyboard is still smeared with the oils from Billie's hands. Her sneeze marks spot the screen. The laptop hums softly as Billie's start-up programs spring open one by one. Where to start? He already glanced through her laptop right after she died, retrieving any critical contacts and files, but he didn't go much deeper than that. It seemed like a form of torture he didn't want to face at the time.

Now he takes a look at the chaotic mess of her desktop. Every square inch is cluttered with folders and files, tiled so thickly on the screen that they overlap at the edges. He starts with the abyss of Billie's email program, an archive that runs 681MB deep. He types in *Shasta,* then *Yosemite,* to see if anything pops up. Nothing does. He doesn't see any unfamiliar male names cluttering her in-box, at least not on a quick glance. Her address book runs to more than two thousand entries; he clicks through a few pages, then gives up.

What else? His wife always shunned social media— "I just don't see why everyone needs to know my business"—so there's no Facebook profile or Instagram feed through which he might pore in search of mysterious strangers' comments. Instead, he clicks over to her calendar. There they are, the trips in question: Shasta, Yosemite, Mendocino, and a few others he made Rita identify before he left the diner.

But her calendar yields nothing else that adds clarity, no secret initials or private notations.

It should be reassuring, but it's not. He can't shake this crawling sensation: *There's something you're missing.*

He considers the files and folders scattered across her desktop. Her laptop's memory is maxed out, each digital crevasse crammed with the ephemera of Billie's day-to-day existence: family photos, work designs, a lifetime's worth of MP3s, plus hundreds of trail maps, recipes, long-forgotten grocery lists, recommendation letters for old babysitters, an eleven-year-old workbook for online traffic school. He clicks around helplessly, not even sure what he is searching for. It's like looking for a needle in a haystack without knowing what a needle even looks like.

He is about to give up and put the laptop away when he stumbles across the folder. It's in the lower corner of her desktop, hidden underneath another folder labeled PLANETRX MOCK-UPS, easy to miss. The folder has an oddly cryptic, abbreviated label: RR. It is password-protected.

Something inside his chest clenches. Nothing else on her laptop has been deemed worth hiding behind a protective wall, not even her email account. He looks at the history of the folder: created February 11, nine months before her death.

He clicks and clicks and clicks at the folder, testing out passwords, but it refuses to let him in. And still he prods at it. Frustrated, he finally gives up, closing the lid of the laptop and tossing it on the bedside table. The computer knocks a book—Billie's unfinished Tana French mystery—to the floor. The bookmark spills out.

Jonathan picks up both book and bookmark. He flips through the novel in order to put the bookmark back, looking for some kind of indentation in the pages, a gap in the spine that might reveal the correct spot. And then he realizes what he's doing. He hurls the book toward the line of bags sitting in front of the closet. It hits the one marked DISCARD and flops, pages bent, onto the carpet.

Next to Jonathan, the light of the laptop's electronic eye blinks slowly, in contrast with his own rapid breath, thrumming with promise of the secrets inside.

5

THE TEMPERATURE GAUGE in her mother's
Subaru says that it's fifty-two degrees out. A dismal
day to be at the beach. Olive gazes out at the ocean,
her face stinging with the salt whipped off the waves
by the wind, her jeans heavy with the damp. A ceiling of clouds hangs so low that Olive thinks she
might be able to insert her hand right up to the wrist
and watch her fingers disappear. The ocean is steel
gray, pissed off, huge and foamy.

Natalie sits nearby on the closed-up lifeguard
stand, a puffy parka wrapped around her, its hood
yanked up over her ponytail; her hands are wrapped
around a vanilla mocha latte that went cold ages
ago. Olive can see her friend shivering from where
she wanders along the low-tide line, collecting bits
of trash. Olive's cold, too, but she's too wound up to
feel it. She skirts the water, the sand coarse beneath

her sneakers, tiny sand crabs scuttling out of her way. The air smells like eucalyptus and seaweed.

At the far end of the beach are the tide pools. A man and his little boy are clambering across the rocks, bundled up in their parkas. The boy is poking anemones with his finger, and Olive can see the father crouching next to his son, pointing out starfish and sandcastle worms and clusters of acorn barnacles. The waves fling themselves against the rocks that the kid stands on, sending up fans of froth-flecked spray.

At the other end of the beach, a giant rock shaped like an arch sits just off the shore, its base submerged in three feet of water. An old woman is walking her Labrador up and down the sand before it, throwing kelp bulbs into the waves for the dog to retrieve. The dog is old and limping and crusted with wet sand, but he plunges into the waves with his teeth bared in a sort of canine smile.

Otherwise, the place is empty.

It *is* the beach from her visions, isn't it? It has to be. The last day trip that they took together as a family before Billie disappeared, the day they came to see the monarchs. Her mom cried when they watched the butterfly migration. Maybe there was some significance to her mother's decision to come here that day; a reason that had drawn her mom back here, subconsciously or not.

But today there are no butterflies—this year's migration hasn't arrived yet. The beach is deserted; not even the surfers are out. Olive and Natalie have been at the beach for two hours, but it took only half a minute to figure out that her mother isn't here. She certainly isn't standing on the edge of the sea in a filmy white dress, surrounded by butterflies, waiting for Olive to find her. Maybe it was naïve to think that bringing her mom home was going to be as easy as zipping down the Peninsula to Santa Cruz and picking her up; but OK, yeah, Olive had *hoped*. Would that have been any crazier than the other stuff that's going on in her head?

One thing is clear: If her visions are some sort of a mystical puzzle, she's going to need more help interpreting the pieces.

Natalie comes up behind her. "Hey," she says. "I stole some fancy gin from my parents' liquor cabinet. Want some?"

Olive shakes her head, her tennis shoes sinking in the waterlogged sand. A Styrofoam cup washes in on a wave, and she pins it under her toe so that it won't drift back out to sea. Next to her, Natalie steps right and then left, watching the impressions of her feet melt away. Olive worries that she's disappointed; that she, like Olive, believed she was about to have a thrilling encounter with the paranormal. Olive feels like she's let Natalie down.

"You OK?" Natalie asks, peering into her face. "I know you were hoping that your mom would be here."

Olive turns to look at the breaking waves and the giant arch standing sentry over the sea, and for a moment she feels herself swell with the wonder of it all—the world is so vast and so beautiful and so forever—and then she remembers that she is supposed to be sad, too. How can she feel both of these things at once? The loveliness of being alive and the knowledge that it can never last? She feels like she has to let one drop in order to really examine the other one, and yet she isn't sure which one she is supposed to let go of first.

She closes her eyes and tries to see herself the way her mother might if she were watching right now: a tiny figure on a cold beach. Standing there with the mist lapping at her face, Olive thinks of the days when she was a kid and her mother manned the Snack Shack on Olive's grammar school playground, lording over platters of home-baked treats. (Her mom's Pinterest-worthy cupcakes—fondant ladybugs, green aliens with mini-marshmallow eyes— were always the first to sell out.) Olive would huddle with her friends in a corner of the playground, pretending to be embarrassed about her mother's presence across the yard, but secretly proud that her mom was the most beautiful, the most creative, the most *interesting* of all the school moms.

Whenever Olive peeked over at her mom with the plates of cupcakes, she would almost always catch Billie studying her. Just by the way her mom pursed her lips or tilted her head, Olive would know whether or not she approved of her behavior. She would find herself adjusting accordingly: walking away from the girls who giggled too much; shouting a little louder on the soccer field; climbing to the highest bar of the jungle gym. Because as much as Olive wanted the other girls on the playground to like her, she wanted her mom to admire her even more. With her mom just over *there,* watching, guiding, Olive experienced a clarity that she didn't when she was all alone.

Her mother isn't watching today. Olive can't feel her here at all.

"I'm fine," Olive says now, pushing back her melancholy, grasping for the optimism she started out with this morning. "It's just our first try, right?"

Natalie puts her arm around Olive's waist and leans her head on her shoulder. Her hair smells damp and honey-sweet. "This is why I'm a Hindu. They believe in immortality via reincarnation: You can never truly die. So even if your mom is dead—which I'm not saying that she *is*, but if she *were*—she's still alive somewhere."

Olive doesn't find this as comforting as Natalie wants it to be; nor does the doubt in her friend's voice—*even if your mom is dead*—go unnoticed. "Since when are you a Hindu? Last I checked, you were Presbyterian."

Natalie pulls back. "Well, maybe not at the moment, but I reserve the right to be someday."

They watch the waves frothing at the base of the rock bridge. Natalie speaks again: "So, you ready to go home?"

Olive reaches out and steals the bottle of gin from her friend's hand. She takes a quick gulp that burns off a layer of her throat on the way down; fortified, she turns to regard a row of homes on the bluff above the beach. "No way," she says, and points at the first house, a friendly-looking cedar-shingled bungalow with white trim and a picket fence politely keeping beachgoers from wandering onto the property. "Now we go up there and start asking around."

Olive marches up the street, Natalie trailing slightly behind her, and through the gate of the shingled house. A faded sign, hand-painted with bumblebees and monarch butterflies, hangs from a nail by the front door: THE TEMPLETONS. Olive knocks firmly on the door and waits.

A bespectacled elderly woman opens the door and peers at them. She's wearing a fuzzy blue house-coat and purple old-lady slippers embroidered with flowers, and her eyes are enormous and rheumy behind thick prescription lenses. "Can I help you?" she asks.

Olive holds out a photograph of her mother. "I'm sorry to bother you, ma'am. But my mother's gone missing, and I think she may be in the area, and I'm wondering if you could tell me if you've seen her? Any time in the last year?"

"Oh, how awful. Let me see," the old lady clucks, and pulls Olive's hand closer to examine the picture. Her hand is papery and porcelain-thin on Olive's own. "I'm— Well, I'm not sure. It's possible she looks familiar, but my eyes aren't what they used to be." She releases Olive's hand. "People come and go around here. Tourists and vacation rentals; the faces change so much." Mrs. Templeton grips the side of her door, slowly pushing it closed. "Well, then. Good luck."

"Thank you!" Olive calls as the door clicks shut. She turns to face Natalie. "I'm thinking it's overly optimistic to chalk that one up as a *maybe*. We'll say *inconclusive*."

Together, they walk down the street, knocking on doors. Most of the oceanfront houses are vacation homes, shuttered for the winter with blinds closed tightly against the light, like sleeping giants. Alarm-system signs bristle from the tiny gardens planted with juniper and ice plant and moss rose. Could her mother be hidden away in one of these homes? She imagines Billie befuddled with amnesia, being care-taken by a love-struck millionaire who has stashed her in his vacation home to recover her memories of her past life. (OK, yes, this does sound suspiciously like the plotline of a made-for-TV movie she recently watched; but wasn't that supposedly based on a true story? So: possible!)

Olive leads Natalie inland, away from the beach, where the immaculate waterfront rentals segue into a more motley collection of homes. These houses show signs of full-time occupancy—a sun-faded plastic tricycle on its side in the front yard; a garden hose trailing across a driveway; laundry drying in the wind. They knock and knock; whenever some-one answers, Olive displays her picture. The people who live in the homes shake their heads and look uniformly befuddled. *No, no idea. Never seen her. Couldn't tell you. Maybe? Isn't that the lady who works in the grocery? Oh, no, wait, maybe not.* It's all maddeningly useless.

Afternoon gives way to evening. Olive picks up the pace. They stop at a green bungalow with surf-boards pitched against its clapboard walls and wet-suits hanging like empty snakeskins from an upstairs balcony. The windows are hung over with tie-dyed bedsheets. Even from the street, Olive can smell the pot smoke emanating from the house. Natalie looks at her and raises an eyebrow.

They pick their way up the driveway, past a rusting truck with a SnugTop capping the bed, and knock on the door. It swings open to reveal a young blond guy in torn sweatpants and three-day stubble, his blue eyes at half-mast.

"Hey, look," Sweatpants drawls, staring down at them. He puts a hand up against the doorjamb. "Please tell me you're selling Girl Scout cookies? Because I could kill a box of Thin Mints right about now."

Next to her, Natalie lets loose a startled giggle, and Olive turns to stare at her in surprise. Her friend is tugging at her jacket with one hand, pulling it down over the waistband of her jeans, and smoothing back the frizz at her hairline with the other. *Seriously, that?* Olive feels betrayed. She looks back at Sweatpants, trying to see what Natalie clearly sees, the thing that is turning her feminist-minded, super-achieving friend into a ridiculous, self-effacing bubblehead. But all Olive sees is some *dude,* maybe kind of good-looking but nothing particularly special.

It's not like she's never kissed a boy. There was a Berkeley High student named Isaac whom she met volunteering at the Berkeley Nature Conservation Network a while back. He was cute enough, and had a kind of nerd-cool Jew-fro thing going—he was smart, and funny, and safe-seeming—and really *into* her for some reason. So she went with him to a party and then let him kiss her, more out of curiosity than uncontrollable lust. She kept waiting for a rush of excitement, the promised amorous tingle, but the experience mostly reminded her of a trip to the dentist. As Isaac tongued her molars, Olive kept visualizing the slides of amoebas they were studying in her biology class—his germy pseudopods spelunking in her mouth.

Olive knows that Natalie has kissed four boys, mostly guys she's met at the sleepaway AcadaCamp where her parents send her every summer to hone her debating skills. She recently told Olive that she wanted to start going to more Berkeley High parties because she really wanted to lose her virginity before she went to college. "You know, knowledge is power, better to start out with *that* under my control," she explained somewhat apologetically. Olive digested this statement unhappily, feeling a gulf open between them that she didn't know how to cross.

Sweatpants is now joined by a friend, also college-age, this one with a deep tan and long salt-damaged brown hair straggling down his back. He wears a faded shirt that reads DISCO BISCUITS across the front. A damp joint smolders between his fingers, slowly burning down. "How can we help you ladies?"

Olive thrusts the picture under their noses. "I was wondering—have you seen this woman?"

Disco Biscuit reaches out and grabs the photograph and peers at it closely. His eyes roam curiously across Olive's mom's face, and then his own pink-rimmed eyes light up. He turns the picture toward Sweatpants. "Check it out," he says. "Could this be that chick, the one with the McTavish longboard? You know, the one who was getting cleaned up out at the Hook last month? You almost ran over her, remember?"

Sweatpants steps back, trying to focus on the picture under his nose. "Nah. That's not her. She's blond. And her hair is short. She's not, like, a *mom*."

"No, check it out." Disco Biscuit puts his thumb over the top of Olive's mom's head. "Imagine her with different hair. Don'tcha think?"

"You're tripping, man."

Disco Biscuit is clinging to the photo, squinting at the picture with one eye closed and then the other, as if he can't figure out how to focus. "Why you need to find her?"

"She's my mom," Olive says. Her heart rate has tripled. Her mom doesn't surf—*hadn't* surfed—but she *would* surf. It is a Billie Flanagan kind of thing to do. Could she have bleached her hair blond, too? Cut it off? Maybe she is in disguise, trying to disappear. But that just raises another, thornier question: disappear from whom?

Disco Biscuit takes a step backward, tucking the joint behind his leg as if only now aware of it. "Well, if she's who I think she is, she's a local." He points down toward the ocean. "I used to see her down at that break a lot, but not so much lately."

"If you see her again, will you call me?" Olive asks. She reaches into her pocket and pulls out a square of paper with her phone number inked on it, pushing it into Disco Biscuit's hand. He stares smearily at Olive.

"Your mom. Huh. What a bummer," Sweatpants mutters. He hooks a thumb over his shoulder. "You want to come in? Get warm? Smoke a joint?"

Next to her, Natalie starts to nod, but Olive reaches out and grabs her friend's waist. She can feel

Natalie twisting under her grasp. "No, thank you," Olive says. "We're on a mission."

"Your loss," says Sweatpants. The two of them stand in the doorway, watching the girls head back down the driveway, Olive dragging Natalie by the fabric of her jacket. Natalie turns for one last wave over her shoulder—a silly, girlish flap—as the boys, leaden with stoned lethargy, watch them go.

"Olive, *honestly*? It wouldn't have killed us to take a little break," Natalie complains as soon as they are out of earshot.

"Can we just focus, please?" Olive eyes the houses on the block, trying to decide which one to tackle next. The Mediterranean villa? The Cape Cod? The light is starting to wane, the gray of the overhanging clouds fading slowly into a deeper gloom. "I want to hit up a few more houses."

Natalie stops in her tracks. "OK. Look. I don't want to sound like I'm questioning your credentials as an amateur psychic, but this is starting to feel like a pretty futile endeavor."

"It was your idea," Olive points out.

Natalie pushes her hands deeper into her pockets, refusing to meet Olive's eyes. "I wasn't really thinking it through."

"That guy thought he recognized her, Natalie!" Olive insists.

"He was *stoned*." Natalie huddles in her parka. "Sorry, Olive. But I'm cold, and it's getting late. My mom will have a conniption if I don't get home for dinner. C'mon." She stalks off up the street.

The optimism that has kept Olive going all day departs her in a rush. She looks around her, counting the number of homes left on this street; multiplying that times the number of streets stretching back from the sea; and then that times the number of beaches and neighborhoods in this area alone; and concedes defeat. Her leads are flimsy. Her one avowed supporter is starting to waver. The loneliness of this pursuit is growing clear.

The next thought lands like a sledgehammer. What if her mom *is* simply biding her time down here, her hair bleached blond, surfing? Yes, it's possible she has amnesia and doesn't know who she is, but how often does that *really* happen? Wouldn't someone have figured out her identity by this point? And sure, it's possible that she's disguised because she's in some kind of trouble—held against her will?—but hanging out on the beach doesn't exactly seem like a call for help. So what has she been doing for the past year? What if Olive finally locates her and it turns out she doesn't really want to be found?

The truth, Olive recalls unhappily, is that they had not been getting along as well as they used to in the year before her mom disappeared. Some invisible rift had opened up once Olive hit high school. It's not that she wasn't close to her mom, or that she didn't love her, but she could feel herself pulling away, chafing at her mother's lofty expectations and immovable opinions. Her mother—maybe in response?—started going off on her all-weekend sports adventures with Rita, and the gap widened.

Not long before she died, Billie had insisted on a mother-daughter hike along the John Muir Trail, which was probably an attempt to compensate for all those other weekends when she didn't invite Olive along. Except it turned out that Olive's mom considered the hike to be some kind of lesson in conjuring your inner warrior, a test that Olive was doomed to fail. Billie raced ahead, trying to make it to the next camp before nightfall, while Olive limped behind her, nursing her blisters. At first she worried that her mom was disappointed that she'd invited Olive to come; and then, as the hours passed, Olive began resenting her for thinking that Olive would be OK with this. At camp that night, Olive called Billie a slave driver, and Billie accused Olive of being afraid to challenge herself. By the time they got back to the car, they were barely talking.

Just as Olive was unloading her backpack, though, she felt Billie's hands on her shoulders. Her mother murmured in her ear: "I'm sorry I push you so much. You're not me, I forget that sometimes. And you *shouldn't* be me. You can be anyone you want to be. Don't ever forget that, no matter what, OK? *Anyone*."

Olive knew she could turn and give her mom a hug and everything would be OK again; but in that moment, she was still angry at her mother for assuming that the things that were easy for her—being beautiful and strong and so sure of herself—were easy for Olive, too. And so she stiffened her body and fiddled with the buckle of her backpack and ignored her mom's invitation. She felt powerful, knowing that she had the ability to hurt her mother like that. Eventually, Billie's hands slid off her shoulders. "Fine," Olive heard her mother say under her breath. "Be that way." Then Billie walked back to the driver's seat and started the car, waiting impatiently for Olive to climb in.

And then a few weeks later, she walked off into Desolation Wilderness, and Olive never had a chance to make it up to her. That has remained a painful penumbra around Olive's memory of her mother: the mystery of whether Billie was still upset with her when she died.

But *this* scenario would be even worse: If her mom *wants* to be gone. If Olive is the reason she fled.

Thinking of this possibility, she begins to feel ill, a weird throbbing nausea that spreads from her stomach straight up into her head. She notices dizzily that Natalie has vanished around the corner and hurries to catch up with her, stumbling a little, catching her balance against a streetlight. The light flickers on just as she touches the post, and she pauses to look up at it and marvel: *Did I do that?* She feels stoned; maybe she has a secondhand high from those surfers.

When she looks back down, her mother is sitting there, on the edge of a planter box a few feet away. She's wearing a neoprene wetsuit, her hair (not blond, not short) wet and slicked back, her knees tucked up under her chin as if she's just sitting there contemplating the view. She lifts an arm and points in the direction of the ocean: "Surf's up, Olive."

Olive looks at where her mother is pointing— there's actually a pink stucco monstrosity blocking the view—and then back to her mother, who is shimmering in the damp fog like lamplight reflected in the mist. Not real. Of course not. Her heart sinks.

"I can't surf," Olive says. "You know that."

"*I can't.* You'll never catch up with me if you keep thinking like that," her mother says. "Repeat after me: I can. I can I can I can I can I can I can I can I can I can I can I can." Her mother goes on like this in a singsong voice, a stuttering recording, until her words start to sound less like encouragement and more like taunting. Olive feels like crying; what's she supposed to do now? She closes her eyes and puts her hands over her ears. This isn't her mom at all, not the way she wants to remember her. What happened to *I miss you, why aren't you looking for me?*

But then she feels something wrapping around her, barely perceptible, like tendrils of fog, a finger of mist across her cheek. Some kind of ethereal embrace; is she imagining it? Probably. Yet somehow she feels better, even when she opens her eyes and discovers that her mother has vanished again. Because why would her mom keep showing up like this if she was angry with Olive? That first vision, it was a summons. So there's *got* to be an explanation for her mom's absence, she tells herself, one that doesn't involve Olive driving her away.

Natalie is right: The surfer was stoned. That blond woman isn't her mom.

She jogs up the road, looking for her friend. When she turns the corner, she bumps into Natalie, cold and annoyed.

"Sorry," Olive says. "I'm ready to go. I'll try another beach next weekend."

They trudge down the street, along the wind-blown cliff back toward the beach. In the distance, Olive can see where the Subaru sits, alone in the middle of an otherwise deserted parking lot. A wooden staircase leads back down to the beach, and Olive follows close behind Natalie as she picks her way down, clutching a weathered handrail worn smooth by surfers' hands.

Natalie stops halfway down the stairs as if struck by a thought. She turns to look back up at Olive. "What if you're not seeing the *present* in your visions," she says. "What if it's the future? Maybe your mom isn't at this beach now, but she *will* be in a month."

Olive thinks of her mother in the neoprene wetsuit. "They call that precognition. I hadn't even considered it. But how would I know?"

"You should consult with a real psychic. You know? Someone who knows how the whole thing works and who can help you interpret your visions. Or even teach you how to have *more* visions, clearer ones."

Olive thinks about this. Where would one find a legitimate psychic? She knows better than to ring up one of those $9.99-a-minute late-night TV hotlines; and while there is no shortage of tarot readers in Berkeley, the neon signs that hang in the windows of their peeling bungalows don't exactly inspire confidence.

A blast of freezing wind blows up the cliff, whipping sand into their eyes. Olive reaches out to steady herself against the wooden rail as she jabs at her tear ducts with her thumb. With the arm of her jacket, she wipes off a fine film of grit that the wind has deposited on her face. And then she looks down at the rail gripped in her hand, noticing for the first time that the soft wood has been completely carved with graffiti up and down the stairway. It's some sort of surfer signpost. *TONY G 11/2/12*. *Santa Cruz Tablista Piratas*. An *MK* inscribed in a heart. *ANGELA DA WAVE HOG*. Olive steps slowly down the stairs, examining the surfers' cryptograms. And then her eyes catch on one particular piece of graffiti, the wound of this one deep and bold in the weathered rail.

She reaches out and grabs Natalie's shoulder and spins her around. "Check it out," she says, pointing at the carving in the rail. Natalie looks at it and then raises a hand to her mouth, her eyes huge above her flattened palm. They stare at each other, connected with electric thrill:

SYBILLA

WHERE THE MOUNTAIN MEETS THE SKY

My Life with Billie Flanagan

——

BY JONATHAN FLANAGAN

The problem with being married to a beautiful woman is that other people are also going to notice that she is beautiful. At first you'll feel almost flattered by the attention to her—as if the nimbus of her beauty includes you inside it, a reflection of your own good taste, of your own desirability. Because, after all, this glorious creature chose *you*.

A decade in, though, as the novelty wears off, this will start to become a kind of test of your marital confidence: How strong do you believe your union is? How much do you trust in the *us* that you are? Because it's inevitable that other people will want to try to break inside that equation, to claim some of your partner's beauty for themselves.

Men looked at Billie all the time, and Billie looked right back at them. She *liked* to be admired.

There was a guy in our neighborhood who used to come watch Billie stretch in our front yard before she went on her runs. Seven A.M., like clockwork, the creep would somehow always be walking his dog right outside our house, letting his terrier urinate on the lantana while Billie loosened up her calves on our steps. He'd ogle her rear end in its black spandex, her breasts strapped tight in the jog bra. Balancing there against the post, she would casually stare right back at him, a wry little smile on her face. Like, *Go on, fool. I know you're looking.*

It happened one time too many, and one day, after watching this play out through the window, I marched out to the street to tell the guy off. But Billie grabbed me as I passed and held me back. "Oh, let him get his kicks," she said breezily as the guy scuttled off down the street. "It's probably the highlight of his day. Sad little man."

Honestly, though, the gawking strangers weren't the ones that bothered me. It was the besotted friends who were harder to stomach.

After Harmony moved to town with her boyfriend, Sean, we found ourselves spending most Saturday nights with them. Potluck dinners that ended in drunken games of Monopoly or Rummikub, Olive passed out on the couch in front of a movie. The two of them stumbling home in the dark long past midnight.

At some point in the evening, a drink too far gone, I would often notice Sean was leaning away from Harmony and in toward my wife. His face would be a hair too close to hers, his eyes firmly locked on Billie's, as if utterly absorbed by her. He loved to draw her into long theoretical debates, in that academic way he had, and the former activist in Billie was happy to engage—*Is there such a thing as acceptable cultural appropriation? Can radicalization ever be a social good?*—but I also couldn't help noticing how much attention he paid to the movement of her lips when she talked.

I remember one night, after goading my wife into a political argument of some sort, Sean abruptly cut her off mid-speech. "What is a woman like you doing here, baking cupcakes in Berkeley?" he demanded. "Why aren't you off running the world?"

"That's *incredibly* dismissive," Harmony interjected, but Billie just waved a hand at her friend as if she weren't at all bothered.

"Ah, but see," Billie said, leaning in toward Sean, her eyes fixed on his. "I *do* run the world."

"You run *a* world," he clarified. His mannered bow tie was askew, shirtsleeves pushed up to his elbows. He rubbed a finger across his dry lips, and when his hand dropped, he let it land on her arm. "But I can't imagine that's a big enough world for a woman with your brains and beauty and self-regard."

My wife's eyes flickered toward me, widened just enough for me to notice: *Can you believe this guy?* And then she turned back to Sean, batting her lashes coyly. "Is this how you think you flatter a woman? With insults? Or are you attempting to *neg* me?" She laughed, and dropped her hand on top of his, and then gave the back of his hand a sharp little flick with her fingertip. He winced but didn't look away. "It's not working, in case you're wondering. I like myself enough not to be cowed by a man who thinks he knows more about me than I do."

Sean grinned. "Oh, *really*."

I remember that Harmony looked helplessly over at me, and I rolled my eyes at her as if the whole thing were a four-handed game of bridge rather than a one-on-one challenge. "Believe me," I said to the group, "no one's holding Billie back. If Billie wants something, she gets it."

"Indeed," Billie drawled, and sat back in her chair. "And

what I want right now is another cocktail." She snapped her fingers in Sean's face.

"Oh, yes *ma'am*," Sean said, and stood up. He looked over at me and shook his head as if to say, *That woman of yours*, and then disappeared into the kitchen.

Once he was gone, Billie raised an eyebrow at me. "Methinks that man has been overserved. Harmony, please cut him off *earlier* next time, for all of our sakes." She reached over and laced her fingers in mine, and then looked at Harmony and laughed, as if we were all in on the joke together.

I remember feeling drawn in by her: Sure, she'd been flirting with a mutual friend right in front of me, but I had been included, so what was the harm?

I must have watched this performance, or a variation on it, hundreds of times during our marriage. With the other dads at Claremont Prep; with my friend Marcus; with my father once. I always felt safe because of the final act of the routine: the flirtation Kabuki that broke the fourth wall to include me. The wink, the widened eyes, the fingers intertwined in mine: This meant that Billie wasn't trying to hide. It meant that there *was* nothing to hide.

6

"MAYBE THE FOLDER CONTAINS super-secret spy plans," Jonathan's friend Marcus is saying. Billie's laptop lies on the desk between them as the two men sit in Marcus's office in a tech campus on the Oakland waterfront, the door closed against any errant employees who might wander in. "Maybe Billie was working for the CIA, assassinating Colombian drug lords on behalf of the government."

"Ha ha?" Jonathan says, failing to match Marcus's forced levity.

Marcus doesn't seem to take Jonathan's hint. "Or maybe the folder has pornography in it," he continues. He leans back in his desk chair, his bulk threatening to tip the whole seat backward. "Selfies! Naked self-portraits, dirty home videos. That would be worth password-protecting. You guys do anything naughty that you've forgotten about?"

"I'm pretty sure I wouldn't forget something like that," Jonathan says drily. He runs his hands across the laptop's titanium cover, feeling the tiny dings and scratches it incurred during its lifetime in Billie's bag. He spent the rest of his weekend methodically spelunking through his wife's digital junk pile but found no obvious evidence of an affair. No compromising emails, no naked selfies or photos of strange men with six-pack abs. After a while, he began to doubt the very premise of what he was doing. Maybe those mysterious trips in their calendar *could* be explained away. *Was she just ditching Rita in order to go hiking by herself?* he wondered hopefully. Perhaps her lies were a forgivable feint rather than a deliberate deception: She didn't want him to worry about her being out there all by herself.

And yet there is that *RR* folder, a second secret that Billie deemed worth keeping. Plus, dug up from her computer, a few additional odds and ends that give him pause:

1) Photographs of a house that he has never seen before: a small cottage, its bottle-green paint job feathering along the edges of the clapboard. A tangle of bicycles in the front yard; a faded decorative flag with a blue whale on it, hanging from the eaves; a dusty kettle barbecue parked between two patio chairs on the lawn. There are three daytime photographs, taken from different angles and, judging by the movement of the objects, on different days; and then two more, taken at night. In these

last, you can just make out the silhouette of a person through the curtain of the front window. Jonathan squinted at this shape, trying to determine identity or age or gender, but the picture is blurry and dark. The photos disturb him with their murky stalker quality. Had his wife taken these?

2) A bookmark, buried deep in a folder of Billie's browser, for a company called Lim & Partners Research Services. When he clicked over to the website, he discovered that Calvin Lim was a private investigator based in San Francisco. What on earth would Billie have needed with a private investigator?

3) An email from the corporate offices of Motel 6, dated seven months before Billie's death. *Dear Mrs. Flanagan,* it reads, *I was informed about the bedbug problems you experienced during your April 20th stay at one of our motels. I'd like to extend you our apologies and offer you a complimentary night during your next stay with us at any of our many locations across America.* Jonathan cross-referenced the date—it was the same weekend that she was supposed to be backpacking in Yosemite with Rita. Why would she be staying at a bedbug-riddled Motel 6 when she was supposed to be camping in a national park? And yet this also didn't exactly seem like a romantic choice for a tryst (he couldn't

imagine his wife voluntarily choosing a budget chain hotel under any circumstances). Which Motel 6 had she stayed at and where? But the email offered no clues, and the Motel 6 website listed 165 locations in California alone. A dead end.

4) An Amazon.com receipt for a product called Mr. Zog's Sex Wax. At first glance, he assumed this was something kinky—evidence of the affair he was seeking? Certainly, she hadn't used whatever it was with him—but on closer examination, it turned out to be a wax for surfboards. And yet, as far as he is aware, his wife didn't know how to surf.

Small things, but taken together, they paint an alarming picture.

There was something else, too, something more disconcerting, that he found jammed in the inner pocket of one of Billie's purses in a manic final tear through her possessions: a condom.

They hadn't used condoms in years—she'd gotten an IUD not long after she turned forty and they officially decided that another kid wasn't in the cards. He turned the condom in his palm, wondering. The wrapper was flattened and worn, its expiration date rubbed off. How long had it been there?

He keeps turning back to the *RR* folder. Is it possible that it contains the explanation for everything? But he's been unable to crack the password. It isn't Billie's maiden name, Olive's birthday, the date of their anniversary, or the password that they used for their shared bank accounts. He's tried her lucky numbers. Her Social Security number. Nothing.

"So, how hard would it be to hack into that folder?" he asks Marcus now.

"Not that hard. I can't imagine that Billie used strong encryption." Marcus's phones pings, but he ignores it, tugging distractedly at his waistband. When Jonathan met Marcus during their undergraduate years at Stanford, Marcus had been a smart-ass string bean with long hair that he pulled into a ponytail, so broke that he owned only one pair of jeans. Twenty-five years later, the ponytail has been lopped off, swapped out for a kudzu-like beard; his paunch has grown in direct proportion with his bank account; and although he now owns at least a dozen pairs of overpriced jeans, he has a far more difficult time keeping them hiked up over his rear end.

Jonathan envies Marcus for his fortuitous ability to exist within a hemisphere in which his physical appearance is completely irrelevant: In the tech industry, one's sex appeal is predicated entirely on the mysterious wiring of one's brain (and its subsequent ability to generate profit). And Marcus has an impressive brain, apparently, its gray matter unique enough to propel him into CTO positions at a succession of unicorn-aspirant start-ups. His friend lumbers through the world with the grace of a man who knows that he has been blessed: blessed by being the right *kind* of person, with the right skill set, in the right city, in just the right era.

Marcus is eyeing him. "But, I'm sorry, can you explain to me again what you're doing this for?"

Jonathan looks out the window of his friend's office and notices that San Francisco's afternoon fog is starting to encroach, fingers creeping down the distant hills to enfold the skyscrapers below. Here, on the other side of the bay, they're in the sun, but within the hour that will be gone, too. "You know. For the book." Marcus keeps staring, saying nothing. Jonathan sighs. "OK. I'm finally going through all of Billie's stuff, and before I box up everything and put it in the garage, I want to tie up any loose ends."

Marcus frowns. "And tying up loose ends involves breaking into her computer? I'm not sure I see it."

"How do I know that the folder doesn't contain something important? Financial documents, a final will."

Marcus grunts as he uprights himself, the front wheels of his chair slamming down to the floor. "Why would she password-protect that? Wouldn't the logical thing be to make it easily accessible if you die?"

"You're not answering my question. Will you crack the password for me?"

Marcus reaches out and runs his hand across the edge of the laptop's case, his fingers surprisingly delicate. "Jon. What's up? You're acting weird. Is there something going on that I should know about?"

"Look, Marcus, if you're not comfortable doing this, that's fine. I'll find someone else."

Marcus winces. "No, no. I'll take care of it. But I'm busy right now, we're gearing up for a new software release, so you'll have to be patient. It's going to take a week or two until I can get to it."

"Fine," Jonathan agrees. Outside the window, in the middle of the bay, a barge has floated into view, carrying a giant stainless-steel cube emblazoned with a glowing neon question mark. It's an advertisement for some sort of new social media app. He read somewhere that it's costing over $1 million a day to keep the question mark floating out there. A fugitive shaft of pink light is shining directly on it, and he wonders if the cube purports to answer all the world's questions or if it is intended as a repository of universal doubt and anxiety.

He thinks of the giant question mark in the middle of his own existence: *What were you up to, Billie?*

He's barely looked at *Where the Mountain Meets the Sky* in days; the act of sitting down to memorialize his wife suddenly feels dishonest. As if he's just turned on a flashlight and is pretending not to see all the dark creatures that are scurrying out of the light. *Surely a few lies don't change everything,* he keeps trying to reassure himself; *she's still the same person you loved. You always knew she was a complicated woman, even if you've been glossing over that in your memoir.* But something has shifted internally, and he's not sure how to set it back to where he began. The discontents he had in his marriage—the ones he's been ignoring out of, what, respect for the dead? convenience for his book?—are starting to creep through in his writing. How is he supposed to write a love story when he's clearly been deceived by his own protagonist?

Marcus is talking as he bundles Billie's laptop into his own messenger bag. "Just promise me that you won't get worked up about anything that I dredge up." He lowers his voice, going unexpectedly earnest, and it's as if he's reading Jonathan's mind: "This makes me uncomfortable, you know, undermining someone's digital privacy. Even if they're dead. For what end? We all have parts of ourselves that we don't necessarily want everyone to see. Doesn't change who we fundamentally are, right? Doesn't mean we didn't live the life we did. The traces we leave behind don't mean anything on their own; they're open to interpretation. Eye of the beholder. And without Billie here to explain to you what you find—well, I hate to think you might get upset about something that's ultimately inconsequential."

"I won't," Jonathan lies, knowing full well that it's already too late.

Back at home, Jonathan finds a package from his lawyer on the front porch, delivered by courier in his absence. He takes this into the kitchen and clears a space on the table, pushing aside the fruit bowl full of blackening bananas and the dirty dishes from breakfast. A precariously balanced pile of mail goes cascading to the floor, and he notices a long-missing (and possibly overdue?) water bill stuck between the pages of a Sweaty Betty catalog.

He tears the package open to find a stack of freshly creased Sunday newspapers. He stares at these, momentarily perplexed. Then, realizing, he flips through the top paper in the stack—the *San Francisco Chronicle*—discarding Arts and Business and Sports, until he arrives at the cluttered, mostly forgotten section at the very back.

There, he finds his classified ad in a bottom corner, easily overlooked:

> If you are—or have any information about the current whereabouts of—SYBILLA "BILLIE" THRACE FLANAGAN of Berkeley, California, please contact (510) 555-0131. Your family has petitioned for a declaration of death in absentia.

He sits at the kitchen table and stares for a long time at the anachronistic newsprint, idly rubbing the words with the tip of his finger until they smudge and turn his finger black. He hates the very premise of this ad, a plea for a dead woman to get in touch, the way it generates a sense of hope where there is none. He should throw these newspapers out before Olive sees the ad and uses it to fuel her delusion that her mom is alive.

He examines the dirty whorl of his fingerprint. Strange, unwelcome thoughts whisper in the back of his head. And then, gripped by some mad impulse, he picks up his cellphone and dials the number in the ad.

It rings twice, three times; Jonathan is just about to come to his senses and hang up when a man with a raspy, smoke-coated voice answers. "Detective Morley, Berkeley PD," the man says tersely.

"Hi," Jonathan begins. "Detective Morley? This is Jonathan Flanagan. I'm calling about the Billie Flanagan case from last winter? She—my wife—

died hiking up in Desolation Wilderness last November. Well, we assume she died, although we never found her body. I'm sure you remember."

There's a long silence on the other end, presumably the police detective running backward through his mental files. "Oh, right. How can I help you?"

"I know that this is going to sound nuts." Jonathan hesitates, not sure where he's going with this, and then forges ahead. "But—have you received any calls about my wife in the last day or two? I'm only asking because I put a classified ad in a few newspapers, seeking information about her current whereabouts—not because I think she's alive, of course, but because I'm required to in order to receive the death certificate." He realizes he is babbling and stops. "Anyway, I thought I'd just check in."

"No," Morley says slowly. "No calls. I'm sorry."

"Look, I don't know why I bothered you with this. The whole thing is just a formality; of course you're not going to get anyone calling about Billie." He is aware that he is starting to sound like an insane person. "Forget it. I'll be in touch if I need anything else."

Jonathan hangs up before Morley can respond. He sticks the phone back in his pocket, feeling as if he's done something unclean. What the hell was he thinking?

He sits there, staring at the ad, reading it over and over. *If you are—or have any information about the current whereabouts of—SYBILLA "BILLIE" THRACE FLANAGAN of Berkeley, California, please contact (510) 555-0131.*

It's impossible. Or is it?

He realizes that a strange seed has planted itself deep in his cerebellum, and it is sending out tentative tendrils. *Let's say, for the sake of argument, that your wife was having an affair, could she have decided to run off with her lover? Could she have disappeared herself, instead of dying?* It's a wild leap to make; and yet he keeps coming back to the absolute certainty in his daughter's face as she uttered those words: *I saw Mom. She's alive.* Putting aside the bizarre supernatural aspect of Olive's claim, is it at all possible that she could be right?

The answer comes to him like an icicle driven through his chest: Nothing is impossible. Improbable, but not impossible.

What would drive Billie to do something so extreme? He runs his finger across the edge of the kitchen table, lost in damning thoughts. *She was still the Lost Years Billie at heart, and she needed more thrills, and there were no more thrills to be had with you. Maybe there were more thrills to be had with someone else. Your marriage wasn't perfect, no matter how much you've been making it out to be that in your memoir.* Still, he reasons, people don't just up and vanish because of ennui. They don't fake their own death simply because they're having an affair, not without trying couples therapy or—for God's sake—*divorce* first.

Or do they?

He recalls an argument they had a few months before her death. He'd been working in the downstairs office at midnight, his eyes dry and stinging with exhaustion, when Billie suddenly stumbled down the stairs. She stood in the doorway, mussed and bleary, wearing an old Stanford tee of Jonathan's that was more hole than shirt.

"Still working?" she said incredulously. "Don't you ever sleep anymore?"

"Sleep is overrated," he said.

"Exhaustion is boring," she retorted. "Seriously. Don't forget that Olive and I exist, OK? We're getting tired of looking at the back of your head. I'm not just here to serve you meals while you work."

He stopped typing and turned around, chagrined. "Shit. Am I doing that? I'm sorry. This job is killing me."

She came closer, leaning on the back of his chair, so close he could smell the sweaty musk of sleep coming off her. "And frankly, I'm tired of hearing you say that. For years now, and it only ever gets worse. I don't know why you don't just quit. Go write a book, do something creative, change the world. You used to talk about that all the time."

"Quit?" He looked up at his wife, who was raising her eyebrows at him as if he were a particularly clueless child. He stared at her for a long time. "It's not like I can walk away from a paycheck. A stable job, that's nothing to take for granted. And health insurance—you have any idea what that costs nowadays?"

"You can *always* walk away," she said. "What are you so afraid of? What's the worst that's going to happen?"

"I won't sell a book and we won't be able to pay the bills and we'll lose our house? We'll end up homeless? We'll have to use Olive's babysitting money to pay for all the pesticide-free kale she insists on eating. You'll have to sell your eggs on the black market."

"No one will pay for my eggs, they're all dried up." She ran a hand through his hair, her warm palm cradling his scalp but tugging on the follicles a little too hard. "Really, I don't care about all *this*. It's disposable."

"What?" He twisted around to study her, confused.

She seemed to backtrack. "You know what I mean. Like they say, it's just *stuff*." She withdrew her hand from his head. "But that's not my point. You always wanted to be an artist, a revolutionary. Big idealistic talk. Now all you do is complain about brogrammers while you edit articles about Wi-Fi-enabled juicers."

He laughed a little uneasily. "C'mon. *Everyone* wants to be an artist when they're young. And then reality kicks in."

"Seriously, Jonathan. Don't be spineless."

"It's not about being spineless, it's about being responsible," he said, bristling. "I need to take care of you and Olive, don't you remember?"

"You don't *need* to take care of me. That's an anachronistic delusion you've always had."

This stung a little; and c'mon, he'd been paying the bills all these years, he *was* supporting her. Still, he couldn't help wondering if she was right. *Was* it such a terrible idea? To quit because he felt like it? Throw caution to the wind? He was unsure why he was protesting when his wife had just offered him a hall pass. Was it that he didn't like this image of himself as a useless appendage? If he wasn't offering his family financial stability, what *was* he offering?

"I've been at *Decode* for eighteen years; there are people counting on me," he thought out loud. "I'd need to give them a good long time to replace me."

Billie threw up her hands with frustration. "They'll cry when you leave and buy you a Costco cake with your name on it and then forget about you ten minutes later when they replace you with some-one younger and fresher and cheaper."

There was a sour taste in his mouth. "That's a shitty attitude."

"That's *life*," she said. "You only get one. Don't waste it. Don't be average." She leaned across him and, with one hand, flicked the lid of his laptop closed. She calmly watched as he scrambled to open the laptop again, checking the state of his work in progress. Then she disentangled herself from his chair and plucked her underwear out of the crack of her butt, drifting out of the room and back up the stairs.

At the time, he tried to put her words out of his head, the way they tipped at some hidden contempt. *She's just tired of holding the family together, she's tired of listening to me complain,* he convinced him-self. *Totally understandable. I'd be sick of me, too.* But now, as he recalls their conversation, he wonders if her words that night weren't about him but about her: *You can* always *walk away. . . . It's disposable.* Had she already been planning to start over with someone else? Is this what she was masterminding during those days when she was pretending to be off hiking with Rita?

Even if she wanted to disappear on me, she would never *do that to Olive,* he thinks. Billie had her issues, but she wouldn't do something so cruel, so phenomenally fucked up, to their daughter. And yet. He thinks of the gaps in her calendar, the missing weekends, and a voice in the back of his head whispers: *If she was capable of lying like that, what else was she capable of? It's clear you didn't know her as well as you thought you did.*

Sitting there in the kitchen, amid the overpowering smell of rotting bananas, he understands all of a sudden why he has been so resistant to Olive's suggestion that Billie might be alive. Because if she's not dead, then she's also not the person he has written her to be: There's no rational explanation for his wife being alive that doesn't point to her being some kind of monster. And he's not ready to change the point of view of his entire life story.

He stares at the fruit bowl for a long time, noting the green fuzz that's slowly enveloping a withered clementine, until he can't take it anymore. He jumps up and marches the fruit to the overflowing garbage can, bags it up, and then grabs his car keys.

I hope Billie is dead, he thinks as he drags the garbage out to the curb. *Because I can't begin to imagine what it will mean if she's not.*

As Jonathan walks back through the door of his house a few hours later, burdened down with grocery bags, he hears conversation and smells sautéed onions coming from the kitchen and recalls that Harmony was coming over to cook dinner. He stands in the doorway for a minute, gathering himself, trying to shed the black doubts of the afternoon.

In the kitchen, he finds Harmony at the stove, fiddling with a pot of soup. She's making conversation with Olive, who sits on the edge of a stool, one foot sliding tentatively toward the door.

"Hey, Dad," Olive says. "You didn't tell me Harmony was coming over for dinner." He registers a distinct note of complaint in her voice.

He glances over at Harmony, whose face is pink and shiny from the heat of the stove, her body humming with activity. She's wearing a low-cut top that reveals a faint sheen of sweat in the valley of her cleavage. He can't help thinking that she looks vaguely postcoital. "Sorry, slipped my mind," he says. He averts his eyes and begins unpacking groceries: cheese, almond butter, bananas, dish soap, the dried seaweed that Olive likes . . . and dammit, no toilet paper. How did he forget the toilet paper again?

The pot on the stove is starting to boil, and Harmony adjusts the knob down to simmer. She rifles through a drawer, seemingly as familiar with their kitchen as he is, and digs out a wooden spoon. "I should have waited before I let myself in. I think I scared Olive."

"I wasn't scared," Olive objects, her voice polite but strained. "Just surprised. Dad didn't tell me you had a key."

"I don't," Harmony says as Jonathan chimes in: "She knows where we keep the hidden key."

"Oh." Olive takes a green banana from the top of

a grocery bag and unpeels it, avoiding both of their gazes. He's momentarily frustrated with his daughter. She's usually so sweet and considerate; what's her issue with Harmony, of all people?

"You know what?" he says. "Harmony, you *should* have a key. I'll get you one. You're practically part of the family."

Harmony flashes a grin at Jonathan, then turns back to busy herself at the stove.

"I was just asking Olive if she'd be interested in having a girls' day sometime soon," she says as she stirs her soup. "Get pedicures, go shopping, facials, you know." She glances over her shoulder and smiles at Olive, who in turn takes a giant bite of banana and glances questioningly at Jonathan, as if asking for permission to pass on this female bonding. Jonathan raises his eyebrows in encouragement. Olive looks at him for a long minute and then turns back and gives Harmony a tiny nod of acquiescence with a beleaguered smile. Jonathan feels a pang of affection for them both: for Olive, who, as long as he has known her, has never painted her toenails; and for Harmony, who is trying so very hard to befriend his daughter.

Harmony points the wooden spoon at Olive. "Ball's in your court. Just let me know a good day."

"Yeah, I'll do that," Olive says quickly, and Jonathan sighs, knowing she never will. Teenagers are like skittish forest creatures that dance away at your approach, snarl if you dare to confront them head-on. You need to wait, patiently, for them to come to you; though odds are they never will.

Olive shoves the banana peel in the trash can and

then looks back at Jonathan. "Dad. I've got tons of homework tonight. . . ."

"We'll call you down when dinner's ready."

She disappears out of the room. Jonathan wanders over to the stove and peers over Harmony's shoulder. "Is that a turnip?"

"Jerusalem artichoke." She twists around to look at the door. "Olive's just patronizing me, isn't she? Maybe I should have suggested something besides pedicures. What do you think she'd want to do?"

"Plant trees? Go to a fracking protest? Read aloud BuzzFeed stories about beached walruses?" He shrugs. "Don't worry. It won't kill Olive to give something frivolous a try for once." He opens a bottle of wine, then settles in to watch Harmony cook. She is sloppy, enthusiastic, voracious, food flying in every direction, one finger constantly in her mouth. He can recall Billie at the stove, much more intense and focused—she was a good cook, her *Bon Appetit*s always heavily marked up with sticky tabs, the resulting dishes always photo-ready—but also somehow dutiful about food where Harmony is passionate.

He slides a wineglass across the island to Harmony. "I have a delicate question for you," he says.

Harmony pauses from her cooking, the wineglass at her lips. "About what?"

"Was Billie having an affair?"

Harmony slowly lowers the glass of wine and wipes a bead of sweat from her hairline. "An affair? Why would you think that?"

He hesitates, aware that he's about to tarnish Harmony's own memories of her friend. "Well. It turns out Billie lied to me a few times. She told me she was off hiking with Rita for the weekend, but Rita just informed me that she wasn't with her."

"Really?" Something sharp and fleeting passes across Harmony's face, her focus drawing abruptly inward. Then she shakes her head. "I'm sure it's nothing; she was probably just off hiking by herself. You know Billie, she could be like that sometimes, off in her own world and not particularly worried about what other people might think."

This should be reassuring, but it's not. If Billie was lying to him, who's to say she wasn't lying to Harmony, too? "But did you ever notice that she was acting oddly right before she died?"

Harmony's whole body goes tense. She turns back to the stove, fiddling with the temperature of the burners. "Well, yeah." Her back is to him as she tosses generous handfuls of something green into the soup. "But you know why, right?" She turns around to face him and lowers her voice to a whisper: "What happened with *us*. Back then."

And there it is, finally unearthed from the coffin in which the subject has been buried for the last year. The Thing That Neither of Them Has Wanted to Talk About.

When had he first noticed it, the way Harmony lingered in their house even when Billie and Sean weren't there? Really, it was there from the very beginning: the way Harmony stood slightly too close to him whenever they chatted, the way the heat of her seemed to trigger something chemical in him. The four of them would be on a double date, Sean and Billie caught up in some heated debate, when

Harmony's blue eyes would lift to meet Jonathan's and he would feel a mix of profound discomfort and giddy shock, as if they shared a secret that he did not at all intend to convey.

But there was something so fecund and female about Harmony, all soft hair and curves. And while Billie was more beautiful—she had a sharper, glittery edge—they were years into their marriage. They were *parents* together. Heady sexual desire had faded out long ago: For years now their sex life had been about the comfortable quick release, familiarity breeding a definite pleasurable ease but also failing to offer any real thrilling highs. And in those days, with Jonathan's late-night work schedule and Billie's early-morning sports regimen, their schedules never overlapped anyway. How was sex supposed to fit into that?

Still, he would have gone on forever, ignoring this vague attraction to Harmony. It wasn't like he was ever going to do anything about it. Other opportunities for infidelity had presented themselves throughout the years—Claremont Moms, four G&Ts in at the spring fundraiser, who let their hands linger too long on his forearm; women at his gym who met his eyes in the mirror and didn't let go—and while it was always flattering, even a little titillating, it certainly didn't seem worth blowing up his marriage over. He adored his wife and kid. He *liked* being a paragon of husbandly virtue. He had the life he'd always wanted, and he wasn't about to screw that up.

About seven months before Billie's accident, Harmony and Sean suddenly broke up, and for a long time after that, Harmony vanished from their lives. "I think she's licking her wounds," Billie said, shrugging, when Jonathan asked. "Feeling vulnerable. Probably a little embarrassed for sticking with Sean so long when anyone could see he was so ambivalent about her. I mean, *you* saw how he used to flirt with me." Jonathan didn't spend too much time thinking about this; Harmony's absence was, frankly, a bit of a relief, as if he'd been trapped inside a pressure cooker and someone had lifted the lid.

But then in early September, two days after the late-night argument with Billie about quitting his job, Billie had gone off for the weekend, hiking Mount Shasta with Rita. Olive was at a sleepover birthday party at her friend Ming's house, leaving Jonathan at home alone on Saturday night, doing battle with a *Decode* editorial about the future of bitcoin while polishing off the better part of a six-pack.

By the time the doorbell rang, he was already half drunk. Maybe that's the reason why, when he realized that Harmony was at the door, he didn't follow his better instincts. Or maybe he was annoyed with Billie and following some subconscious self-destructive urge. Either way, when he saw Harmony there, clutching her cellphone in her fist, he opened the door wider instead of turning her away like he should have.

"Hey! This is a surprise," he said, hearing a note of excessive enthusiasm in his voice. "You looking for Billie? Because she's off hiking this weekend."

Harmony stood awkwardly at the door, looking fruitlessly at the screen of her cellphone as if it should have informed her of this. "Oh," she said. "I was just stopping by. I should have called first." She took a sheepish step backward. "I'll go."

He hesitated only briefly. "Well, *I'm* here. And I'm pretty sure there's a bottle of wine in the fridge."

Two hours later, the bottle of wine was gone, along with most of a second. Jonathan found himself sitting on the couch with Harmony, listening to her talk about the breakup with Sean, the struggle to find a new apartment, the monthlong forgiveness-centered meditation retreat in Sedona from which she'd just returned. "I needed to find my emotional center again, let go of all that toxic anger. I was feeling so"—she lifted a hand and made a jittery motion with it—"unbalanced." She dropped the hand abruptly and then glanced at him sideways. "Sean cheated on me, did you know that?"

He sat up. "Seriously? I had no idea. What an idiot."

She looked at him for a long time, her translucent eyes studying his. Finally, she threw herself back on the throw pillows and sighed. "He already has a new girlfriend, too, some grad student who's half my age. And I'm stuck online-dating. Getting on Tinder now that I'm over forty, it's just laughable," she said. Her bare feet rubbed up against each other, little round toes painted a metallic cerulean. Her blond hair, loosened from its braids, billowed out in shiny waves behind her. "It doesn't matter what you look like or how interesting you are, once there's a four in front of your age, you're basically invisible."

"I can't imagine you ever being invisible," he said, his voice raspy.

She smiled blearily at him. "You're so sweet. No, I need one of those online matchmaking dating sites. You know, 'People Past Their Prime Dot Com.' 'People Who Need Help Because They Usually Date Losers Dot Com.' 'People Totally Ready to Settle Dot Com.'" She looked like she might cry.

He looked at her appraisingly—he couldn't help it—and tried to imagine someone swiping left on her. It seemed unfathomable. "Come on, Harmony. Stop being so hard on yourself. You're a beautiful woman." Had he gone too far in saying this? He settled himself tighter into his corner of the couch as if erecting an invisible barrier of fortified air between them.

"Doesn't matter, anyway. The good guys"—she lifted a wobbly finger to point at him—"the nice guys like *you* are already gone. Snapped up years ago. By the smart women who had foresight, the women who didn't spend their twenties and thirties thinking, *Well, maybe the next one will be better,* only to discover that with each passing day the men get a little bit worse."

"Jesus, Harmony." He was shocked to hear that coming out of her mouth. He flailed desperately for something, anything, that might take the uncomfortable sting out of her words. "You're going to meet someone eventually. Anyway, I'm not that great. I'm sure Billie has told you about my many, many flaws. The workaholism, the obliviousness, the risk aversion."

"Oh, *please.*"

"Seriously. Billie thinks I should quit my job and do something more creative and adventurous, and instead I make a million excuses to avoid it because I'm scared of failing. You must have heard about *that*." He realized that a certain bitterness was creeping into his voice, and he laughed to counter-balance it.

Harmony stretched her legs out on the couch so that her toes were inches away from his thigh. "Billie doesn't tell me everything."

"C'mon, I see how you guys talk, always whisper-ing to each other." He took a long drink. "Plus, the two of you have all that shared history."

"History. Yeah, we have a *lot* of that." Harmony gave a curious laugh and fiddled with her wineglass. "Our relationship—it's complicated. You know, back in Oregon I used to think she just tolerated me. Maybe she still does. Maybe she keeps me close now because I know too many of her secrets."

"Secrets?" He laughed at this, imagining interne-cine Claremont Mom drama from which he'd been thankfully excluded. "Anyway. I'm sure that's not true. You're her best friend."

"You know what Billie's like," she continued, a flush stealing up her cheeks. "You spend all this time with her, talking, and you feel like you're getting *in* there; and then when you walk away, you realize she hasn't told you anything real about herself at all. She's mostly just reflected you back at yourself. What you most want to see."

Jonathan felt an unexpected, unpleasant jolt of recognition. They looked at each other from oppo-site ends of the couch, and he felt Harmony's toe making electric contact with his thigh. It was excru-ciating. A red alert was going off in his head—*bad* idea *bad* idea—and he began to shift himself up and off the couch, far away from her, when all of a sudden she was right there, pressing against him, her tongue in his mouth.

Kissing her was a full-body rush unlike anything he'd felt since he and Billie first started dating. He'd almost forgotten this kind of primitive joy, the pleasure of kissing someone new, your body primed and loose with alcohol. For a few critical seconds—a half minute?—he forgot himself entirely in the surprise of it all, the flat-out decadence of desire, his tongue tangling with hers; and then his conscience battled valiantly back, triumphing over primal lust.

He jerked away. "Stop!" The room was spinning, and the reality of what had just happened gripped him hard. "I can't . . . sorry . . ." He recoiled and then scrambled across the living room toward the powder room in the hallway. There he pressed his face against the sobering porcelain of the toilet and threw up the hamburger he'd eaten for dinner. Afterward he washed his face in cold water and stared at himself in the mirror, horrified. *You stopped in time,* he told himself. *She kissed you. You didn't do anything wrong.* Still, there was no denying that he'd liked it, that he'd felt tempted, and this felt almost as bad as infidelity itself. He could see himself teetering on a precipice: divorce, a custody battle, Olive's tears; the lonely nights with a bottle of bourbon in a bachelor pad in a generic high-rise apartment building; the spare bedroom made up for Olive but mostly standing empty. *I don't want that,* he thought. *I love my family more than anything else.*

When he came back out, Harmony was sitting in

the corner of the couch with a pillow clutched to her chest. He sat down in an armchair safely on the other side of the room.

"I'm not going to lie and say I'm not attracted to you," he said. "But I'm married. I love Billie. I don't want to do anything that would hurt her."

She nodded and looked like she might burst into tears. There was a smudge of mascara under her left eye, pink gloss smeared outside the lines of her lip.

He wanted to go over and give her a hug but knew better. "I hope we can still be friends," he continued. "And I hope this doesn't damage your friendship with Billie, either, if that's possible. I'd hate to drive a wedge between you."

"Sure." Harmony's voice had gone flat, and he wasn't sure who she was upset with: Him? Billie? Herself? They sat in silence for a few minutes until Harmony finally stood up and straightened her shirt. "Look, this was totally my fault. I don't know what I was thinking. Whatever you do, don't blame yourself." She walked to the door and then hesitated, turning back to study him. "Billie doesn't deserve you," she said, and then left before he could respond.

When Billie returned that Sunday, he said nothing about what had happened. What would that accomplish? And yet he couldn't help sensing that something in his behavior had shifted: He had a secret from his wife, and it felt like a sharp stone lying at the bottom of every interaction, every benign kitchen-sink exchange. It had to be glaringly obvious to Billie that something was different. And despite Harmony's reassurances, he *did* blame himself. Surely Harmony wouldn't have kissed him if he hadn't given her reason to think it would be recipro-cated?

He wasn't sure what to do. The impulse to make it up to his wife with flowers and expensive gifts and orgasms was a clear giveaway of his guilt, but nei-ther did he want to avoid her by burying himself in his work, because wasn't that part of her problem with him in the first place? Nothing he did felt natu-ral anymore. Instead, he felt like an imposter; the gnawing ache of his guilt and self-recrimination was as painful as an ulcer, eating him alive.

At last he couldn't take it anymore. He came into the bedroom one night and found Billie sitting in bed, reading a novel. He sat cross-legged on the edge of the mattress, staring at her: the soft furrow of her brow, the fine lines around her wide-set eyes, the first strands of gray in her hair, all the result of the care and attention and stress that went into raising their family. His beautiful wife, his partner for so long. He'd let her down.

"I need to talk to you about something," he said.

She looked up at him, startled, her dark eyes fiery with some undefinable emotion. Fear? She folded the page over carefully and closed her book. "Go on," she said.

"Harmony and I kissed," he said, his voice croak-ing. And it was almost a relief, the way all that pent-up guilt came flooding out of him, the release of an opening valve.

Billie pushed herself upright on the pillow. She tilted her head, puzzling this. "You. Kissed. Har-mony?" He waited for something else—recrimination, tears—but she just studied his face. Was this a test?

The words began to pour out of him. "It was a huge mistake. And I know it's no excuse, but we were both drunk, it was while you were off hiking with Rita," he said. "And I stopped it before anything really happened. There was no—"

"Sex?" she interrupted sharply, not looking at him.

"No. Just a kiss. The whole thing lasted a minute, tops. And look, I know that's still bad, and I don't blame you for being furious—" He strangled, running out of words.

Billie stared at him, her mouth slightly open. And then, unexpectedly, she began to laugh, a tight joyless laugh that cut out almost as soon as it began. She dropped her face into her hands. "Why are you telling me this?" she said, her voice muffled.

"Because I couldn't stand lying to you," he said. "We don't have that kind of marriage, and I don't want to start. Dishonesty is what kills relationships."

Billie lifted her head out of her hands. Her eyes were bright and glittering. "We won't talk about it again," she said.

He hesitated, unsure what this meant. "Maybe we should, though," he said. "Maybe it's time to talk about couples therapy. This thing, it didn't come out of nowhere."

"Couples therapy? Seriously?" Billie stared at the wall across from the bed for a long time, thinking. Then she turned and offered him a curious conciliatory smile. "No. It's already the past," she said. "It happened and that's that. Rehashing it with a stranger isn't going to change anything. Let's move on." She reached across the bed and grabbed Jonathan's hand and tugged it toward her mouth, bending to kiss it with dry lips. Then she lay back and opened her book again, paging through until she found the marked corner.

He was rendered speechless, her lips still burning on his palm. Was it really going to be that easy? Wasn't there something more that needed to be done or said? Yes, it was a minor transgression in the grand scheme of things, but wasn't he supposed to suffer more?

He waited for a delayed fallout. But things between them remained fine; they were maybe better than they'd been in years, as if the kiss had illuminated everything that truly mattered. He cut back his hours at work so he could spend some much needed time with his family: weekday dinners with Olive and Billie at their favorite restaurants, a family day trip to the butterfly beach, warm fall evenings sitting on the porch drinking wine and talking about Olive. He and Billie had a few bedroom sessions that left them drenched and gasping, like the old days. One Friday he even came home from work to discover Harmony and Billie sitting in the dining room, their faces flushed with wine and the scattered remains of a box of cookies on the table before them. "Oh, good, you're home early," Billie said mildly, and they went back to their conversation as if nothing at all had changed, even though Harmony couldn't quite meet his eyes across the table.

Whenever he tried to bring up the subject of the kiss—obeying some nagging sense that something between them remained unresolved—Billie would brush it aside. Things stayed that way until the very last day of her life, when she kissed him goodbye, picked up her backpack, and headed out for Desolation Wilderness alone.

At the time, he'd felt enormously relieved by her reaction: It could have been so much uglier. Better his wife's curious, cheerful forgiveness than a festering, palpable anger. But when he looks back from his current vantage point, Billie's nonchalant attitude seems far more suspect. Especially knowing what he knows now: that on the night he kissed Harmony, the night when Billie was supposedly hiking Shasta with Rita, Billie wasn't actually hiking Shasta with Rita at all.

Maybe the reason Billie didn't get upset about his transgression was because she knew her own was so much greater than his.

He lifts his eyes now to meet Harmony's. She's staring at him with bright, measuring eyes, the wooden spoon dripping in her hand, as if trying to gauge his temperature now that she's turned up the heat. The Thing That Neither of Them Has Wanted to Talk About. Harmony was the first person he called, panicked and frantic, that Sunday night last November when Billie failed to return home from her hike. Harmony showed up within minutes and hugged him wordlessly, as if she were still Billie's best friend, and they'd proceeded that way ever since. The kiss was seemingly buried by the avalanche of grief, a hallucinatory mistake that neither of them wanted to exhume and examine.

And yet. Here it is, somehow alive. Because he

can see it now in Harmony's earnest expression, the faint trembling of her lips: that she would, if given the chance, kiss him again.

And judging by the rebellious stirring in his groin, he might just kiss her back.

7

OLIVE IS ALONE at the top of a mountain, pine trees rustling around her, the sharp bite of snow in the air. She sits on a fallen log overlooking a valley, the setting sun in her face. At her feet sits a baby deer with its ears twitching in nervous anticipation. Someone is coming.

"You have a choice to make." She turns her head and sees her mother beside her on the log, legs stretched out before her, boot-clad feet crossed at the ankles. She's got sunglasses on, zinc oxide on her nose, her face deeply tanned. "Do you like things the way they are? Because if you do, by all means, carry on. But if you don't, nothing's going to change until you decide to make it change."

"What are you talking about? Change *what*?" Olive says. She turns to get a better look at her mother but is blinded by the glare.

Her mother turns her head toward the sun. "Sun feels nice," she says, tearing open a granola bar. "It shines on us all, no matter where we are."

"And where are *you*? Are we in Desolation Wilderness now?"

Her mom starts to laugh. And for a moment, it's almost like old times, the two of them sharing a secret; and then the forest begins to fade away, and the mountain breeze deposits Olive gently back in the driver's seat of the Subaru. Billie vanishes into Olive's backpack, which is jammed with books on the passenger seat; the deer rearranges itself into a canvas grocery tote, long abandoned in the foot well. Olive looks up and tries to reorient herself: the gladiolus-lined driveway, the McMansion with its two-story entrance and windows etched with dancing grapes; the row of anorexic cypress trees tilting toward the ground. *I am in front of Sharon Parkins's house,* she reminds herself.

It's her second vision that day alone. They are coming like that now: nothing at all for days and then clusters of them, each resolving briefly into sharp focus before fading into the background, like tuning past a radio station. There she'll be, sitting in her physics classroom, and then abruptly, she'll be somewhere else entirely, her mother beside her making enigmatic observations. Sometimes Olive will recognize where she's landed (her mom's favorite café; the top of Tilden Park), and other times the places are too vague to identify (a beach; an unrecognizable stand of pine trees). The visions are frustratingly cryptic and uncontrollable; they shimmer across her existence like layers of cellophane rather than offering any useful information. They feel like fragments of clues, signs pointing toward a bigger picture she can't quite grasp. What does it all mean? She attempted mirror-gazing, following the instructions in *Connections* to the letter, but all she ended up with was sore eyes from staring into a mirror for three hours straight. She even located an old Ouija board in the attic and sat in the dark, begging the spirits for answers—*Where'd you go, Mom?*—but the planchette under her fingertips remained stubbornly rooted in place.

Other than returning to Santa Cruz and parking herself at the base of the wooden stairway—for, what, weeks? in the hope that her mother will finally stumble past?—Olive has no idea what she should do next.

This, she hopes, is where Sharon Parkins might help.

Olive climbs out of the car and makes her way across the paving stones to the front door, where a small plaque, inscribed in calligraphy, hangs over the portico: *No Solicitors, Please*. She tentatively rings the doorbell, hearing it chime across some vast empty space behind the door.

A tiny thirtysomething redhead in workout gear opens the door so fast that Olive has to jump backward. The woman looks at Olive, eyebrows furrowing. "Oh," she says. She looks over Olive's shoulder, confused. "I was expecting my trainer."

"Are you Sharon Parkins the psychic?" Olive asks, taking in the woman's tennis bracelet and the enormous diamond hanging off her ring finger. She has the crème anglaise complexion of a woman of leisure, her hair pulled back into a shiny waterfall. She's wearing an awful lot of makeup for a workout.

The woman winces. "I'm not a tarot card reader, if that's what you're looking for." Her hands are poised on the jamb of the door as if preparing to close it.

"I'm not." Olive wonders whether the surprise she feels is as obvious to Sharon Parkins as it is to her. She thought a psychic would be more . . . mentorly? Motherly? Spiritual, maybe. At one with the universe.

Sharon certainly does not look like what Olive expected to find when she typed the phrase *Bay Area Psychic* into Google. (Then again, what *did* she expect? A head scarf, dangling gold Gypsy jewelry, a velvet-draped crystal ball nestled in her arms?) Olive's initial Google search turned up 117 hits; she narrowed these down to 33 by modifying her search to *Best Bay Area Psychic,* turning up a psychic who specialized in finding lost cats and a guy named Dr. Wisdom who had a sideline in closet organization.

Olive tried again: *Legitimate Bay Area Psychic.*

Bingo. The top hit was a *San Francisco Chronicle* story: "Bay Area Psychic Leads Police to Body of 12-Year-Old Missing Boy."

Manuel Alvarez had been missing for eleven days when Sharon Parkins, a housewife in Palo Alto, began seeing his face. She had no idea who the boy was that she kept seeing in what she describes as "waking dreams," but she knew he was important. So she called the local police station and asked to go through their missing persons files. It took less than ten minutes for her to identify Manuel as the boy she'd been seeing, and less than twenty-four hours for her to lead the police to the empty lot in San Bruno where Manuel's body was lying under a pile of abandoned mattresses.

"Sharon Parkins is totally legitimate," says Detective Fred Politsky, who has consulted with Parkins on past missing persons cases. "I don't know how she knows what she knows."

A psychic with a sideline in finding missing people: perfect. Olive typed *Sharon Parkins Palo Alto* into Google and retrieved an address, which led her here, to this faux-Mediterranean villa with a white Mercedes sedan parked in front.

"My name's Olive Flanagan," Olive tries again. "I was hoping you could help me find my mom, who's missing." The muscles around Sharon's jaw twitch and tighten, but Olive presses on: "But first I should tell you—I think I've been communicating with her telepathically." Olive watches as Sharon Parkins raises one of her perfectly arched eyebrows in apparent surprise, although it's hard to tell because of all the Botox.

Sharon Parkins peers past Olive, noting the sturdy Subaru parked in the driveway, then looks her up and down, taking in the freshly laundered school uniform with the Claremont Girls College Prep logo emblazoned on the breast pocket. Finally, she sighs and glances at her watch. "Oh, honey. OK. I guess I've got a few minutes. Come on in."

She leads Olive down a terra-cotta hallway and into a living room with a hulking marble fireplace and a chandelier the size of a car. The couches are leather and dense with pillows. Every surface is cluttered with objets d'art—jade vases, porcelain statuary, bronze urns, framed oils—ranging from ancient to modern and East to West, as if the sheer abundance and variety are intended to offset any doubts about the collector's taste. Olive looks down and realizes that she's standing on a rug made out of a real bearskin, head and all, which makes her feel sick to her stomach. She chooses a seat on the couch where she won't have to touch it.

Sharon Parkins settles into an armchair across from her and leans forward, chin in hand. Her eyes scan across Olive's face, flicking left to right, eye to eye, and Olive wonders if she's trying to "read" her. Uncomfortable, Olive glances away, making eye contact with the milky pupils of an antique carousel horse, skewered by a brass pole, over by the fireplace.

"Is—*this*—all from doing psychic work?" she asks, gesturing at the room.

Sharon laughs. "I don't *do psychic work*. Not that I get paid for. No—my husband's in venture capital."

"Oh."

"I don't advertise my abilities, let alone try to monetize them. Especially since I often can't do anything to help. But people keep finding me and ringing my doorbell anyway. Although"—she glances at the backpack at Olive's feet—"they're not usually schoolgirls. Aren't you supposed to be at school right now?"

"Staff development day," Olive lies. In fact, she skipped her afternoon classes in order to drive across the bay, and she has to be back by five P.M. in order to make it to her appointment with her new therapist. It's the first time she's ever cut class, which makes her skin crawl—surely she's going to get in trouble?—but she reminds herself that this variety of insubordination is exactly the kind of behavior her mom would have encouraged. (Anyone *can follow the rules. Find your own thing.*)

"So, should I start by telling you about my visions?" Olive asks.

Sharon kicks her sneakers off and then crosses her legs, sitting back in her chair. "Start wherever you feel like starting."

"OK, well, it began about a little over a week ago," Olive begins. She quickly tells Sharon about her mother's disappearance and the first vision. About her mother's name carved in the wooden rail at the beach. About the rest of the visions, increasing in frequency, right up to the mountaintop vision of a few minutes earlier.

"So what does it all mean?" she finishes. "I'm not sure how it all adds up. Am I seeing the present or the future? How do I know if something I've seen is important or not? Is it all related?" Sharon nods, and Olive waits for her to speak before realizing that this is a nod of the *Yes, go on* variety and doesn't signify any particular answer on Sharon's part. Olive continues more pointedly: "I thought maybe *you* could tell me how to interpret everything. Since you're the expert."

"*I'm* an expert?" Sharon laughs, exposing tiny

teeth as even and white as party mints. "I can't even interpret most of my *own* visions. There's an awful lot of noise and not a lot of signal, if you know what I mean. So I'm not going to be able to help you interpret yours, sorry. Really, I wish I could help you. But if you're looking for *logic,* you're not going to find it within the unexplainable. Like I said, most people who come here leave unhappy." She shifts forward as if the conversation is over. "Is that it?"

Olive remains rooted in place. "But you find people, right? Missing people?"

Sharon sits back again and looks down at her hands, pressing against the spandex of her workout pants. She wipes gently at the nap, smoothing it all into place. "I found Manuel Alvarez, if that's what you mean."

"So how did you do that?"

"It's hard to describe. I woke up one day and just knew where to go; I had a strong mental image where we'd find him, and then . . . God." Sharon presses her lips together. "It's not a skill I can teach you, if that's what you're asking. And remember that I also see a lot of things that make no sense whatsoever, things that I never figure out. Like I said—noise."

Olive's throat tightens. "OK. But even if you can't teach me what to do, *you* still found Manuel Alvarez—right? So you *could* find my mom." Sharon is shaking her head, looking very tired, but Olive presses on. "I thought maybe we could tap into her—what would you call it, energy?—if we worked together, with both of our . . ." She stumbles for the right word.

Sharon's lips twist back into a bemused smile. "Powers? Look. I'm not a superhero, honey. And besides, this isn't exactly something you can do *together*. It's not like 'Wonder Twin powers, activate!' "

Olive doesn't know what she's talking about. She looks down at her hands, clenched in her lap. "You don't believe me about seeing my mother, do you?"

Sharon reaches out to touch Olive's knee. "That's not what I meant. I'm getting definite energy off you. You've got *something* going on. And I would love to help you find your mom, I really would, if I could. But I can't, not like that. In my experience, visions aren't about communication; they're a one-way street. Nor do I often get to choose what I see. It's not like flipping to a TV channel to watch the eight o'clock movie."

"But you just said you find people."

"It's more like they find *me*."

"So? You could at least try." Olive realizes that she's tearing up. "I don't know who else to ask for help."

Sharon seems flustered by the sight of tears. "OK, OK. But no promises." She sits there twisting the giant rock on her finger. "Do you have anything with you that used to belong to your mother?"

Olive thinks about it for a minute. "I drive her old car."

Sharon puts her sneakers back on, and they walk out to the driveway. Sharon stands looking at the bottle-green Subaru with the dent in the driver's door where Olive opened it into a pole last week, and three years' worth of Earth Day stickers flaking off the rear bumper. The paint job is pebbled with rain-specked mud that is slowly eating away the finish because Olive thinks it's wrong to wash your car during a drought, no matter how much her father has been nagging her about it. Sharon rubs her hands together and then places her fingertips lightly on the hood of the car. She stands there with her eyes closed, the sunlight playing on her skin. For a moment, looking at the glow of the woman's face, Olive is hopeful; and then Sharon opens her eyes and shakes her head.

"Sorry. All I'm getting is spark plugs and piston rings."

Olive persists. "It might be better if you got inside the car? Since she spent most of her time in the driver's seat."

Sharon looks around as if waiting for someone to come to her rescue. "OK," she says reluctantly. Olive opens the driver's door for her, and the woman lowers herself into the seat, avoiding the corner where tufts of foam bloom from a fresh split in the leather. She places her manicured fingers at ten and two on the steering wheel, fingertips grazing the plastic. As Olive stands beside her, she peers straight ahead, out the windshield toward the Monterey Colonial across the street. She closes her eyes. The edges of her mouth twitch.

A long minute passes before Olive finally breaks the silence. "Are you seeing something?"

Sharon looks up at Olive with a glassy expression. Her voice, when she finally speaks, is low and slurred, belonging to a different person entirely. "Did you ever stop to think that maybe there are things that are just better not to know?" she growls.

Olive recoils. Before she can gather herself, a BMW pulls into the driveway and parks on the other side of the Subaru. There's a young guy in a black hoodie behind the wheel, mirrored sunglasses and carefully groomed stubble. At the sound of his tires squeaking to a stop, Sharon seems to return to herself. She carefully extricates herself from the front seat and adjusts the straps of her workout top, flashing a brilliant smile at the man now climbing out of his car.

"What did you see?" Olive persists, scrambling after her. "Look, if you're trying to protect me, you don't need to. I can handle it."

Sharon takes in Olive's face for a beat too long. "I got nothing," she says. "Sorry."

Sharon begins to walk back to her front door, trailed by the trainer with a BOSU ball in his arms. Olive watches her go in frustration, and just as Sharon is about to cross the threshold, she lurches forward and grabs the woman's arm. "You're lying to me. You saw something."

Sharon turns to face her, her face compressed into a tight knot of frustration. "I don't know. Maybe. Honestly—I'm really sorry about your mom, but I think you should let it go. Go spend some time with your friends, kiss someone, be a normal high school kid for as long as you can. If you're really psychic, this is only going to get harder. The grown-up world is cruel and unfair, and you don't want to spend any more time there than you're going to have to."

For a moment, Olive hates this woman and her platitudes. Doesn't she understand that nothing is "normal," not for Olive? That without her mom, the world is already "cruel and unfair," and until she gets her back, she is never going to figure out how everything is supposed to work? "Just tell me this one thing," she blurts. "My mom—she *wants* me to find her, right?"

Sharon stops. A bead of sweat slips down the edge of her hairline and swerves underneath her ear. She looks at Olive for a long time, and Olive can see a familiar sympathy creep into her eyes. "Oh, honey. Of course she does," she says softly, and then extricates herself with a little shake.

At that moment, the trainer brushes past Olive on his way into the house, and Sharon slips in with him, tipping the door closed behind her.

And with that, Sharon Parkins is swallowed up by Villa Valparaiso. Through the door, Olive can hear the squeak of the woman's sneakers echoing along the Spanish tile.

Is it a victory? Not exactly, but Olive feels like something has been achieved. *My mom wants to be found.* It's a validation, at least. She jumps happily back in the Subaru and put her hands at ten and two, just where Sharon's were. The steering wheel is still warm. Olive thinks she can feel her mother's presence lingering there in the car before she turns the key in the ignition and prepares for the rush-hour battle back across the bay.

Dr. Albright's office is a converted garage in the back of a Victorian painted a cheery mint green, down a path lined with wild lavender and creeping fig. Olive waits in the therapist's anteroom underneath a series of photographs of Balinese children. She looks at the pictures, wondering how Harmony knows Dr. Albright; are they friends? Is Dr. Albright her therapist? That would be awkward.

Olive stares at the clock on the wall, impatient for the next hour to be over. What a colossal waste of time.

Somewhere deep in her backpack, her cellphone is ringing. She fishes it out and examines the unfamiliar number before answering it.

The male voice on the other end sounds like it's emerging from the spin cycle of a washing machine. "Hey, um . . . Olive?"

She holds the phone gingerly. "Who is this?"

"Yeah, this is Matt. You came to my house the other day. Asked about that woman in the photo?" *Disco Biscuit,* she realizes. The roar in the background resolves itself: the sound of waves and wind.

On the other end of the line, Matt is yelling at someone, his voice muffled as if he's pressed the phone against his shirt. *"Hey! C'mere!!"*

"Right! Hi," Olive says quickly. "What's up?"

Matt comes back. "Yeah, I found her. The blonde with the McTavish. She was out at Steamer Lane. . . ." Once again the phone is muffled. She can hear him talking to someone in the background, his voice rumbling in his chest. Inside her own chest, her heart lets out a hopeful hiccup. *Could it be?*

The phone abruptly changes hands, and a woman's voice comes over the line. "Hello?"

It doesn't sound like her mom's voice, not at all. Her mom's voice was low and spiky, and this woman's sounds more nasal. And yet she hasn't heard her mom speak in a year; memory could be deceiving her. "Mom?" she asks, testing.

The woman on the other end of the line sounds puzzled. "God, I hope not? What's this about?"

Olive's eyes sting, hope dashed. The voice, it is definitely wrong: all drawling uptalk, a question mark in the words. Billie always talked like she knew exactly what she was talking about, no question about it. Olive clears her throat. "Sorry, I'm looking for my mom, and Matt thought you might be her."

"No," the woman says. "I think I'd know if I had a kid? Good luck, though."

Matt comes back on the line. "Dude, sorry," he says. "Now that I'm looking at her, yeah, she's probably not old enough to be your mom."

"Are you high? I'm twenty-five." Olive can hear the woman in the background. "I would have had to give birth when I was, like, in grammar school."

"Whatever. Sorry." Olive isn't sure if he is apologizing to her or to the blond surfer. "Well, I tried. OK, bye!"

He hangs up. Olive looks at the cellphone in her hand with chagrin. What now? All is quiet in Dr. Albright's office.

She punches out a quick text to Natalie:

Disco Biscuit called with blond surfer. She is DEF not mom.

Her phone vibrates with Natalie's response. ☹

Maybe mom wasn't at that beach at all. Maybe I interpreted vision wrong.

What about the name on railing?

??? FIIK. Coincidence?

Olive thinks and types again. *Or she IS there but this was the wrong way 2 find her.*

There is a long pause.

Maybe she wrote her name B4. When ur family had ur picnic there last yr.

Olive hadn't considered that possibility. She ponders this dispiriting idea, feeling her paltry leads wink out one by one.

Her cellphone vibrates once more: *So now what?*

Good question. Out of ideas.

The door to the therapist's office swings inward, revealing a woman about Olive's mom's age. She has wild, curling black hair and wears an off-white cardigan that hangs to her knees over loose linen pants. Olive jumps to her feet, shoving the phone deep into her backpack.

"Olive Flanagan?" Dr. Albright says brightly, reaching out to shake Olive's hand. "I've heard a lot about you from Harmony. Let's go into my office. What's on your mind?"

WHERE THE MOUNTAIN MEETS THE SKY

My Life with Billie Flanagan

———

BY JONATHAN FLANAGAN

M y wife wasn't exactly an *easy* person—I knew that from the very beginning—but that didn't mean she wasn't fun to be around. In fact, it was exactly the opposite; she always knew when she'd gone a bit too far and it was time to swing back in the other direction and do something thoughtful or spontaneous. And in those whirlwind moments, the high moments, I couldn't have been happier or more in love.

We'd get in a fight, and then next morning I'd wake up to an elaborate breakfast in bed, the final course being an unsolicited blow job. She'd be moody and selfish and irritable all week, but then on Friday she'd show up at my office with Olive in tow and whisk us away for an impromptu weekend trip to a mountain town where she'd heard we could get the world's best apple pie. She'd be cold and thoughtless to me as I was leaving for work, and when I opened my laptop an hour later I'd find a sticky note taped to my screen: *Don't be mad. I love you.* I never could stay mad. I always forgave her. I always loved her back.

When I think of Billie now, I often imagine her behind the wheel of her car, taking Olive and me on some unanticipated adventure. She drove with her seat tilted back, loud music blasting over the radio, the windows rolled down as far as they would go. Living life in the minute. *That* was the kind of person she was at heart, and for me, that made it easy to gloss over the rest.

But lately, I've also been thinking of an observation that a friend of Billie's made to me: *Billie liked to be surprised.*

For all the spontaneity that Billie liked to surround our lives with, after sixteen years together, was there really anything surprising about *us* anymore? Is it even possible, after all those years of marriage, to truly surprise someone? At that point, they are already intimate with everything that is you: the smell of your shoes, the way you drink your coffee, the sound you make when you sneeze. The way you are impatient with your elderly parents on the phone and the way you repeat ad nauseam the same handful of injustices that they have inflicted upon you. The quotes you recycle. The cherry-picked memories from your childhood repeated so many times that your spouse can now recite your best anecdotes on your behalf at dinner parties.

You grow predictable, your quirks no longer interesting but expected. Like a board game that you've played too many times to truly enjoy, a favorite movie that you don't feel compelled to watch all the way through anymore. You're comforted by your spouse's presence; yes, you still love them; but you are no longer thrilled by them, not in the way you once were. You are no longer surprised.

Of course I didn't surprise Billie anymore.

Because—let's be honest—I wasn't particularly surprised

by *her* anymore, either. Her unpredictability had become . . . predictable. Annoying, even. But that was OK. It was OK, because I'd always believed that the cornerstone of a strong marriage was a lifelong commitment to putting up with your partner's faults—the ability to move past those things that tickled at your distaste. Even when you grew weary with your wife's inexplicable moodiness, or her too-cold judgment, or the way she assumed that you were always there to pick up after her: You took a deep breath, smiled with forbearance, and did something generous to sweep the negative feelings away. Instead of rejecting your partner's flaws as imperfections, you were supposed to cover them with understanding layers of nacre, build a protective pearl around them. Love wasn't supposed to be simple; it was supposed to be something you did regardless: *I love you anyway*.

Besides, wasn't everyone flawed? I believed that divorce was for cowards who used their partner's failings as an excuse to avoid looking too closely in the mirror.

I always assumed that Billie felt the same way, that she was fine with things the way they were—the inevitable, unavoidable progression of marriage—but maybe she wasn't.

So what happens if you and your spouse are striving for two totally different marriages? One built on a belief in forbearance and another on surprise? What if the ideal that one of you thinks is keeping you together is actually something that is driving the other one away?

What happens then?

8

THE OFFICE OF LIM & Partners Research Services is on the eighth floor of an aging building in a Tenderloin-adjacent neighborhood, at the far end of a hallway whose doors otherwise advertise accountants and tax advisers and cryptically titled consulting services. The building is dead empty—the sound of Jonathan's footsteps echoing dully across the stained marble lobby, the elevator ascending directly to his floor—as if Jonathan has entered some anachronistic ghost town, far from the bustling new economy.

Behind the Lim & Partners burnt-orange door, Jonathan finds a large square room with windows looking out toward downtown. A bank of brushed-steel filing cabinets flanks one wall and a mostly empty bookshelf lines the other. In one corner a portable water fountain burbles, not quite masking the honking horns and the jangle of streetcars eight floors below. A schoolroom clock above the fountain silently jerks away the passing seconds.

Exactly in the center of all this sits Calvin Lim, slim and neat, his hair freshly shorn around exposed pink ears, his button-down shirt tucked snugly into pale trousers. He sits perfectly upright on a backless ergonomic stool, which closely resembles a bicycle saddle on wheels. The glass-topped desk before him is bare except for a closed laptop, a cellphone, and a perfectly aligned stack of printouts.

Lim stands to shake Jonathan's hand, directing him to another of the saddle stools positioned directly before his desk. "Happy to meet you," he says, his words clipped and careful. "What can I help you with?"

Jonathan settles himself gingerly on the stool. "It's not about me, actually. It's about my wife. I think she might have talked to you at some point last year," he begins. "I found your website bookmarked on her browser. Her name was Billie Flanagan. Ring a bell?"

Lim's left eye twitches. "I can't confirm or deny that. I'm sorry."

Jonathan expected this. "If it makes a difference, she's dead."

Lim blinks. "I'm sorry for your loss."

"Yes, well, thank you," Jonathan continues. "I'm dealing with some estate issues. And I was hoping that you could tell me what she hired you for."

Lim folds his hands together, carefully positioning each finger an exact distance from the next, and studies them. "My company confidentiality policy is very strict. I have to maintain the privacy of my clients. Or else I won't have any clients."

"She's *dead*." Jonathan repeats the words slowly. Underneath his rear, the stool rolls gently back and forth in agreement. "She's dead, and you still can't confirm that she came to see you?" Lim shakes his head. "Look, I understand—and appreciate!—your commitment to discretion. But it's not like she's going to come in here and be angry with you."

Lim frowns slightly. "Well, anyone can come in here and *say* that their spouse died, you see. Do you have a death certificate you can show me?"

Jonathan almost laughs. "Not yet; there are some legal loopholes we're trying to address. That's part of why I'm here."

Lim nods as if this isn't unusual in the least. "Without proof, I can't help you. Sorry, but the policy stands. Anything else I can assist you with?"

Jonathan spins wordlessly on his stool, thinking, and finds himself facing the filing cabinets. He scans for a drawer marked *F,* half inclined to make a mad dash and tear through it until he finds Billie's file; and then he realizes that the cabinets aren't even marked. In fact, judging by a drawer that's slightly ajar, they are all empty. Just for show? He rotates further and finds himself staring at his own reflection in a narrow mirror adjacent to the office door, looking unshaven and rumpled in third-day khakis and an old zip-up that reads, in faded lettering, DECODE THE FUTURE! And then spins further to regard the near-empty bookshelves containing a handful of software manuals and some abstract black-and-white photographs that look suspiciously like IKEA prints.

He spins back to face Lim. "Where's all your surveillance equipment? Isn't that what private investigators do, mostly? Follow around cheating husbands and wives, catch them in the act?"

Calvin Lim smiles tightly, revealing crooked incisors. "That is an antiquated idea of the services I provide, Mr. Flanagan. My business is rather more *modern*. I do almost all of my work online." He rests a hand on his laptop. "I do a lot of work with records investigation, missing persons, real estate transactions, database searching, personnel histories. I don't spend my time"—he laughs drily—"sitting in *automobiles* eating *doughnuts*."

"Interesting. Then my wife didn't hire you to, say, follow someone." Who would she have wanted to follow? Him? The putative mystery lover?

"Again, I cannot confirm or deny that she hired me."

"OK, I get it." Jonathan stands up, and the stool rolls silently toward the wall of bookshelves. His cellphone is ringing in his pocket, and he pulls it out: *CLAREMONT*. He mutes it; it's probably Gillespie, after her tuition. "Well, thank you for your time."

"Not at all." Lim stands politely. "Sorry I couldn't be of more assistance."

Jonathan walks to the door and then pauses as he looks at the detective reflected in the mirror, a pucker between his eyebrows as he frowns down at his laptop. Something that Lim said lingers on the periphery of Jonathan's consciousness, nagging at him.

He whirls around. "You investigate missing persons."

"Yes," Lim says. He closes his laptop again.

A rabbit hole is opening up before Jonathan—*Do you really want to do this?*—but he opens his mouth anyway and asks. "How hard would it be to disappear?"

Lim cocks his head. "Elaborate, please?"

Jonathan rolls the stool back to the desk and sits down. "Let's say I wanted to vanish off the face of the earth. No trace of my existence. Everyone thinks I'm dead. What would it take? Would it even be possible?"

Lim stares at him, the muscles around his jaw clenching and unclenching almost imperceptibly. "Would you like to hire me to locate a missing person?"

"What do you charge?"

"A hundred an hour," Lim says.

Jonathan winces. "What if I gave you twenty-five dollars for fifteen minutes of your time? Just a quick bit of consultation?"

Calvin Lim shrugs and glances at the clock. "Sure. We start now."

"So?"

"So, it's not terribly hard to disappear if you really want to. There are online markets—probably you've heard of the Darknet?—where you can buy entire identities, stolen Social Security numbers and fake passports and driver's licenses and the like. Piece of cake to find if you know where to look, and it's not even that expensive. Eight hundred dollars, maybe a thousand, to become a whole different person. And planning it—it's easy to mask your trail these days if you're careful, with prepaid phones and anonymous email accounts. Slip over the border into Mexico, and you've disappeared off the grid. The tricky part, though, is *staying* disappeared."

Lim is leaning forward now, his breath fogging the pristine surface of his glass desk as he grows more animated. "You have to leave behind anything that's GPS-enabled—your car, your phone. You have to stay away from email and social media linked to your old identity, of course, because we can tell if you've logged in. Avoid places you might once have gone. Leave behind absolutely everything, including photos and sentimental mementos that might give you up. Give your laptop a thorough scour of anything suspicious. And when you set up your new identity, you have to make sure you don't rely on any giveaway details from your old life that might wind up in a searchable database." He smiles, gleeful. "I've caught people because they just transposed their Social Security number, or made a new name out of an anagram of their old one, or signed up for a new online account with the same login name. I know all the mistakes."

Jonathan thinks about it. Was *this* why Billie hired Calvin Lim? Did she come to him and ask him to help her lose herself in a way so complete that she would never be found? He imagines her with a prepaid phone and an untraceable email account, carefully staging her exit; starting a new life somewhere with a fake passport and a name bearing no resemblance to her own and a shelf bereft of sentimental photographs.

He tries to wrap his head around this, struggling to reconcile it with the wife he was married to for so long. And yet. He thinks of Billie's words again: *You can* always *walk away.* Didn't she do that before, more than once? She'd left several lives behind by the time he met her. But those were bad situations, lives that *should* have been left behind.

And yet how can you ever really know the truth about another person? We all write our own narratives about the people we know and love, he realizes. We choose the story that's easiest to tell, the one that best fits our own vision for our lives. We define them in the way that's most convenient for our own sense of self-aggrandizement. Glossing over anything that doesn't fit into that neat little narrative because we don't want the whole fiction to fall apart. In his own happy Billie-Olive-and-Jonathan narrative, theirs was the ideal life that Billie would never want to walk away from. In *her* version, maybe it wasn't.

He feels ill. He stares at the slightly flushed face of Calvin Lim and can't help wondering if this stranger actually knows something about his wife that he does not. If he knows that Billie is alive and, if so, where she is.

"OK," Jonathan says slowly. "Let's say I don't have access to the databases that you do. But I want to figure out if someone I thought was dead is actually alive and just pretending to be dead." He studies Calvin Lim's face to gauge his reaction—*Does this scenario sound familiar to you, hmm?*—but Lim gives him nothing in return. "What clues would I need to look for?"

Lim is quiet for a moment. "Well, the first place

to look would be electronic bank transactions," he says, drawing his words out. "If you want to disappear, you need cash, right? So a history of suspiciously large cash withdrawals, or even smallish ones that stretch over a prolonged period of time."

Jonathan thinks of their depleted savings account. "OK. And?"

"Go through the person's laptop. Web history, emails, calendar, photos, anything that doesn't look quite right."

"I've done that. That's how I found you."

Lim looks hard at him and then glances at the clock. "Sorry, that's fifteen minutes."

That's not enough, thinks Jonathan frantically. "One last question?" he asks.

Lim folds his hands again, pressing his thumbs together until the tips of both fingers turn white with pressure. "OK, just one."

"What would *you* do to catch someone—this person?" Jonathan asks carefully. "If they don't want to be found. One trick that you would use to trip them up."

Lim releases his hands from their grip and flexes his fingers as he thinks. The fountain burbles and slaps against its decorative stones; outside the office door, a burst of voices disappears slowly down the hall. Finally, Lim speaks. "I'd make an IP address trap," he says. "Mock up a website about the missing—the *dead*—person, you know, memories of them, or asking for information, or something along those lines. And then track the IP addresses of the people who come to check it out. People who disappear themselves—they want to know if they've gotten away with it. They can't resist looking themselves up on the Internet to see what friends and family are saying about them. So you set up this site and then watch to see if there's an IP address that comes back over and over. Odds are, that's your man." He looks at Jonathan, assessing. "Or woman."

"Thanks," Jonathan says. "That was very helpful." He stands up and pulls out his billfold, counting out a fistful of bills and placing these on the desk. Lim glances at the pile of money and gives a small nod. As Jonathan walks to the door, he hears the soft murmur of Lim's voice behind him:

"Good luck," he says. "I hope you find her."

Jonathan drives blindly back across the bay, his mind so muddled that he barely registers the locked-in traffic or the formidable rotting smell from last week's spilled latte emitting from the backseat of his Prius. The victorious white spire of the new Bay Bridge passes overhead; in the distance, the cranes of the Port of Oakland crouch like praying mantises, surrounded by the carcasses of empty freight containers.

He arrives back home just before five and pulls into the empty driveway. He cuts the engine, momentarily incapable of leaving the confined safety of the car, the warmth of the seat against his back. Outside the car, the street is dark, the lights in the crumbly old Craftsman homes ticking on one by one. Across the street, in a house owned by an old-school Berkeley hippie holdout, an army of rainbow flags—pinwheels, fish kites, whirligigs, windsocks, sticking out of the lawn and hanging from the oak trees and jammed in among the ferns—flap in a synchronized frenzy as the wind picks up.

His own house is dark. Olive isn't home. Looking up at the void of her window, he remembers that Olive is at her first appointment with the therapist, Meredith Albright. It strikes him with a wave of guilt that he's been trying to get Olive to stop believing Billie is alive at the exact moment when he has seized on the same thread.

He sits there, his mind filling with hypothetical scenarios: his wife, instead of dying out there in the middle of Desolation Wilderness, hiking back out and back to life. And what, catching a bus? There wasn't exactly a lot of public transportation out in the woods, and there was a manhunt going on, so someone surely would have noticed her. No, the more likely scenario was an accomplice of some sort, someone with a car. Presumably the person she was spending her weekends with.

He climbs from the car and shoulders his way through the damp air to his front door. Inside, he clicks on the heat and walks directly to the office, depositing his laptop on the desk. He begins yanking out desk drawers, pulling out file folders and examining their labels, marked in Billie's neat penmanship. PHONE BILLS—REPORT CARDS—CABLE—BANK STATEMENTS. He disgorges the contents of this last folder, fanning out several years' worth of account statements before him.

It doesn't take very long to find what he's looking for. He releases a long rush of air, only then realizing that he's barely breathed since he left Calvin Lim's office. In the last year of her life, Billie started making regular cash withdrawals from their savings account. At first just a few hundred here and there, and then sums up to a thousand. All in, roughly $19,500 disappeared this way, putting the dismal state of their savings account in a whole new light. (He also flags, with grim confirmation, two payments made to LPRS, Inc., in May and then again in October. Of course: Lim & Partners Research Services.) Maybe Jonathan would have noticed the money slowly vanishing if he'd bothered to do their monthly accounting. But he never did, and Billie would have known that, so the slow attrition had slipped right past him.

Almost twenty thousand dollars—it's not enough to live on forever. But perhaps long enough, especially if she fled somewhere cheap, like Mexico. Or had someone else to share expenses with.

There it is, proof of some sort. He stares at the pile of papers and then, with a swift swipe of his palm, sends them tumbling to the floor. His whole body is quivering with fury, and when he tries to still his shaking hands by gripping the edge of the desk, he notices the battered wedding band on his ring finger. He slides the ring off and shoves it among the paper clips and dried-up pens in the cluttered depths of the desk drawer, then slams the drawer shut.

Mexico. He recalls another of the curious fragments that he unearthed from Billie's laptop. He pulls his laptop out of his bag and boots up the browser. He clicks to the website of Motel 6 and types *Mexico locations* into the directory and waits for the results, his heart flipping back and forth.

There are no Motel 6 locations in Mexico. He stares at his browser, trying to figure out what to do next. So maybe his wife didn't go on a secret scouting mission to Mexico that weekend, planning her tropical escape. But where else might she have gone?

He hears the rattle of keys and gets up from his chair just as Olive comes through the front door. She peers around the door and then steps quickly into the room, scanning his face with her clear wide eyes. There is a smear of blue ink on the side of her nose, faint, like a thumbprint. He feels a stab of love for his daughter, so visceral, so alive and present. Without thinking about it, he folds her inside his arms and squeezes her tight, his eyes blurring. He realizes that he hasn't hugged his daughter in far too long, and it's not only because she isn't coming to him for hugs anymore. It's also been easier to simply forget what it feels like to have someone's arms around him, especially someone who, day by day, more closely resembles his absent wife.

Olive hugs him back wordlessly, her backpack slipping out of her hand and hitting the floor with a thump behind his feet. She clings tightly, as if to compensate for all the hugs—paternal, maternal—that she's been missing over the last year. *What's the best thing for Olive?* he wonders as he carefully disentangles himself. *For her mom to be alive and have left us intentionally, or for her to be dead and gone forever?* He needs to proceed carefully, he realizes. If he goes down this path, the odds are good that whatever he discovers—whatever dark-blind creatures are scuttling around underneath these rocks that he plans to overturn—isn't going to be pleasant. What's that going to do to his daughter? How will he protect her from the ugliness they might find?

It can't be helped. There's no way he can stop now.

OK, let's do this, he thinks. *Let's go figure out if Billie is alive and what she was doing in the year before she disappeared.*

He steps back and examines Olive. "You're coming from seeing Dr. Albright, right? How was it?"

She bends to fiddle with her backpack. "I liked her," she says, her face buried inside her bag. He can feel her disappearing into herself again, and he wants to drag her back. "She had a pretty good sense of humor."

"What'd you talk about? Am I allowed to ask?"

"Mostly about Mom, you know, but also about school and stuff." Olive still isn't looking at him.

"Did it clarify anything for you?" he asks, glancing at the bank statements lying in disarray on the floor, and the open laptop with the browser querying *Motel 6 Mexico*.

She frowns. "About what?" she asks, following his gaze toward the mess on the floor and giving him a quizzical look.

"About your mom . . ." he begins. But Olive isn't looking at him anymore. Her face has gone pale, her pupils dark and wide; with one unsure hand she reaches out and clutches an armchair as if to hold herself upright. Her eyes scan left, then right, skimming past Jonathan as if something interesting is happening just behind him. Worried, Jonathan stoops to peer into her face. "Olive?"

She doesn't seem to register his presence in front

of her. He grips her upper arms, unsure whether he should rouse her. It's like the other evening in Olive's bedroom, the way she rose from her desk with the same unfocused expression. He realizes now what that was all about. *Oh, hell,* he thinks. "Olive? Are you OK?"

He feels a quiver pass through her, the muscles in her body making a series of tiny adjustments, and all at once she is back. She looks at him, her pupils glazed over, as she slowly releases her grip on the chair. "I'm fine, Dad."

He shuffles back through the same set of possibilities he's been ruminating over the past two weeks—*Is she having hallucinations? Or seizures? Or is it grief?*—before he decides, somewhat reluctantly, to draw one last card. "Can you tell me about it?" he asks.

She blinks at him, feigning innocence. "What do you mean?"

"You just had another"—he stumbles over the word, not quite reconciled to it—"*vision*. Right?"

She studies him as if searching for a sign that she's stepping into a trap. "If I tell you, you're going to send me back to the therapist."

"You don't have to go to see the therapist again if you don't want to," he says.

"Oh, *good*." She stops, confused. "Wait—*what*? You believe me about the visions now?"

Does he? She's the one who set him on this road in the first place, he realizes. He thinks about something he wrote a few years earlier in a *Decode* story about dream research scientists: *The mind is neither sensible nor scientific. As the quantum physicist*

Max Planck once wrote, "Science cannot solve the ultimate mystery of nature. And that is because, in the last analysis, we ourselves are a part of the mystery that we are trying to solve."

He gives up, lets go. "I'm suspending disbelief," he says. She's looking at him, not understanding. "Look. I think it's possible—*possible*—that your mom is alive. Enough that I'm willing to explore it with you."

He expects Olive to get excited, but she just offers him a wobbly smile and then, bit by bit, her face collapses. She sinks down on the couch and presses the heels of her hands into her eye sockets, breathing hard. Jonathan sits down next to her and puts a hand on her shoulder, feeling her body quivering. They sit there, at a loss for words, for a long time. "So—*did* you see something just now?" he asks.

"Yes," she says quietly. "I see weird stuff all the time, Dad. I see *her*. She talks to me. It feels like, I don't know, telepathy or something."

"And you still believe that she's alive."

"Yeah," Olive says softly. "I know it doesn't really make sense, Dad. But I just do. She needs me. I think she must be in trouble."

"OK." He cocks his head and examines his daughter, trying to imagine what she must be seeing in her head, the ephemeral signals flickering through the dark. Is it comforting for her to see Billie again after all this time, to hear her voice? "The vision you just had right now—she was there?"

"Yes. We were on"—she closes her eyes, thinking—"a farm?"

"A *farm*?" Jonathan's mind paints a picture of a

cheerful red barn and a white picket fence, some moony cows and a clutch of freshly shorn lambs. "As in 'Old MacDonald'?"

"No." She opens her eyes again. "Not the cliché. More like dust bowl. Failing."

The image in Jonathan's mind clears, replaced by a different farm that he has seen far more recently. Almond trees, a lopsided chicken coop, a tire swing: a photograph currently sitting in a pile in the kitchen, waiting to be framed.

He walks back over to his browser and clicks back to the Motel 6 web page, scanning the list of locations in California until he recognizes a name that rings a very faint bell. Schuster, California. He clicks on the address, and the mapping tool sends a red arrow down on a side street alongside a highway in the middle of the Central Valley of California. He scrolls right and left on the map, waiting for something to jog his memory. There. Roughly five miles to the east of Schuster, California, is the tiny hamlet of Meacham. The town where his wife lived until age seventeen, the town where her parents—as far as he knows—still live. He zooms out again until it's abundantly clear: The Motel 6 is the closest hotel to the town where Billie grew up.

"What are you looking at?" Olive asks, peering over his shoulder. Her voice is steady again, growing animated. "Are you seriously saying that you believe me now? Because, Dad, this is great—I could really use your help. For a while I thought maybe there was this surfer down in Santa Cruz that was her, plus I found Mom's name carved into a staircase down there, but that hasn't panned out. Not yet, at least.

Oh, and I have to tell you about this psychic I met today; she saw *something*—she wouldn't tell me what. But she says Mom definitely wants to be found. I'm not sure how it all adds up, but maybe—amnesia? I'm thinking that, or . . ." She is babbling, but the words slide over Jonathan, who has clicked into a track that's set him flying off in a new and very interesting direction.

"What do you think," he interrupts her, "of you and me going on a road trip tomorrow to meet your grandparents?"

9

THE ROUTE TO OLIVE'S grandparents' house is lined with almond trees. They march precisely out toward the horizon, their branches reaching out for the sky, bereft of leaves, dormant. As Olive turns to watch them fly by, the individual trees dissolve into rhythmic noise. The ground beside the highway is brown and cracked; a sign attached to an abandoned trailer reads PRAY 4 RAIN.

The drive from Berkeley to Meacham has taken four hours, and Olive's father has spent most of that time peppering her with questions: *How's school? What are you thinking about college? Are you considering possible careers yet? Do you worry about the future?* She bats his questions back haphazardly, too wired to really focus on the answers she's giving. Still, she feels oddly happy: the sun through the windows warming the car, Coldplay on the radio, her dad nodding intently at everything she says as if it all matters.

Her father guns the Prius and veers around a lumbering semi. "Is it weird if I ask you whether there's someone you like?" he asks.

"*Dad!* God. Yes. It's weird."

He glances sideways at her. "You know, I barely dated at all in high school, too. I didn't *get* girls, and they didn't get me. It wasn't until I got to college that I felt comfortable with myself and grew up, sexually speaking. At which point I went a little crazy with the girls, but that's another story." He clears his throat awkwardly. "My point is, it's OK if you feel like you're still trying to understand those kinds of feelings. That's normal."

"Dad, *seriously*. TMI. I don't want to know how and when you lost your virginity, OK? Please change the subject."

He laughs. "This is nice," he says. "We should spend more time talking this way."

She nods and looks out at the orchards and thinks of the way her mom used to creep into her room in the middle of the night when she was little, crawling into her bed and prodding her awake to whisper hungrily in her ear: *Tell me everything. Tell me what's in your heart today.* Protected by the dark, in that vulnerable twilight state of semi-sleep, she found it a relief to spill everything for her mother's consumption: the way other girls could be so casually cruel, the times when her teacher made her cry, how the collective pain of the world sometimes made it hard to breathe. Her mother would listen intently, the heat of her body warming Olive's side until Olive finally slipped back into sleep, teary-eyed and depleted.

At some point after she started at Claremont, though, Olive grew tired of these emotionally exhausting nocturnal talks. She wanted more privacy, and she wanted to *sleep*. She started locking her door at bedtime. The first night her mother tried to come in, Olive cowered guiltily under the covers as she heard her mother rattling at the doorknob, softly calling her name. Hating herself for her betrayal, yet feeling like there was something precious that she was protecting. At breakfast the next morning, she could barely meet her mother's eyes, which were puffy and pink, even though Billie smiled as if nothing was wrong while she was buttering her toast.

Olive unlocked her door again after that, but her mother never came back.

After a while, her father pulls off the freeway at a sun-bleached freeway exit north of Bakersfield. They buy drive-through burritos from Taco Bell, and then her father parks the car on the side of the road in front of a peach stucco Motel 6. Plastic grocery bags blow through the mostly empty parking lot and catch on the edges of the hotel's concrete portico. The rooms on the upper floor appear to have an excellent view of the interstate, a hundred yards away.

"I'm pretty sure your mom stayed here the April before she died," her father says. "I think she must have been visiting your grandparents."

Surprised, Olive cranes her neck to look at the motel. She tries to imagine her mother stepping out from under that portico, a duffel bag slung over her shoulder. "She stayed here? How do you know?" she asks.

Her father leans forward and wraps his arms around the steering wheel, looking up at the windows of the hotel. "Something I found on her computer recently," he says.

"But why would she visit them? I thought she hadn't talked to them in like thirty years."

He shakes his head. "I have no idea. But maybe they'll be able to answer that."

Olive looks at her father. Behind his glasses, the skin around his eyes is tender and raw, and for the first time, Olive wonders why her father does not seem as excited about the possibility of Billie's ongoing existence as she is. Does he know something she doesn't? She is trying to figure out how to ask him when he starts the car and, with one final flick of his eyes toward the motel, pulls back on the interstate. The moment passes.

A few minutes later, he exits to a country highway where closed-up fruit stands advertise strawberries on splintered signs, and disused harvesters sit in ditches, gray with road dust. Distant hills bookend the flat expanse of the valley. Her father slows the car as they pass an orchard where drought-damaged almond trees have recently been bulldozed; the dead trees lie in rows like body bags at a disaster site. Two migrant workers with bandannas tied over their faces are feeding limbs into a wood chipper.

Finally, he turns right at a row of mailboxes and begins bumping down a country road, passing the occasional clapboard farmhouse. In every direction, Olive sees indistinguishable trees and cold dirt and a featureless sky that looks like it's been painted on with a roller brush. The land feels separated from modern times, a place where existence still founders on the elemental and cruel. *Save the earth,* she thinks reflexively, but this earth doesn't seem like it particularly wants saving. The foreign objects planted in its soil will flourish, or they will wither, and everything will continue on regardless.

Nonetheless, she likes the idea that she has this in her family history: something rural, connected to the land, people who once coaxed food from the earth. "I didn't realize that Mom grew up on a *real* farm," Olive says.

Jonathan frowns. "It wasn't a working farm. Her dad was a preacher, actually. I seem to recall that they sold off most of their land before she was born. Kept the house, though; your mother said it had been in the family for generations."

They pass a small horse farm where a woman in riding gear is slowly circling a paddock on a steaming black mare, churning up pillows of yellow dust. Finally, the GPS informs them that they've arrived at their destination, and Jonathan slows, turning up a driveway.

"This is it," he says.

The farmhouse that stands before them is falling to its knees. White paint curls from the edges of the house; the wraparound porch has collapsed at one end. A fraying rope hangs from the branch of an almond tree near the front door, but whatever once hung from it—a tire swing, maybe?—is long gone. A rusting Pontiac sits in the front yard, weeds growing up through its missing engine block. It's the farm from her vision, but a far more run-down version.

Jonathan cuts the engine. He's quiet for a minute. "You know that your mom didn't like her parents very much," he says. "Her father did some pretty bad things. I'm not sure they're nice people. They may not be happy that we're here."

"I know, Dad," Olive says. She can hear the wind in the branches of the almond trees, whispering about their presence. A chain-link fence surrounds the farmhouse, separating it from the orchards that lie beyond.

She pushes the car door open and climbs out, looking up at the house. The car door slams and her father comes to stand beside her. They gaze at the house together, and the house seems to stare sullenly back at them, its windows shrouded in yellowing lace curtains. The air smells faintly of burning wood and fertilizer.

Olive struggles to remember stories that her mother told about her childhood here. There aren't many. But she recalls, when she was much younger, playing treasure hunt in the garden with her mom, and asking if this was something she had done with her own mother. Something hard passed across her mother's face. "My mother didn't *play*," she said. "She believed in only two things: chores and prayers. I spent every minute that I could outside, so that I could get away from her." She was holding Olive's hand, and all of a sudden her grip was too tight. Olive whimpered, and her mother released her. She turned to Olive, smiling reassuringly. "It's OK. The trees were my friends."

Olive has always liked this image of her mother playing in the almond trees, like the little boy in *The Giving Tree*—swinging in their branches, making crowns from their papery white flowers. Olive looks around now at the cold, bare trees that stretch in every direction. They do not come off as particularly friendly.

"I can't imagine who would want to buy this place," Jonathan says, looking at a sign half buried in weeds: FOR SALE BY OWNER. He starts up the porch, stepping gingerly on the collapsing steps, Olive close behind him. He presses a doorbell, then, when that doesn't seem to work, knocks loudly.

No one answers.

Olive peers through the window closest to the door. The house is half abandoned, as if someone began to remove their belongings and then gave up halfway through. Each piece of furniture left behind suggests the absence of another piece, making the room feel even more barren than it would were it completely empty. Olive can see dining room chairs but nothing to eat on, a coffee table but no couch, a TV stand but no TV. On the far wall, over a solitary folding chair, hangs a painted cross, Jesus' face twisted up serenely despite the blood dripping down his cheeks.

On the other wall, she notices a collection of drawings in cheap frames, hung crookedly above the spot where the couch probably once sat. "Look." She points. "Are those some of Mom's drawings?"

Her father cups his hands to the glass. "I guess so."

She pushes at the window to see if it will open,

but it's locked tight. "It doesn't look like anyone is actually living here." She is whispering, though she's not sure why.

Jonathan shakes his head. "Her parents would be in their mid- to late eighties at this point. It's possible they're dead."

Olive thinks about this. "Maybe that's why she came here," she realizes. "For their funeral. She thought it would be too depressing for us, or that we would feel obligated to come with her, so she didn't say anything about it."

Her father gives her a funny look and then lets out a quick, surprised laugh. "I hadn't considered that." He cups his hands and peers in through the window on the other side of the door. "Well, clearly, your mom isn't here."

He steps back and wipes his dusty hands on the legs of his pants, his face contorting with some emotion that Olive can't identify: Relief? Disappointment? "Did you think she'd be here?" she asks. She remembers how she felt that day on the butterfly beach with Natalie when her mom failed to appear. She knew better this time. But still—there's got to be a reason her mom directed them here.

Her father shakes his head. He looks around, examining the trees, the state of the porch. "I don't really know what I thought," he says, turning to Olive. "Run me through what you saw again? Anything more you can remember?"

"I didn't see anything specific. Just the farm, like this, except not so run-down. She was swinging on a tire swing." Olive points to the rope hanging from the tree. "She said, 'What's taking you so long?' And that was it."

The fascinated way her father is looking at her—as if she's a delicate creature that requires careful handling—makes her uncomfortable. She feels like some kind of a freak show, and she begins to suspect that he's humoring her. "Dad?" she says. "Why did you change your mind? Why do you believe me now about Mom being alive?"

Her father waits a beat too long. "I believe you because I love you, Bean," he says.

"Gosh, thanks, but that's not a very convincing reason," she says. Then she hears the high-pitched squeal of slowing brakes. Olive and Jonathan turn to see a pickup truck idling at the foot of the driveway. The woman from the horse farm down the road sits in the front seat, her arm hanging out of the rolled-down window.

"Are you looking for Mrs. Thrace?" she calls. "Because she's not here anymore."

Jonathan and Olive step down off the porch, the boards of the steps creaking ominously under their combined weight. "She's alive?" Jonathan asks.

The woman shrugs. "Far as I know. She moved out after her husband died."

"When did he die?"

"Back in February of this year. He had a heart attack."

Olive watches her father take this in, doing the math, his Adam's apple working up and down. She figures it out quickly—February means that her mother didn't secretly come here for a funeral in the year before she disappeared. Maybe she *was* just visiting her parents, then? But why?

The truck belches a plume of black exhaust. "You relatives or friends or something?" the woman asks.

Jonathan puts his arm around Olive and gently grips her upper arms, framing her. "I'm Jonathan. This is Olive. She's their granddaughter. I'm her dad, I was married to the Thraces' daughter."

The woman cuts the engine. She puts a hand up as a visor to shade her eyes and examines them closely. Her short hair is matted from the riding helmet and ringed with drying sweat. "How about that. I didn't know they even had a kid."

Olive speaks up. "Her name was Billie. Sybilla. You never met her? She never came by?"

The woman shakes her head. "I wouldn't know. I wasn't very tight with the Thraces. They kept to themselves." Her pale eyes dart to the farmhouse and back. "I heard there was some scandal a long time ago, back when he was still a preacher. People around here leaved them be, no one wanted to have much to do with them."

Jonathan nods. "So what happened to Rose?"

"Well, she came down with dementia a few years back. Sometimes I'd find her in my barn, wandering around confused, convinced it was her living room. Things were pretty bad here, I think; your grandfather didn't seem to be handling it very well." She coughs wetly and then turns and spits out the window. "And then your grandfather finally had his heart attack in February." She squints at them. "I found him, you know. Out in the road by the mailbox. So I felt some responsibility. Did what I could, contacted some agencies on Rose's behalf, but she couldn't stay here alone, of course. There weren't any relatives who could take her in. Except you, I guess. But I didn't know about you."

"Where is she now?" Jonathan asks.

"A government-run nursing home in Oildale. Up on Chester, across from the BK." She hesitates. "You've never met her? Rose?"

They shake their heads in unison.

The woman starts her car. "Well, let me warn you: She's not much of a conversationalist these days."

When Olive was young, Billie set out a tiny table and chairs underneath a giant fern by the back fence, gave her a spade and a magnifying glass, and declared this Olive's "private exploration zone." Her mother kept their garden wild and overgrown, and its dark soil was a source of endless fascination, so rich with life and decay. Olive would sit there in the dappled shade, absorbed in the treasures that she'd unearth: a waterlogged earthworm; a rotting camellia; the bones of a sparrow she'd buried the summer before; the remains of a dehydrated beetle.

Olive's grandmother, collapsed in the wheelchair, reminds Olive of the things she used to examine in her garden laboratory: There is more death in her than life, as if she's a translucent husk outlining the space where a human once existed.

Rose Thrace sits in a corner of the community room at the nursing home in Oildale. Someone has wheeled her over to the window to take in the view, but she has obstinately turned her head away, so that instead of looking at the expanse of the parking lot and the Burger King across the street, she is staring blankly at a paper Halloween skeleton pinned to the community room wall. Her features are buried underneath an avalanche of wrinkles; only her tiny dark eyes peer out dimly from within the withered flesh.

She fixes these eyes on Olive and flicks them across her granddaughter's features, taking in the gold hoops in Olive's ears, the green clip that holds back her hair. She seems more interested in the individual parts than their sum.

The air smells like disinfectant and urine. Olive glances around, saddened by the institutional nature of this place; couldn't someone have *tried* to make it more cheerful for these poor people at the end of their lives? The couches are covered in a shiny stain-obscuring plaid fabric; the floor is carpeted in faded blue that doesn't conceal the spill marks scattered across it. The room is quiet except for a talk show blaring on the TV, which only a handful of the residents seem to be watching. Many of the rest sit motionless in wheelchairs like hibernating bears, chins drooping to their chests. A few of the more alert women, playing bridge on a battered folding table, have stopped their game to watch the visitors cross the room. They smile at Olive with hungry eyes, and she smiles guiltily back at them, feeling like she should try to compensate for all the visitors who have failed to walk through the doors today.

Beside Olive, on one of the chairs that the nurse dragged over for them, Jonathan clears his throat.

"Mrs. Thrace," he says slowly, his words wincingly loud in this silent room, "I'm Jonathan, Billie's husband. This is your granddaughter, Olive."

Rose's eyes slide briefly over toward Jonathan before settling back on the paper skeleton.

"Hi, Grandma," Olive says softly, self-conscious in the face of her grandmother's disinterest. But she's senile and probably can't understand. Olive thinks of Grandma Annie, her dad's mom back in Wisconsin, who is in her seventies and needs a walker because of her arthritis but still calls weekly and recently attempted a Facebook profile so that she could "keep up with my grandbaby." Olive has often wondered about *this* grandmother, the woman her mom loathed so much that she barely ever mentioned her. Imagining Rose, Olive used to envision someone tall and intimidating, a granite face in a Sunday suit with a hat pinned to her head like the nasty aunts in a Roald Dahl book. But the woman who sits before her is concave and balding, with stains down the front of her robe, a poster child for elder negligence rather than the formidable monster Billie insinuated. She bears no resemblance at all to Olive's beautiful mother.

"I'm really glad to meet you," Olive says, carefully enunciating each syllable.

Rose reaches one hand up and clutches at the neck of her robe. Still she says nothing.

"This is Billie's daughter, Mrs. Thrace," Jonathan repeats even more slowly.

"No it's not." Rose's voice is tinny and small.

Olive looks at her father just to check: Do they have the wrong person, or is this the disease talking?

But then Rose's face abruptly snaps into focus. She turns her head across the room to watch the nurse who wheeled her in and drops her voice to a whisper. "That nurse over there, she stole my cross. Solid gold. She took it from me when I was sleeping, from right around my neck. You see, she's a *spic*." Olive flinches at the racial slur, but Rose smiles sweetly and continues, dropping her voice. "I think she's under Satan's power. But I have the light of the Lord within me, so I can help her."

Flummoxed, Olive looks at her father with raised eyebrows. *How am I supposed to respond to that?*

"I'm sorry your necklace is missing, Mrs. Thrace." Jonathan leans in close to the old lady, placing a gentle hand on her knee. "We'll find it later. But, Mrs. Thrace—Rose—did you hear me? This is your granddaughter, Olive."

Rose looks down at the hand on her knee. She tries to move her leg out from underneath. "That's *not* my granddaughter," she says weakly as Jonathan pulls his hand back. She calls out to the nurse in a cracking voice, "God sees everything!"

The nurse makes a huffing sound but keeps her back turned. Jonathan and Olive exchange glances, and Jonathan shrugs, his eyes telegraphing a lack of concern that Olive can't quite match. Is no one else bothered by what the old lady is saying? Is this *normal*?

"Rose, did your daughter come to visit you?" Olive watches her father's eyes scan Rose's face, waiting for a reaction. Her grandmother's torso rises and falls from the exertion of shouting at the nurse, but she says nothing.

Olive can see the struggle in her father's face: the impulse to be kind, battling his impatience with Rose's bigoted senility. "Look, I'm sorry to have to tell you this, but Billie"—he hesitates, thinking—"I mean, *Sybilla*—she's dead."

Rose swings her face back at them, finally looking directly at Olive. For a moment she appears frightened and lost, as if she might cry. "Sybilla," she says, her tongue tangling up in the name. Her watery eyes fix on Olive's, and her hand darts forward to grasp Olive's forearm. "You came back." She lowers her voice to a whisper: "I don't want God to punish you."

Olive is afraid to pull her arm away. "Don't worry—" she begins.

But Rose interrupts her. "You have to ask God's forgiveness!" She tries to stand up, and the force of her effort causes the wheelchair to jerk back and forth in impotent semicircles. "We'll pray! I can save you! It's not too late!"

The nurse is now making her way across the room as Olive, standing, begins to back away. Her father, also upright, presses Olive protectively behind him with the flat of his hand, as if Rose is capable of launching herself from her seat and forcing Olive to her knees. "That's really not necessary, Rose," he says, the gentle quality gone from his voice.

The nurse, her comforting bulk smelling like lemon soap, passes between them. She grabs the handles of Rose's chair, pushing her back toward the window. "Now, Rosie," she chides, "these nice people came to visit you. I don't think you want to be saying things like that to them, do you? I'm sure God doesn't think they need saving right now."

Rose looks up at the nurse helplessly. "Give me back my cross," she mutters, but the spark of life inside her has dimmed again. She drops her head to the right so that, once more, she's looking at the paper skeleton. It leers back at her, doffing its top hat in a mockery of respect.

The nurse escorts them to the facility entrance. Olive notices that her scrubs are decorated in goggle-eyed cartoon frogs, as if she is working in a pediatric unit, which makes Olive feel marginally better. The name tag over her heart reads MARGARETA.

"Sorry about that," Margareta offers. "She raves like that a lot. Religious mania. It's pretty common with dementia, you know, a fixation on God and punishment." She wrinkles her nose. "'Course, all the Jesus stuff just drives the other residents away. And visitors, too, I suppose. Rose doesn't really get any."

"No one comes to visit her?" Olive finds this tremendously sad—does her grandmother really have *no one*? How awful to end your life like this, unloved and alone, even your happiest memories stripped away from you by a failing brain. A swell of pity makes her look back at Rose, who has fixed her eyes on the television set, where a transgender actress is giving makeup tips.

The nurse frowns. "Well. There's one woman who's come round—a relative, I have to assume. But she's only visited once, a couple months back. And she didn't stay long, either. Went to see Rose in her room and bolted a few minutes later."

Olive watches her father draw his cellphone out of his pocket and turn it so the nurse can see. It's a photograph of Billie and Olive on his home screen, taken on vacation a few years back, smiling by a swimming pool. "This woman, by chance?" he asks, jabbing his finger at Billie's face.

The nurse examines the photo. "Gosh. It's been a while, obviously, but— Yes. Sure looks like her."

Olive looks at her father; he looks back at her with his eyebrows knitted together, as if doing some complicated computation. Olive's own mind feels liquid, all the conflicting details too slippery to grasp. It's what she wanted to hear, isn't it? That her mom might have been spotted alive? And yet the meaning of this—that Billie might have come to visit the mother she supposedly hated, but not her daughter and husband—makes Olive ill. She looks at a plastic jack-o'-lantern sitting on a side table, its mouth painted in a shocked O of surprise, and wishes they hadn't come here.

"Do you have a record of the people who come to visit?" her father is asking.

"Sure, but we're not allowed to show you," the nurse replies. She uses her thumb to push the tiny hairs around her hairline back into place. "This place has bureaucracy like you wouldn't believe. And I thought the *hospital* where I worked was bad. Government-run is the pits."

Jonathan writes his email address on a piece of paper and thrusts it into the nurse's hand. "Look. I don't want to get you in trouble. But we'd really like to know the name of Rose's other visitor. And the date she visited, if that's possible. We're trying to locate"—he glances at Olive—"a missing person, and this would be a huge help."

The nurse holds the paper with the tips of her fingers. "Well, I don't have access to front-office files. I'm a floor attendant." She looks back up at them. "I suppose I could ask around," she says.

Jonathan grips Olive's shoulder as they leave the nursing home. "Don't get too excited," he says softly. "There's a reason they say that eyewitness identification is unreliable: People are suggestible. Memory is a reconstruction, not a record; that's one of the first things you learn in journalism school. So unless we get a name, that woman could have been anyone. We don't know it was your mother."

Olive nods, not sure how to feel about this. On the way to the car, she glances back at the nursing home. The glare of the sun off the asphalt parking lot has faded the front of the monolithic two-story stucco building to an indeterminate greige. The windows are coated with reflective film that makes it impossible to see what's going on inside. Olive wonders if this is by design, so that passersby won't be forced to make inconvenient eye contact with the dying.

But one pane on the left side of the building has lost its film. Through the triangle of exposed glass, Olive can see her grandmother, in her perch by the window. She could swear that Rose is looking right at her and crying.

WHERE THE MOUNTAIN MEETS THE SKY

My Life with Billie Flanagan

BY JONATHAN FLANAGAN

So maybe that psychologist wasn't right about love being something that can be manufactured between any two people. And maybe love isn't magical, either. Maybe love comes down to your issues aligning with someone else's, tongue into groove. Your neuroses, all that baggage from your past, somehow the perfect match to theirs: You need someone to take care of, and they need to be taken care of. You long for someone creative, they need someone stable. And so forth.

If that's the case, then the reason why I fell in love with Billie probably starts with Jenny. My sister.

Jenny was the one who suggested we sneak into the neighbors' pool. It was an oppressive summer day, heavy with Midwestern humidity, and our own shrubby backyard provided no relief from the sun. Our mother had forbidden us to leave the house while she was off doing the shopping—Jenny was ten, I was eight, and we were only just allowed to stay at home alone. After a half hour of playing listlessly with our Atari with a fan positioned at our feet, my sister suddenly lifted her head.

"Let's go swimming," she said.

"Now? Where?" I asked.

"The Wilsons'." She was already standing at the window on her tiptoes, peering out over the hedge into the yard of our neighbors, whose crystalline blue pool had remained woefully unused all summer. "They're both at work, they'll never know."

My sister had always been the scrappy one, her knees scabby from her skateboard and her report card filled with admonishments from her teachers; whereas I was the good kid, bookish, rule-bound, depressingly dutiful. "I'm glad you know better than that," my mother would whisper to me when my sister came home with yet another bloody nose from a fight at school; but sitting in my room, with only books and my *Star Wars* action figures for company, I wasn't sure that this was really true. Jenny always seemed to be deeply immersed in life, whereas I was skating along the edge, dipping my toe in.

So that day, I followed her into the Wilsons' yard, clambering over the ornamental hedge, which scraped our shins raw. We left our shorts on the lounge chairs and danced across the hot concrete, jumping into the water in our underwear and T-shirts. The water so cold that it felt like a slap, leaving us breathless and laughing; the sun beating down mercilessly on our faces when we burst up through the surface, spraying diamond droplets in every direction. It was one of those moments when you know what it really means to be alive, to have every cell in your body attuned to the astonishing fact of your existence.

"This is amazing," I called to my sister.

"Hell yeah," Jenny replied.

I'll always remember my sister the way she looked as she climbed out of the pool: her cropped blond hair a shiny cap against her head, the soaked T-shirt clinging to the boyish planes of her chest, her face shining with happiness. She walked back toward the hedge, crouched down like a sprinter. "Double backflip," she announced, and then broke into a run, her knees flying, feet akimbo. She was on the steaming concrete and then her toes were gripping the tile edge of the pool and then she was impossibly high in the air and then she was deep under the water and she wasn't coming up. Or, rather, she *was* coming up, but in a very strange way: upside down, her limbs floppy, her short hair drifting aimlessly around her head.

Dead man's float, I told myself, waiting for her to stop joking around, and yet something looked wrong. "Stop it," I said out loud from where I sat frozen on the steps of the pool. "Stop it, Jenny, stop it." I kept saying this to myself, over and over, as if when I'd said it enough times Jenny would finally roll over and laugh at me, *Such a scaredy-cat, such a sucker, get your nose out of a book and get a life.*

Even once I knew for sure that something was terribly, terribly wrong, I still sat there, paralyzed. Thinking, *I have to call 911 no I have to swim in and rescue her I'll do the Heimlich no CPR which one is it I don't know how anyway I have to call Dad at the office he'll know what to do no he'll know we broke into the neighbors' and we'll get in trouble no that doesn't matter.* It was probably only a matter of seconds, and yet it felt an eternity had passed before I thrashed my way into the water, spluttering through my tears, and tugged my sister's horrifyingly leaden body to the steps, propping her there half out of the water. I whacked at her back with the flat of my hand, tried to breathe into her lungs; but her empty eyes told me that it was already too late.

And yet I kept shouting *Stop it Jenny stop it* as I scrambled back over the hedge to call 911, this time getting a nasty gash on my thigh that would go unnoticed in the days to come and would ultimately fester before it was treated, leaving a faint scar that I can't bear to look at even as an adult.

No one blamed me; no one except myself. "Your sister was older, she was the one in charge," my father said as he sat on the edge of my bed, his red eyes the only clue to his own swallowed grief. "Even if you had known CPR, it wouldn't have helped. She broke her neck, the doctors said it was instantaneous." But I knew he was wrong; I knew that those crucial seconds when I sat there, useless, had to mean *something*. And even earlier than that: I was supposed to be the smart one, the responsible one, I should have cut Jenny off when she came up with the idea in the first place. *I knew better than that.*

In the years that followed, I tried to make up for the death of my sister by being even better behaved, as if doubling my achievements might somehow mask the loss of an entire child. I learned how to be charming and funny, so I could make my parents smile again. I became editor of my high school newspaper, graduated at the top of my class, went to Stanford, got a job in Silicon Valley. Dated a string of nice girls with admirable résumés. *He must be a real consolation to them,* I could hear the neighbors whisper, but I secretly knew that I was no consolation at all.

So was it any surprise when, at age twenty-six, I met a woman who reminded me of my dead older sister, all grown up—living on the sharp edge of convention, self-assured down to the bone—that I would thrill to her? That I would leap to make up for all my past failings? To protect her, sacrifice myself to her, think that by doing so I was somehow being *noble*?

Maybe it was inevitable that I would fall for Billie. Maybe it was inevitable that I would willfully ignore all her faults. Only someone fearful of his own ordinariness would buy, so unquestioningly, someone else's extraordinariness.

Maybe this is why they say love is blind: Who you want people to be makes you blind to who they really are.

10

WHEN HE STARTED at *Decode,* just out of Stanford, Jonathan hung his favorite Graham Greene quote over his desk: *A story has no beginning or end: arbitrarily one chooses that moment of experience from which to look back or from which to look ahead.* The job of a writer, he'd learned over time, was not to try to tell a story in its entirety, but to tell an inevitably abbreviated version in the most interesting way one could. Giving shape and direction to something otherwise formless and elastic. Cause and effect. Action and reaction. Lede and kicker.

The story line of his life with Billie: Where did it truly begin? Was it at the moment when she climbed aboard the J Church and made a beeline for the seat next to him; the moment she turned and made an inaudible comment about the weather? Or did their story together actually start years earlier, when his

sister drowned and the trajectory of his life permanently shifted? Or earlier even than *that*, perhaps as
early as the moment he was born, when the twin
forces of nature and nurture started forming a path
before him that would eventually lead him straight
to his future wife?

Or would a more accurate version of their life
story now begin at the very end? Or what, at the
time, he *thought* was the end of the Billie-and-
Jonathan narrative: Billie's memorial service, four
hundred friends and relatives jammed into the auditorium of a yoga center rented out for the day, Olive's hand clenched tightly in his own, his body
shaky and sweating as if he were going through
some kind of opiate withdrawal. He believed until
recently that this was going to be the closing scene
of *Where the Mountain Meets the Sky,* a hell of a
kicker; but now he wonders, thanks to the facts that
have come to light, if it should be his lede.

How many times can he write and rewrite the
story of his life with Billie before he'll know what
was really true?

Jonathan sits at the desk in his home office, blinds
closed against the light of a fairly pleasant Monday
morning. Three fingers of bourbon in a glass next to
him; a buzz on from the four fingers he's already
consumed. Peering at his laptop, the empty cursor
blinking on a blank blog template: his IP address
trap awaiting its latest entry.

Setting up the IP address trap has turned out to
be Internet 101 kind of stuff: The "trap" is simply a
blog enhanced with a free Web server log analysis
program called ipTracer, which captures the IP ad-

dress of every visitor to the site. As for the content of the blog—the "memories of Billie" that Calvin Lim suggested—that was even easier. He already has hundreds of pages written about his wife, and more coming every day; although the tenor of his latest pages has shifted dramatically, to something darker and far less adulatory.

He takes a fortifying slug of bourbon and begins to type a new section.

When Olive turned eight, Billie and I took her to Six Flags Marine World for her birthday, which turned out to be a mistake for many reasons (the resigned elephants in their concrete enclosures; the roller coasters that Olive was too small to ride; the hour-long lines for the dolphin show). Not long after Olive barfed up a funnel cake, she vanished entirely. Billie and I were distracted, burnt out, bickering, cleaning the vomit off our tennis shoes, and studying the map for the quickest routes to the exit, and when we looked up, our daughter was gone.

I panicked. There was water all around us, and I thought instantly of Jenny. I started running in circles, hollering Olive's name. Flailing about in the bushes, throwing aside trash cans. I accosted some kid in a Six Flags uniform, probably all of eighteen years old, and demanded that he DO SOMETHING NOW OUR DAUGHTER MAY BE DROWNING.

I was about to take off my tennis shoes and dive into the murky water of Seal Cove when I heard Billie's voice over a loudspeaker. I turned, and there Billie was, standing on the roof of the root beer float stand, holding a megaphone that she'd commandeered from a passing tram driver. God knows how she'd gotten up there.

"Olive," she said, her voice so loud and urgent that the flamingos in their lagoon rose as one and flapped their wings. "Bean. Please come out. We aren't mad at you, OK? We love you. Show us where you're hiding."

All across the area, people came to a stop. Like me, they couldn't help but stare at my wife up there on the roof, her dark hair flying in wild glory, the setting sun behind her almost blinding. So calm, so magnetic, so sure of herself. A moment later, Olive came creeping out from behind the barricades by Monsoon Falls, tears clinging to the sugar smears on her face. She looked at her mother making her way down from the concession stand, and then ran to me and threw herself into my arms.

I pressed Olive to my chest as people clapped. Billie, now back on the ground, just stood there watching us. A strange look crossed over her face, something hard and furious—as if Olive had betrayed her by running to me first instead of waiting obediently at the bottom of the concession stand for her mom to climb down—and then it passed. She gave a little ironic bow to the crowd and then sauntered over, nice and calm, as if she'd never been worried at all; as if the whole thing was a lark, already a story we would tell in the years to come.

When she got to us, she rubbed Olive's head, tangling her hair. "It's OK, Bean. You're going to be just fine," she said to Olive, then looked around her, assessing the scene. "Let's get the hell out of here."

For a moment, I almost hated my wife in all her radiant bravado. Did she really fear so little, or was she just covering it better than I did? Was it so terrible to her to show weakness? Was it possible that the feelings she felt were not ones that I understood at all?

I don't remember much about what we did next—

whether we fought or not. Whether I felt blessed that our daughter was OK or ashamed at both of our failings as parents. But to this day I still remember the moment when I looked at Billie, up there in the sky, this intimate stranger, and thought, *Who the hell are you? How did this happen? How did we end up choosing each other? How will we ever really know each other?*

Jonathan studies the words that he has just written. He never told Billie any of this. How could he? These were the thoughts that he never even admitted to himself; the inconvenient doubts that flickered through his mind before he pushed them away. He wonders now if marriage is about balancing on that fragile intersection between the said and the unsaid, sharing just enough to satisfy the need for intimacy without crossing over into dangerous territory. Shoving everything else under the rug, hoping it doesn't accrue high enough to trip you up.

He scrolls back up to the top of the standardized blog form and clicks Post. His latest entry goes online to join the forty-six he uploaded over the weekend. The vast majority of the memoir is now up there for Billie's perusal, assuming she bothers to find it.

Hi, Billie. I think you're out there somewhere. Show me where you are. Show me why you disappeared. Explain to me how on earth you could do this to us. Show me who you really are.

Now there is nothing to do but wait. How long? A day? A week? A month? A year? How long before Billie, wherever she is, succumbs to curiosity and does a vanity search, unintentionally setting out her trail of bread crumbs?

He takes another slug of whiskey and then downloads the ipTracer app. He installs it on his cellphone and then checks his stats: *Your page has been visited by 0 unique IP addresses.*

The phone rings as he's holding it—CLAREMONT—and he jumps. He clicks Accept before he can think better of it. Vice Principal Gillespie's voice is on the other end. "Jonathan?"

"Hi," he says, steeling himself.

"Yes. I'm following up on my message from last week, which you haven't returned." Her voice drips with displeasure, as if he's been a naughty schoolboy indeed. "Are you aware that Olive cut class last Friday afternoon? You realize that we have a no-tolerance policy for this at Claremont Prep?"

"Really?" He remembers the call that he failed to answer last Friday when he was at the private investigator's office. He momentarily perks up at the unlikely image of his rule-abiding daughter sneaking off in the middle of the day (to what? go to the movies with Natalie? go shopping on Telegraph Avenue?) before realizing that this is an inappropriate response. He musters up a more parentally disapproving tone of voice: "I will talk to her about that."

"Good. Be sure she's aware that future infractions will mean suspension and, if they continue, expulsion," Gillespie says. "And while I'm on the phone with you—can I expect the tuition check this week?"

Shit. He pulls his laptop close and opens his latest bank statement: $3,123. That's barely enough to cover the month's mortgage, and there are property taxes and grocery bills and car payments to think about. He'll have to pull from his 401(k) again, just for basic expenses. "Soon, I promise," he says.

Gillespie makes a grim noise, neither approval nor disapproval. "We can't do this much longer, you know," she says.

"Believe me, I enjoy this even less than you do."

Gillespie laughs, a small bark of surprise. "OK. And talk to Olive about her absence, please."

"I will."

He hangs up the phone and immediately dials a New York number. His agent answers the phone with booming cheer: "Jonathan! How's the writing going?"

"Oh, great," he says. "Look, Jeff, I'm wondering—I know I'm not supposed to get my next advance payment until I turn in the book, but do you think the publisher might possibly pay out some of it to me now? I'm really strapped for cash."

Jeff laughs. "Sure," he says. "It's possible. But only if we can show them the progress you've been making. You getting close? Got anything I can see?"

Jonathan glances at the last chapter, open on his desktop: his wife standing at the top of the concession stand as a younger Jonathan questions the very nature of their marriage. Not exactly a real-life *Love Story*. "Not yet," he says. "Still tinkering with tone."

"It's gonna be great," Jeff says. "Now get off the phone and get back to writing. That's the fastest way to get us *all* paid."

Jonathan laughs drily, thinking, *Jerk,* and hangs up. He takes another slug of his bourbon, mulling his options. Then, with increasingly clumsy fingers, he dials Marcus.

Marcus sounds like he's speaking from the far end of a tunnel. Jonathan can hear traffic noises in the background, the rush of wind through an open window. "Jonathan, can't really talk. I'm late to an investor meeting in Palo Alto."

"Two questions?" he begs. "I'll be quick."

"Shoot," his friend says.

"First: You crack Billie's password yet?"

A moment of silence. "Shit. Forgot all about that. I'll get to it soon, sorry. It's been nuts."

"I get it, I get it. No pressure." He clears his throat. "Second: Can I borrow a little money from you?"

Marcus coughs. "How much are we talking?"

Thirty thousand dollars, Jonathan thinks, but he doesn't have the guts to say it. How did he get to this place in his life? Forty-three years old and having to borrow rent money, worrying about the price of toothpaste. (*What's the worst that's going to happen?* Billie asked him last year. *This,* he thinks now, humiliated.)

"Ten grand," he says, equivocating. Maybe Claremont will settle for a partial payment.

"Whoa, Jonathan—I had no idea you were struggling."

"It's just to cover expenses for a little, until I get my next book payment or the life insurance settlement. Whichever comes first." As he says this, it hits him: *If I prove that Billie isn't dead after all, then there is no life insurance. And, for that matter, no book.* Christ.

"OK, I can swing that," Marcus says.

"I'll pay you back as soon as I can," Jonathan says, feeling himself choke up. The bourbon is making him feel emotionally diffuse; it's all too much to take in.

"I know you're good for it."

After they hang up, Jonathan finishes off his drink and stares forlornly at his computer, knowing that the fastest way to dig himself out of this hole is to finish the goddamn book. But how can he do that when his head is swimming with apocalyptic visions of his wife with her faceless lover in various exotic locales? A man's arm wrapped around her waist on a sunny beach; pornographic positions in a darkened motel room; mai tais at breakfast. Jaunting around California, visiting her incoherent mother in between spa visits. Living the high life on stolen money while he sits here and tries to keep everything together, his whole world slowly slipping underwater.

Oh, the irony: He quit his job in order to somehow please his dead wife, only to end up broke and desperate and unsure whether his wife is dead at all.

How could you do this to me, Billie? He lets the fury in, feels it rush through him like a drug coming on, all the anger he has spent his life pushing away. Anger at his wife, at all the ways she'd failed him during their marriage, at the way she's hurting him even now. There's other anger in there, too, anger at the way his life choices have betrayed him; and, going back even further, buried anger at Jenny, for dragging him to the swimming pool that day and making him complicit in her death. Anger has always made him anxious, but in this moment, it's not frightening anymore: It's freeing.

He hears footsteps on the front porch and then a soft knock on the door. UPS, he assumes; but then there's the sound of a key in the front latch, and he jumps up from his chair.

He gets to the entry just as Harmony lets herself in with her new house key. She stands in the doorway, holding a coffee cup and a bag of pastries, a startled expression on her face. "Hi! I was at Market Hall and thought I'd stop by with some sustenance for you." She thrusts the cup at him. "Is it terrible of me to just let myself in like this? You can kick me out if you're busy writing."

He takes the coffee, reeling backward so she can come in. He realizes that it's not even noon and he's already fairly drunk. "I'm not really writing," he says.

She follows him into the house. She's wearing some kind of snug cottony dress that drapes across her hips and chest. If you look close—even if you don't look *that* close—you can see the line of her underwear. It's most definitely a thong. Her nostrils flare as she smells the bourbon wafting off him. "Missing Billie a lot today?" she asks. She peers past him into the study, where the laptop glows in the dark like a beacon.

"What makes you say that?" The words tear violently out of him.

She tilts her head, a confused expression on her face. "Oh. You were saying the other day, about hitting the bottle . . . maybe you want to talk?"

"I'm tired of talking about Billie," he says thickly,

interrupting her. "Shouldn't we talk about something else?"

"Like what?" She smiles faintly.

"Like . . ." He can't think of what he wants to talk about at all. And he realizes that talking is exactly what he *doesn't* want to do. He doesn't want to think at all anymore; he doesn't want to assess the risk factors, or worry about what anyone else needs from him, or analyze the overall trajectory of his life. He just wants to do what he wants to do.

And what he wants to do right now, very badly, is to kiss Harmony.

So he does.

Her mouth is hot and yielding. It's strange how familiar it feels, as if his fascia has somehow retained the memory of her flesh despite the intervening year. Kissing her is like sinking into a warm bath; his whole body sighs with relief.

Harmony puts one hand on the back of his neck and grips it tightly; her other hand goes to the buckle of his jeans. He kicks the front door closed with his foot and stumbles a little, then pulls her in closer, pressing his body to hers so hard that it feels like he's about to push himself straight through to the other side. His hand slides up until it encounters her breast and then stays there, riveted by its fullness. It's all so decadent and unexpected that he thinks he should stop, give himself a minute to process, except that what he's really doing is tearing the dress off her shoulders as he pushes her toward the staircase. He feels like he's losing himself, like he's let go of the string of a balloon and is watching some old version of himself disappear off into the atmosphere.

He pulls back once to take a breath and looks at her face, flushed and heavy-lidded: "This is OK with you?" he asks her, suddenly concerned.

"Don't be ridiculous," she says, and she grabs his hand and drags him up the stairs to the bedroom.

He swims back to himself an indeterminate amount of time later and finds that he's tangled in sodden, oceanic sheets. His heart still rattling in his chest, a naked woman beside him who is not his wife. His body smug with pleasure. What just happened? Was that infidelity? A betrayal of his wife's memory? A revenge fuck? Or simply a well-deserved rediscovery of his sexuality after an appropriately mournful interval? He feels quite sober now, but no less disoriented.

He rolls over and looks at Harmony, prostrate and panting, on the side of the bed where his wife used to sleep. She reaches out and presses a finger between his eyebrows. "Stop looking so worried," she says. "You just got laid."

"You make us sound like rutting teenagers," he says, sliding an arm across her naked waist.

"I don't know about you, but I didn't have sex like *that* in high school." She smiles contentedly, long blond strands of hair stuck in her bruised mouth. The skin of her belly is a revelation, creamy and endless. He can't stop running his hand across it.

"This was somewhat unexpected—" he starts to explain.

She cuts him off, tugging his arm tighter across

her body. "If you're feeling guilty, don't. Billie's been dead a year. You're not doing anything wrong."

"I know," he says.

He can feel her eyes, searching his face. "I need to tell you something," she says.

He smiles. "What?"

"You asked the other day if Billie was having an affair." Jonathan's smile freezes. *Oh God.* "Well, she slept with Sean. That's why he and I broke up."

He jerks upright. "What?"

"Didn't you notice that Billie and I didn't talk for, like, six months, that year before she died? That's why. She slept with Sean. I found her bra in our bed." She sits up so that she's at his eye level, and he can see that her face has flushed a valentine red. "When I confronted her, she said Sean had been hitting on her for years, and eventually he caught her in a weak moment on a day that you guys had gotten in a big fight; she was angry at you for some reason and just made an impulsive decision." She puts a consoling hand on his chest. "She begged me not to tell you. And then told me I was better off getting rid of Sean before I wasted any more of my life with him because he wasn't good for me." She gives a light little laugh, but he senses something darker festering underneath. "I was so angry for so long, until I went off and meditated on compassion in Sedona. The night I came over here last year, the night you and I kissed, I was going to tell her that I forgave her, but then—" She runs her hand meaningfully across Jonathan's chest. "You know what? I think she did me a favor. If I was still with Sean, I wouldn't be here with you right now, would I?"

The sensation of her hand on his skin is suddenly unbearable. He removes her hand from his body and holds it tightly in his own. *A big fight?* he thinks dumbly. *What did I do to her?* And then—*Sean. Of course. That motherfucker.* "Why didn't you tell me this sooner?" he manages.

She tugs on her upper lip with her free hand. "I almost told you that night we kissed, but, well. And then she died, and after that I didn't think there was any point in dredging it up. It would just hurt you. I can't bear to hurt you."

His stomach gurgles unhappily, sour with alcohol. *Sean.* He tries to put Sean's arrogant face on the head of the stranger he's been imagining with Billie. "So that's where she was, those missing weekends I was telling you about. She was with *him.*"

"Oh! No." She shakes her head. "I don't think so. She said it only happened once. And once Sean and I broke up, he found some new girlfriend within the month. I ran into him with her a few weeks ago, down on Telegraph. She's pregnant. He always told *me* he didn't want kids."

His head is fogged and throbbing, his mouth dry. If Sean wasn't with Billie those weekends, was it possible that there was yet *another* man? Christ, at this point, anything seems possible. He leans over to retrieve the glass of water by the side of the bed, at which point he notices the clock. "It's almost three. I have to go pick up Olive from school."

Harmony frowns. "I thought she was driving herself these days."

"Subaru needed an oil change. Shit. I'm going to be late." He extricates himself and climbs out of bed. His shirt is inside out on the floor, and his underwear is underneath an armchair overflowing with dirty laundry. He can't locate his sweater, and then he remembers that it is on the staircase, along with Harmony's bra and dress. He grabs a dirty sweatshirt from the pile on the chair and pulls it on.

Harmony draws the sheet up over her chest, watching him. "Should I be here when you get back?"

He freezes. "Not today, no. Olive will be with me."

She nods glumly. "I shouldn't have told you about Sean and Billie. I should have just kept my mouth shut. I *knew* it was a bad idea."

"Not at all," he lies. "I'm glad you told me."

She tucks her knees up under her chin like a schoolgirl. "Just tell me this, please, and be honest. Was this a onetime thing or something we'll do again?"

He sits down on the edge of the bed and puts a hand to her cheek. "I'm not a jerk, I promise," he says. The sideways light through the bedroom window illuminates her face, warming her skin under his hand. Her eyes are still heavy-lidded with sex. She looks like a depraved angel. "I'll see you soon," he says, and kisses her one last time before racing down to his car.

He speeds through Berkeley in a daze, taking wrong turns. He feels disassembled, as if his entire life is tearing apart at the seams. The loss of control makes him giddy, sick to his stomach with dread but also a strange kind of exhilaration. He wonders darkly if this was what Billie felt when she was sleeping with Sean, those weekends when she wasn't actually hiking Shasta and Yosemite, when she was leading her secret double existence: The reckless freedom in knowing that the direction of your life has veered off course and might be headed straight off a cliff.

She screwed Sean. Right under my nose. And I never even noticed. He thinks bitterly of the condom in her purse. How long had his wife kept it there in anticipation? Were there others?

There is something in the pocket of his sweatshirt, a sharp edge poking through the fabric. He pulls it out and realizes it's the Lost Years Polaroid of Billie and her ex-boyfriend, Sidney. Two kids wrapped possessively around each other, staring defiantly out at the future. He glances at it and tosses it aside in the passenger seat.

. . . And then picks it up again, struck with a possibility he hadn't considered before. A different face for that faceless man in his apocalyptic visions: Sidney.

He came back, didn't he?

His mind reaches back to the day, three years ago, when an envelope arrived in the mail with a return address for a correctional facility up in Oregon. Jonathan fished the letter out of the pile of catalogs lying in a heap below the mail slot and carried it, curious, to where his wife stood in the kitchen prepping dinner. He popped it in her line of sight and watched as her mouth went tight.

"Do you think it's from Sidney?" he asked.

"Who else?" She carefully cleaned her fingers with a kitchen towel, plucked the envelope from his hand, and examined it. Then she reached over to the stove and turned on the gas burner, holding the edge of the envelope to the flame until it blackened and ignited. Turning, she walked back to the sink and let the letter burn until it was nearly scorching her fingers before dropping it into the stainless-steel basin. The envelope smoldered for a moment, the neatly inked capital letters of her name and address—MRS. JONATHAN FLANAGAN—flaring bright against the paper; and then it collapsed into ashes. Billie turned on the faucet, sending a sludgy black spiral down the kitchen drain.

He watched her, shocked. "Jesus. Not feeling very conciliatory?"

She turned back to face him, wiping her hands dry on her jeans. She leaned against the sink, gripping the edge of the basin behind her. "Whatever's in there, it's nothing that I need to read." There was something false about the calmness of her voice, as if she had to work very hard to stay in control.

"You aren't curious?" *He* was curious.

"I'm sure it's some attempt to make amends, one of those Alcoholics Anonymous twelve-step things." She shrugged. "Honestly, I really don't want to know. All that is so far in the past now, and I'd like to keep it there. So why open a door if I'm not planning on walking through it?" She turned back to her cutting board and resumed slicing bell peppers into neat finger-sized ribbons.

He lingered behind her for a few moments, strangely disturbed by what she'd done. The way she'd held the envelope to the flame suggested a violence of emotion that surprised him. It felt almost as if she'd burned the letter to shut Jonathan out of some critical part of her past. *That's silly,* he told himself at the time. *She didn't even read the letter. She didn't even know what it said.*

But now, as he stares at the Polaroid—a picture his wife had hidden from him their entire marriage—he wonders if she *did* know what the letter said. If it wasn't the first one she'd received. If, in fact, she'd written Sidney back.

The car behind him honks, rousing him. He accelerates as alarming questions start to fill his mind. How had Sidney even known where to send the letter? Why was it addressed to Mrs. Jonathan Flanagan, her married name? When *had* Sidney gotten out of jail? What if they'd rekindled some sort of romance since then? Is it possible that Sidney came to Billie's memorial not to mourn but to check it out and report back to *her*?

As he mulls this over, his phone begins to buzz. He glances at the display—it's an unfamiliar number. Punching Accept, he turns onto College Avenue just as a woman's voice comes over his car's speaker system: "Is this Jonathan Flanagan?"

"That's me," he says.

"The police gave me your number." The woman is speaking in a rush. "My name's Cheryl? I saw your classified ad in the *San Francisco Chronicle*. Asking for information about Sybilla Thrace? And I just called the number and the guy on the other end, the policeman, he wasn't very helpful. But he gave me your contact information."

Jonathan lets the car slow to a crawl. "You know

where she is?" he asks. The car behind him honks, and he turns blindly onto a side street.

"Sybilla? No!" she says. "I didn't mean to give that impression. It's been, what, thirty years since I last spoke to her. But she was my best friend, see? Back in high school." She laughs, a nervous *Haw! Haw!* "Anyway, I saw the ad and it was like—*wow!* You know? Memories. And I thought, well, heck, I always wondered what happened to her. So did she disappear again, is that what the ad's about?"

"Again?" His disappointment tempered by curiosity—*Is this the friend her dad molested?* he wonders—he continues in the general direction of Claremont Prep.

"Yeah. She disappeared on me, too, back then." The woman laughs again.

"She disappeared. On you. Oh—when she ran away in high school?" Something about the woman's laugh—*Haw! Haw!*—puts him on edge. He realizes he is driving down a dead-end street, so he does a U-turn and ends up stuck in traffic on Ashby Avenue. The back of the van in front of him is papered with bumper stickers. He fixes on one: YOUR IGNORANCE IS THEIR POWER.

The woman isn't laughing anymore. "I tried to find her; everyone did. Back then. She really left me in a bad place. I mean, I don't blame her! But yeah, it was . . . hard."

Another bumper sticker: YEP, WE'RE FUCKED. "So wait," Jonathan says slowly. "Can you tell me—"

"STOP THAT PLEASE, GUYS?" Cheryl's voice is suddenly overly loud in his ear. "HENRY, I CAN SEE WHAT YOU'RE DOING, DO NOT HIT YOUR

BROTHER WITH YOUR CLEATS. PLEASE, GUYS. DON'T MAKE ME BEG." There's a muffled conversation in the background, a shrill insistent yapping, and then she comes back on the phone. "Sorry, my kids just got home from school, chaos is breaking out, I gotta run. Maybe we could get together, though? And talk?"

"Yes, please," Jonathan says. "Where do you live?"

"Fremont."

Claremont Prep looms ahead, a thicket of cars stretching out into the street, the usual pickup gridlock. He can see a pack of moms clustering together in the parking lot, wielding commuter mugs, steeling themselves for the onslaught. Jonathan slows his Prius to a crawl, wanting to finish this conversation before Olive gets in the car. "Fremont. OK, that's not so far. I can come to you, maybe tomorrow evening—"

"No, no, it's nuts here in the evenings. You're in Berkeley, right? I love Berkeley. I'll come up Thursday afternoon, I don't work that day, and the kids stay at school late for soccer practice. Be nice to have an excuse to get away."

"Black Top Coffee, at one? They make a great cappuccino."

"Oh, I don't drink caffeine," Cheryl says. "But I love herbal tea."

He hangs up and pulls up to the school, too late to park, stuck at the end of a line of idling cars. The big shaggy mansion expels girls in clots, their heads bent together over iPhones, uniforms drooping from the day's exertions. Olive's far-too-handsome English teacher, Mr. Heron, hangs out at the top of the steps, collecting the bits of wreckage—dropped sweaters, forgotten notebooks—that drift along in the girls' wake. A pack of junior girls clusters around him, flipping hair, adjusting skirts, testing out their nascent sex appeal.

Finally, Olive appears in the doorway to the school. Her coat is unbuttoned despite the chill in the air, and she wears her hair in twin braids that make her look three years younger than she is. There's a wilting daisy tucked behind one ear.

Olive heads to the top of the stairs, avoiding the gaggle of girls flirting with her teacher, and then stops, as if distracted. Jonathan taps his horn, a soft beep to snag her attention. Every girl at the front of the school turns to look for the source of the sound—every girl, that is, except Olive, who just stands there, swaying slightly, her gaze fixed on something in the distance. *Oh, shit,* Jonathan thinks, recognizing the expression on her face.

His daughter takes a single step forward, misses the top stair entirely, and collapses.

11

"SEE THIS DARK MASS here? It's possible that you have some sort of contusion on your right infero-temporal cortex, some gliosis. It might be from your fall on Monday, but it could also signal a previous minor brain injury of some sort that's causing your visual anomalies." The neurologist taps at Olive's MRI scan with the end of his pen. *Tick tick tick.* "On the plus side, there's no sign of edema."

Olive and Jonathan stand in the dark in the neurology clinic's exam room, staring at the slices of Olive's brain hanging on the wall. Jonathan steps up close to peer at the nebulous dark cloud, his face illuminated by the glow from the light-box. He nods as if everything the doctor has said is acutely clear, although Olive, looking at the same scan, sees nothing obvious at all. Gazing at a cross section of her own head, all she sees is a blobby pattern of grays and blacks, like a bloated branch of coral.

It's weird to see the inside of your own body, not at all what she expected. You'd think a glimpse of your own gray matter would be mysterious and magical, but instead it feels like Olive is looking at a bowl of meaningless cottage cheese. Even the shape of her head looks unfamiliar, more round than oval, slightly misshapen rather than perfectly symmetrical. Lumpen. Distressingly organic. Is *this* what makes her who she is? How can an MRI machine possibly capture anything truly interesting about a unique human existence?

The technician warned her that the MRI would be unpleasant, but she still hadn't expected it to be quite so awful and claustrophobic, all that science fiction buzzing and banging and grinding just inches away from her face, which was immobilized in some sort of sadistic metal bracket. Trapped in the tube, her eyes winched closed, she tried to imagine the hydrogen protons in her body obediently turning in unison, spinning like tops in response to the giant magnets surrounding her. Mostly, though, she felt like a hot dog in a movie theater's warming tray.

She doesn't understand it: Why does she even have to be here? Yes, she collapsed in front of the whole school; an ambulance was summoned as Mr. Heron stood watch over her, keeping the pack of girls at bay. Of course they had to go see a doctor. But she thought she'd get her routine checkup and then leave; she didn't expect her dad to take all this so seriously, to make the follow-up appointment with the neurologist and then to tell him about her visions.

She thinks of what she saw right before she collapsed and feels her heart pick up its pace, thumping nervously in her chest.

"Olive?"

She realizes that her father and Dr. Fishbein are both looking at her expectantly. "What?"

Dr. Fishbein repeats his question: "Any recent accidents that might have caused this? Car collision, sports injury, particularly bad trip-and-fall? Remember anything like that?"

Her father studies her, his expression masked by the ghoulish shadows from the light-box. "She hurt her head at school a few weeks ago. Remember?"

"That?" She turns to the doctor. "It was no big deal. I walked into a wall."

"She had a pretty big goose egg." Her father points to the spot on Olive's forehead where the bump turned purple, then blue, then faded to a sickly yellow before disappearing entirely.

The doctor frowns. "You might have suffered a concussion."

"I didn't black out."

"Doesn't matter. Stuff can still get rattled around in there." The doctor raps on his own skull with a knuckle. "Sometimes the damage doesn't make itself apparent until a little later."

"I started seeing Mom *before* I bumped my head," she objects.

But her father and the doctor are back to studying the MRI. "So, there's nothing there that's not supposed to be there? No growths, say?" her father asks somewhat cryptically.

The doctor shakes his head. He taps the MRI with his pen. *Tick tick.* "You mean a tumor? No. Definitely not. The only irregularity I'm seeing is this mass here, which, like I said, *could* be scarring. There's no certainty, of course, but it seems like a possible cause of the visual anomalies your daughter has been experiencing. Maybe it's triggering a type of temporal lobe epilepsy."

"They're not *visual anomalies*," Olive interrupts, looking to her dad for help.

But he's squinting at the doctor: "Wait—she has epilepsy?"

"Temporal lobe epilepsy. It's possible. Temporal lobe seizures, they're very different from the tonic-clonic variety; you know, they're not—" Dr. Fishbein rolls his eyes in the back of his head and begins to jitter in a rather disarming impersonation of a grand mal seizure. Olive wants to hit him. "With TLE, it's more like visual, emotional seizures. People who have it experience auras, odd smells or tastes, strange physical sensations, déjà vu, even hallucinations. Sounds similar to what you've described. So that's my guess."

Olive touches the MRI scan with the edge of her finger, pressing her thumb against the tiny gray blob that Dr. Fishbein has singled out. Seizures? "But there's no certainty."

"Not unless we slice your brain open, no. Perhaps not even then."

She doesn't buy it. That very morning she awak- ened to the sight of her mother standing at the end of her bed, looking straight at her. "You're going to be just fine," she said, clear as day, and Olive felt so relieved that she started to cry. That wasn't a random hallucination, a misfiring of damaged neurons; it couldn't be. Because those words were *exactly* what her mother used to say all the time, typically delivered in the same matter-of-fact tone. A skinned knee, a bad grade, a fight with a friend: With Billie, it was *You're going to be just fine,* followed by a little push on the small of Olive's back, as if she were a baby bird who needed to be tossed right back out of the nest. The thing was, her mom was right; everything usually *was* OK. The scab fell off, the grades improved, the friend made up. It used to drive Olive crazy. Not so much now.

Besides, she thinks, even if the visions are a random firing of neurons in her brain, does that make them any less real? Isn't her whole personality a random firing of neurons, anyway? Just bits and bobs in the gray mass on that MRI, bumping against each other, making her *Olive,* whoever *that* is. What makes *any* of her real? Who says that a vision can't be as important as anything else she thinks or feels? Isn't life itself kind of a hallucination? Just atoms clumping together and then coming apart, firing into life and then falling away again.

Dr. Fishbein has pulled down the MRI scans and is stacking them in Olive's file. He leans over and flips a light switch, and the three of them blink in the fluorescent wash, taking in the glaring white lacquer of the cabinets and the informational posters on the walls. Brain vivisections in acid-trip colors.

"There's a whole lot we don't know about the

brain. Even *I'm* baffled sometimes." Dr. Fishbein seems amused by his fake self-deprecation. "But I'd guess your brain is accessing your memories, repurposing them as hallucinations. That's where you keep your memories, you know: the temporal lobe. Memories and emotions. So, with this gliosis, this possible TLE, it's like you've accidentally turned on a tap that you don't know how to turn off." He reaches for his prescription pad and begins to scribble. "But the good news is, *I* know how to turn it off for you."

He tears the prescription off the pad and hands it to Olive's dad. Jonathan glances at it and folds it in half. Olive is annoyed: Do they think she is a child who can't be trusted to hold her own prescription?

"What if I don't want to turn it off?" she demands.

Dr. Fishbein turns with a look of mild surprise on his face. "I wouldn't recommend that." He absently clicks the top of the pen. "So, we'll start you with a hundred and twenty-five milligrams of Depakote, three times a day, take it with food. Plus, you might want to consider lifestyle changes." He turns to Jonathan again. "Is she sleep-deprived? Under a lot of stress?"

Jonathan laughs. "She's a junior in a private high school. What do you think?"

Dr. Fishbein turns back to her. "Well, both of those are seizure triggers, so stop worrying so much, OK, kiddo? Get some sleep! Try to have some fun!"

He pats her on the shoulder and then abruptly leaves the room. Jonathan opens the prescription in his hand, reads it, and tucks it carefully in his wallet.

Olive leans back against a cabinet and folds her arms across her chest.

"I'm not going to take it," she informs him.

"Yes you are." Her father closes his eyes wearily. "I'm sorry. But you heard the doctor."

"What happened to believing me?" she asks him, her eyes brimming with tears of disappointment. She thought they had an alliance. She thought he was *on her side.*

Jonathan picks up a plastic 3-D model of the brain that is sitting on the bank of cabinets and pulls a lobe out. He turns it in his hand. "Try to see it from my perspective, Bean," he says. "This is your brain we're talking about. And I'm not going to take chances with my daughter's brain. Yes, we *both* liked the idea of you being psychic, but doesn't this make a lot more sense? Let's be honest."

"So, what now? You've decided I'm just brain-damaged, so you're going to stop looking for Mom?"

Jonathan peers into the model of the brain as if he might find it full of jelly beans or lost keys or the answer to the question she's asked. He gently fits the lobe back into place. "I didn't say that."

"But why would you bother looking for her if you think that what I'm seeing is just a result of misfiring neurons?" Her father is blinking a suspicious amount, and she stares at him, suddenly under-standing. "There's stuff you know about Mom that I don't. Isn't there?" Her father gives a tiny ambiva-lent shake of his head. " 'I believe you because I love you.' That wasn't true, was it? You think Mom's alive because you found out something that you're not telling me." She's growing excited. "Dad, you have to tell me."

He shifts uncomfortably. "Well, there was the nurse at the home who saw her."

She shakes her head. "You already told me you thought she was an unreliable witness. There's something else, right?"

He puts the brain model back and neatly aligns it with the edge of the sink. "Olive. I can't tell you everything."

"Why not? I thought we were a team."

He sighs. "Because I'm not sure what everything means yet, and the last thing I want is to cause you even more unnecessary anxiety. You heard the doctor. *No stress*." Then, recognizing her unhappiness at this: "Please, just . . . let me do my thing for a bit, and you take the Depakote and try to get more sleep, and we'll see what happens." He steps in closer, turning so that he is leaning up against the cabinet next to her, and puts his arm around her shoulder. "If you take the pills and you're still having your visions, then we'll know Dr. Fishbein was wrong, won't we?"

She looks away from her father and shivers, suddenly cold from the blasting air-conditioning. She has a terrible feeling that her father believes something about her mother that she will not like at all, something so awful that he isn't willing to say it aloud. She senses them sliding apart again, as if they are standing on opposite staircases in a bank of escalators, one rising as the other sinks, watching unhappily as their faces fall into darkness.

You're going to be just fine. Her mom was always

right about that, wasn't she? Right up until the day when nothing was fine at all.

Her father drops Olive off at school just as the lunch bell rings. The classroom doors bang open one by one and release a murder of Claremont Girls, skirts flying in their haste to raise their blood sugar levels. Olive wanders through the Sunshine Wing toward the cafeteria, acutely aware of the orange vial of Depakote nestled in her backpack. She just won't take it. Who will know if she doesn't, anyway?

The cafeteria is serving avocado sandwiches and chocolate pudding and a lentil salad studded, alarmingly, with bloody-looking beets. She gathers her tray and locates Natalie sitting at a table under the big window with Ming and Tracy. Her heart sinks—she hoped to find Natalie alone.

When she approaches, Natalie slides down to make room for her. Olive puts her tray down across from Ming and Tracy, who are leaning their heads together and talking in lowered voices, their hair falling in protective curtains around their faces. The Smart One and The Pretty One, that's how the Girls always refer to them; Olive suspects that Ming and Tracy cling to each other because they complete each other, together making a whole person that is better than the sum of their parts. She remembers how she used to sit behind that curtain of hair with them, giggling and gossiping. Was it only a year ago? It's not that they aren't nice to her anymore; it's just that they've shifted Olive to the periphery since her mom disappeared. She wishes Natalie didn't still hang around with them.

"Where were you this morning?" Natalie asks Olive. Her hair circles her face like a halo, wild and out of control, clipped haphazardly over one ear with a kid's butterfly barrette. Olive looks at the barrette admiringly—Natalie never seems concerned about what anyone thinks of her—and then takes a bite of her sandwich, resisting the urge to reach out and smooth down a particularly unruly curl of Natalie's hair. The avocado sandwich is unpleasantly soft and squishy in her mouth.

"Doctor's appointment," Olive says with her mouth full, glancing at Ming and Tracy, who, thankfully, seem less interested in her than in vigorously stirring their chocolate pudding into syrupy goo while discussing the plot of the latest episode of a zombie show that Olive has never watched.

"Because you fainted on Monday?" Olive winces at how loud Natalie's voice is, wishing for once that her friend had a volume control.

"Yeah," she says, lowering her voice. "Dad took me to a neurologist. So ridiculous. He made me get an MRI."

"Hard*core*." Natalie puts a hand on Olive's arm, giving it a squeeze that tingles even after Natalie pulls her hand away. "You should get a copy of the MRI and frame it. That's so cool."

Ming and Tracy have stopped talking and are listening intently. Ming turns to examine Olive, her eyes widening. She's got a giant crusted pimple on her nose that she's attempted to conceal with coverup; her black hair is as shiny as patent leather except for the frizzled bits where she's dyed it in violet streaks. "I saw you fall! What was *up* with that?" Ming turns to Tracy. "She, like, pitched straight down the front steps. Mr. Heron was freaking out, he called an ambulance and everything."

"Oh, it was nothing. I just fainted. Probably dehydrated or something." Olive picks at her sandwich, extricating a particularly stringy bean sprout. "So, did I miss anything this morning?"

But it's too late. Ming and Tracy are looking at her with more interest than they have in ages, and Natalie's brow is rumpled with concern. "So wait—did you tell the neurologist about your visions?" Natalie asks. "Is that why you had to get an MRI?"

"Visions?" Tracy's voice is whispery and dramatic. She peers curiously at Olive. Her hands tug at her blond hair, which is burnished to a trophy shine in the filtered sunlight. The shimmer in her face lotion sparkles in a distracting way.

"Guys, Olive is *psychic*. She's been talking to her mom and . . . stuff." Natalie glances sideways at Olive, eyebrows raised as if she's asking for approval for this revelation, although clearly, it's too late for that. She leans across the table, sliding her hands palm-down toward Ming and Tracy, as if inviting them into the secret. Olive shrinks in her seat, uncomfortable with this. "So wait, did you have another vision on Monday? Is that why you fainted?"

Olive nods, her face burning. Ming is staring at her, brow furrowed, as if Olive has just revealed herself to be a peculiar new life-form, and Tracy's jaw is ajar in a fairly moronic expression that she is attempting to conceal by drawing her hair across her mouth. Olive knows they are going to talk about her the second they leave the table.

"Of, like, what?" Tracy breathes.

Olive glances at Natalie for reassurance. Natalie is smiling back at her, seemingly unconcerned, so Olive relaxes a bit. "Fire," she says. "I saw a giant wall of fire."

Tracy's face falls. "Just—fire?"

"It was a huge fire. Really hot," Olive says, feeling defensive. The tiny hairs at the back of her neck tingle as she recalls the dread that she felt in the moment when she first came out the front door of the school: The familiar falling sensation, the burning smell, and then her mother suddenly standing next to her. Trees all around them, so dense that the sky was blotted out and the whole world seemed to go dark.

Something in her mother's hand: a match.

Her mother had looked at her sideways: "Whatcha think? Should I do it? Burn it all down?"

No, Olive thought. *Don't.*

But it was too late, because already a wall of flames was jumping across the horizon, so real that she could have sworn she felt the heat of it pressing her backward. She could hear an ominous rumble nearby of something collapsing, or maybe just the sound of the flames devouring the oxygen; a sickening sense of danger hung in the air, a sensation of bodies at risk. Her mother's? Her own? And then the next thing she knew, she was lying on the ground surrounded by a circle of girls, punctuated by Mr. Heron's uncharacteristically worried face.

"So, what? Is that supposed to mean something?

The school's going to catch on fire?" Ming does not bother to conceal the note of skepticism in her voice.

Olive shrugs, looking at Natalie for backup. But Natalie leans back on the bench, her hands braced behind her, waiting for Olive's explanation.

What *is* the vision supposed to mean? A fire is just a fire unless you know where or when or how or to whom. As the three girls look at her, demanding logic or mystery or insight, Olive thinks of the vial of Depakote in her backpack, of the amorphous gray mass in the MRI, of the neurons in her head pinging erratically. Her specialness sliding away, leaving her as just a mental case with a dead mom.

And yet even with the pills sitting in her backpack in rebuke, nothing feels as true as—no logical hypothesis or medical technology can compare to—this *feeling* of her mother lurking somewhere just out of sight. It has lodged there, in her chest: the tether binding them. She isn't going to give anyone—not the doctor, not Ming and Tracy, not her father—the opportunity to take that away.

She squints at Ming and Tracy. "I think I saw you in the flames," she says to Tracy. "You were screaming and your hair was on fire."

Tracy clutches at her precious hair, her eyes wide, and Ming throws Olive a disgusted look; but Natalie giggles beside her, and Olive feels a little surge of vindication.

"Oh, come on, that's such bullshit," Ming says. "You're faking."

"Swear to God," Olive says, but she's lost the high ground already, so it comes out as a squeak.

"Whatever, wacko."

"*Language.*" Olive feels a hand on her shoulder and looks up to see Vice Principal Gillespie looming over her. She's wearing yet another of her scratchy-looking suits, the ones that Olive suspects she wears to repel any unwanted bodily contact. The girls all freeze in their chairs, running through the rest of their conversation to see if anything un-Claremont-like has been uttered. Gillespie's index finger taps gently on Olive's collarbone. "Can I speak with you for a moment?"

Olive stands and grabs her backpack. Ming, Tracy, and Natalie watch her go with sympathetic eyes, and then their heads inevitably swing toward each other, their hair once again forming privacy curtains for their whispered conversation.

Olive follows Gillespie out of the cafeteria to the courtyard. It's sunny out, a respite from the rain, the air clean and crisp.

"I just spoke with your father," Gillespie says. She smells faintly of lemons and damp wool. "He told me about your appointment with the neurologist; that you're having seizures. Are you feeling OK?"

Olive nods, flustered.

"You have your medication on you?"

"My father told you about that?"

"Of course," Gillespie says briskly. "School policy. No medication on campus unless we've been informed. We'll keep a copy of the prescription on file, so there's no misunderstanding, and monitor its consumption. You've taken it already today?"

Olive shakes her head. "I'm supposed to take it with food."

Gillespie gestures toward the cafeteria. "I'm pretty sure I just saw you eating your lunch."

Olive stares at her, uncomprehending. "You want to watch me take it? Seriously? Because honestly, that's a very Orwellian move, Vice Principal Gillespie."

Gillespie laughs toothily. She runs her hands along the edges of her skirt as if making sure there aren't any errant fibers or dust flakes. "You're a *good* student, Olive. I know that. But lately you're failing to show up to class, and your teachers are saying you seem distracted. I assumed it was related to your . . . family situation and was going to suggest some more sessions with Mrs. Santiago. But, well, seizures, that's a different story. It's my job to make sure that whatever health issue you're dealing with doesn't get in the way of your education. And the first step is making sure you're taking your medication. So"—she forces a smile—"let's not wait."

Olive reaches slowly into her backpack and pulls out the bottle of pills. "I don't have water," she says.

Vice Principal Gillespie points at an ancient water fountain on the edge of the courtyard, jammed with abandoned gum and soggy leaves. "I see a water source right there, Olive."

Olive trudges over to the fountain. It smells like mold and rust. She glances over her shoulder to check if Gillespie is watching. She is. Olive fishes out a pill and puts it on her tongue and then takes a gulp of water from the fountain, surprisingly cold and crisp. The pill sticks briefly in her craw, making her gag, but with a second gulp it slides down her throat. She stands there staring at the shingled siding of the cafeteria wall, royally pissed. What will happen now? What if the visions *do* stop? What if her vision that morning was the last time she would see her mother?

She turns around and shoulders her backpack. "Please tell me we aren't going to do this every day, Vice Principal Gillespie. Is it too much to ask for a little trust here? I'm sixteen, not twelve."

"Don't think of it as a trust issue," Gillespie says. "It's about taking good care of one of my favorite girls." She pats Olive crisply on the arm and walks back into the cafeteria.

As the door to the cafeteria swings open and closed again, Olive can see Natalie staring at her through the glass, eyebrows wrinkled into furry question marks. *What's going on?* she mouths. Olive shrugs, so Natalie repeats herself—*What's going on?*—as if Olive didn't understand her the first time. Olive gives up and turns away. She takes a shortcut across the lawn and around the edge of the building, grinding her sneakers into the soggy grass, leaving muddy size-seven divots marking her path. She thinks she's walking aimlessly until she reaches the front entrance to the school and finds that she is still walking, right out onto the sidewalk, and only then does she realize that she is leaving for the day.

Let them expel me, she thinks. *I don't care if I ever go back.*

WHERE THE MOUNTAIN MEETS THE SKY

My Life with Billie Flanagan

———

BY JONATHAN FLANAGAN

When Olive was eleven years old, Billie left us. That's really what happened, isn't it? For years I've been painting the whole episode as "Mom needed time to herself," just a hiccup in the history of our lives together, but the fact of the matter is this: She left and didn't tell us where she was going. For three days, she didn't answer her phone. And then, out of the blue, she was back.

So where did she go?

The day that she left, she and Olive got in a fight. It wasn't their first one. They weren't joined at the hip anymore, not since she started at Claremont, but I figured, well, that's what happens with moms and daughters, right? The daughters hit puberty and pull away. They need to individuate. They get in screaming matches about skirt length and curfew and doing their own laundry.

But the thing was, they weren't fighting about that kind of stuff.

"Natalie invited me to go to church with her this Sunday," Olive announced at breakfast on the morning that Billie left.

Billie, busy getting food on the table, dropped the milk jug down with a thud. "Oh, Jesus Christ," she said.

"I think that's the general idea," I quipped.

Billie didn't look amused. She sat down on the other side of Olive. "You are not going to go to church, OK? You know who goes to church? Sheep. People who can't decide things for themselves. People who are too cowardly to take responsibility for their own lives, so they shunt it all off on some deity. You are stronger than that, Olive."

Olive frowned. "Natalie goes to church."

"Maybe it's time to find a friend who doesn't, then." Billie picked up the milk and poured a giant glug over the Rice Krispies in Olive's bowl. "You forget, I was raised in the church. I know things that you don't know."

Olive's face brightened. "But, Mom, it's different, see? Natalie's church—it's *progressive*. So it's OK."

"God is God." Billie stood up, milk in hand. "We'll go hiking on Sunday instead, how about that?"

"I hate hiking," Olive muttered.

Billie froze halfway to the fridge. The cereal in front of Olive fizzed and popped in the silence.

I jumped in. "Hey," I said. "If she's supposed to be deciding things for herself, we should let her start by deciding about church."

Billie turned to face me, her face red with fury. "Don't. Undermine. Me."

I was acutely aware of Olive sitting next to me, a soggy spoonful of cereal dripping en route to her mouth, wide eyes flicking between us. I felt something then, a faint but distinct pressure on my toe; the heel of a sneaker making deliberate contact with mine. A message from my daughter.

Maybe she was trying to thank me, maybe she was trying to tell me not to worry, maybe she was warning me to back off: The exact intention being expressed through her foot wasn't clear. What *was* obvious was that some invisible shift of alignment in our household had just occurred; and where once it had been Olive and Mom, with Dad watching from the perimeter, there was suddenly the possibility of an Olive-and-Dad alliance.

"If you want to go to church, go to church," I told Olive, and then looked at my wife, who stood there with a hand on the hip of her jeans, staring death at us. "One sermon. It's not going to kill her. Bore her to tears, maybe, but it won't kill her." And then, gentler, because I thought I knew what this was all about: "Not everyone in the church is like your father. I know you're worried about that."

But instead of softening, Billie went stiff, as if someone had shoved a garden rake up the back of her T-shirt. "I don't appreciate you using my past as a weapon against me," she said. Her voice was neutral, but underneath there was something deathly sharp. She turned deliberately away, putting the milk back in the refrigerator, sweeping the cereal box back in the cupboard. By the time she turned back to face us, she was smiling again. "Banana, anyone?" she asked, dangling a bunch from her forefinger.

That night, when Olive and I got home from school, Billie was gone, along with her suitcase. A note: *Back soon*. So that's what I told Olive: that her mom was taking a little time to herself. That she'd be back soon. Wasn't that what Billie said in her note? I didn't have any solid reason not to believe her, even after Friday turned into Saturday, and Saturday became Sunday, and soon became not soon at all. Annoyance turned to worry, and then to hurt, and then to fury.

And then Billie came back. She walked into the house

Sunday evening with her arms full of groceries, as if she'd just popped out for some milk. Acting as if nothing had happened at all.

I remember standing there in the kitchen when she waltzed in the door and feeling like I'd been hit in the face with a plank. Staring at Billie, tanned and glowing and beautiful, like a model advertising some fancy lifestyle retreat, I was filled with a kind of rage: *How can you look like that after what you just did to us?* And yet, as she locked eyes with me, lighting up with apparent delight at my presence, I felt her emanating some curious magnetic draw on me. It reminded me of how I felt that first day on the J Church in San Francisco, as if I were being sucked blindly into her vortex.

"Where have you been?"

"Nowhere worth mentioning," she said. She dropped the groceries on the counter and slid her arms around me. "Don't be mad," she said. "I just needed space to breathe. Which I deserved, you know. But I missed you two!" As if that were a sufficient explanation. And like the sucker I was, I let it be sufficient—because that was the answer I *wanted* to hear.

At the time, I didn't directly connect the two events—the fight and Billie's departure. And maybe the two events *weren't* connected; maybe there was another reason she left us that weekend. Maybe she was having an affair even then. Maybe she did just need a little space for herself. But maybe, just maybe, the confrontation with Olive and me gave her an excuse she was looking for: evidence that we were aligning against her. A reason to leave.

Another truth I haven't wanted to admit: As anxious and angry as I was about Billie's disappearance, it was nice to have her gone. It was like coming out from under a shadow, feeling the light on your face again. Olive and I spent the weekend together, ice cream sundaes and the sci-fi films Billie would never, ever watch, reading books together in comfortable silence, ordering takeout. Solidifying our fledgling alliance with an unspoken understanding, that we two were more alike than we'd ever been given the space to realize.

And yet. That Sunday morning, when church time rolled around and I offered to drive Olive over to Natalie's house, Olive hesitated. She looked around the room, as if her mother might have materialized behind the couch or in the doorway, and then down at her bare feet. "That's OK, Dad," she said softly. "I don't really want to go after all."

No wonder I pretended that Billie didn't really leave us. I did it for Olive. I did it for me. I did it so that we could survive as a family, because Olive wanted us to.

12

CHERYL IS FIFTEEN MINUTES late to their meeting. Jonathan sits in the window of the café on College Avenue, just a few blocks from his house, nursing a coffee. A waitress with a Frida Kahlo hairstyle and a turquoise nose stud is wiping down the marble-topped tables in the wake of the lunchtime crowd. Three Chinese Cal students sit quietly in the back of the café, studying organic chemistry. Outside, a little boy on a Kickboard scooter whips back and forth past Jonathan's window, from the Nepalese clothing boutique to the Italian gourmet grocery and back.

The appointment with Dr. Fishbein has left him queasy; the sight of his inert daughter sliding inside that grinding machine has liquefied something critical inside him. Even though the diagnosis is less terrifying than it could have been—temporal lobe epilepsy, it's not great, but it's also not (*thank God*) a tumor—he still doesn't like to imagine his child's vulnerable brain marred. It was prettier to let himself believe that something more magical was happening in her head, that she could really see things that he couldn't. He should have known better. It was selfish of him to have indulged the fantasy: He stupidly spurred Olive into action instead of keeping her safe in the dark until he was sure there wasn't a monster waiting behind the next door.

(And yet. Olive had picked up on *something*, hadn't she? His brain seizes up whenever he considers this apparent conundrum.)

Ten more minutes pass. He orders another coffee and checks his ipTracer app: 0 visitors, not a single hit yet, despite three more days and four more chapters. The dark memories are spilling out of him now like a previously undetected cancer that's metastasized: Writing them down makes him feel sick, yet he can't seem to stop, even though it appears that no one is paying attention. He is starting to think Calvin Lim has sent him on a fool's errand; maybe he warned Billie in advance to avoid vanity Google searches.

He checks his watch again. Cheryl is a half hour late. He is about to give up and leave when a woman rushes through the door, slamming a voluminous battered purse into the doorjamb and ricocheting back off it. She looks around with embarrassment, makes eye contact with Jonathan, and then teeters toward him, falling into a chair across from him.

"Jonathan, right? Sorry I'm late, I forgot to put the dog out this morning and he vomited all over the carpet and I had to clean it up before I left." She ri-fles around in the purse, looking for something. "And then I didn't have any change for the meter, I had to ask someone, and I'm pretty sure they didn't give me the right amount—" She opens a fist and stares at the coins lying there with bafflement; then looks directly at him, her eyes wide. "Oh! You're handsome, aren't you? Not that I'm surprised about that. Sybilla always got the cute guys."

He feels like he has whiplash. "Can I get you a tea?"

"No, no! You don't have to do that, I can get it myself." She spins back out of the chair and heads to the espresso bar, scattering spare change beneath her feet.

He watches her go. Cheryl is tall, but she tips forward when she walks, as if someone is giving her a little push from behind. A ponytail sprouts from the back of her head, a blond stalk rooted with several centimeters of gray-threaded brown. She wears pink leggings and UGGs and a mumsy cardigan sweater, but as she pays for her tea, Jonathan can see tattoo sleeves covering her wrists. A constellation of wilting holes decorates her earlobe, from oversize studs that have long been removed. She was probably pretty once, but a road map of wrinkles marks the route of some hard-living years.

"So you saw my ad in the *Chronicle*?" he asks when she sits down again. "I'm amazed anyone reads the print edition anymore, let alone the classi-fieds."

She stirs a heaping spoonful of sugar into her tea. "Oh, I don't read the paper. I work part-time as a pet groomer, and we use newspaper to line the cages. It happened to catch my eye, you know? Her name jumped out at me?"

"And here I thought you were a sign that newsprint had a viable future." She gives him a baffled look. "Forget it."

"Can I see a picture? Of Sybilla?"

Jonathan pulls one up on his phone, a snap of Billie and Olive taken a few summers earlier. Their two faces side by side, Olive's a faint echo of her mother's, their hair loose and eyes squinting in the sun. "With our daughter," he offers.

Cheryl grabs his wrist to pull the phone closer to her face. She stares at it for a long time, silently. "Wow. Wouldn't have thought she'd end up one of those yoga-mommy types."

"Yoga wasn't really her thing, actually," he says. Cheryl is still gripping his wrist, pinning him uncomfortably in place.

"Oh, don't get me wrong, I love yoga, I would do it if I had the time. God knows I need it, twin nine-year-old boys, I could use a little more Zen in my life. *Haw! Haw!* My husband would probably freak out, though, he thinks it's all too culty. We met in AA, you want to talk culty, but whatever." She releases his wrist. "I'm blabbering too much, aren't I? Shit, I'm sorry. I do that when I'm nervous."

He massages his wrist under the table. "So, about Billie?"

"*Billie.*" She says the name slowly, letting the *L*'s roll languorously off her tongue. "Funny, no one called her anything but Sybilla back then. She hated nicknames."

She told me she hated the name Sybilla, he re-members. He tries to remain neutral: an objective journalist, collecting facts about his subject. *Start at zero, build a picture, see if it matches the one you already had in your head.* "Tell me more," he says. "What was she like back then?"

Cheryl blows across her tea to cool it. "Oh," she says. "I was hoping you could tell *me* about *her*. How she did in life." She looks around her, at the marble-topped café tables and the signboards advertising sixteen-dollar salads; at Jonathan's button-down shirt and the laptop tucked into the leather bag at his feet. "She did well, didn't she? I always knew she would. She had that *thing*, you know?"

He takes a careful sip of coffee. "What thing?"

"You know. She was the girl everyone wanted to be. Or be around." Cheryl casts her eyes aside, smiling to herself. "She and I, we were the pretty ones in our class, right? Strolling through that school like we owned the place. I have a picture, if you want to see it? From sophomore year of high school." Cheryl reaches into her purse, rummages around, and pulls out a snapshot, discolored with age, of two pretty, big-haired teenagers: bangs sticky with aerosol hair products, eyes popping with neon eye shadow, jeans tight as Saran Wrap around slim thighs. They're sitting on a curb, feet folded into the gutter. The blond one, Cheryl, is splayed across the brunette's lap, laughing; the brunette is holding a cigarette over her friend's head, an ash in danger of igniting all that hairspray, and looking at the camera with a be-mused, tolerant expression, as if she's waiting for all this to end. It's Billie, but not a version of her that he's ever seen. He stares at it.

"We were the bomb, right? Except what Sybilla had that no one else did—*definitely* not me—was that she was cool. As in cucumber. She didn't get worked up about regular shit the way the rest of us did. You know, she got voted to homecoming court? And she didn't even show up for the dance. She was already on to bigger and better things."

"Like what?" He tries to imagine.

"Like *anything*." Cheryl exhales hard. "She liked being ahead of the curve. Older guys, obscure music. Things she'd read. She'd study something, get all intense about it, and then get bored and move on to something else." She pauses. "You have to understand where we came from. It was nothing. Farms and churches, migrant workers and struggling families; and nothing to do on the weekends but drive two towns over to hang out in the parking lot of a Stop and Shop."

"I've been to Meacham," Jonathan says, thinking of the dilapidated farmhouse collapsing into the earth.

"So you know. Sybilla's dad was kind of a big deal in town back in the day, preacher at the Episcopal church everyone went to." She looks down at her hands, fingernails chopped pragmatically short. "Her parents were pretty tough on her; they would have locked her up until she got married if they could have."

"Didn't they?" he asks, catching the edges of Cheryl's story and making them meet up with the one he's already familiar with. "In the basement."

She looks up with a confused expression. "The rumpus room? We used to get stoned down there. But I mean, yeah, they were *strict*. They'd punish her by making her copy out Bible verses freehand. Her father didn't let her wear short skirts or go on dates or listen to the music she liked, so she was always sneaking around behind their backs. She just loved pulling one over on them." Cheryl takes a gulp from her tea, winces at the heat, and sets it down, leaving a coral lip print smeared across the rim of the cup. "Starting our junior year, she told her parents she'd joined an after-school Bible study group, and she and I started hitchhiking in to Bakersfield and hanging out at the mall. Slim pickings, but that was the best we could do. Her parents found out eventually, and they grounded her."

"Can you tell me about when she ran away?"

She tilts her head. "Which time?"

This is jarring. "She did it more than once?"

Cheryl reaches down and fishes in her purse and pulls out an electronic cigarette. "Sorry, talking about the past really makes me need a cigarette. Don't worry"—she waves away the Frida Kahlo waitress, who is immediately by her side with a disapproving expression—"I'm not going to smoke it, sometimes it helps just to hold it, OK?" She rolls it between her fingers. Back and forth. "So. Sybilla did not like being grounded. But this is the thing about Sybilla—she never got hysterical, you know? She just got *focused*, all intense. So one day she comes up to me in school and drags me into the bathroom and says, all serious-like, 'I'm going to run away.' And she's not just saying it. She means it." The cigarette slides back and forth, back and forth. "I talked her into taking me with her. We just packed some stuff and slipped out the back door of school and jumped a bus to Los Angeles." She laughs: *Haw! Haw!* "Turned out that Sybilla had been stealing money from the collection plate at her dad's church for *years*. She had a whole stash of cash. She called it her fuck-off money."

Jonathan thinks of the missing weekly withdrawals from his own bank account, seeing patterns play out across decades. *Fuck-off money.* "Yeah, sounds like Billie," he mutters.

Cheryl shoots him a quizzical look. "Anyway, we checked into a cheapo motel in Los Angeles, and for ten days, we totally lived it up, partied on Hollywood Boulevard. Sybilla met this guy at a party we went to. And then one day there was a knock on the hotel door and my parents were there." She blinks, remembering. "See, Sybilla had warned me that we needed to pick new names—she was going to be Elizabeth, and I was Laura—but I forgot and booked the motel room in my real name, and I guess our parents called around until they found us. Sybilla was so pissed at me. We got dragged back to Meacham, and that was pretty much the end. Her parents decided they were going to send her off to some Bible school for wayward girls."

Jonathan takes another sip of his coffee, now cold. Billie had never told him this part of the story. "But they didn't end up sending her," he says.

She gulps at her tea. "No. She took off again before that happened. And her parents never found her." She makes a strangling sound and stares into her empty cup. Jonathan notices that the tips of her fingers on the table are vibrating.

"That must have been hard on you," he says.

Cheryl looks up at him with big wounded eyes. "She left me behind, see? She thought I was too much trouble. She didn't think I was worth it." She takes a ragged breath. "Anyway. That's the story."

Jonathan nods, assembling all the moving pieces in his mind. Though it's not exactly how he imagined Billie's childhood, it's not a radical departure. But what was he expecting, anyway? Another person's past spreads out like a vast sea, impossible to grasp in its entirety; all you get is brief glimpses of the things hidden down in its depths, the things you drag up one by one to examine before throwing everything back.

Then he remembers something else. "Sorry to pry, but . . . Billie told me that her father got in trouble for sexually assaulting one of her friends. Was that you?"

The e-cigarette slips out of Cheryl's fingers and clatters to the floor. She drops to her knees, scrabbling around under her chair. When she sits back up, she doesn't meet his eyes but instead stares at the e-cigarette. "Yeah," she says. "That was her idea."

He puts the coffee cup down too fast, and it slips in the saucer and spills the tepid remains across the table. He dabs at the spill with a napkin. "Excuse me? Billie's idea?"

Cheryl pushes up her sleeve and scratches nervously at the tattoo on one arm, running a fingernail up and down the belly of a belligerent Japanese koi. "After they dragged her back from L.A. She was furious that her dad was going to ship her off to Wings of Faith, or whatever that school was called," she says. "So it was, like, revenge, right? She said I should go to his office in the church and cry a little bit, tell him I wanted to repent for my sins and then go sit in his lap and see what happened. Just to freak him out, she said." Cheryl goes quiet. "And she was already pissed at me for the L.A. thing, and I didn't want to disappoint her anymore, so yeah. I did it."

Jonathan's cellphone begins to ring, but he quickly mutes it, flipping it on its face. "You just— sat in his lap."

"Yeah." Cheryl folds the cigarette into her palm, like a magic trick, and then opens it again. She stares at it dolefully, as if she expected it to disappear. "I mean, it was the *way* I sat. I think Sybilla must have known something about her dad that she didn't tell me. Because when I did it, when I slid into his lap and put an arm around his neck, he didn't act freaked out or upset. He got pretty . . . excited. And then, suddenly, he had one hand up my skirt and the other inside my blouse and I didn't know what the hell to do. Like, did Sybilla want me to keep going or stop? You know? But then a church deacon came racing through the door and saw us. And yeah, you can guess the rest. Huge scandal. Her dad was pretty much destroyed. I mean, I was barely sixteen." She pauses. "I always wondered if Sybilla sent that deacon in to get her dad in trouble. Never got a chance to ask her, because right after all this went down, that's when she disappeared."

"Jesus." His voice is too loud, and it echoes off the marble tabletops, the tile floor, the wall of glass.

A few tables down, one of the studying students looks up and frowns, showily flips a page in her textbook. He lowers his voice. "I'm so sorry."

Cheryl sits up straighter. "Oh, it's OK," she says cheerfully. "I mean, it screwed me up for a long time. But I got my life together now, right? Got a husband, two kids who aren't *always* complete monsters, a good enough job. Haven't had a drink in ten years. I did all right. I don't blame her for anything."

You should, he thinks. He feels disoriented: These are Billie's life legends, the familiar stories she always told about herself. He realizes now that someone else was telling the exact same stories her entire life, but in a wholly different way. Perhaps both versions equally true to their tellers. So which one should he believe?

He is momentarily distracted by a familiar silhouette walking along College Avenue, a blazer he recognizes, the sluggish gait from a too-heavy backpack. Is that Olive? He picks up his phone and glances at the time. Is his daughter cutting class *again*? He notices that the phone call he missed was from the front office of Claremont Prep.

He lifts his hand to rap on the window and hesitates, reconsidering the scenario, just as Olive passes the café and notices him sitting there. There is an uncomfortable moment as they stare at each other through the glass, each waiting for the other to do something. Olive looks at Cheryl, back at Jonathan, and then back at Cheryl. She turns around and walks back to the door of the café.

"Sorry," he says to Cheryl. "That's my daughter. I think she's cutting school."

Cheryl watches Olive approach their table and whispers under her breath, "She looks a little like her in the eyes."

Olive sidles up to them. "Hey, Dad."

"Why aren't you in school?"

She shrugs. "I felt lousy."

"You can't just take off like that, Bean. Claremont has a no-tolerance policy for cutting. You'll get yourself suspended." It's hard to be indignant when his daughter looks so miserable. She is pale and shaky, her uniform half untucked, straggling bits of hair falling loose from her hair clips. He wonders if she's taken her Depakote yet but doesn't want to ask her in front of Cheryl.

"Can we not talk about it right now?" Olive is baldly staring at Cheryl, who sits there with the unlit electronic cigarette lodged between her fingers. "Um—hi?"

"This is Cheryl—" Jonathan looks at Cheryl. "Sorry, what's your last name?"

"Lutz. I know, awful, right? But that's what happens when you get married, you get their name, too, along with all their baggage." She releases another of her braying laughs.

Olive stares at Cheryl, her eyes widening slightly. She seems to be on satellite delay.

"So, look, Olive, we'll talk back at home—" he begins, but Cheryl is already talking over him.

"I knew your mom back in high school."

"Really?" Olive perks up. She grabs a chair and sits down. Her backpack lands at her feet with a thump. "OK if I join?"

"We're pretty much done," Jonathan says, turning to Cheryl. "Aren't we?"

But Cheryl is rummaging around in her purse, her eyes trained on Olive's face. "Your mother, she was really something. I still think about her all the time." She extricates a folded piece of paper and slides it over to Jonathan. "I thought maybe you'd want to see this."

It's a note, written on smudged binder paper that's faded almost to yellow with age, its creases soft and worn. He unfolds it carefully, and instantly recognizes his wife's spiky handwriting.

Cheryl

People in this town want me to be small. They want to squeeze me into the tiny box of their expectations even if it kills me in the process. Anyway, I'm not going to let that happen anymore, so I'm off. Everything about this place is stagnant.

I know you want me to tell you where I'm going, but honestly, I don't think I can trust you. Not after what you did. Just know that I'm going to a place where people think a lot bigger. There's a whole world of people out there, people like Sidney, who see the big picture and know that their lives are good for more than sitting around eating Doritos and talking about who's the hottest Bon Jovi.

So, listen: The earth as we know it is teetering on the brink. It's going to collapse, sooner than we think. We're draining her dry, leaving nothing behind, and pretty soon we are going to be facing massive shortages of resources, and then the cataclysms are going to happen— the global warming and the depletion of the forests—and then everything is going to go to hell. Like nothing you could imagine. So yeah, Sidney and I are going to do something about that.

I'd say I'll see you again soon but I'd probably be lying. Don't worry, I don't hate you. But buck up, OK? I'm sure you'll be fine. Lips zipped, chin up, don't look back.

Sybilla

He looks up, snagging on that name again. "You knew Sidney?" he asks.

Cheryl nods. "That's the guy she met at the party in L.A. Honestly, he kind of creeped me out, he was all intense and, like, fixated on Sybilla. Loved to hear himself talk, you know? Thought he was soooo radical, save the world, all that crap. Hippie punk shit." She makes a face. "Of course, Sybilla soaked that up. I didn't realize they'd kept in touch until I found her letter. She'd stuck it in my math textbook and I didn't find it for a month."

Jonathan absorbs this uneasily, thinking of the Polaroid, still wondering. He glances over at Olive. She is staring at the letter in a way that makes him uncomfortable. He feels oddly queasy about the teenager who wrote those words: He used to feel protective of that girl, a victim of untenable circumstances, but now he isn't entirely sure that she was the victim she made herself out to be.

Cheryl is standing up, balling her belongings

under her arm as if she's about to make a dash for the door. "Gotta run," she says. She leans over and tugs the letter away from Olive, folding it back to a rectangle. "Kids will be home from school soon."

He thinks quickly, running through the questions piling up in his mind, settling on the one that seems most critical. "One last question," he says. "Did Billie ever come back? To Meacham?"

Cheryl already has the electronic cigarette pressed between her lips in anticipation of flight. It dangles there as she mulls over his question. "I'm not totally sure," she says finally. "I heard a rumor, maybe five years later? That she was back. I even went to her house a few times to ring the doorbell, but no one ever answered. So." She edges toward the exit. "Look—I'm sorry, but—I gotta . . ."

He stands. "Thanks for coming."

He watches her leave. The sideways afternoon light through the windows illuminates her face: the way her skin sags under her eyes, the limp straw hair stuck in the coral gloss of her lips, but despite all that, something earnest and hopeful in her eyes. Billie's words echo across the decades: *I'm sure you'll be fine*. This woman, she's really trying. He wonders what she's trying to prove and whether she's doing it for a ghost.

"Dad," Olive says softly. "Sidney's the guy who's in jail, right? The drug dealer?"

"*Was* in jail. He's not anymore. He came to your mom's memorial."

She sits straight up in her chair, looking past him at some point in the distance. "What if Sidney kidnapped Mom?"

He is struck momentarily dumb: This is a scenario he didn't consider. Finally, he laughs, a little uneasily. "That's ridiculous," he says. "Why would he do that?"

"You heard Cheryl. He was *obsessed* with her," Olive says, her voice pitching high and hot. "It makes sense, doesn't it? He's a criminal, he came after her! God, Dad, it would explain everything! I *told* you she was in trouble."

"Slow down, Olive, you're getting way ahead of yourself."

"We have to find him!"

"I don't even know his last name," he says.

"Then invite Harmony over for dinner tonight and ask her," she says, crossing her arms. "I bet *she* knows."

That night, after dinner has been cleared and the dishes piled up in the sink where they will be ignored for the next few days, Jonathan turns to Harmony. She sprawls next to him on the living room couch, reading a book. Olive is upstairs, safely ensconced in her room, where she fled the minute dinner was finished; still, just to be safe, Jonathan has positioned himself on the opposite end of the couch from Harmony. Close enough to register the heat of her, far enough away to stay out of trouble.

He notices that Harmony is reading Billie's old Tana French novel, apparently retrieved from the corner of his bedroom where he flung it two weeks earlier. When did she find that? The bookmark has been moved back to page one. He tries not to let this bother him. The tangle of their relationship—his dead wife, Harmony's ex-boyfriend—gives the whole scenario a weird undercurrent that he isn't sure how to process.

"Sidney," he says to her. "You knew him, right?"

"Sidney? Billie's old boyfriend?" She flips a page, her index finger tracing its way along the words. "Yeah, I knew him. He was kind of a mess. Had a drug problem."

"He got arrested for dealing, right?"

She looks up from the novel, considers a point on the opposite wall. "Among other things. I was gone by then."

"Is he . . . dangerous?"

She turns to stare at him, her brow wrinkling in a distractingly appealing way. "What? That's a weird question. Why are you asking that?"

He thinks quickly. "I was just remembering that I saw him at Billie's memorial last year. I didn't really talk to him, but I was curious. He gave off a vibe."

Harmony drops the book and stretches out toward him, questing with a toe until it makes contact with his shin, moving it slowly up the inside of his leg. "I'm sure that's what all those years in jail will do to you."

"What was his relationship with Billie like?"

The toe hesitates precariously near his crotch. "It was kind of a love/hate thing. Intense. She sure didn't love his drug problems. They fought a lot about that."

What part should he be more concerned about? The love part or the hate? "Do you know where he lives now?"

"Why would I know that?" She laughs. The foot makes contact with his groin. "It was a pretty nomadic scene back then. People came and went a lot; got arrested, moved off to the woods, ended up on the street, died of drug overdoses. No one really kept tabs. We've all gone our own ways since then. I mean, he could be anywhere."

Jonathan thinks of the burned letter; Sidney's fleeting presence at Billie's memorial. *Not anywhere,* he thinks. *Somewhere around here.* "Well, what's his last name? I was thinking I'd look him up."

She slides closer and slips a hand between the buttons of his shirt, tugging gently at the hair there, sending electric shocks across his torso. "No clue," she says. "Everyone had nicknames back then; no one even liked to use their real first names, much less last ones. They were all about 'reject the patriarchal authority,' 'anarchy not hierarchy.' Anonymity was big. Remember? Sparrow? Sidney went by Maverick. A much better name for a radical than Sidney, don'tcha think?"

He's distracted by her hand on his chest. "And who were you?" he asks.

She laughs as she straddles his lap. "Harmony," she whispers. "I've always been Harmony."

There's a small mewling sound, and they look up to see Olive standing in the doorway, watching them. They quickly disentangle themselves, but it's too late.

"Well, that explains a lot," Olive says flatly.

She turns and bolts back up the stairs. They can hear her bare feet slapping across the wooden floors upstairs, and then the slam of the door to her room.

Harmony looks at Jonathan. Her eyes are dilated and dazed, her mouth slightly agape. She slaps a palm across it, suppressing whatever words are trying to come out.

"Shit." Jonathan pushes himself off the couch and dashes after Olive. By the time he gets to her door, breathing heavily, she's already locked it. Through the crack, he can see her shadow, just on the other side of the door.

He knocks quietly. "Go away," she calls out.

"I'm not going away," he says. He waits a minute and knocks again, harder. "I can do this all night."

He hears her exasperated groan through the door—"God. *Fine*"—and then the door swings open, revealing Olive, her face red with self-righteous fury.

He pushes into the room and sits down on the desk chair, kicking aside a pile of books and a filthy-looking towel. Olive remains standing, her arms hanging limply by her sides. Next to him, on her desk, her laptop is open to Google; the search field reads, heartbreakingly, *Sidney Oregon Drug Dealer*. There are 2,770,000 results.

"I'm sorry, sweetheart. I know that what you just saw probably feels like a, a—"

"Betrayal?"

He winces. "Olive. Look. We were already heading into treacherous waters, with the one-year anniversary coming up. And now with all this—speculation—about your mom, and the things you've been seeing . . . I'm sure it's confusing for you, because it's confusing to me. Who knows what any of it really means? There's a lot of big emotions at play here right now. Meanwhile, Harmony, she's been a real comfort to me, and it's natural that I would want to feel—something—again—"

She cuts him off. "When we find Mom, how's she going to feel about you hooking up with Harmony?"

How would *she feel?* He swallows. "I can't live my life based on speculation. Your mom's *not here.*" His voice is sharp, his jaw working up and down.

"Not *yet.*"

He throws up his hands. "What do you want me to say? That I'm going to sit here like a monk forever, just in case?"

She lifts her square chin stubbornly. "No. I want you to say that you're going to find Sidney."

The laptop next to him glows bright in the dim light of her room. It draws his eyes back to it like a beacon. The top Google search result is a recent news story out of Florida: "Mexican Mafia Tied to Car Lot Drug Bust." He can see that she's already clicked through the top seven links, and he understands that his daughter intends to sit here all night, methodically poring over every one of those useless pages. It's painful to imagine.

He gently closes the lid of her laptop, putting the search engine to sleep. "OK," he says. "I will."

13

OLIVE WAKES UP IN the dark with a start, her heart pounding. She lies there as the panic subsides, settling into a familiar sensation—*the feeling of the dreams still clinging to the edges of her mind*. At first she can't pin down what's wrong, just that something has changed in the night. An absence. It's like that memory game you play as a kid: a tray full of objects and you have to close your eyes and open them again and determine which object was removed; and you stare and stare at the tray, an invisible void nagging at you, until the answer hits you.

Mom is gone.

The Depakote has kicked in. Olive lies motionless in bed, taking inventory of the drug's side effects. Weak, slightly queasy, an odd metallic taste in her mouth: check. She feels like a dull pencil. She

tests herself, reaching out with her mind for the reassuring presence of her mother buzzing imperceptibly around the periphery of her consciousness, but
Billie has disappeared. Almost like she was never
there; which maybe she never was. Maybe the visions *were* all a matter of misfiring neurons, a bruise
on the brain and a bad case of nostalgia, the search
for her mother just a wild-goose chase.

She lets herself cry a little bit.

Time passes, she's not sure if it's been minutes or
hours; she's exhausted, but she can't make herself
fall back to sleep. She lies there trying to make her
mother materialize again—trying to *picture* her—
but the image in her head already feels like it's fading, like a photograph left too long in the sun.

Eventually the morning chases the night away, a
thin sunrise leaking gray under the curtains. She can
hear the murmur of voices downstairs—Harmony is
here. Did she sleep over last night? Or did she come
back this morning? Both unappealing scenarios.

After a while she smells breakfast cooking—eggs
and hash browns. Her father never bothers cooking
on weekday mornings, which means that either Harmony has taken over in the kitchen or her father is
showing off. In the cage above her desk, Gizmo burbles happily, rings her bell, waits for Olive to get up
and feed her.

She pulls the covers over her head, and when her
father knocks on her door, murmuring her name,
she doesn't respond. She can hear him come into her
room and pick his way across the minefield of discarded laundry on her floor; and then she feels the

weight of his body depressing the edge of her mattress.

"Who are you hiding from?" he asks.

"I'm not hiding," she says from under the covers.

He gives her foot a little squeeze. "Why don't I believe you?" Then, his voice pleading: "Olive, please. Talk to me, Bean."

"I feel sick," she says into her pillow.

"What variety of sick are we talking about? Sick like the flu? Pinkeye? Or do you mean side effects from the Depakote?" He peels back the covers to expose her face, and she blinks unhappily in the light. Despite her father's expression of concern, he seems distressingly lively this morning, as if he's already polished off a pot of coffee. His cheeks are flushed; he's shaved. She notices that he's holding a cup of water.

"It's the Depakote, I think," she says. "It's making me feel weird. Like, groggy. Queasy."

He looks down at his feet and fishes the Depakote pill bottle off the floor, where she dropped it last night. "Dr. Fishbein said to expect that." He turns the container slowly in his hand. "We'll see where you're at after the weekend and give him a call if you're not feeling better. Until then—" He tips a pill into his hand and hands it to her, along with the glass of water.

"Come *on*, Dad. I'm perfectly capable of taking my own pills." She swallows it down, staring at him balefully over the rim of the water glass. "Why does everyone treat me like a child?"

"Sorry," he says, but he doesn't sound particularly sorry at all. "If you're feeling that bad, you shouldn't go to school today. I'll call the front office."

"Thanks." She rolls over and picks at the peeling tape on one of the photographs above her bed, a snapshot of her and Mom making an igloo up at Lake Tahoe, back when she was just a kid. She still remembers that igloo: They spent all day building it, her mom insisting that it had to *really work,* and when they were done, they built a fire inside it and roasted marshmallows and drank hot apple cider. It was magical, as if they were picnicking on the moon, even though she was sore and her snowsuit was soaked from spending the whole day digging in the snow. Her mom wanted to camp out in it that night, too, but her dad argued that Olive was going to catch pneumonia if she didn't get inside to warm up. "Party pooper," her mom teased him, although Olive felt vaguely relieved that she didn't have to sleep in the snow.

"I have to go into the city today, but I'll have Harmony stay here in case you need anything," her father says.

"*Dad.* Did you not hear what I just said about treating me like a child? I don't need anything. Especially not her." She stares at him accusingly.

Her father sighs. "Call me if it gets any worse."

"I will." Olive pulls the sheet back over her head.

"I love you," he says. She hears him leave the room, but she stays under the covers in the dark until, her head swimming, she falls back asleep.

When she wakes up again, the house is silent. It's somehow already midday. Her stomach growls, so she puts on her fuzzy slippers, wraps herself in an old bathrobe of her mom's that she rescued from her father's discard pile, and goes downstairs to the kitchen. She's shaky and disoriented—maybe from hunger, maybe from Depakote—so she descends slowly, clutching at the railing to keep from falling over.

As she reaches the bottom, she realizes that she's not alone in the house after all: Her father is back; he's in his office, opening and closing drawers. She walks down the hall in his direction.

She swings the door open and stops, confused. Harmony sits at her father's desk, her hand stuck deep in the back of a half-opened drawer. She starts at the sound of the squeaking hinge and turns, freezing when she sees Olive. They stare at each other for a few seconds before Harmony withdraws her hand.

"Looking for a pencil." She laughs, sweeping a chunk of blond hair from one shoulder to the other. "You two seem to have a boycott against them."

Olive points at the pencil jar on the top of the desk. "Take your pick," she says.

Harmony stares at the jar. "Oh gosh, I'm going blind," she says. She selects one and sticks it behind her ear and then stands up. "Can I make you something? Cup of tea? Omelet?"

Olive doesn't move from the doorway. "Why are you here?" she asks pointedly.

"Your dad had a meeting in the city," Harmony says. "He asked me to stay and make sure you were OK. I'm not working today. I was just going to do the crossword."

"That's not what I m—" Olive starts to say, but the

words die in her throat as Harmony walks toward Olive. She stops when she's inches away. Olive tips back, fearing a hug; she can smell Harmony's body lotion, coconut, cloying.

"Olive, look. I don't want this to be awkward between us. I know you miss your mom; we all do. I know this—him and me, together—may seem strange for you. But you have to cut your father a break. Your mom's been dead a year now. We're all just trying to find new paths toward happiness."

Mom's not dead, Olive thinks instinctively, but the urgency of this belief already seems like a relic of a past lifetime. She can't think of anything to say that doesn't sound petulant or childish or insane. The Depakote has fuzzed her edges so that she can't even remember why she felt the need to lash out at Harmony in the first place. Her mind is a muddle.

Harmony blinks at Olive, waiting. Her lips are full and shiny, gloss bleeding out from the faint smile that plays across them; it's the mouth of someone who spends a lot of time thinking about what goes in it. She reminds Olive of a custard, sweetly bland and inoffensively nice. Still, something about her makes Olive feel uneasy. Like she's not as benign as she's pretending she is.

"Yeah, I'll have an omelet," Olive says, and turns and walks back upstairs to her bedroom.

The day inches by with excruciating slowness. Harmony brings an omelet to Olive's room and then quietly, unceremoniously, leaves the house. Olive hears her car start in the driveway and then creeps downstairs to watch nature shows on the Discovery Channel. She can't recall the last time she was home alone during the day. It's so empty that her breath sounds like a hurricane.

Natalie sends her a text at lunchtime—*Why aren't u at school???*—but Olive doesn't respond; Natalie's question requires an answer that seems far too complicated for her to type out on the phone. She pushes the phone under the pillows of the couch and ignores its buzzing as she watches a show about Alaskan hunters who kill animals for their fur. She feels bad for the poor dead animals; and then she feels bad for the hunters, who are, after all, just trying to survive; and then she feels bad for herself most of all.

At three, after Claremont Prep has gotten out for the day, Olive pulls a hoodie over her pajamas and digs the keys to the Subaru out of the drawer in the front hall. She drives herself to Natalie's house, a few miles up into the Oakland Hills.

Natalie lives in a two-story Tudor with timber frames and leaded glass, a tidy English garden in front, manicured ivy and roses. Wisteria creeps up the facing, a few last withered leaves clutching the vines. The plants have all been cut back for the winter, and the front grass smells like cow manure.

She texts Natalie from the car, suddenly unsure of herself: *U home? I'm here*

Why r u sitting outside my house in ur car, silly

OK coming in

Natalie meets her at the front door in skull-and-crossbones sweatpants and a T-shirt that reads THIS IS WHAT A FEMINIST LOOKS LIKE. She is mid-manicure, waving her hands in the air to dry the polish. She steps aside to let Olive in. "You missed fetal pig dissection today," Natalie says. "It was pretty cool, actually."

Olive shudders. "Not so cool for the poor pig."

"They give their life for a greater cause." Natalie ushers Olive to her bedroom with a sweep of her arm. "Come into my boo-dwoir."

Natalie's room looks like a Pinterest page, all throw pillows and drapery and framed art prints, a duvet cover with her initials monogrammed in purple, and an egg chair upholstered entirely in fake fur that Olive is pretty sure she saw listed for eighteen hundred dollars in a Restoration Hardware catalog. Natalie is doing her best to trash the place. There's a big black footprint right in the middle of the duvet, a torn Bikini Kill poster Scotch-taped over the Monet print that Natalie's mom hung there, dirty tights hanging off the top of the chair.

Olive flops back on the bed and kicks off her shoes. Natalie curls up at the other end of the bed and resumes attacking her fingernails with a bottle of particularly hideous neon-orange polish.

"We going to do anything for Halloween this year?" Natalie asks. "I was thinking I'd be Maleficent. Maybe you could be the Evil Queen from *Snow White*?" She squints, assessing Olive. "Though I don't know if you're capable of pulling off *evil*."

Olive thinks of the depressing pumpkins that are sitting uncarved on their front porch. "I'm boycotting Halloween this year."

"Too many ghosts in your life right now?" Natalie catches Olive's wounded expression. "Wow, that was totally insensitive of me. Sorry."

"That's OK," Olive says. "It's kind of true."

Natalie finishes her left hand and looks at Olive. "Want me to do your feet?"

Olive nods, sitting up. Natalie picks up Olive's right foot and plops it into her lap. Her hand, holding Olive's heel, is cool and sure.

"Stop giggling," she says. "You're going to make me mess up."

"It tickles," Olive says.

"Think about getting Odor Eaters? Your feet stink." But Natalie keeps applying the polish in tiny strokes as Olive's foot warms in her hand.

"My toes look like they belong to someone else," Olive says, staring at her orange nails. "Like a clown or a Japanese schoolgirl."

"Camouflage," Natalie says. "It'll help you blend in with the natives."

"Is that the goal? To blend in?"

Natalie wrinkles her nose. "Depends on who you ask." She furrows her brow and rubs at a smear of polish. "You're not exactly disappearing these days, if that's what you want to be doing."

"Who says I want to disappear?"

Natalie gives her a long look. "So are you going to tell me what's up your butt? You bailed out of school yesterday and then didn't show up at all today and you didn't even text me why. Mrs. Santiago is walking around wringing her hands like you're dying of consumption in a Romantic novel. Ming thinks you just want attention."

"Oh, great." Olive stares at a bug on Natalie's

ceiling, clinging upside down to the decorative molding. "I so don't give a shit what Ming thinks."

Natalie makes a face. She examines her handiwork and then pushes Olive's foot off her lap. "So are you going to tell me what's going on?"

"The Depakote that the doctor gave me made my visions stop," she says. "I can't see my mom anymore."

Natalie frowns. "What does that mean?"

"It means I'm not psychic after all. Just brain-damaged. Some kind of epileptic or whatever he called it. A mental case." She says it flippantly, but the muscles around her mouth seem determined to tip downward; a fresh torrent of tears bursts forth from her eyes, and suddenly, she's just a puddle of woe in the middle of her best friend's bed.

"Oh," Natalie says, understanding. "Oh, *shit*."

She scoots closer to Olive, her still-wet fingernails leaving a sticky streak of orange polish across the duvet cover, and puts her arms around her.

"You just ruined your bedspread," Olive says, sobbing into Natalie's shoulder. "It's such a nice bedspread. Like a thousand thread count or something."

"I don't give a crap about this hideous bedspread." Natalie squeezes Olive tighter. She smells scalpy and sweet, like she didn't shower after PE today. "Look. I know this sucks for you. But maybe it's still possible that your mom is alive, even if she wasn't actually communicating with you, like, clairvoyantly?"

Olive shakes her head and sniffles. "We never really found anything conclusive." A curl of Natalie's hair ends up in her nostril, and she sneezes wetly. "Sorry. Now I got snot in your hair."

Natalie shrugs. "Doesn't matter." Olive pulls back a little to look at her. Natalie's face is flushed and pink, the tip of her tongue probing the top of her lip. She takes Olive's hand. "I wish I knew how to make you feel better."

Olive can feel Natalie's heartbeat, hot and fast and pulsing, just below the surface of her skin. She is acutely aware of Natalie's breath a few inches away from her face. She turns her own head, catching on to an electric thread, something sizzling and magnetic passing through her, and before she can stop herself, she presses her lips against Natalie's.

Natalie's lips are smooth and surprisingly cool, like soft-serve ice cream on a hot day. Olive thinks she might pass out because her heart is beating so fast. In those fleeting few moments, a whole new future opens up before Olive, like a door opening to reveal a view whose existence she always suspected but could never quite see.

I love you, she thinks. (But . . . oh shit, did she say that out loud?)

And then Natalie lurches away, and there's only empty air where her lips were a minute earlier. Olive is left hanging there in space, and she vainly wishes to freeze this moment in time, because she knows that in the next second everything is going to change forever and not for the better.

"That's not what I meant," Natalie mumbles. She's gone pale, her freckles flaming bright against her face. She scoots away until her back is against the headboard.

"I'm sorry," says Olive, as humiliation balloons inside her until it feels like it might burst through her skin. "I don't know what that was about."

Natalie gives her a sideways look. "C'mon, Olive. Even *I* know what that was about. You're a lesbian. Which, whatever, I figured that out a while ago. Totally cool, you know? Yay for rejecting heteronormativity. But, see, I'm *not*."

Olive imagines a needle pushed into her chest, pinning her to a display case, the label below her: LESBIAN. It doesn't hurt, exactly. It's more like something inside her is spilling out through the hole that's opened up, and it's kind of exciting and mind-boggling. *Is it true?* she asks herself. *Is that what I am?* But she can't stop to answer this question, because the more pressing issue right now is the imminent loss of her best friend. Because despite what Natalie just said—*Yay lesbian!*—when Olive looks at her friend backed up against the headboard, it looks like she's a million miles away.

"Got it," Olive says. "Anyway, I'll go now." She flings herself off the edge of the bed, almost falling over from a head rush of dizziness—the Depakote side effects kicking back in at the least opportune moment—and fumbles for her shoes.

"You don't have to leave," says Natalie, but something stiff and awkward has crept in around her words, and Olive senses that she *does* have to go, and fast, before this all gets worse.

"Mmm, yeah, gotta run." She shoves her feet into her shoes, marring the fresh paint on her toenails, and leans over to find the car keys that have slid off the mattress to the floor. She finds them under the dust ruffle, stippled with the tears that slip out of her eyes once she's safely out of Natalie's line of sight.

Wiping her face, she stands and turns. "How did you know? That I was a lesbian. Because *I* didn't even know. Not really." Maybe she *did* know, though, because she can feel the logic of it all clicking into place, like a critical piece of a puzzle she's been staring at for the better part of the last year. *Did my mom see it?* she wonders suddenly. Maybe that's what her mom meant when she lectured Olive about finding her own thing and being whoever she wants to be; maybe that was why she got so frustrated with Olive all the time. Maybe Billie could see in Olive the things that Olive was incapable of seeing in herself. For a moment, before she can think straight, she imagines going home and asking her mother about it, maybe even crying in her lap a little, and then she remembers that her mother isn't there anymore and apparently never will be again.

Natalie shrugs. "Well, you don't really care about boys. And that's kind of a giveaway."

"Right." Olive backs toward the door. She stops, thinking of something else: "You won't say anything, will you?"

Natalie frowns. "It's not like it's something to be ashamed of. In fact, it's kind of cool, you know? Lesbianism is very on-trend. Even more so if you decide to, like, cross-dress or transition—"

Olive cuts her off, feeling queasy. "Please?"

Her friend looks abashed. "OK, sure."

As she's halfway out the door, she hears Natalie's murmur: "I'll see you at school Monday." Olive thinks she hears something hopeful in Natalie's voice, something that makes her wonder if she should turn around and go back to her; as though Natalie is as worried about everything that was just forever-fucked as Olive is.

But it's too late.

"Probably not," she says.

She drives back down the hill toward her house. Under the shivering canopy of oak trees that line Tunnel Road; past the Claremont Hotel, which looms over the road like a colossal wedding cake; through the parking snarl by the monstrous new Safeway. She cruises down into her own neighborhood, slightly shabbier, more bohemian, but when it comes time to turn right onto her own street, she keeps going.

It feels good to be in her mother's car, cocooned, the heat blasting, the worn-in foam of the seat molding to her rump. The overcast sky speckles a thin sheen of moisture on the windshield. Halloween pumpkins rot into goo on the porches of the houses she passes; plastic ghouls drag themselves out of landscaped lawns; skeletons jangle from tree limbs. She usually loves Halloween, but this year, the shivery promise of the dead coming back to life just makes her feel depressed.

She turns the dial of the radio until she gets to the Berkeley college station, which is playing some kind of retro funk, and lets the music guide her west toward the bay. Then south; and west again, over the San Mateo Bridge. The sun sets; traffic thickens and slows like clotting blood. She tells herself that she's not going anywhere in particular, just driving, but when the Subaru finally sputters to a stop, she looks up and isn't at all surprised to see that she's in front of Sharon Parkins's house.

It's dark out now, but every window in Sharon's house is illuminated. The cypress trees sway in the evening breeze, describing lazy circles in the sky. As Olive walks up the driveway, she can hear the faint sounds of opera, something Italian and dramatic. Her teeth chatter: She's still in her pajamas, not even a coat.

She knocks and waits.

The person who opens the door is a man, older, about her dad's age. He's got bulgy eyes and a square chin and is wearing a button-down shirt and slacks with fuzzy plaid slippers. He stares at Olive, perplexed. "Can I help you?" he asks.

Just then Sharon appears behind him, holding a brimming glass of red wine in her hand, her breasts nearly toppling out of a low-cut fuzzy yellow sweater. She slips around her husband and grips Olive's elbow, tugging her into the house. "It's OK, honey. I know her," she says as she steers Olive toward the living room and away from him.

"Make it fast," she says in a low voice. "My husband doesn't like me doing this. He says it creeps him out. Plus, the legal liability, you know?" She holds the wine aloft so that it won't spill. "So what's up? Did you see something?"

Olive drops down on the couch in the same place she sat last time. Nothing in the room has changed since she was here last: the skewered carousel horse still cantering in space, the skinned bear still staring, stoic, into the distance. "No," she says. "That's the problem. I'm not seeing her anymore." And she bursts into tears.

Sharon freezes. She sits down next to Olive on the couch, setting the wineglass on an agate coaster on the table. "Oh, honey. I warned you," she says softly. "There's nothing logical about this. It's not predictable."

Olive wipes her nose with the back of her sleeve. "My doctor said I was having seizures. They put me on Depakote."

Sharon's face goes flat. "Oh. *Hell*." She picks up her wine and drinks half of it down.

"And the visions stopped. So that means they're right, doesn't it? My mom was always just a hallucination? There was no significance to any of it, the visions or the butterfly beach or the woman at the nursing home, it was just my mind making connections because I wanted them to exist."

Sharon sets down her wine and tentatively reaches out to rub Olive's back, her hand moving in small, stiff circles. It's clear to Olive that Sharon hasn't spent much time around kids or she'd know that this is the correct time for a maternal hug. "I'm not a doctor. But think about it." She gives Olive's back a last pat and quickly withdraws her hand. "Of course you're going to stop seeing your mom when you start taking medication. Depakote—that stuff's no joke. It's messing with the chemistry of your brain. You're blunting *everything* going on in there." She glances at the door and drops her voice. "Look. I drink too much for a reason: same effect. It turns it all off when I don't want it there. And Depakote is way stronger than a glass of wine."

Olive's phone is ringing insistently in the pocket of her hoodie. She pulls it out and glances at it—it's her father, probably wondering where she is. She hits Decline and looks up at Sharon. "Then how do I know if the doctor is right or not? How do I know if what I saw was real?"

Sharon shrugs. "Does it matter? It was real to you. Maybe that's the only thing that counts." She leans in closer. "No one else can tell you what's happening inside your head. You're the only one who could possibly know. They can't. I can't." She looks over again at the doorway, where the shadow of her husband is hovering, as if he's trying to stay out of sight in the hallway.

Olive leans in conspiratorially. "But you saw something, right? That day in my mom's car?"

Sharon picks up her wine and stares into the bottom of her glass, swirling it so hard that it looks like the remaining wine might splash over the edge. "You love your mom, right? You really miss her? That's what this is all about?"

Olive nods, not liking where this is going.

Sharon gives a little shake of her head. She stands up, finishing off her drink with one smooth tilt of her neck. "Let's leave it that way, then. Look, I've got dinner on the stove. And your dad is trying to get in touch with you, isn't he? He's probably wondering where you are. *Go home*. I can't solve anything for you."

Olive refuses to budge from the couch. "That's it? That's all you've got for me? 'Go home'?"

Sharon wipes up a spilled drop of wine from the coffee table with the edge of her hand. She licks the wine off her skin with a shockingly pink tongue. "What do you want me to say?"

"Tell me what you would do."

"You tell me what *you* think I'd do."

Olive thinks. "You'd toss the drugs."

Sharon shrugs. "I'm not going to say that. I just think—" She hesitates and then leans down and whispers in Olive's ear, so quietly that Olive isn't sure if she's heard correctly. "I wouldn't let anyone stop me from seeing something I really want to see."

She starts walking to the doorway, where the shadow of her husband has vanished; but halfway there, she stops. She turns around to face Olive. "And don't worry about your friend, she'll get over it soon enough," she says. She offers a faint apologetic smile. "Someday soon you're going to find someone who loves you back."

WHERE THE MOUNTAIN MEETS THE SKY

My Life with Billie Flanagan

BY JONATHAN FLANAGAN

F our hundred people attended Billie's memorial. At the time I thought this was evidence that my wife had been universally beloved, but looking back, weren't they mostly gawkers who wanted to claim their little piece of the most exciting thing that had happened to a Claremont Mom since that time Sofia Drumm got arrested for tax fraud? How many of them really know the first thing about my wife?

It should have been obvious to me on our wedding day that Billie didn't let *anyone* get close to her for long. That day in Big Sur, our guests predominantly filled my side of the aisle—my parents, my work colleagues, my college pals—whereas hers was populated with a smattering of art school friends, friends who would vanish entirely in the years to come.

Back then I figured that Billie was a bit of a lone wolf, struggling to ground herself after all those itinerant years, and working too hard to establish much of a social network of her own. Another reason she needed my love and support. Another reason we needed to have a kid and build our own cozy little unit of three.

But the years passed and the pattern continued. She was always surrounded by people, and her social calendar was packed; but close friends tended to come and go as Billie grew impatient with their shortcomings and moved on. I can still see the faces that passed through our house, and I remember their flaws as Billie articulated them to me: Jane, the anti-vaxx hardliner with no understanding of *science;* Emma, the depressive who talked incessantly about leaving her creepy exhibitionist husband but never did anything about it; Trudi, who launched a GoFundMe to raise fourteen thousand dollars for cancer treatments for her eighteen-year-old blind Chihuahua but refused to buy Girl Scout cookies when Olive came around *because sugar*. These women would sit at our dining room table, stuffing envelopes with Claremont spring fundraiser invitations, gossiping with Billie as they worked their way through a bottle of pinot; and then one day, out of the blue, they'd be gone.

"I just *couldn't* anymore," Billie would say when I asked about someone, and she'd make a face. "I have no patience at all for her special brand of bullshit."

The thing was—I secretly *liked* this about her. I liked the way it made me feel so chosen. Other people might come and go, but *I* was the one she really loved. She held the bar so very, very high, and Olive and I were the only ones who made the cut. It made me feel closer to her.

But now that she's gone, I have to wonder: Was that bar so impossibly high that no one, not even Olive or I, could hang on to it for long? Did our particular brand of bullshit finally cross the threshold of her limits? Should I have realized, that day in Big Sur when I smiled blindly out at a crowd comprised almost entirely of my friends, that I was marrying a woman who didn't want to be known by anyone—not even me?

If I dig back far enough in Billie's history, will I finally find someone who knows what was really going on inside her?

14

THE *DECODE* MEDIA OFFICE is on the eighth floor of a generic building in a neighborhood of San Francisco that a few years earlier was known for its transients and nightclubs but now features a dozen blindingly new office buildings and luxury condo towers, with more on the way. In order to get to the *Decode* entrance, Jonathan has to pass through a scaffolding walkway, kicking aside neon-pink flyers advertising escorts and tarot readings. The air smells like urine and roasting coffee.

He hasn't been here since the day, eight months earlier, when he quit his job. Looking around, he experiences an unexpected pang of nostalgia. The daily trudge from the BART station, the cheese roll from the café in the foyer, the early-morning hum of a hundred computers in an empty office: the soothing *normalcy* of it all. What exactly was it about this place that he grew to loathe, anyway? Why did he throw it all away? From his vantage point now, *Decode* is as inviting as a beanbag chair, as if he could sink back in and stay there forever because it's too damn hard to get back up.

At the front desk, the receptionist, a blue-haired kid Jonathan doesn't recognize, asks him to sit down while he summons Desi, Jonathan's former investigative assistant. Jonathan settles stiffly into a couch as magazine staffers pass by, waiting for someone to recognize him. They look harried, focused on the vital urgency of whatever tidbit of news the world is obsessed with today.

They'll cry when you leave and buy you a Costco cake with your name on it and then forget about you ten minutes later when they replace you with someone younger and fresher and cheaper.

He sips at his complimentary bottle of water, pecks around on his cellphone, idly checking the ip-Tracer app without much hope. He's uploaded the entire memoir to the website at this point, hundreds of pages of increasingly vitriolic ramblings about his wife; what more of a lure can he give her?

Your page has been visited by 1 unique IP address.

He has to read this twice before he's sure he's not hallucinating. He stares at the IP address, just a string of meaningless numbers, and then realizes he can click on the number for further information. He clicks.

The app churns for a half second, then spits back an answer:

Continent: North America
Country: United States
City: New York
ISP: Random House

It's his *publisher.*

Oh, crap, he thinks. On cue, the phone in his hand starts to ring, his agent's name appearing on the screen. JEFF FREELS.

Reluctantly, he answers. "Hi, Jeff," he says, forcing sunshine into his voice.

"Jonathan, what the hell?" The spit in his agent's voice sizzles on the line. "Your editor just called me, he says he just stumbled across the manuscript of your book online? He says you're self-publishing it as a . . . as a blog? Is that right?"

Jonathan stares at a stain on the rug that's the exact shape of Brazil. "It wasn't self-published, exactly. I didn't expect anyone to see it."

"Yeah, well, your editor came across it easy enough with a Google search on your wife's name. Don't you understand that you *do not own* that book anymore? You cashed a check, *they* own it. You don't have the right to self-publish. They can sue you for that."

"I'll take it down," Jonathan says.

"Good, but that's only half the problem." His agent sounds on the verge of apoplexy. "Apparently it's not even the book you told him you were writing. He says it makes Billie sound like some kind of raging bitch. Like you're hashing out all your marital issues with her on the page. Like maybe you're not so sad that she's gone after all. Is that true?"

Jonathan considers this. "It's all a little complicated right now."

Jeff's voice hits high volume; Jonathan has to hold the phone away from his ear. "Jesus, Jonathan. This is supposed to be a *grief* memoir. What happened? This was your great lost love?"

The blue-haired receptionist is staring at him. Jonathan lowers his voice. "Things . . . changed."

"Well, Elliot says that if this is the book you plan to turn in, he doesn't want it. So you better rethink your direction fast. You've only got, what, three months to finish this thing?"

"I don't know if I can write that book anymore," Jonathan says quietly.

There's a long, slow intake of breath on the other end of the line. "OK, I get that maybe you're feeling something you weren't expecting to feel when you started writing this thing. That happens. But can't you put that aside for the purposes of the book? It's called artistic license."

Jonathan's stomach turns as he considers the question he's been avoiding for the last few weeks. Can he fake it? For the sake of his book deal? For the sake of his very livelihood? He thinks of a line he read in *The New York Times Book Review* not long ago—a review written by Gregory Cowles, of a Mary Karr book—that landed painfully close to home: *All memoirs are lies, even those that tell the truth. They can't help it, because the longer we live the more our fixed pasts keep changing.* And yet he doesn't even have a narrative to seize on anymore; he can't get a grip on his own protagonist. Was she a fundamentally good person? A monster? Something in between? Both at the same time? How can he possibly finish a book about her when he doesn't know who she really was? Or still *is*?

"I don't know," he says at last.

There's a long silence. When Jeff speaks again, he sounds completely deflated. "You realize what this means? You'll lose your contract. You'll have to pay back your advance. Do you even have that kind of money lying around?"

Jonathan swallows back the bile that rises at the thought of this sum.

"Jonathan?" Desi stands in front of him. From where he sits on the couch, he's eye level with her big black boots and a sweater that sweeps down to her knees.

"Jeff, look, I've got to run. Just . . . tell them I'm sorry. I'll figure something out." He hangs up and then pushes himself upright so that he's towering over her; when she hugs him, he feels something pushing against him. "Desi . . . You're . . . ?"

"Pregnant," she says. "You'd think I was a leper, the way the kids here treat me. No one wants to sit next to me at the story meetings. I think they believe they might catch it if they accidentally touch me."

He follows her through the maze of cubicles, which has shifted since he was here last: new routes leading to entirely new destinations and a sea of faces he doesn't recognize. A few people pop up to call his name from across the room, wave a quick greeting, but everyone's too lost in deadline to chat. "A lot of new hires?" he asks hopefully. *If Decode is doing well, maybe they'll be able to hire me back.*

Six months back on salary and I'll have enough to reimburse my publishers.

She rolls her eyes. "Last spring it was all about longform, right? Then upper management starting freaking out that investigative journalism cost too much money. As of this fall we're going for utility: all explainers and charts. The new guy who replaced you brought in a bunch of kids from L.A. to make video content, but honestly, it's a sinking ship. I think layoffs are looming." She sighs.

"*Decode* always pulls through," he says, trying to remain positive. "*Decode* is the cockroach of the digital media age, you just can't kill it."

She laughs. "You had the right idea, go do your own thing, write a book. All that glorious *time*. Going to bed before midnight. No middle-of-the-night emails or six A.M. deadlines. It sounds like heaven."

"You have no idea," he says.

In her cubicle, Desi clears magazines off a stained IKEA armchair and motions him to sit. A strange whirring noise: He looks up and sees that someone is flying a toy drone over the heads of the writers. It hovers a few cubicles away; he hears someone swear, and a hand pops up in the air and gives the drone the finger. The drone swerves out of reach, wobbles a bit, and then zooms off toward the conference room.

"So, show me what you need." Desi settles in before her screens.

He slides the Polaroid toward her: Sidney and Billie peering out at him from 1992. Maverick and Sparrow. Desi picks up the photograph by its edges and peers at it closely. After a minute, she does a double take. "Is that *Billie*?"

"I'm interested in the guy she's with," he says. "I need to figure out who he is. All I know is his first name—Sidney—and that he was in jail in Oregon for drug dealing. Early nineties. Can you help me dig up his full name?"

"Shit, pre-Internet, huh? Well, there are options," she says. She puts the photograph in her scanner and loads it up on her screen. She crops his face out of the picture and opens a new Photoshop window, zooming in for a close-up portrait. "I can try an image search in a few databases, run it past NICAR. Let me see what that turns up."

He sits in the chair behind her and waits, flipping through a three-month-old copy of *The Atlantic*. The newsroom buzzes and clicks and murmurs around him, a familiar white noise. Eventually Desi whispers something under her breath and then turns around. "Found him. Check this out."

She tilts the screen of her computer so he can see. It's a mugshot of a man—a boy, really—in front of a blue background, staring crookedly at the camera with a stunned, glassy expression. His hair is longer than it is in the other photo, his beard bushier, and his face more gaunt, but there's no question: It's Sidney.

"Sidney Kaufman," Desi reads. "Arrested in Bend, Oregon."

"Convicted of drug dealing?"

She types again and frowns. "Yes, and a whole lot of other things."

He peers over her shoulder. "Like what?"

"Arson, attempted manslaughter."

"*Manslaughter?*" He watches as Desi plugs some keywords into a database and pulls up an old news brief from *The Oregonian*.

Sidney Kaufman was convicted today of four charges, including attempted manslaughter, conspiracy to use fire or explosives to damage corporate and government property, and possessing a controlled substance with intent to sell. Kaufman and his co-conspirator, Vincent Sparto, were arrested earlier this year for setting a series of firebombs that destroyed several properties, including a wild mustang shelter and a U.S. Department of Agriculture dam. Caught in the act of sabotaging a ski resort, Kaufman critically wounded an officer of the law. Estimates put the amount of damage at $18 million. Sparto pleaded not guilty by reason of insanity and was committed to psychiatric care. Kaufman faces 25 years in prison.

"He was an ecoterrorist," Jonathan says out loud. His mind spinning, adding up the details. The years out in the woods. His wife's talk about being "scared straight" when she left the Pacific Northwest; her alarming reaction when she got the letter. His stomach drops. Jesus, was *this* why she fled the Pacific Northwest all those years ago? She found out her boyfriend was some kind of sociopath?

"Sounds like it." Desi sits back and distractedly runs a hand across the taut weave of her sweater.

"Can you find out when he was released?"

She turns back to her computer and types again. "About two years ago." Just when Billie's string of deception began, he realizes. Christ, maybe Olive was right: Maybe Billie *was* in danger. A murderous sociopath, who reportedly had an obsessive relationship with his wife, gets out of jail; and within the year, she disappears? It can't be a coincidence. He feels like he might throw up.

Desi looks over her shoulder at him. "Is this for the memoir or something? He was an old friend of Billie's?"

"He was her boyfriend."

"Oh, wow." She spins her chair to face him, sliding down in her seat to take the pressure off her belly. "Did she know what he was doing?"

The drone passes overhead again, stopping to hover a few feet above Jonathan's head. He notices that there's a GoPro camera attached to its frame, and it's aimed at his face. He wonders who's watching him and what that person thinks he's seeing. Jonathan stares directly into the lens for a minute, the drone shivering in the air above him; and then abruptly, he stands up and bats it across the corridor. The drone smashes into the wall and falls, whining noisily, to the ground.

"Only one way to find out." He sits back down. "Can you figure out where this guy lives now?"

He calls Harmony as he winds his way across San Francisco, tailing a Muni streetcar up over Noe Valley and toward the outer Mission. (The J Church, he notices, with no small amount of irony.) Harmony answers on the third ring. "Hey, baby," she says. "I'm not at your place anymore—"

He cuts her off. "Did Billie know that Sidney was an ecoterrorist?" he asks. "I just found out the guy was setting off bombs! He was convicted of attempted *manslaughter*!"

There's a long silence on the other end of the phone. "How did you find that out?"

"Newspaper reports. I was doing research for the memoir," he says. "So *did* she know?"

Harmony's voice goes cool in a way that he's never heard before. "Why do you think she left him?"

The streetcar squeals to a stop in front of him, and he jams on the brakes. "Did she leave him before or after he got arrested?"

It takes a long time for Harmony to respond. "Jonathan," she says carefully. "Billie *turned him in*."

He feels disoriented, the world flipping upside down again. Could Sidney have gotten out of jail and come looking for vengeance? The missing money—maybe it was some sort of emergency fund that Billie started, thinking she might have to flee from Sidney in order to save her own life. Was she in hiding from *him*? Or worse: Jonathan closes his eyes and sees his wife hiking up in Desolation Wilderness, Sidney tight on her heels, waiting for the right moment to strike.

A kid getting off the J Church stares through the windshield at Jonathan, probably wondering why the guy driving the Prius looks like he was just punched in the face. "Why didn't she tell me?"

There's another void-like silence, as if a thumb has been pressed over the receiver. When Harmony speaks again, her words are sharp and precise. "Billie wanted to put all that behind her. She wanted to forget it ever happened."

The streetcar lurches forward again and Jonathan creeps along behind it, growing impatient with its glacial speed, with Harmony, with everyone. "And you? You could have told me the other day, when I asked you about him."

"She made me promise not to say anything. I was just being true to her request." She is pleading now. "Don't be upset. Honestly, Jonathan, it was all so long ago. Decades!" Her voice gets small. "Are you mad at me?"

He *is* mad at her, irrationally angry. *Don't you see? All this time I might have been going down the wrong path, furious at Billie when I should have been worried about her.* But then he reminds himself, *That's not fair.* Harmony doesn't know what he's been going through. It's his own fault for not filling her in.

"No. I'm not mad at you. Don't worry about it." He sees his destination looming ahead. "Sorry, I gotta go. I'll call later."

Sidney Kaufman lives in a peeling gray apartment building in the outskirts of the Excelsior District. Jonathan parks in front of a boarded-up corner store and walks up the street to Sidney's building, past a salon called Gla-more Nails and a café painted in graffiti portraits of hip-hop stars with oddly macrocephalic heads. The area is socked in by dense fog, and by the time Jonathan gets to the front door, his wool coat is dripping with condensation.

He locates Sidney Kaufman's name written in slanted handwriting on a piece of peeling tape next to buzzer number six. He steps back and peers up at the windows of the building, all of which have their backs turned against the outside world. One set of windows is covered over with cardboard, another with broken venetian blinds; then there are paisley curtains; sun-faded Ron Paul campaign signs from several elections back; a sagging sheet; peeling tinfoil. Jonathan considers the windows, wondering which one belongs to Kaufman. Does he have something up there that needs to be hidden?

(My wife?)

Jonathan presses the buzzer. The bell sputters, an electric crackle. No one answers. He cups his hands against the scratched glass of the vestibule and looks in, but the only thing to see is a water-damaged telephone book, dismantled in pieces on the floor, and a pile of take-out menus for a Chinese restaurant.

A powerful smell of curry wafts on the fog from someone's apartment, and Jonathan realizes he hasn't eaten anything since the breakfast that Harmony cooked for him this morning. He heads back down the street to the café, which turns out to be fairly cheery, a neighborhood kind of place with cling-wrapped pastries the size of his head. Scone and coffee in hand, he walks back and settles in a doorway across the street from Sidney's apartment, waiting for him to show up.

An hour passes, and no one comes in or out of

the building. It's not even five o'clock, but somewhere beyond the fog, the sun is already setting. A persistent wind picks up, blowing down the hill, piercing through the lapels of his coat. The trickle of pedestrians picks up, mostly Chinese and Latino commuters making the trek back home from the Balboa Park BART station.

As he sits there, he finds himself thinking, oddly, of Jenny. For a long time after his sister died, he clung to the idea that she might be a ghost: still by his side, keeping him company, even if he couldn't see her. Later, he grew to think of her as a kind of invisible cheerleader, urging him on when he got drunk for the first time, asked out a girl he liked, learned to snowboard. Her voice in his head, cutting through the self-doubt: *Don't be so afraid.* But that stopped once he was in his late twenties, with Billie in his bed and Olive the next room over. Instead of being a tangible presence, Jenny faded into something more abstract, a pang that would strike him at unexpected moments and make his eyes tear up at the half-forgotten sensation of loss.

What would it be like to have Jenny here now, as his sounding board? Would she have been a voice of reason, able to put this mess into perspective? Would she have instinctively understood Billie in a way that he apparently can't? He closes his eyes and tries to envision her as an adult, but all he can see is a ten-year-old girl frozen in time, a tanned tomboy worried about nothing more than sprained ankles and missing homework. She has no advice to offer him today. Who knows whom she might have turned into; who knows whether they even would have been close.

He is alone in this.

He startles when the door of the building across the street slams with a loud bang. He looks up and sees a young woman in a rainbow-colored sweater-coat exit from the building across the street. She heads toward a hatchback Volkswagen and fumbles for her keys.

He darts across the street, intercepting the woman in front of her car. She's holding a pet carrier under her arm, and a very angry cat mewls from inside it. "Hi, can I ask you a quick question?" he asks.

She whips around, taking in his damp hair and limp clothes, and takes a step back, holding the pet carrier between them as a shield. He holds up his hands. "I'm not a stalker or a weirdo, I swear. I'm just trying to find someone that I think lives in your building."

She hesitates, long enough for him to dig the photograph out of his pocket. When he holds it up, she glances at it quickly, and her face relaxes. "Oh, him. Yeah, he lives a floor below me."

"What's he like?" he says. "Scary? Dangerous?"

"What? Um, *no*?" She frowns, still backed up against the Volkswagen. "I mean, I don't know him well. But he says hi in the stairway. Not everyone does that."

"He nearly killed a police officer," Jonathan says sharply. "He set off a bunch of bombs and spent twenty-four years in jail."

"*Really?*" The girl looks horrified. "Him? Are you sure?"

Jonathan nods. "You wouldn't happen to know if he has a woman hidden up there, would you? You ever hear strange sounds, like, you know, someone's being held against their will?"

The girl's eyebrows rocket north. "Ohmygod, no!" She frowns. "Do you think I need to move? Is he a predator or something?"

"I'm sure you're fine," Jonathan reassures her.

She doesn't look convinced. "Sorry, but I have to go. I've got a vet appointment, and I'm going to be late," she says, swinging open the driver's door. Before she climbs in, though, she takes one glance back down at the photograph in his hand. She hesitates. "I've seen her, too," she says.

His heart flips. "Her?" He stupidly points to Billie, as if there might be another woman in the photo.

"Yeah," she says. "She looks a lot different now. Older. More conservative. But yeah, I'm pretty sure I saw her. A few times."

He looks back up at the apartment building, with its rows of blinded windows. "Recently?"

The girl shakes her head. "It was a while back, definitely not in at least a year. I remember because the last time they were yelling at each other so loud you could hear them in my apartment?"

He looks at the picture. "And then what happened?"

The girl shrugs. "She left. I watched her drive off." She slides into the driver's seat and turns the key in the ignition. The cat in the backseat lets out a furious yowl. "Gotta go. My cat ate an M&M."

He watches her pull out of her parking space, lurching inch by inch until she's free, and then creep slowly off down the street. It's starting to get dark. The streetlights flip on, *click click click,* casting the street in a sickly sulfurous glow. His phone beeps with a text message from Olive: *At Natalie's, home soon.*

He digs in his coat pockets until he finds the crumpled receipt from the café and a stub of pencil. He thinks for a minute, questions spinning in his mind. But the paper is too tiny for nuance, so he writes six words—*I need to talk to you*—and adds his name and phone number. Then he slips it into Sidney's mailbox.

He examines the apartment building windows one last time. The tinfoil, he decides. Maybe the cardboard. And then he jogs back toward his car to try to beat the rush-hour traffic home.

15

OLIVE IS PRETTY SURE that her dad is hungover when he takes her out to brunch on Sunday morning. His breath still has alcohol on it, there's a suspicious smell of cigarette smoke threading his hair, and his eyes are bloodshot. This worries her: The last time she saw him like this was in those awful months after her mom first disappeared, when she would sometimes hear him stumbling around the house in the middle of the night like a confused poltergeist.

He sits across from her at some fancy new restaurant a few blocks from their house, the kind of place where the egg dishes have French names and the salt on the table is pink. It's the exact opposite of the café they used to go to all the time with her mom—a local institution dating back to the People's Park days that sold fruit Danish and tofu scrambles and had a bunch of old guys playing bluegrass on weekends.

Her father nurses a black coffee, the hollows under his eyes slowly disappearing.

She picks at her breakfast. "My eggs are runny," she observes.

He peers over at her plate. "No, they're just cooked the French way."

"I don't know why we didn't just go to Emmy's," she says, stirring them into goo on her plate.

"I needed a change from Emmy's," he says as he lifts a spoon of bruléed oatmeal to his mouth. "We've been there too many times."

She drags a triangle of toast through the mess on her plate and sucks the egg off. There's some kind of early Halloween festival taking place on the street, little kids in costumes thronging the stores, collecting candy in plastic jack-o'-lantern buckets. Queen Elsa and Spider-Man toddle past the window, their mouths stuffed with lollipops. Elsa stops and peers in the window at Olive, then sticks out her tongue.

Startled, Olive makes a face back at the girl. The little girl rolls her tongue from left to right. After a moment, Olive realizes that the girl can't even see her. She's just examining her purple tongue in the reflection.

"I wonder if their parents know that food coloring is toxic," she says out loud. She looks back at her father and realizes that he's staring intently at her, as if he's trying to see right through her skin and skull and into her brain. "Dad, stop it," she says finally.

"What?"

"You're staring at me," she says.

He blinks. "Just wondering if you're feeling any better today."

"Lots," she says truthfully.

He looks relieved. "Maybe you just needed to stabilize. Have you had any more seizures?"

"No," she says, thinking of the pill bottle in her room at home. Of how she tipped the Depakote pills into the toilet when she got home from Sharon Parkins's house; of the pretty way they swirled on their way down. She picked through the old medicine bottles in the cabinet until she found something that looked vaguely like the Depakote—a blister pack of expired allergy pills—and refilled the bottle with those. Just in case anyone bothers to watch her. Like Ms. Gillespie. Or her dad.

She's feeling more clearheaded already; that hopeless dulled-pencil feeling of the past few days was gone when she woke up this morning. She can feel herself vibrating around the edges again, as if her molecules are in motion, ready to tune in to whatever the world is sending her way today. Her mother is just out of sight; Olive can sense her again, creeping back in closer, almost in view. This makes everything else that's too unbearable to think about—her father kissing Harmony, the whole fiasco with Natalie, the fact that her mother may have been kidnapped by her criminal ex-boyfriend—somehow more tolerable.

Her father taps at the sugar crust of his oatmeal, peering underneath as if there's something meaningful to be gleaned from the curds. "Well, I guess that means the drug is working."

"I guess so," she lies.

He presses his lips together. "I worry about you, sweetheart. You're all I've got."

She looks at his fingers gripping the spoon and notices for the first time how wrinkly his skin is compared to her own. Not old-man hands, not yet, but closer than she remembered them being. It freaks her out. "Don't worry about me, Dad. I'm going to be just fine." She smiles, buoyed by her secret. "Like Mom used to say, right?"

He makes a strange face. "Speaking of." He clears his throat. "The court date, the hearing, is this Wednesday. I know you were planning on coming, but I don't think that's such a good idea after all. Everything considered."

It takes her a minute to figure out what he's talking about. "You mean the hearing about Mom's death certificate? That's still happening?"

"Of course it is," he says.

"But we think she might not be dead," she says in disbelief. Her father says nothing, just keeps toying with his oatmeal. "What are you going to say?" she asks.

He shakes his head. "I'm not sure yet."

"Call it off!" The thought of the court issuing her mother's death certificate horrifies her, as if the act of signing a form will somehow undo any possibility of her mom being alive.

Her father sighs. "It doesn't work that way. They don't let you do that. Besides, we've waited all year for this hearing."

Olive drops her fork. It bounces off the plate and clatters to the floor, sending bits of egg splattering across the table. Her father blinks at her. "You don't even care, do you?" she says. "You're *glad* she's gone. So now you can be with Harmony."

She stands up and walks out the door of the restaurant, leaving her father scrambling to flag down the waiter for the check.

She is almost back to their house when she hears his feet slapping the pavement behind her. He comes up alongside, breathing hard, his hands pressed to his waist. "Hey," he says. "I get that you're mad at me. But you're not being fair. This isn't about Harmony. And it's not about looking for your mom, either. This is about a legal process that I have little say over." He stares at his feet and then bursts out: "For chrissake, Olive, it's about paying the bills. We need the life insurance money."

Her hands reflexively go up to cover her ears. She doesn't like to think about things like this, the invisible mechanisms keeping everything moving. The way you don't ever want to eat sausage again once you know what's in it. "You have to be honest," she says. "You get to say what you know."

"What I *know*? Olive, I know your mother had an ex-boyfriend who got out of jail. I know she did some unexplained things before she died. I know she wasn't particularly truthful with me. And I know you've had what you think are visions but that a doctor believes are epileptic seizures. So what does that all add up to? I honestly have no clue." He stops in his tracks. "*Christ*," he mutters, staring at something up ahead.

She follows his gaze and sees a strange man sitting on their porch. Maybe a junkie who needed a place to sit? He's gaunt, with long hair pulled back into a stringy ponytail, a receding hairline exposing several inches of pale scalp. A neck tattoo—it looks like a bird—peeks out from the hood of his khaki army jacket, which he wears over a faded T-shirt with a Greenpeace logo on it. He's sitting on their steps, drinking something out of a paper take-out cup, fingering the dying camellia bushes next to the steps with a blank expression.

The man stands when he sees them coming up the walk. Her father reaches out and grabs Olive's hand. She tries to shake him off, but he's insistent, gripping her so hard that she can practically feel the bones crunching against each other.

"Ow," she says. "What's the problem?"

"That's Sidney," he says under his breath.

"Sidney?" She turns to goggle at the man. "You found him?"

Her father nods uneasily. Her heart is fluttering in a way that makes her feel dizzy. She realizes that Sidney is looking right at her, squinting slightly. Does he *look* evil? She can't tell. He lifts a hand in acknowledgment of her stare, and before she can stop herself, she reflexively waves back.

Her father glances behind him, at the garden full of rainbow flags across the street, and gives Olive's hand a tug, as if he's considering stashing her there for safety. But Sidney is already walking toward them. He's smiling now, a lopsided grin that transforms his face from something broken into something almost charming. His eyes are almost hypnotically black.

"Jonathan? I think we met briefly at the memorial service." Sidney is sticking out his hand for a shake, and her father hesitates, drops Olive's hand, and takes it. "And this is . . . Olive?"

"That's right," she says, disarmed.

"Go in the house, Olive," her father says. But she stands rooted in place, since she's a little queasy, anyway; *that* sensation has returned, as if there's something inside her about to burst through her skin. The world slightly too bright, shimmering around the edges. An aura pulsing in and out with her breath. Her mother, nearby.

The guy sips from his coffee cup, seemingly at home in their front yard. The barista has Sharpied CINDEE on its side in loopy handwriting, with a smiley face. "You really need to fertilize your camellias," he says. "Try Dr. Earth. It's organic, lots of probiotics."

Her father has a puzzled expression on his face. "Why are you here?"

"I got your note," Sidney says to Olive's dad.

Her father's hands are sticking out slightly from his sides, as if he's keeping them at the ready. "How did you know where we live?" he asks.

The man grins. "There's this thing called the Internet. You're all over it."

"So are you," her father says darkly.

"Not very up-to-date, though, is it? That's what happens when you spend a few decades in jail. You vanish. It's like to the outside world, you've stopped existing altogether." Sidney puts a fist up and then opens his hand, his fingers flying out—*poof*. "So what's up?"

Olive can't stand it anymore. "What did you do to my mom?" she demands. "Did you kidnap her?"

As the words come out of her mouth, she realizes how ridiculous they sound and how unlikely the scenario is. If this guy absconded with her mom, why would he show up at their doorstep? Nor does the guy really *look* like a hardened ex-con. He's skinny-fat, his shoulders sloping in his faded T-shirt, a paunch jutting over the top of his Goodwill jeans. He's wearing a string shell bracelet around one wrist, the kind she used to make in summer camp. Honestly, he looks more like someone's aging hippie uncle, the kind of guy who spends his weekends trying to register Green Party voters outside the medical marijuana dispensary on Telegraph Avenue, the kind of guy who slices your goat Gouda at the Cheese Board Collective.

Indeed, the expression on Sidney's face is one of utter bewilderment. "*Kidnap* her?" he repeats.

"Olive," Jonathan says under his breath. "Please let me deal with this."

Sidney's brow furrows with confusion. "Is there something I'm missing here? She's dead. I saw it on TV. I came to the memorial."

Her father squints at Sidney, sizing him up. Finally, he seems to realize that his hands are still dangling in midair, and he shoves them in his jacket pockets. "Yes, of course, right, you're right," Jonathan mutters. He's quiet for a moment, thinking. "OK. Tell me this: Why did my wife come to visit you last year?"

"She told you about that?"

"No. I figured it out myself."

Sidney seems to relax. He sits back down on the edge of their porch, facing them, his jeans rising up to expose hairy ankles. "Well, I called her after I got out of jail. I wanted to catch up, reminisce about old times."

Her father remains standing, stiff as a plank. "Like how she fled town after you blew up a dam and killed a bunch of horses?"

"Wait, *what*?" The words burst out of Olive's mouth.

"I didn't *kill* the horses!" Sidney objects. "Jesus!"

"Olive, go inside," her father says.

"No way," she says, riveted.

Sidney tilts his head, looking a little embarrassed. "What *do* you know about me?"

"I read the news clippings from when you were convicted."

Sidney laughs. "Then you know nothing at all. The biased idiots in the corporate media didn't get anything right."

Her father crosses his arms, plants his feet, settling in. "Tell me."

Sidney hunches over, cradling the cup in both hands. He stares at his feet, in tattered TOMS, for a long time before he starts to talk.

"Billie—well, I first knew her as Elizabeth Smith. That's the name she gave me when I met her in Los Angeles all those years ago. I was hanging out with some friends down there, post-college, and I saw her at a party and thought, *Wow*. I knew she was a runaway—the name was fake, that was obvious— and that she was underage to boot, but I didn't really care." He laughs. "She was a quick study; she took it all so seriously. This beautiful girl from nowhere, marching right into town like she owned the place. Soaking up every word I said until she was even better at it than I was. It was flattering, you know? Three weeks in and you'd never know she hadn't been there forever. New haircut, new clothes, whole new persona. I turn around and suddenly I've got this girlfriend, and how the hell did that happen?" He shakes his head admiringly. "Sheer force of will.

"I helped her out. I knew people who could fake documents." He flicks his eyes at Olive. "You meet a lot of people when you deal drugs. Don't deal drugs, OK? It's bad news. I had a degree from UCLA, you know? And then I fell into *that*—because, well, philosophy major, what else was I going to do?—and now look at me." He stares morosely at the coffee cup in his hands. "Anyway. We bummed around L.A. for a year or two, until she seemed to get restless. Saying that my friends and I were acting like a bunch of posers, sitting around on our asses, talking about changing the world but mostly just smoking too much dope. And that's when she said it was time to move to the Pacific Northwest, where the *real* action was.

"Thing is, she was right about the Pacific Northwest. We got up there just as the whole scene was starting to take off."

"Like Nirvana?" Olive asks tentatively.

He makes a face. "No, not *Nirvana*. Jesus. No, it was radical up there. Yeah, you had your emerging grunge scene and your gutter punks out to *fuck shit up,* but there were also legit activists up there. We were closer to nature, you could see what was at stake, we wanted to make a *real* difference. Civil disobedience, right? Making a loud enough stink that the world would see what really mattered. Stick it to the man." He makes a fist with one hand and drives it into the air for emphasis, managing with the other to splash milky coffee out of the hole in the lid and onto his T-shirt. "One of the first things she and I did when we got up there was chain ourselves to a tree in this old-growth forest in Cascadia. There were fourteen of us, chained together for three months, living on gorp and pissing in buckets, really making a statement!" His smile falters. "Yeah, OK, they eventually cut the forest down anyway. But still.

"We lived like that for a long time. Kind of itinerant. We'd head into Bend, or Olympia, or Portland, and I'd deal acid or pot or heroin to the local college kids, save up money; and she'd get odd jobs, paint some pictures, maybe audit a few classes. She liked to do that." He screws up his face, remembering. "We'd help stage protests in town, these kind of theater sit-ins, with costumes and everything. And then we'd hear about some urgent action out in the woods, tree-sitting or protestors lying down in front of logging trucks, and we'd head back out."

Olive smiles, imagining her mom trussed up in craft-paper feathers, living in a redwood tree, but her father interrupts: "We know most of this already. Get to the point. To the part where you start setting things on fire."

"That was Sparrow's idea, actually."

Her father stiffens. "*Her* idea?"

Sidney smiles. "Yep. We were up in Oregon at another protest, against this new dam that had stopped the salmon from swimming upstream to their breeding grounds. Standing around dressed up like fish, giant signs that said 'My Existence, Your Subsistence.' And a few days in, Sparrow, she yanks the salmon head off, and she looks out at the government hacks, who are totally ignoring us, and the one local newspaper journalist who's still there, and she says to me"—he raises his voice in a painful mimicry of Olive's mom—"'This is getting us nowhere. If we want the dam to go away, we should just blow the stupid thing up.'

"So that's what we did! Got together a little group, along with my friend Vincent—he went by Pangolin, you know, after the anteater—and put together a plan. It was shockingly easy, actually. Sparrow got her hands on a copy of *The Anarchist Cookbook,* which taught us how to assemble a firebomb. We did some surveillance on the dam for a few weeks and then sneaked out there in the middle of the night when no one was around. And bam"—he slams his hand on the porch stair, jolting Olive upright—"the motherfucker was toast."

"My *mom* did that?" Olive feels dizzy: the charming tree forts and paper feathers suddenly incinerated, replaced by crumbling concrete and shattering glass.

He winks at her. "Your mom was a natural, you know? She was the one who figured out how to do it right. How to set up a 'clean room' where we made the firebomb: basically just a camping tent we'd set up in a motel room, but we had to wear a surgeon's mask and a shower cap and gloves whenever we went inside. So we wouldn't leave fingerprints or DNA on the bombs, see? And then we just gave the tent to a homeless person, and presto! No trail, *and* we helped the disenfranchised!" He smiles at this. "Next we targeted a wild mustang preserve, which was selling the older horses as meat to a Moldavian sausage factory. We released the animals and blew the place up. That one was *my* idea." His eyes glitter darkly with the memory. "It was pretty spectacular. Those beautiful horses, finally free, galloping away into the woods, lit up by the flames."

Olive tries to imagine this, but mostly, she keeps seeing her mother like she was in the vision that Olive had on the steps of school. The match in her hand: *Should I do it?* She reaches out and clutches her father's arm, fighting off the wooziness that is threatening to buckle her knees. Her dad reaches his arm around and covers her hand with his own.

There's a thick hot ache in her head, as if someone has poured pea soup in her skull. She can't wrap her mind around these stories. On the one hand, isn't it just like her mom to have done something so *badass,* so extreme, once again trumping Olive's own timid efforts to make the world a better place? Then again, this guy ended up in prison for doing the same things. Why didn't her mother?

Could it be true? she asks herself. *Is this guy lying to us because he hates her for some reason? How would we even know?*

Sidney is still talking. "After we freed the horses, we had to go off the grid for a while. We were out there in this cabin in the Oregon woods, the three of us on top of each other, kind of driving each other nuts, frankly. Pangolin, well, it was starting to grow obvious that he was not mentally altogether. He would conduct long conversations with people who weren't there: just him and Bakunin and Nietzsche, sitting by the fire, having a long chat about nihilism and social change. As for me"—he glances at Olive—"let's just say that I had my drug use under control for a while, and then I didn't. I wasn't at the top of my game.

"Meanwhile, we learned that the actions we'd taken hadn't really had the impact we'd wanted them to. The feds rebuilt that dam within months, made it even bigger. And the mustangs we freed— well, they rounded them all up, and this time they slaughtered them all because they no longer had a preserve where the horses could be stashed."

He sighs. "So, yeah. I was arguing that was why we needed to do something even *bigger* this time. Get the man where it hurts, you know? His pocket-book! There was this fancy-pants ski resort upstate that was clear-cutting an old-growth forest in order to build more ski runs. Killing these ancient trees so that some rich assholes could get their adrenaline fix, right? I said, 'Blow that fucker up.'

"Anyway. We had everything all prepped, and then right before go time, Billie got sick. Throwing up. So Pangolin and I left her behind. The plan was, she'd clean up the cabin where we'd been living, gather up the cash we had stashed—which, by the way, was about thirty grand, those U of O under-grads *loved* their hallucinogens—and meet up with us afterward in Olympia." He takes a sip from his coffee and makes a startled face: *Cold.* "So, anyway. Pangolin and I head out to the ski resort, but just when we're almost there, we get pulled over. Broken taillight. The cops ask to inspect the van—which of course was packed with incendiaries—and I'm, you know, not so sober, maybe not making the best decisions. . . ." He stares at the camellia bushes, remembering, his face slackening. "See, I thought, if I just . . . drove away." His voice drifts off. "Well, *that* didn't work. I ran over the cop—which, don't believe the press accounts, was *not* intentional—and broke both his legs. They slapped me with attempted manslaughter on top of the arson and conspiracy charges. Oh, and the drug charges for the five sheets of acid I forgot I'd stashed in the trunk." He shrugs: *Oops.*

"It turned out that Pangolin was schizophrenic; he ended up in a psych ward, talking to the walls. I got twenty-five to life. And Sparrow—for a long time I thought she'd gotten away. That she'd somehow made it to Olympia with all the cash we'd stashed, and the feds had never figured out that she was involved. I was *glad* she made it out, see? No way in hell was *I* going to turn her in."

He makes a wry face. "Life goes on, right? I'm doing my time, it's not *so* bad, I started a meditation group and got to work in the prison garden. And then a few years ago, I'm on the computer in the prison library, clicking around on *Decode*—it's the site's twentieth anniversary, lots of pictures of their big gala—and there's this woman in one photo who looks familiar. She's on the arm of some normalish guy, she's laughing, not even looking at the camera, she's a middle-aged brunette. But I could tell." He wags a finger. "The caption read: 'Senior editor Jonathan Flanagan and wife.' I couldn't stop thinking,

Wife? That's all she is now, someone's wife? It didn't seem like the Sparrow I knew. So conventional."

"We're not *conventional*," Olive bristles.

He laughs, reaching back to tighten the elastic on his ponytail. "Well. Comparatively speaking, let's say. Anyway, I searched her out, sent her a letter. She never answered. So when I got out of jail, I headed down to the Bay Area to find her. Just friendly-like."

"Friendly-like." Her father looks skeptical. "Even though she's the one who turned you in?"

"You know about that?" Sidney frowns. "She told me you didn't know *anything* about what was really going on in Oregon."

Olive looks from her father to Sidney and back. Where is this coming from? "I've been made aware," her father says carefully.

Sidney looks like he's trying to decide what to say, but Olive is having a hard time paying attention. She's feeling weirder by the minute; she's pretty sure she's about to have a vision—and increasingly she wants Sidney to stop talking and go away. She has a feeling she's not going to like what he has to say.

Sidney carefully places the cup on the ground next to him. "OK, well, yeah. She turned me and Pangolin in. Took all our money and split. Maybe she was trying to save her own ass; she told *me* that she suddenly grew a conscience about what we were doing. Regardless, she really screwed us, you know?" His eyes light up with a flash of anger. "But it wasn't until *after* I got down to the Bay Area that I even found this out. An old mutual friend filled me in. Pretty fucked up."

Her father sighs as if he's come to some conclusion. "So *that's* what you were fighting about," Jonathan says. "You weren't, say, threatening her?"

"Dude, I'm a *pacifist*." Sidney looks wounded by the very suggestion. Then he looks Olive's dad up and down, taking in his jeans and sneakers, the cable-knit fisherman's sweater that Olive gave him last Christmas. "You're a nice guy, aren't you? Straight as an arrow? Bet you never even dropped acid. Bet you've had a steady job your whole life. Paying your mortgage. Supporting your family."

Her father looks like he's trying not to hit the guy. "Yeah, and? What's your point?"

"My point is . . ." He sighs. "Billie never told you anything about what really happened up in Oregon all those years ago. And of course she didn't. Because what would she have had to gain? Billie never did anything unless she stood to benefit from it." He glances over his shoulder at their house, giving it a quick assessment. "Like you. She found herself a good provider, didn't she? Someone who wouldn't ask tricky questions. Someone who would buy into her Saint Billie act. A chump. That was her MO even back then." He twists his mouth into a wry smile that doesn't look amused at all. "Sorry to say that about your dead mom, kid, but it's true."

Sidney's insults seem to hit her dad like a physical blow. He takes a small step back. Olive feels a burst of sadness for her dad, can feel the soft things inside him bruising like fruit. She doesn't like this guy and his stories; doesn't like them at all. Sidney clearly doesn't know where her mom is—which is a good thing, right? she wasn't kidnapped, she's not in danger, at least not from him—and yet the things he's saying about Billie feel like someone shoving splinters under her fingernails. Her mom, some kind of *snitch*? Turning her friends in to the authorities and then taking off with all their money? She shakes her head, as if this might dispel the unpleasant mental image of her mother that Sidney is painting in her mind, but it just makes her feel dizzier.

Sidney studies Olive's father, looking gloomy. "Hey, don't take it personally. I was her chump long before you were," he says, and something in his voice breaks. And then Olive understands: Sidney was in love with her mom once. Like, *really* in love. She watches as Sidney hunches over and turns his head, pulling the ponytail aside so they can get a good look at the tattoo covering the back of his neck. Olive peers at it: It's blobby and misshapen, a pretty bad interpretation of the real thing, but Olive recognizes it anyway. It's a sparrow.

Looking at the tattoo, the stringy graying hair in its sad little ponytail, she feels sorry for him. Maybe he used to be cutting-edge once, but now he just seems pathetic. Like he's trying to relive his glory days of anarchy and rebellion because he doesn't have anything newer to cling to. *Of course he couldn't have kidnapped Mom,* she realizes. *Mom is stronger than he is. She broke his heart, moved on to bigger and better things, and he hasn't forgiven her.*

"See, there's other things about her—" Sidney begins, but then he stops, as if transfixed by something he's seen over Olive's shoulder. He abruptly stands up, the empty coffee cup clattering to the ground. "Well, shit. What are *you* doing here?"

Olive turns around and sees Harmony standing

behind her. Canvas bags full of farmers' market bounty dangle from Harmony's wrists. Her blond hair is wound in twin braids that she's pinned up around her head in a crown. She appears to be wearing one of Olive's father's button-down shirts under her puffer.

"Maverick," Harmony says slowly, tilting her head sideways, her forehead puckering with concern. "What kinds of stories are you telling them? Don't you think they've suffered enough this year?"

Sidney looks abashed. "Of course," he says. "Just, well, don't you think they should—" He stops as if realizing something. He swivels his head to stare at Jonathan and then back at Harmony. "Hey, are you two together now? Wow. Sparrow would not have liked *that*."

Harmony sets the market bags carefully on the ground. "Honestly, Sidney, I told you this was a bad idea." Her voice is dangerously soft.

"*He* wanted it." Sidney points at Olive's dad. "He *asked* me to get in touch."

"Wait." Her father is looking at Harmony, confusion on his face. "Have you two . . . kept in touch? You didn't mention that the other day."

Olive watches this interaction as if through a plastic shower curtain, disembodied; she is oddly glad for Harmony's presence, as if some crisis has been narrowly averted. She teeters slightly, feeling like the ground has just tilted under her feet. And then it's on her. The dizzy feeling that's been lingering on Olive's periphery all morning is pouring through her as if a dam has finally broken somewhere within. She's vaguely aware that she's made a strangling sound—that her father and Harmony have turned to look at her, that Sidney has broken off mid-sentence to stare at her—but their presence isn't real anymore.

What's real: her mother, sitting in a lawn chair a few feet away from her, pants rolled up to her knees. Smoking a cigarette. (A fleeting, dismaying thought: *Mom smokes now?*) A smell of the sea, sand stretching out beyond them both into the distance. There's a tree hanging over Olive's head that wasn't there a few seconds before, its leaves rattling in a breeze.

Mom's back, Olive thinks happily.

Her mom takes a long drag of the cigarette and scratches at a scab on her shin. "Don't believe a word he says," she says, exhaling. "He's not to be trusted." She makes a sweeping gesture with the lit end of the cigarette. "Your father, either."

Did all that stuff in Oregon really happen that way? The question in Olive's mind is so loud that it makes her head throb.

"Ancient history," her mom says, and stubs the cigarette out in the grass. "Pay it no mind. It holds no bearing on the present."

But the past piles up, it builds a ladder to where you are now; without it, how would you get anywhere? Without it, who would you be? Can you really start new and leave your past behind? Because I want to, Mom. I want to start over. I want to be someone totally new. Show me how.

Her mother doesn't appear to hear this. She shakes out her hair, turns her head beatifically toward the light filtering through the tree. It dapples her skin, shadows her eyes. A whisper on the breeze, even as her mother's mouth stays closed. "You're closer than you know, Olive."

Olive realizes she's stopped breathing. Her lungs lurch open and she's suddenly dry-heaving, on the verge of vomiting. She drops to the ground, her knees giving way beneath her.

"Shit, man," she hears Sidney say. "What's wrong with your daughter?"

She feels her father's hands grasping her shoulders, smells the oatmeal on his breath. "She's having a seizure," her father says, his voice so close that it makes her head throb. "Olive, sweetheart, can you talk to me?"

Her mother's outline fades sharply and then vanishes. The vast stretch of sand sifts away, resolving itself into their sodden, half-dead lawn. The world rushes back in.

"I'm fine, just a little dizzy," she insists, taking her father's hand and pulling herself upright. She wobbles a bit as she stands. The grass below her feet buckles strangely. Sidney is staring at her, agog.

"Should we call the doctor?" Harmony's cool hand is on her forehead and Olive turns her head to shrug it off.

"I'm going to take her inside." Her father grips Olive's elbow and steers her up the path toward the house despite her weak protests that she's OK, just give her a minute, she'll be fine.

Sidney steps aside to let them by. He picks his empty coffee cup off the ground and cradles it in his hands. "Sorry," he says. "I'll leave." He turns to survey the three of them, stopping at Olive. Studying her face as if looking for someone else inside her. "It was nice to meet you, Olive. Maybe I'll see you again sometime."

Olive cranes her neck to watch Sidney head down the path toward the sidewalk. His jeans sag around his hips when he walks, catching on his pelvic bones in a way that suggests the skeleton underneath. He stops at the end of the driveway to throw the empty cup in the recycling bin.

"Hey," her father yells. Sidney freezes with the lid half open. He looks down into the contents of the recycling bin with bafflement and then back up at them. Her father lowers his voice just slightly: "You don't know where Billie is now, do you?"

Sidney's face puckers with confusion. "How would I know that? Heaven? Hell? Reincarnated as an elephant? Daffodil food? Is that what you're asking?" He starts to gently lower the lid of the recycling bin, then changes his mind and lets it drop. The lid slams shut, making Olive jump a little.

"Wherever she is," Sidney finishes, wiping his hands clean on his jeans, "I can't imagine she's happy about it."

WHERE THE MOUNTAIN MEETS THE SKY

My Life with Billie Flanagan

—

BY JONATHAN FLANAGAN

One thing I remember
She used to
Billie was
I know
I thought
I
I
I

16

AFTER SIDNEY LEAVES, THE three of them gravitate numbly toward the house and then into the kitchen. Harmony unloads the vegetables from her market bags onto the counter while Jonathan, stunned, pours a glass of water for Olive. Olive sits at the kitchen table and immediately puts her head down, nose pressed to the wood.

Harmony's chirpy chatter fills the silence. "Well. How about that. So strange of him to show up on your doorstep. What did he have to say for himself? God, he looked *awful*. Poor guy."

Jonathan sits at the table next to Olive and puts a hand on her back, feeling her heavy breath through the fabric of her shirt. "Be honest with me, now," he says to her. "You stopped taking the Depakote, right?"

Olive nods, her forehead tapping the table.

Harmony comes closer and stands behind him, placing a warm palm on his neck and giving it a little squeeze of sympathy. "Should she go to the doctor?" she asks in a low voice.

Olive's head rockets back up. "No. She shouldn't." She stares at Harmony, her pupils slightly dilated, until Harmony's hand slides off Jonathan's neck. Olive abruptly stands. "I'm going to go lie down," she says, and disappears out the door.

"Hey," he calls after her. "We're going to talk about all this, OK?"

"Whatever." Jonathan hears her feet trudging up the stairs and then the click of her door latching.

Harmony picks up Olive's water glass and places it in the sink, then looks around the kitchen uncertainly. "Should I go?"

"You didn't mention that you'd kept in touch with Sidney." This comes out more accusingly than he intends it to.

Her fingers fuss at the sleeve of her shirt—is he crazy, or is it one of his own?—buttoning and unbuttoning the cuff. "Oh, I wouldn't say we keep in touch. He looked me up when he first landed in the Bay Area. I felt sorry for him. I met him for coffee and connected him with an old chef friend of mine about a job as a prep cook. That's really the last I saw of him. Well, maybe we chatted a little at Billie's memorial service last year." She shrugs. "Why, are you upset about that?"

He buries his head in his hands, taking this in. "Tell me this: Were you involved in all *that*, too? Up in Oregon?"

"No." Harmony slowly gathers her empty market

bags, folding them into neat squares. "*No*. I mean, I knew what they were doing. I begged Billie to let me be a part of it, even followed them up to that cabin outside Bend, but Billie wouldn't let me get involved. She told me that I was"—she screws up her face as if trying to recall the exact words, even though her expression suggests that she remembers quite clearly—"*amateur-hour*, and this was the big leagues, and I should go back to college and be a good girl and finish my degree and stay out of trouble." She wrinkles her nose as if amused by this former version of herself. "At the time I was hurt—I worshipped her, you know?—but later, after everything went down, I was *so thankful*. I really dodged a bullet on that one."

"So did Billie, sounds like," he says.

"Well, yes. For different reasons."

He's silent for a minute, trying to piece together all the conflicting stories he's heard at this point. "So how did you know that Billie turned them in if you weren't around by then?"

"I read the news reports after they got arrested, and I just knew. Sidney and Vincent just *happened* to get pulled over for a broken taillight, and Billie just *happened* not to be there?" She laughs. "Please. Maybe I was naïve, but I wasn't stupid. I'd visited them out there in that cabin in the woods, I saw how messy things were getting. It was obvious what had happened. Well, maybe not obvious to Sidney, but he was too besotted and way too high to see straight." She looks down at the folded market bags in her hands, aligning them in a stack. "After Billie and I reconnected in Berkeley, I confronted her about it. She told me she was afraid that Sidney and Vincent were going to accidentally kill someone if they kept it up. That they needed to be stopped and she couldn't think of another way to stop them. . . ." Her voice trails off, as if she's still puzzling her way through the logic of this explanation.

Jonathan sits there taking this in. He can feel Harmony studying him, waiting for his reaction, but he can't bring himself to meet her gaze. He thinks of Billie, a suitcase full of money, fleeing Oregon; heading where?

The heater ticks on as the temperature drops, and a blast of hot air from the vent sends dust bunnies skittering across the kitchen floor. Upstairs, he can hear the creak of the floorboards as Olive moves around her room. "I should probably go talk to Olive," Jonathan finally says.

Harmony nods quickly, glancing up at the clock. "That's OK, there's a yoga class I'd like to hit up anyway. I'm really feeling like I need to get centered right now." She leans over and kisses Jonathan on the cheek. "Call me later?" She spins off, out the door before he can respond one way or the other.

Jonathan finds himself alone in the kitchen. He stands there motionless for a minute, incapable of mustering the willpower to go upstairs and face his surly daughter. He jerks open a cupboard above the refrigerator and pours himself several fingers of bourbon, which he swallows in one quick gulp. It burns going down, and then the dull heat spreads through him, loosening him until he feels like he can breathe again. He leans against the refrigerator, noticing the shabbiness of the room—the chipped paint along the floorboards, the tilting faces of the cabinetry, the grime stuck in the grout of the tile. He is struck with an unlikely desire to fix the place up.

He pours himself another drink before going to retrieve his toolbox. For the rest of the afternoon, he bumps around the kitchen, fiddling with the loose hinge on a saggy cabinet door that won't quite close; daubing lacquer into cracks; tackling the tile with Comet and a toothbrush. Mindless, meditative manual labor. And yet his mind won't comply, persistently buzzing with the subjects he doesn't want to think about: lies and betrayal. His wife's secret and highly problematic history; his not entirely forthcoming new lover; his daughter who refuses to take her meds. The money he will have to pay back to his publisher, the financial hole that he continues digging deeper.

Mostly, though, he thinks about Billie. If Sidney doesn't have her hidden somewhere, if he's not her lover or her abductor, then where did she go? Is she even alive? Or has he been forcing tangential evidence toward a conclusion it doesn't deserve, spurred on by his hallucinating daughter?

He keeps coming back to the same question: Who *was* the woman he lived with for all those years? Billie's identity keeps shimmering and changing in his mind, like a fish slipping through the sea; he can't seem to fix his perspective on her anymore. Scrubbing the tile, he wonders: Do all the new things he's learned about his wife change who she really was, or is it that he's simply seeing her from a new angle?

A memory bubbles to the surface: a conversation they had a while back about Billie's then-friend

Emma. Emma had installed a nanny-cam and, in the process, accidentally discovered that her husband had been indecently exposing himself to both their teenage babysitter and the Guatemalan cleaning lady.

"How can you be wrong about someone for so long?" Jonathan marveled. They were sitting on the back sunporch, drinking manhattans, watching night set over the garden.

At this, Billie set her drink down on the arm of her chair and squinted at him with an expression of amused disbelief. "Easy. You can be wrong if they want you to be wrong. Look. All people are unknowable, no matter how close you may think you are. Of the millions of thoughts we all think every day, of the millions of experiences we have, how many do we allow other people to know about? A handful? And no one willingly shares their worst, do they? The flaws you see, those are like the very tip of an iceberg. So we're all just poking around on the surface, trying to figure out the people we love with a kind of, I guess, naïve idealism."

He looked out at the garden for a long time, listening to the crickets call to each other, digesting this. "That's the cynical view, maybe," he finally replied. "But I think you can know someone if they want you to know them. That's not naïve idealism; that's trust. That's the foundation of love." He turned to her with a pang of fear. "I know *you*, don't I?"

Billie laughed and leaned across the arm of the chair to kiss him. "You've always been a glass-half-full kind of guy," she said. "I love that about you. It's so *pure*. Olive is definitely your daughter."

Only now, picking crumbling grout from the cracks of the kitchen counter, does he realize that his wife never answered his question.

When Jonathan is done cleaning, he stands back and studies his handiwork. The kitchen doesn't look any different than it did three hours earlier; its issues are too deep to be fixed by a quick paint job. What it really needs is to be brought down to the studs and rebuilt. *What the hell,* he thinks. *If I don't get that death certificate, we may be losing the house anyway.*

He nudges the sagging cabinet door closed with his toe, and when it swings open again, he kicks it hard. Then he cracks a beer and goes upstairs to Olive's room.

He raps on the doorframe with his knuckles, sticking his head around the door to see Olive sitting at her computer, her back to him. "Hey," he says. "You ready to talk about this morning? That was a lot to take in."

She turns quickly, closing the lid of her laptop with one hand as she does. "Can we do it later?" she asks. "I'm not really in the mood."

"Oh." *She's still angry about Harmony,* he realizes. "Maybe you want to go to a movie?"

She looks at her computer and back at him. "I'm kind of in the middle of something."

"Maybe tonight," he says. "You're home this evening? Or are you going over to Natalie's?"

"I'm not hanging out with Natalie," she says quickly.

There's something in her face when she says this that makes him stop; is she fighting with her best friend? He stands there a minute longer, weighing the possibility of pressing her for details, afraid of pushing her too far and making everything worse. He's never really understood the hothouse intimacy of female friendships, the way women consume and then repel each other. How can he help his daughter with those kinds of inscrutable relationships? Is it better to just stay out of whatever's going on and assume they'll work it out themselves?

"All right, then. Well, we'll talk when you're ready." He slips back down the hall, aware that he's letting cowardice prevail over good parenting.

He retires to his room with his laptop and Netflix, listening to Olive tapping away on the other side of the wall. He imagines them as planets, living in the same galaxy but spinning in their separate orbits. This makes him ineffably sad. Just when it seemed like they were starting to connect, he screwed it all up, for the most selfish of reasons. *Am I a bad father?* he asks himself. *Billie made all this look easy. Maybe I didn't have a chance to realize what a shitty dad I am until she wasn't around. No matter what else she might have been, she was better at this than I am.*

Lying on his bed, he frets about the legal hearing on Wednesday: a quarter million on the line, and he still doesn't know what he's going to say. *The truth, like Olive says, you have to tell the truth.* But what will that accomplish? It's not going to bring Billie back. Will it soothe some vestige of his belief in the righteousness of honesty, of doing the right thing? Or will it just mean that he loses the life insurance money that's his best shot at pulling their lives back together?

You need a plan, the voice in his head nags. He silences it with a beer, and then another, until his confusing past and indeterminate future are both a blur, numbed by the warm immediacy of intoxication.

When he gets a text from Marcus—*Meet me for a drink at Bacaloa? I've got your check & something to show you*—he is grateful for the shock back to life.

Marcus is waiting for him at a tapas bar on Shattuck with big doors that open out to the street during the summertime. Tonight the doors are tightly shut against the cold. Most of the bar's patrons seem to be soccer fans, gathered drunkenly in a huddle at the bar, watching a game on the muted big-screen television on the back wall.

Marcus sits at a table directly under the TV, his bulk precariously balanced on a stool, with an empty pint glass in front of him. He has half-moons of exhaustion under his eyes; a nascent beard creeps across his chin and cheeks. He's determinedly working his way through a bowl of french fries.

"Sit," Marcus says as Jonathan approaches, and points at an empty stool.

Jonathan sits, and Marcus immediately slides a check across the table. "Ten grand. Pay me back when you can, but don't stress about it, OK? There's no rush."

"Honestly, I can't thank you enough," Jonathan

says thickly, as he slips the check into his pocket. He notices Billie's laptop sitting on the table next to Marcus, and this cuts through his buzz, momentarily sobering him up. "Wait—you cracked the password?"

Marcus nods, picks another fry out of the bowl. "Are you going to tell me what's going on now?"

A waitress veers over to their table, dropping two more beers in front of them. She smiles brightly at Jonathan and then spins around to the tables behind them. He waits until she's out of earshot before he responds. "A lot," he admits. "Where do you want me to start?"

Marcus points to the laptop. "How about with this."

Jonathan takes a sip of his beer, slowly licks the foam off his lips. He can't see the point in being coy anymore. "What if I told you I thought that Billie might still be alive," he says.

Marcus absorbs this with surprising aplomb, gazing thoughtfully into the depths of his drink. Jonathan waits for the inevitable expression of concern—*You're crazy, man; you're imagining things*. But after a second, Marcus shakes his head, slumping in his stool as if all that weight is too much to keep upright. "Shit," he says softly. "You think she took off. Faked her own death."

"Yes," says Jonathan.

"You have proof that she did that?"

"Nothing conclusive. Missing money. A possible sighting. A lot of lies. She cheated on me, at least once that I know of. She was definitely sneaking around behind my back that last year of her life.

And it turns out she had a criminal past that she completely failed to mention to me."

Marcus exhales a long puff of beer-scented breath. "That's messed up."

Jonathan's drink is somehow already gone. "You don't seem surprised," he observes. "Which makes me think you found something on the computer that confirms my suspicions."

Marcus slides the computer closer. He boots it up, presses a few keys, and then spins it around so it's facing Jonathan. "Maybe, depending on how you want to parse this."

The television overhead explodes with sound as the bartender turns the volume on. The low happy-hour clamor in the room turns into a dull roar of protest. Startled, Jonathan looks up and sees the entire bar staring at him; and then he realizes that they are riveted by the activity on the TV just over Jonathan's shoulder. Someone has made a goal.

Jonathan turns back to the laptop, studying the document on the screen before him. It's a letter.

Dear Ryan—

I've waited a long time to write you this letter: too long, I know. I'm so sorry I didn't want to see you before, but you have to understand that I just wasn't ready yet. Not a day has gone by when I didn't wonder if I'd made a mistake, though. Walking away from you was the hardest decision I've ever made.

I hope you haven't been angry at me. I hope you can see that I did what I did for you, too.

My life was complicated, and I knew that you'd be better off without me.

Have you been?

I think about you all the time. I wonder where you might be, who you're with, what you're thinking and doing and feeling. I close my eyes and I can see your face looking back at me. Do you think about me, too?

I want another chance, but it's up to you to decide. I'll be waiting to hear from you.

I've always loved you.

Sybilla

The soccer-fan screams on the TV above him reach a fevered pitch, a crowd of thousands with their hearts torn from their chests, their hopes dashed on blood-splattered Astroturf. Something inside Jonathan turns to stone. *Of course. She left me for someone else,* he thinks. *Occam's razor, the simplest explanation. I knew it from the very start.*

He realizes that Marcus is asking him a question. He looks up, still disoriented, and Marcus repeats himself: "So. Who's this Ryan guy?"

Jonathan looks back at the letter. "Hell if I know," he says.

His equilibrium is precarious. He has a hard time getting the key in the hole of his front door, what with the way his body keeps tipping sideways. The house is dark; Olive is already asleep. His grasp on time grew tenuous around when Marcus ordered a third round of tequila shots. But he looks at his phone and it's only eleven.

Jonathan bumps into the house, his throat raw from the tequila, and his feet get tangled in Olive's hoodie, abandoned on the floor of the entry. He stumbles; rights himself. The walls of his house slip underneath his hands as he makes his way to the kitchen. Leftover pizza from Olive's dinner, congealing in a box on the counter. He devours a slice, then forages in the fridge, finds some leftover lasagna that Harmony brought over, eats that cold straight from the Tupperware.

Harmony. He thinks of texting her. A booty call. When was the last time he did that? He remembers those days back in college: the buzzy late-night fumblings, a scented candle fugging the air by the bed, mascara smears on the pillows in the morning. Hair of the dog with a michelada. That sense of life as an endless cornucopia, yours for the taking. All the time in the world.

He pulls out his phone and starts to compose a text with slippery fingers before thinking better of it. *You can't act like a teenager,* he thinks, putting the phone away again. *You* have *a teenager.* The thought sticks to him; is sticky; so he scrawls it on a sticky note that he finds on the counter and sticks it to the front of his shirt.

He tiptoes up the stairs and stands outside Olive's darkened room. "Olive," he whispers in a raspy voice, tapping softly at the door with his naked ring finger. There's no response. He remembers how his wife used to just let herself into Olive's room as if it belonged to her; crawl right into bed with her without asking permission. Why is he always so careful?

He pushes the door open a crack and peers in. Olive is sprawled facedown on her bed, one hand dangling off the side, the sheets wadded around her feet. He tiptoes closer, swearing when he trips over the books lying in a jumble on the floor. She doesn't wake up. The room smells sweet and gamey, the way an unwashed baby smells behind the ears. He kneels on the floor next to her bed.

Looking at his supine daughter, the limp looseness of her limbs, the sugary innocence of her sleeping face, he is filled with a sharp, hot fury at his wife. *How could an affair with Some Guy Named Ryan possibly be more important than this?* He thinks of his daughter's helpless yearning for her mother, the echoes of grief muddling Olive's head. A bitter thought: *Billie doesn't deserve our daughter's devotion.*

Catsby-the-cat slips around the open bedroom door and leaps up onto the bed next to Olive, curling herself into the pillow behind Olive's hair. The cat gazes steadily at Jonathan, marking her territory in a way that reminds him unpleasantly of his wife.

Fuck this, he thinks, standing up. *I'm done looking for Billie. Let her be dead if she wants to be dead.*

He pulls the sheets up over Olive before he leaves the room.

". . . hopefully Your Honor has had the opportunity to review the documents that we filed last month. To review, these include affidavits from both police detectives and search-and-rescue experts, interviews with relatives and friends conducted over the last year, and phone and computer records that we believe conclusively demonstrate that Sybilla Flanagan died while hiking in Desolation Wilderness on November seventh of last year. Additionally, we filed public notice about our petition for death in absentia in several national newspapers, per Code 12406(b)(1), and have had no response. Mr. Flanagan and his daughter have already experienced undue distress due to the nature of Mrs. Flanagan's death, and we hope that you will expedite the death certificate process so that they are not forced to wait six additional years before they can properly move on with their lives."

Jonathan sits next to Jean, his attorney, his head throbbing, his throat parched. He's been on a bender since Sunday night, and even with a handful of aspirin in his system he can still feel last night's bourbon poisoning his bloodstream. His eyeballs feel like they've been seared with a blowtorch. He somehow managed to shower and shave, he's wearing his most expensive suit, and yet he feels like a fraud: as if the mess that he is inside has somehow manifested itself in his appearance.

The courtroom is cold, modern, and noisy: His case is just one number on a busy docket today. Behind Jonathan, strangers shift noisily in their seats, waiting their turn, blatantly ignoring the NO FOOD OR CHEWING ALLOWED IN THE COURTROOM and NO READING WHILE COURT IS IN SESSION signs. People constantly come and go, their movements relayed to the room at large by a faulty hinge on the courtroom door. *Squeeeeeak SLAM*. The sound is putting Jonathan on edge.

The judge is an older woman, hair slicked back in a bun, drugstore bifocals perched on the end of her nose. She waits for Jean to finish speaking and then begins shuffling through the papers on her podium. "Thank you, counselor. I have had a chance to review Mr. Flanagan's case and am satisfied with the documentation you've provided." She turns over a page in front of her, scanning it, and then looks back up at Jonathan. "Mr. Flanagan, you have had no contact with your wife since November seventh of last year?"

He jerks out of his chair before his lawyer has the opportunity to nudge him upright. "No, Your Honor," he says, grateful for a question he can easily answer. *Maybe this will be easier than I thought.*

The judge peers over her glasses at him. "And you have no reason to believe that she might still be alive."

Oh. His mouth tastes like glue; the alcohol from the night before is making its presence known in his esophagus. He swallows, opens his mouth to speak, and his parched tongue ties itself up, making him cough painfully. His burning eyes grow watery.

Next to him, Jean magically produces a bottled water from her tote bag. She hands it to him, and then—to his surprise—puts her palm sympathetically on his back. *She thinks I'm crying with grief,* he realizes with some chagrin. He sips slowly, peering over the lip of the water bottle at the judge, and sees on her face the same lenient expression, her eyebrows tugging together in a dutiful show of empathy. *I'm the bereaved widower. That's all they expect to see here,* he understands.

"I'm sure this isn't easy for you," the judge says. "Take your time."

He wipes his eyes dry. He thinks of all the reasons he *does* have to believe that Billie is alive. Of his wife hiking out of Desolation Wilderness and straight into Some Guy Named Ryan's arms. And then he thinks of Olive. Of the things she stands to lose if this insurance settlement doesn't come through. Of the pain she's going to feel if she learns that her mom left her because she loved someone more.

Squeeeeeak SLAM.

"No," he lies. "There's no possibility that my wife is still alive."

Behind him, he hears a familiar mew of distress. He turns quickly and sees Olive sitting three rows back, in her school uniform with her backpack in her lap. Cutting class again; she must have bailed on third and fourth periods. She's staring straight at him. *Oh hell,* he thinks. Their eyes meet and she shakes her head. She mouths something at him, and he's pretty sure he knows what she's saying: *How could you?* She looks like she might cry, probably the most honest emotion in the room right now.

But the judge is talking again, and he's forced to turn back to her. "Thank you, Mr. Flanagan, you may be seated," she says. She presses the bifocals up her nose with the side of a knuckle. "OK. I am satisfied with the evidence provided. This court rules in favor of a judgment of death in the case of Sybilla Flanagan. We will be issuing a death certificate immediately so that your family can begin probate proceedings."

And there it is. He waits for some symbolic act of finality—a gavel pounding, the onlookers in their seats jumping respectfully to their feet—but the judge simply taps the pile of documents into a stack and then slides them to the far end of her bench. The room grows louder, people shuffling into position for the next case on the docket. He's dimly aware of Jean's arm around his shoulder, her voice whispering congratulatory words in his ear.

A death certificate, a life insurance settlement, permission to move beyond the torpid limbo of his life: He feels relief wash warm across him. (Is it relief? Or is it vindictive glee? He doesn't want to examine this emotion too hard.) *It's done,* he tells himself, and it feels like every muscle in his body is relaxing all at once, releasing a vise grip it's held far too long. *You wanted to be dead, Billie? Well, now you really are. Go be with Some Guy Named Ryan. We don't need you.*

Jean bends down and begins collecting her things, shoving folders in her tote. Remembering, Jonathan pivots sharply, looking for Olive in the seats behind him. In the momentary lull between cases, the crowd in the benches has shifted; a crumpled old man with mustard in his mustache is now sitting where Olive was moments before. Jonathan stands and cranes his neck, scanning faces, but she's gone.

Panic prickles up his spine.

But he feels Jean's gentle hand at the small of his back, pressing him forward.

"We're done here," she says.

_____

The first thing he does when he gets back to the house is fire off a text to Olive: *Call me. We need to talk*. Then he opens his laptop and pulls up the folder that contains the manuscript of *Where the Mountain Meets the Sky*. He scans the Word documents, his eyes catching on the most sentimental and sappy lines—*there* was *something magical about my immediate connection with Billie . . . someone finally understood the texture of my heart*. The syrupy words feel foreign, as if they were written by a stranger about a stranger.

He drags the manuscript to his laptop's trash can; and then—why not?—the entire research folder. Then he empties the trash, just to make it stick. Let his publisher come after him for the advance; once December rolls around, he'll have plenty of money to pay it back.

Giddy with his recklessness, he pulls up the blog page where he was posting the book as his ipTracer lure. He dismantles this, too, deleting the entire account. *Cleaning house,* he tells himself. *No: taking it down to the studs.*

What next? He remembers Billie's laptop. Where did he put it when he got home from the tapas bar the other night? He retraces the steps he can recall and finally finds it underneath an empty pizza box in the kitchen. He walks the computer out to the garbage cans by the front curb and unceremoniously dumps it in, atop a pile of coffee grounds and curdled Thai take-out containers.

Back inside, he stands in the empty living room. Now what? *Start a whole new life. Leave all vestiges of Billie behind.* Oh, just that. He squints at the photograph of their family in its place of honor on the mantel. Then he turns it facedown so that he doesn't have to look at it anymore.

The house echoes around him. He can hear the groan of the freezer as it regurgitates another round of asymmetrical ice cubes from its innards. The ticking heater in the hallway, recovering from its latest heroic effort to heat this drafty house. And from somewhere outside, a vague rumbling sound, the urban white noise generated by tens of thousands of people churning constantly forward, battling inertia in an attempt to stave off their own inevitable death.

Christ, stop being so grim, he thinks. But his house is unbearably empty. Four hours until Olive gets home from school. No writing to do; no deadlines; no legal documents to fill out; nothing urgent that needs to be dealt with. He's released from the past now, but he's never felt so aimless in his life.

His cellphone vibrates in his pocket. It's Harmony: *How'd the hearing go?*

He types back quickly: *As well as it could.*

He waits for her response, feeling the solitude of his home settling over him like a particularly stifling blanket. Then he picks up his phone again: *Come over?*

You mean now?

Yes.

Fifteen minutes later, he hears her key in the front door. By that time, he's dug up a dusty bottle of expensive-looking wine from the basement and put some only-slightly-mangy cheese on the coffee table, along with a bowl of crackers and some dried apricots.

Harmony appears in the doorway of the living room, wearing leggings and a soft-looking oversize sweater. He feels a little surge of happiness at the sight of her, a warm blast of life in this cold house. When she sees the wineglasses on the table, her eyes go wide. "What's this for?"

"I felt the need to mark the occasion." He pours the wine and slides a glass toward her. "I think it's really good wine. Maybe a gift I got from *Decode* upper management? Can't think of any other reason we would have stashed it in the basement."

She slips down onto the couch next to him, her thigh close to his, her long lashes obscuring her expression. "I take it this means the judge issued a death certificate?"

"Yes," he says. "It's official."

"Does that . . . hurt?" She doesn't take the glass but instead squeezes closer to him, as if the substance of her body might be capable of absorbing his pain.

"A little," he says. Saying this, he *does* feel some kind of grief that he didn't acknowledge before, a dark knot of loss, though he's unsure whether it's the loss of the woman he once loved or the loss of his belief in her existence at all. Maybe it doesn't matter. "But the death certificate, it marks an end, right? So—what's that saying you see in fortune cookies? 'New beginnings are often disguised as painful endings'?" He frowns, the aphorism familiar but not quite right. "Or wait, maybe it's 'Everything that has a beginning has an end.' No, I think that's from *The Matrix*. Forget it."

She reaches out and takes her glass. "Either way, I'll toast to that." She looks sideways at him. "So what begins now?"

What *is* beginning? He hadn't thought that far. His life seems like a raft of wreckage right now, with nothing to anticipate but the slow, arduous repair of his relationship with Olive. Except that, as he looks at Harmony—wrapping himself in the comfort of her presence—another answer becomes obvious. "Us," he says. "You and me. For real."

She flushes, fiddles with the hem of her sweater. "Are you saying you want me to be your *girlfriend*?"

His eyes flick to the family photograph, facedown on the mantel. He is quiet, thinking of Olive. As long as she keeps believing that Billie is alive, she's going to hang on to the false hope that her mom might come back. And *that* would be more painful for him to watch than the grief he's witnessed all year. It's time to cut it off: frame Billie's death certificate, get past the one-year anniversary, put Olive back on Depakote, and start building a new family. *It's what's best for Olive,* he tells himself. *I need to expel the specter of her mother from this house, and as long as it's just the two of us around here, that's never going to happen.*

He takes Harmony's hand, turning it over and pressing a thumb against the calloused pad of her palm. "I want you to move in," he says. Her eyes fly open wide. "I'm serious. This house is too lonely with just Olive and me rattling around in it. I'm ready for a change."

There's a smile twitching at her lips. "And Olive? Is she going to accept that?"

"Not at first. But she'll get there eventually," he says. "Our life isn't over just because Billie's dead. She's going to have to accept that at some point, like it or not. Maybe Billie's death certificate, plus the one-year mark, will be a turning point. She already knows you and I got together, right? We'll give her a few months to get used to the idea, and then we can tell her that you're moving in."

Maybe he's being overly optimistic; and yet it sounds plausible. And when he looks at Harmony, he sees that she's radiant, as if some kind of internal combustion is lighting her up from the inside out. "I'd be lying if I said I hadn't thought of this. A lot," she says. Her hand comes to rest on his leg, her fingers toying with the seam of his jeans. Her voice goes soft. "I was afraid you wanted something different. I thought maybe Billie, and the Sean situation, all that awkwardness, might be scaring you off."

He hesitates, feeling himself grow hard just from the proximity of her hand. "Well, yes, it's complicated, but it's the past. It's behind us. Maybe that's *why* this could work, because of all that shared history." Harmony lets out a big sigh, as if she's been holding her breath. "So is that a yes? You'll move in?"

"Of course," she says, dragging her fingers up

until they meet his and tangle there. "I love you," she says shyly.

"I love you, too," he says. The sentiment feels strange on his lips—his brain sends an instinctive red alert: *the wrong woman on the receiving end*—but he wills himself into it, sinking into the words until they wrap around him like a warm cloak. He pushes aside a parade of unwanted thoughts—*Is this love or just convenient lust? A forced attempt to close the door on Billie once and for all?*—and focuses on Harmony, who is whispering damply in his ear.

"I've loved you since the moment we first met," she continues.

The timing on that—*since we first met?*—is a little discomforting; and just before he kisses her, he notices something strange about her smile—something that smacks curiously of victory—but he chalks it up to his own balky nerves. *Beginnings, not endings,* he tells himself as he pushes up Harmony's implausibly soft sweater.

And by the time he finally remembers the quote he was searching for—*A story has no beginning or end*—he's in too deep to care.

Later, when Harmony is napping in a beam of sunlight on his bed, he goes downstairs to clean up the mess in the living room before Olive gets home from school.

He puts the wineglasses in the dishwasher and finds himself thinking of his daughter's horrified face in the courtroom, her expression of betrayal. *You did the right thing,* he reminds himself. *She didn't know all the factors at play, and she never should.*

He pulls out his phone to double-check whether Olive responded to his text. There's nothing.

He's about to put the phone back in his pocket when he notices the ipTracer app still in prominent position on his phone's home screen. He punches at his phone, preparing to delete it, but can't quite make himself do it. He tries to resist the impulse; ultimately fails. He opens the ipTracer one last time, just to check.

Your page has been visited by 3 unique IP addresses.

There is quicksand shifting underneath his feet, ready to pull him back in. *It's probably nothing,* he reassures himself, *just like the last time.* He carries the phone to the bottom of the stairs and stands there for a moment, listening for Harmony, but all is quiet.

He goes back into the living room and opens the ipTracer report.

The first IP address is the same number from last Friday, his editor at Random House.

The second IP address is also based in New York; it presumably belongs to Jeff, his agent.

He starts to think he's dodged a bullet as he clicks on the third number. Surely it's another New York address: an agency minion, a Random House marketing person, someone else sent to scope out Jonathan's blog and help mitigate the disaster that is *Where the Mountain Meets the Sky.*

But the ipTracer spits out an unrecognizable location:

Continent: North America
Country: United States
City: Santa Cruz
ISP: Surfnet

His stomach goes sour. *Santa Cruz.* His intuition is sending up bright orange signal flares of distress. *Maybe it's just a fluke,* he tries to reassure himself. *Someone who stumbled upon the site by accident.* But when he scrolls down he sees that this particular IP address has visited his site six times in four days, logging 182 page views in total.

He glances at the clock—it's almost three, Olive will be home from school soon, he really should wake Harmony and make sure she's dressed before that happens. And yet he finds himself out at the curb, rummaging through the garbage can until he finds his wife's laptop. He dusts coffee grounds off its titanium cover and takes it back inside.

The computer hums to life in his lap. Billie's hard drive is still an impenetrable digital hoard—a jumble of billions of irrelevant bytes—but this time around, he knows exactly what he's searching for. *Ryan Santa Cruz,* he queries the computer's search engine.

The laptop immediately spits out an entry from Billie's address book.

Ryan Ratliff
830 Madeo St.
Santa Cruz, CA

RR.

Shit. He looks at this name for a long time, weighing his options. He pulls up Google and types *Ryan Ratliff* into the search field; but he hesitates before he clicks Return, aware of the black hole of misery into which he's about to leap. What is this going to accomplish? Does he really want to know more about his wife's lover? Does he really want to resurrect the woman he spent the morning burying?

No.

With infinite self-control, he closes the search window and quits out of the browser. *Put it back in the trash can and forget about it,* he tells himself. But he can hear Harmony moving around upstairs, as well as the distinct sound of Olive's backpack being unceremoniously dumped on the front porch. And so he slams Billie's laptop closed and slides it under the cushions of the couch, to be dealt with later.

He dashes to meet his daughter at the door.

Olive appears in the doorway, canted sideways from the weight of the backpack that's hanging from the crook of her elbow. She stops when she sees her father standing in the entry, and opens her mouth to speak; and then she stops, distracted by something she's noticed behind him.

He turns to see Harmony standing at the top of the stairs, wearing an old flannel shirt of his, a pair of purple lace panties, and nothing else.

Harmony waves at Olive as if the tableau is perfectly natural. "Hi there!" she calls. "How was school?"

Olive smiles dutifully. "Fine," she says in a voice so small that Harmony probably has to strain to hear it. And then, under her breath, she whispers to her father: "I thought you wanted to talk."

"Right, God, I'm sorry," he stumbles. "I didn't mean her to . . . Poor judgment, I know. She just came over, and . . ."

"Dad, she's *always* over these days." Olive is staring at the purple panties. "Next you're going to be telling me that she's moving in."

He freezes, feeling like a kid caught with his hand in the cookie jar. "Well."

Olive whirls to study him. Her eyes are wet, her lip quivering righteously. *"Seriously?"* She flings her backpack to the floor so hard that Jonathan can hear the aging hardwood splinter under the weight of a $26,720-a-year education. "You suck."

She marches up the stairs and brushes past Harmony, the skirt on her uniform kicking pertly with each step. His daughter gives Harmony's purple panties a long, hard look and then disappears into her own bedroom. The door slams so hard that the house shakes, and an alarming crash echoes through the kitchen. When he peers in to check, he sees that the saggy cabinet door has finally broken straight off its hinges.

"Whoops," he hears Harmony murmur behind him. He makes sure to plaster a reassuring smile on his face before he turns around to face her.

17

SHE CAN HEAR HER father at the top of the landing, talking in a low voice with Harmony. A flurry of activity in his bedroom at the other end of the hall; a toilet flushing; the thump of Dansko clogs on the stairs. The windows of her bedroom shiver as the front door opens and then shuts, and Harmony's Kia coughs to life in the driveway.

Olive stands in her bedroom window, watching Harmony drive away, but she doesn't feel particularly victorious. She won a dogfight, not the war.

She feels like she's back at zero when it comes to finding her mother. Worse than zero; a negative sum. What now? She has no clues left to cling to, just a string of alarming stories about her mom's past, and not even her father or her best friend by her side. She feels like she's been washed out to sea without a life preserver.

After a few minutes, she hears her father rustling outside her door, his knuckles scraping along the grain of the wood. "Olive, I'm ready to talk now."

"I'm not," she says.

"C'mon, Bean. Let's try to do this like reasonable adults."

"I'm pretty sure I'm the only one acting like an adult here."

This shuts him up. Finally, he says quietly, "I'll be waiting downstairs when you're ready."

She knows he's lurking at the bottom of the stairs, waiting to pounce on her the second she leaves her room. She flips onto her stomach on her bed, pulls out her cellphone, and rereads her message exchange with Natalie for the hundredth time.

Hey Nat, didn't see u in german this morning????
stomachache, came late
Oh.

. . .

I'm sorry about what happened last Friday.
It's fine

. . .

What R U doing after school
Plans with Ming sorry

. . .

R U avoiding me?
No

. . .

Is everything OK w us?

. . .

. . .

Nat?

She shoves the phone back in her backpack.

Overhead, Gizmo flies from one side of her cage to the other, stuttering back and forth and back again until Olive can't take it anymore. She gets up and opens the door to the cage. "Come on out," she tells the bird, but Gizmo refuses to leave, huddling at the far side of her cage as if the open door is some kind of trap. Olive sticks her finger in, trying to get the bird to hop on her finger, but Gizmo just flutters from bar to bar, twittering angrily, until Olive wants to cry.

"Olive?" she hears her father calling up the stairs. "I'm making popcorn, you want some?"

She doesn't answer. But a few minutes later, the smell of hot buttered popcorn infiltrates her room, an olfactory diplomat. Not fair. She flips open her trigonometry textbook, refusing to engage. But her stomach growls—she missed lunch period because of her trip to the courtroom—and eventually, hunger wins.

She climbs off her bed and tiptoes down the stairs. She can see a big bowl of popcorn sitting on the coffee table in the living room; she hears her father in the kitchen, doing something with a drill.

She plunks down on the couch, cramming popcorn into her mouth. As she sits, her tailbone makes contact with something hard and oblong. Reaching behind her, she fishes the offending object out from underneath the pillow where it's been tucked.

It's her mother's laptop.

Where did *that* come from? She puts the computer in her lap, popcorn crumbs still falling from her mouth, and runs her hand over the computer's cover: It's warm, thrumming, as if it's hibernating.

She imagines some essence of her mother trapped inside, waiting for her to let it out.

It's a sign, she thinks, brightening.

She flips the laptop open and the screen immediately wakes up. The keyboard is filthy, spotted with spilled coffee and calcified secretions from her mother's hands. She uses the edge of a fingernail to pick an ancient crumb from the crevasse of the *B* key, imagining her mom eating a sandwich while she typed. Olive pops the crumb in her mouth and lets it dissolve on her tongue.

Her mother's desktop materializes, an achingly familiar clutter of folders and files and sticky notes. Only one window is open: a contact from her mother's address book. A name—Ryan Ratliff—and an address in Santa Cruz.

Santa Cruz.

The vectors of Olive's life draw momentarily tight, a month of mystery closing in around one point. SYBILLA carved into a wooden rail and her mother calling to her from a windswept beach. It's as clear as if someone drew arrows around the address and wrote PAY ATTENTION OLIVE in Sharpie above it.

The air around her fills with butterflies, their wings moving in syncopation with her beating heart.

This is the address where I'll find her.

Her father is suddenly beside her, gently tugging the laptop from her hands. "I was going to get rid of that," he says.

She doesn't relinquish her grip. "Who's Ryan Ratliff?" she asks.

She can see a battle taking place inside him, his

jaw twitching as he tests out different responses and discards them. Finally, something in his face collapses, his mouth going slack. He sits down heavily beside her. "I've got something unpleasant to tell you. I've been keeping it from you because I didn't want you to get hurt, but it's time that you know. Maybe if you do, you'll understand the situation a little better."

"OK," she says slowly, not liking where this is going.

"This guy, Ryan—I think your mom might have been having an affair with him," he says.

She closes her eyes and sees butterflies exploding. Fragments of wings flying in all directions, the entire rainbow spectrum obliterated into dust, tiny furry bodies shorn of their plumage, falling softly to the forest floor below.

"No," she says. "That can't be right. Mom wouldn't do that."

He lets out a small sigh of exasperation. "It's true, Olive. I found a letter she wrote to him."

"Show me," she insists.

He shakes his head. "That wouldn't do you any good."

Understanding spreads through her, as sticky and smothering as pancake syrup. "You think that's what happened, don't you? You think she left us for him?"

He stares dully at the opposite wall; the hollows around his eye sockets look bruised and blue. "Olive, please just let it go. Your mom is dead. We have a death certificate. We need to get on with our lives."

She *does* see it all now: why he lied to the judge this morning, why he's been so reluctant to believe her. He thinks her mom betrayed him for someone else. But he can't be right, it doesn't make any *sense*. Wouldn't she have seen that in her visions? Wouldn't she have known? Is it possible he's making this up to get her to let go and move on? Has Harmony messed with his head?

She thinks of her mother's warning during that last encounter, her words as she stubbed her cigarette out in the grass: *He's not to be trusted.*

"That death certificate doesn't mean anything, and you know it," she points out.

He lets out a strangled sound. "Oh, Christ, Olive. Don't make me do this. Don't you see? Even if she's not really dead, she wants us to believe that she is. She's not lost in the mountains somewhere and she's not in trouble and she doesn't have amnesia, sweetheart. She's gone because she wants to be gone."

His words are ragged, they scrape across her heart like a broken fingernail. "That's not true. She wants me to look for her. She *told* me! She said she missed me!"

"She didn't tell you anything, Olive." This is delivered so gently that Olive can hardly bear it. "You were having seizures. You wanted to see her, and your brain obliged. It took your memories—memories of being with your mom at the beach, seeing old photos of where she grew up, pictures of our wedding day—and reshaped them into hallucinations. That's all."

"But I was right about her being alive," she protests. "That woman at the nursing home—she saw her, remember? You said you believed her."

Her father shuts his eyes as if the effort required

to keep them open has just surpassed his abilities. "The only thing I truly believe is that it's just you and me now, and we need to start figuring out how to make that work. Because *this*"—he makes a fist and gently taps her chest with it and then taps his own, as if trying to connect them with an invisible string—"is breaking my heart."

This is the moment when she starts to cry, because she loves her dad, and she wants him to be happy; but she also knows that she can't believe him, because that would be disloyal to her mother. And so she snuffles and wheezes soggily into his shoulder, strung out like a wire between two poles; and as she does, she can feel her father gently slipping the computer from her lap and out of her reach.

"OK, Dad, I'll let it go," she whispers, because she knows that's what he wants most to hear.

She lets him think that he's won. But he hasn't. She's already memorized the address in Santa Cruz.

In the morning, she arrives at school early and finds a senior girl trying to shove a flyer through the ventilation slits in her locker. The girl sees her coming and turns to greet her.

"Olive? Hi, I'm Dominique," she says.

"I know who you are," Olive says, unexpectedly shy. She's noticed Dominique before; how could she not? Dominique has hair an implausible shade of red that is shaved short on one side and falls across her cheek in choppy waves on the other. Her ears are studded with inky black buttons and her lipstick is purple and she has a tattoo of a blue star visible on her collarbone under her uniform. A walking rainbow. She's the kind of girl who surfs easily through the halls, riding each passing swell of girls, never appearing to lose her balance. She is everything Olive is not.

Dominique shoves the flyer at Olive, who takes it out of reflex. She reads it as Dominique looks on, apparently quite pleased with herself.

CLAREMONT QUEER CLUB MEETING
THIS FRIDAY AT 4 PM.
FREE DONUTS.
HOT GURL ON GIRL ACTION.
OPEN 2 ALL!

How did she know? Is it really that obvious already? Olive looks questioningly at Dominique, who smiles wider. "I'm the club president. Loud and proud, right?" Olive isn't sure what to say. Dominique's smile starts to fade. "Oh, shit. You're not out yet? I thought . . ." She shrugs. "Sorry. Someone told me something and I just assumed."

Natalie told. Stung, Olive shoves the flyer into her backpack. "Thanks. I'll think about it," she says.

Dominique swings the hair out of her eye with a practiced flip of her head. "At your own pace. We'll be here when you're ready." She squeezes Olive's arm and then disappears off down the hall.

Olive slowly gathers her books from her locker. The hall is filling with Girls, the humidity rising; she can smell the sharp scent of her own sweat through the layers of wool and cheap uniform polyester. Her head spins. She needs to talk to Natalie.

She races toward first-period German, ping-ponging dizzily through clusters of girls. Is everyone staring at her, or is she imagining that? She doesn't like this feeling at all: like she's been trapped in a terrarium, labeled and put on display. Again. (It was bad enough being Poor Olive Whose Mom Died in a Tragic Accident, now she has to shoulder Olive the Closeted Lesbian, too?) What if she's got the wrong label? What if she has to stay there forever? Why do people always seem to feel like they know more about her than she knows about herself?

"Olive!" Someone is calling her name from the opposite end of the hall. She spins around just in time to see Mrs. Santiago, the school counselor, descending on her from the direction of the administrative offices, knit layers flapping like the wings of a colossal bird. One of those wings sweeps Olive out of the stream of girls and to the edge of the hallway, beside the trophy case. Olive is trapped.

"I already took my medicine today," she says quickly. She digs in her backpack, pulling out the bottle of allergy pills, and waggles it in the air. "I swear. You can count."

Santiago shakes her head. "That's not it. I'm worried about you. I'm hearing things about your problematic attendance record." Her breath in Olive's face smells like Altoids. "Can you tell me what's been going on, Olive?"

Olive gazes deep into the trophy case, hoping it will yield answers. *2012 Indoor Lacrosse Champions. Third Place JSA State League. CIF NorCal Girl's League Golf 2004.* "Family crisis?" she tries.

Santiago shakes her head sadly, as if Olive's problems pain her deeply. "I can't help you if you won't try to help yourself."

Over Santiago's shoulder, Olive sees Natalie walking by, flanked by Ming and Tracy. Ming and Tracy are staring straight at Olive, baldly curious. Between them, Natalie resolutely refuses to look up, her gaze trained on the wooden floor of the hallway.

Olive feels sick to her stomach.

"Olive? Do you understand what I'm saying?"

"I understand," Olive says quietly.

Santiago peers at her face, her voice soft. "Olive, I'd really like to set up a session with you."

Olive can't imagine anything she wants less at this minute than to try to explain herself to the school counselor. "I swear, I'm OK. It was an anomaly. I promise it won't happen again," she says. Then, aware of what Santiago most wants to hear: "And my dad is already sending me to a therapist. I'm just, you know, learning how to process my grief."

Santiago sighs and sweeps a wing of taupe linen across Olive's back, steering her toward her classroom. "Well, that's great, Olive," she says. "Remember, I'm always here for you."

And she pads off down the hall, patting backs and squeezing shoulders as she passes. Olive hesitates outside first-period German, peering at the roiling mass in the overheated classroom, a bevy of girls frantically getting in their last Instagram posts before the final bell rings. Her own desk, next to Natalie's, sits empty.

Natalie is looking down at her phone, her curly hair hanging limply around her flushed cheeks. Olive wonders whom Natalie is texting. It clearly isn't her.

Olive pivots on her heel. She dashes back down the hall, makes a right at the trophy case, and takes a shortcut through the silent auditorium, her sneakers squeaking on the freshly waxed floor. Then it's out to the parking lot, where the dusty Subaru sits wedged between two late-model BMWs, looking like a forlorn goldfish stranded in a tank full of exotic koi.

There's only one place left to go.

It's a clear day in Berkeley, but by the time Olive gets to the other side of the bay, the sky is socked in with gray cloud cover. She drives south and west on 280, getting stuck for a time in Silicon Valley commuter traffic near San Jose; and then she breaks free and she's winding over the mountains toward the coast. A fine mist hangs low between the pines, the road slick with damp. Her tires skate along the hairpin curves. She stays in the slow lane, petrified, as trucks whizz past so close that they rattle her car.

And then she's finally out on the other side of the mountain, accelerating down the hill, turning onto Highway 1. The ocean opens up before her, a blanket of gray rising to blend with the clouds. She knows exactly where she is. Some force keeps bringing her back here, and surely there's a reason for that.

The GPS directs her south, though, away from the butterfly beach, toward the outskirts of Santa Cruz. She winds slowly through a scrubby neighborhood of cottages with unfenced yards, their battered grass creeping out to meet the crumbling asphalt of the road. Station wagons parked on meridians, the salt air chewing holes in the finish of their paint. Faded beach towels slung over porch railings.

Only now does she grow aware of the kick of her racing heart. The car windows are fogging up from the heat of her breath. She realizes that she's in danger of hyperventilating. *This is it.*

"Almost there."

Olive looks to her right, to the source of this voice. Her mother sits in the passenger seat, her feet kicked up on the console, warming her bare toes against the vent of the heater. She's wearing a fleece sweatshirt and a woolly cap pulled down over her forehead. A thick braid dangles along the side of her neck.

The car veers in the roadway as Olive stares. Billie raises an eyebrow, then lifts a foot off the vent and uses her toe to point ahead, through the windshield. "Eyes on the road, Bean. Don't kill us now."

Olive jerks around and corrects course just in time to avoid sideswiping an RV parked by the side of the road. When she looks back, her mother is gone.

And then the GPS on her phone informs her that she's reached her destination. *830 Madeo St.* Olive slows to a stop. She peers through the condensation on the windshield, sees that she's parked in front of a bottle-green bungalow, its paint weathered and peeling, sheltered by a giant oak tree. A faded ornamental flag with a smiling orca hangs over the living room window. The patch of grass in front of the house is cluttered with bicycles and rusting lawn chairs and surfboards still wet from the sea.

She feels her bladder pressing heavily on her groin and realizes she's in danger of peeing her pants.

She gets out of the car and walks up to the front door of the bungalow. There's a line of flip-flops, male and female, jumbled in a pile beside the bungalow's screen door. A fraying hammock, strung between the house and the trunk of the oak tree, sways heavily in the breeze.

She raises a hand to knock and hesitates. Music blasts from inside the bungalow. Cat Stevens, live in concert. *There'll never be another you.* She remembers her mother sitting in the driver's seat of the Subaru, banging her fingers on the steering wheel in time to this song. *There's going to be another story.*

(Why is she so scared of knocking?)

Olive knocks.

Nothing happens.

She knocks again, louder this time. And then she rings the bell, but it seems to be broken; or maybe she just can't hear it over the music. She presses it again, then again and again and again, bearing down so hard that the joint of her thumb begins to protest.

She steps back from the door and then screams at the top of her lungs: *"MOM!"*

The music stops so abruptly that Olive can hear her own voice echoing through the cottage. Footsteps thump through the house and then the front door is yanked open.

Olive finds herself staring into the eyes of her mother.

18

BY THE TIME JONATHAN wakes up on Tuesday morning, it's almost eight o'clock. He lies in bed, listening to the garbage trucks rattling down the street. *Today you begin again,* he thinks. *It's time to start making plans.* Maybe he'll meet with a head-hunter and see what jobs are available for someone with his qualifications. Maybe he'll call up some of his old journalism contacts and see if he can rustle up some freelance work. Maybe he'll start writing a *new* memoir, something utterly unrelated to Billie—travel back further in time, say, and write about Jenny.

Then again, maybe he should take advantage of the life insurance money that is coming his way and take a little more time to figure out what's next. He imagines the world opening up before him, imagines himself shedding the brittle carapace of forty-three years of single-minded focus and trying on some-thing completely new. He could launch a dot-com. Learn a new language. Take up CrossFit. Plan an extended vacation, just him and Olive: some bond-ing time before Harmony moves in.

Take that, Billie, he thinks. *We're going to be just fine without you.*

He wanders down to the kitchen and discovers that Olive has left a pot of coffee for him. A sign of reconciliation? The Subaru isn't in the driveway; she's already left for school. He sits at the kitchen table, flipping methodically through the newspaper, determined to read every word of every article. Be-cause *why not.*

At half past eight, the home phone rings.

"Jonathan?" The taut voice on the other end of the line belongs to Vice Principal Gillespie, and im-mediately his upbeat mood is shattered.

"Yes," he says flatly.

"Olive came to school this morning and then left campus again without permission."

He stalls for time as he dashes up the stairs: "Are you sure?" He pushes open the door to Olive's room and peers in, just to check. Cascades of books lie upended on every surface. Her bed is unmade, the sheets dragged off the bed and halfway across the room, tangling with a pair of boots and some striped tights. An opened bag of barbecue Kettle Chips lies abandoned in the middle of the rug, regurgitating orange crumbs across the floor.

Catsby is curled up on Olive's pillow, keeping guard over the chaos. The cat jumps to his feet and leisurely picks his way through the mess, then slips past Jonathan and dashes down the stairs.

"She cut class yesterday, too, were you aware of that?" Gillespie says.

He thinks of Olive sitting in the courtroom behind him. *I should have written her a note to take to school today.* "Actually, yes. I can explain that one, I was with her—"

"Which makes this the fourth time in two weeks that she's been truant, not including the sick day she took last Friday." Ms. Gillespie's voice is as crisp and tart as a Granny Smith. "Honestly, Jonathan, because of your family circumstances, I've already given her more leniency than most girls would get, but this, in combination with your late tuition payment . . ."

"I can give you partial tuition now," he says quickly, wondering if Marcus's check has cleared the bank yet. "And I'll have the rest shortly."

She hesitates. "The thing is, Jonathan, I'm not sure that Olive *wants* to be at Claremont anymore. She doesn't seem happy, her grades are falling, and her teachers tell me she's struggling with her friendships. She's resisting our efforts to try to help her and refuses to meet with the school counselor. I'm wondering if perhaps a change might benefit her."

"Look, don't do anything yet, OK? We've had a lot going on lately, as I'm sure you're aware. Why don't we set up a meeting, all three of us, to discuss it?"

Gillespie sighs. "Fine. She's suspended for the rest of the week. We'll discuss this further when she returns on Monday."

Where the hell is *Olive?* he wonders as he hangs up and races out to his car. He texts her as he pulls out of the driveway, typing in furious all-caps: *SCHOOL CALLED WHERE ARE YOU? CALL ME NOW!!* Steering with one hand, eyes on his phone, he knocks over one of the garbage cans out by the curb and sends its contents flying across his lawn. Leftover pad Thai noodles glue themselves to the top of his hood. It looks like someone vomited on his Prius. He feels like vomiting, too. *What are you trying to pull now, Olive?*

He drives through the streets of Berkeley, the noodles on his hood collecting gnats and dust, his eyes peeled for a glimpse of the Subaru. He tries the Cheese Board first; they bake pletzels on Tuesdays, and Olive loves their pletzels. But she's not there. Maybe she's at a coffee shop: the original Peet's, Philz, the Elmwood Café? No, no, and no. Mrs. Dalloway's bookstore, Amoeba Music? It's too early; both are closed.

He makes it to the Berkeley library just after it opens, and jogs up to the reading room; but even before he scans the tables, he knows that it's pointless because Olive's car wasn't parked in the library's lot. The reading room is cold and empty and accusingly silent. A solitary librarian watches, baffled, as he races around, checking between the stacks to be sure. Nothing.

He is at a loss. Where else would she go? Why is she such a mystery to him? How can he pull her back to him, how can he climb inside her mind and untangle its cryptic contents? What *does* his daughter care about these days?

Natalie, he realizes. *Maybe they're together.*

He drives back home. From the drawer in the kitchen, he digs out a dog-eared Claremont school directory and thumbs through it until he finds Natalie's contact information. He calls her cellphone from the house line, hoping that she will recognize their number on her caller ID and pick up. Natalie's phone rings and rings as he studies the clock, trying to figure out if he'll catch her between classes. He gets voicemail and hangs up. And then he tries calling it again.

This time Natalie answers right away. "Olive?" she whispers. "Why are you *calling*?"

"Actually, this is Olive's father," he says. "Hi, Natalie."

He can hear Natalie's footsteps echoing in the empty hallways of the school. "Oh," she says. "Is Olive in trouble for cutting again?"

"You could say that," he says. "Natalie, where is she?"

There's a burst of staticky noise on the other end of the line—he can hear the student council president making an announcement over the school's loudspeaker, something about the Fall Frolic—and then Natalie comes back on. "I don't know," she says.

"Did she tell you that she was planning to cut class today?"

A hush on the other end of the line. "No. We kind of, had some problems? We aren't really talking."

Her only close friend. His heart breaks for his daughter. "Where do you think she would go?"

"I honestly don't know." She's quiet. "I have to go. I only got a bathroom pass, and my teacher is going to yell at me if I don't get back soon."

"Wait." He thinks. "How does my daughter seem to you these days?"

She seems flummoxed by the question or perhaps by its source. "Confused," she says finally.

"Confused by what? Do you mean, about her mom or her seizures or . . ." Something else rises to the top of his mind. "Something to do with a boy?"

"A boy?" She's quiet for a beat. "Not a *boy*, no. Look, sorry, I gotta go, bye."

He holds the dead receiver in his hand, thinking. Something about the way Natalie said this—*Not a boy*—gives him pause. Out of nowhere, a critical question that has been gestating in the back of his mind for months finds its form: Is his daughter *gay*? It would explain her lack of interest in talking about boys; it would explain so much, really, about her state of mind, about their growing disconnection. Does she think he wouldn't support her if she told him she was into girls? Doesn't she know him better than that?

A rush of hope. Maybe that's where she is right now: skipping school with a secret crush. Maybe there's someone he's overlooked.

He goes back upstairs to Olive's room, pushing his way in through the mess. He walks over to look at the photographs that Olive has taped to her wall, but there's nothing there that might enlighten him. Besides a few selfies taken with Natalie, the pictures are mostly of her mom. Billie and Olive in an igloo, cheeks flushed with the cold. Olive at her eighth birthday, Billie lowering an elaborate cake in front of her. Billie at the beach, laughing with her head tipped back, chin tilted at the clouds. He pushes a pile of books aside in order to make a closer examination of this photo, and one slips off the top of the heap and lands on his toe: *Connections: Visionary Encounters with Your Beloved*. He looks down at the book, feeling ill, knowing in his heart that his daughter is not off doing something reassuringly normal like cutting class with a love interest.

I've lost my daughter, he thinks. *I tried so hard to do this right, and still, I lost her. I lost her to Billie a long time ago.*

He drifts back downstairs to the living room and stands there, looking out the front window as if Olive might magically materialize in the driveway. Garbage is scattered across the front lawn from his collision with the trash bins. Empty yogurt cups and moldy bagels and the metallic glint of Billie's laptop computer. And then— "Jesus," he says out loud.

He runs back out to the curb and flings aside the trash, his hands growing gritty with coffee grounds, then jerks Billie's computer free from the bottom of the pile.

He sits down on the grass and turns it on, praying that he didn't kill the damn thing when he chucked it in the bin the previous night. The hard drive whines threateningly, and there's an ominous chunking coming from deep in the computer's bowels, but it boots up. He waits, his jeans growing damp from something unsavory underneath his rear.

Then he opens Billie's contact database and plugs the name in: Ryan Ratliff.

Here I come, Billie, he thinks.

The drive from Berkeley to Santa Cruz seems to take ten minutes; anger keeps his foot heavy on the accelerator. He skids through the curves on Highway 17, veers around the lumbering trucks, whips over the summit and back down the other side. It's a small miracle that he neither crashes the Prius nor gets pulled over by the police.

As he drives, his mind churns through an endless list of questions that he wants to ask Billie when he sees her. *How could you leave us? Is anything about you real? Was any of this my fault? Why didn't you trust me enough to tell me the truth about your past? Could we have stopped you if we'd tried? What makes this guy so much more important than us? Are you a sociopath or just a narcissist?*

Did you ever love me? Or was that all an act, too?

He wonders who he'll see when he gets to Santa Cruz; if she'll even be a Billie he recognizes. If she'll try to spin it all in her favor; if she'll have the decency to be ashamed. And—the most disturbing thought of all—what if Billie *does* want Olive back; and what if Olive wants to stay with her mother? What will he do then?

You had your chance, Billie, he silently glowers. *You chose to leave. It's my turn.*

Once he reaches Santa Cruz, he finds himself in a shaggy neighborhood on the edge of town, cozy but unkempt, a surf village that looks like it's seen its fair share of keggers. Not where he would have expected to find Billie, but he's had too many surprises this month to muster up much astonishment.

Turning onto Madeo Street, he immediately notices the Subaru on the side of the road. He slams on the brakes, skids to a stop behind it. The car is parked in front of a green bungalow. It takes him a minute to place it: peeling paint, a whale flag, bicycles in the yard, a giant oak. It's the house from that odd series of photos on his wife's computer. Pieces clicking into place.

He marches to the front door and rings the doorbell.

The door swings open before he can even steel himself, and for a moment, he thinks he might be losing his mind. Because it's Billie standing in front of him. But not Berkeley Mom Billie, with her brown hair cascading around her shoulders, but a much younger Billie, in her mid- to late twenties. A blond duplicate of the girl he met seventeen years earlier. The same cropped pixie hair, the same delicate freckled cheekbones, the same elfin chin. Billie's dark eyes, wide-set and watching. He's disoriented, as if he's stepped into a time machine. Could this be a hallucination, a mirror of the ones that Olive has been experiencing?

The young woman examines him. "Yeah, can I help you?" she says.

His voice finally comes back. "I'm looking for Ryan."

"Lemme guess, you're Olive's dad?" She opens the door wider, an amused smile on her face. Over her shoulder now he can see his daughter, sitting on a futon in the middle of Young Billie's living room. She jumps up when she sees him.

"Dad," Olive says, her eyes bright with excitement. "Mom's not here, she wasn't having an affair, you were wrong. We both were. *This* is Ryan. Dad—I have a sister."

You believe what you think you believe, until suddenly, you realize that you don't anymore. Or maybe you *do* believe, but it's no longer convenient to do so, so you decide to forget. You decide to find other beliefs, ones that more comfortably fit the constantly evolving puzzle of your life.

To put it more finely: There are those beliefs that you will carry with you until the end of your days. A belief in friendliness; a belief in long vacations; a belief in the power of the press and the merits of good coffee. And then there are the beliefs that seem so vital when you are young, but that the passing years steadily leach out of you: a belief in not selling out; a belief in the superiority of the artist; a belief in hardwood floors and staying fit and your ability to change the world. Most of all: a belief that love is forever, that you can climb into a stranger's heart and know that person and be known in return.

What remains, after all those beliefs have fallen away, is this: your child. Olive.

Jonathan sits in a stranger's living room, his daughter's hip pressed against his own, and feels like he's been utterly emptied, a shell of the person he thought he once was. As he looks at this girl in front of him—Ryan, his wife's child?—he grasps that everything he once believed has been turned inside out and will never quite go back to right. The only thing that he knows is true anymore is that his daughter is here next to him, she is safe, and she needs him even more than he needs her.

And in this moment, that's enough.

They sit across from each other, Olive and Jonathan squeezed together on the futon couch, Ryan sprawled out in an armchair facing them. The bungalow reeks of post-collegiate glory: the sour tang of last night's party, marijuana wafting from a wooden box on the coffee table, sulfur and red wax from the Mexican prayer candles lined up along the mantel. There is sand in the shag rug and a pair of men's boxer shorts lying lewdly on the dining room table.

Stunned silent, Jonathan can't stop staring at Ryan. He takes inventory: *Billie's thin nose, Billie's tiny earlobes, Billie's way of chewing her upper lip when she's thinking*. He looks at Olive and back at Ryan, mentally comparing their features, finding it hard to accept that the stranger in front of him resembles his wife so much more than his own daughter does. The magnitude is hard to absorb: *Billie had a kid. Olive has a sister. Billie never told me. What the hell*.

"So Billie is . . . was . . . ?" he begins.

"My birth mom," the girl says quickly. "She gave me up for adoption right after I was born. I started looking for her, let's see, maybe four years back? Not long after I dropped out of State. I was back at home living with my parents in Fresno, which sucked, and I was having a, you know, *life crisis,* and I reached out to her, see—left a letter at the agency that arranged the adoption? And I ended up hearing back from my mom's mom, Grandma Rose. Who was kind of a nutbird, don't know if you ever met her, but God." She huffs out a sleepy little laugh. "*Literally:* God. Anyway, Grandma Rose sent my letter on to my birth mom, but Sybilla didn't respond to me. And then eventually I moved out here to Santa Cruz and stopped thinking about all that for a while." She reaches out with a toe and nudges the reeking box on the table, centering it next to a water-stained copy of *Surfer* magazine.

"So about a year and a half ago, this private investigator calls me out of the blue and says my birth mom wants to meet me. She'd come around, just needed some time, right?" Her words are drawling, there's a faraway smile on her face. "But by that point the adoption agency had closed, and Grandma Rose was, you know . . . senile, so Sybilla had to hire the investigator to track me down." Her hands fiddle in her lap, folding and refolding the sleeves of her oversize sweatshirt. She rubs her feet against each other; she's wearing a man's crew socks that droop off the end of her toes.

Jonathan realizes that his staring is starting to make the girl uncomfortable. He tries to drag his gaze away and fails. "And you actually met her? In person?"

She looks at him like he might be a little bit dim. "Well, *of course*. We met for dinner at first. And then she started coming down and staying with me weekends. She did that a few times. I taught her to surf. You know, she picked it up crazy fast? She told me she felt at home out there in the waves, said it made her feel truly alive again. I could totally relate to *that*. That's why I moved out here, too." She says this with pride, and then her eyes meet Jonathan's, and guilt fleetingly crosses her face. He wonders if it has just occurred to her that Billie's weekends with *her* must have meant weekends away from *them*.

Weekends away from them.

Things start clicking into place for Jonathan. The missing weekends in Billie's calendar. The Sex Wax receipt. Calvin Lim. The stalkerish photographs of the bungalow, probably Lim's handiwork, too. Billie's emotional distance that last year. And the stay at Motel 6—not to visit her *parents,* maybe, but an attempt to track down the adoption agency documents. Even the money missing from their bank account: He looks around the battered bungalow, noting the shiny new big-screen TV and the top-of-the-line stereo speakers, quite likely purchased with guilt money siphoned from his own bank account.

Not an affair, he understands, and it feels like his entire body has just gone light, a boulder lifting off his back. *A search for her long-lost daughter.* His mind reels. How could he have gotten everything so wrong?

"And your biological father?" he wonders out loud.

She shakes her head. "I never met him. She said he was a"—she lowers her voice to a whisper, mouthing the words as if someone might be listening in—"*convicted felon*. He tried to murder a cop. Not a nice guy."

"Sidney," he says, another piece of the puzzle

snapping into position. He wonders if this is what Harmony didn't want Sidney to tell him the other day—did *she* know about Ryan's existence, too? Is this why she was so secretive?

Ryan seems surprised. "Wait—you know my bio-dad?"

"We met him last weekend," Olive blurts.

"Jeeeeezus." Her brow knits itself together as she parses this information. "But Sybilla said he was in jail for life. Not true?" She frowns as they shake their heads. "Huh. Is he as bad as she said he was?"

Olive glances over at Jonathan. "Well, he *is* a convicted felon," she says. "But he seems pretty benign, actually. More pathetic than dangerous."

Ryan frowns, her eyes glazing over. "Sybilla said . . . Are you sure? This is really confusing." The girl's eyes wander back over to Olive, and she gazes at her for a long time, thinking. Then she leans forward in her chair, folds her legs underneath her, and really starts talking.

. . . About how she was adopted when she was two days old and how her parents never told her, she only found out by accident when she was seventeen ("Aunt Didi got loaded one night and spilled the beans, and boy, did my parents *hit the roof*"), and how she'd never really forgiven them for this. She and her mom barely speak these days, you know? Though maybe that's because her mom is still angry at her for dropping out of college; honestly, her mom is just, like, *angry at life,* she really needs to start doing yoga or meditating or something because she's so unbearable to be around. The last time her mom visited from Fresno, she had a conniption when she found the vape stashed under the sink, and threatened to stop paying an allowance if Ryan didn't buckle down and get herself a "real job" (Ryan rolls her eyes at this and jerks her fingers in air quotes). But whatever, *she's* happy with her life, hitting the waves in the morning, waitressing at a restaurant in town, hanging with her boyfriend, beach bonfires and house parties, whatever, her parents can *deal*. She's only twenty-five, you know? She's *supposed* to be having *fun*.

So yeah, she's just hanging out here in Santa Cruz, doing her thing, when she gets the call from a private investigator. And when she meets Sybilla, everything suddenly makes sense. *Of course* her birth mom would be someone so much cooler than her parents, someone who understands her life choices. She's the kind of mom Ryan always dreamed of, more of a friend than a parent, you know? When they get together the first time, they stay up all night talking, and it feels like Sybilla is trying to soak up everything from all the years she missed. And then when the sun rises, they walk out to the beach and go surfing together and it's like a whole new day dawning.

Olive cuts in again: "My mom's name is carved in the rail at the butterfly beach. Who did that?"

Ryan's eyes drift over to Olive's. She offers a lazy smile. "Oh, we did that together. I carved my name, she carved hers. It's kind of a thing at that break, you know? You go out when the surf is really firing, you leave your name behind."

Jonathan tries to visualize Billie and Ryan kneeling on a staircase, laughing as they hacked at the wooden rail with a Swiss Army knife. He wonders what Billie was thinking during those secret visits. Maybe she regretted giving the child away. Maybe she was nostalgic for the girl she had been. Maybe she was trying to recapture her lost youth, out there in the waves.

. . . So anyway (Ryan continues), they get together a few times over the next six months. And Ryan *loves* hearing about her own history, how she is the result of her mom's wild-child youth, how her biodad was this dangerous criminal type who coerced her into doing some pretty stupid things. They were living off the grid like renegades, but when Sybilla found out she was pregnant, she knew it wasn't a good life for a baby. No way she could raise a kid like that, scared of both the baby's father *and* getting arrested. So she turned her boyfriend in and fled back to her parents' house, where she gave birth to Ryan. (Ryan leans in as she tells this part, folding her elbows over her knees and gazing thoughtfully at her socks.) Sybilla gave Ryan up in order to give her a better life, like, the noble sacrifice, you know? But she never stopped thinking about Ryan, not in all those years. The only reason it took her so long to get in touch was that she felt so guilty about her decision to give Ryan away.

Ryan's face is glowing, her eyes misting over as if she's emotionally moved by the drama of her own genesis. Jonathan watches the girl, transfixed, envisioning a twentysomething Billie fleeing Oregon, pregnant and scared and alone. He can't help wondering about the veracity of this alternate narrative, conveniently painting Billie as an innocent victim rather than the author of her own behavior. Then again, it's possible that getting pregnant was a wake-up call for Billie, that she felt stuck and saw only one way out. The truth probably lies somewhere between Sidney's and Billie's interpretations of events; Jonathan would really never know, would he?

Maybe she was just a scared pregnant kid, he tells himself. *Trying to save her own ass after she made some stupid mistakes.*

His anger is leaking away, and yet a last vestige of doubt clings to him. Billie's whole last year of her life was a lie, it can't be ignored; the entirety of their marriage, she was lying. It was fucked up that Billie withheld this critical information from him all these years. But perhaps, he wonders, it was forgivable? After all, it wasn't a lie of betrayal; it was a lie of omission. A lie born out of shame or insecurity, maybe; a fear that he would hate the person she'd been more than he'd love the person she was now.

Christ, Billie, he thinks, *why did you think you needed to keep all this a secret from me? Did you think I was incapable of understanding? Because I wouldn't have judged you.*

His mind races through their last year together. No wonder he felt so much distance between them, with all *this* happening behind his back. Maybe it can even explain why she cheated on him with Sean: some perverse way of flailing against the mess she'd made. He wonders if Billie *did* try to tell him about Ryan and he didn't hear her.

He studies Ryan, wondering: "Did she tell you about *us*?"

"Well, yeah." Ryan looks up to see the both of

them staring intently at her, and a flush creeps across her face before she averts her gaze and goes back to studying her socks. "She said she was waiting for the right time to tell you about me. That she wasn't, you know, sure how open you'd be to meeting me."

The butterfly beach. Jonathan remembers, now, that day at the beach just a few weeks before Billie died, his wife studying the surfers out at the water's edge. *She brought us here. Maybe she was planning to introduce us and lost her nerve.* It's a consoling thought.

"You're the surfer with the McTavish long-board," Olive interrupts Ryan. "I talked to you on the phone."

"You did?" Ryan looks perplexed. "Weird. When?"

"I showed a picture of Mom to this surfer I met, and he thought you were her."

"Oh yeah, I remember that." Ryan smiles, pleased. "Yeah, Sybilla and I look so much alike, right? Here, check this out—" She jumps up and goes to a drawer, pulls out two photographs, and presents them for examination. One is a faded color snapshot dating back to the seventies, the other a much more recent digital print, but the ponytailed little girls in the photos could be twins if it weren't for the twenty-odd years that separate them. "I went to visit Grandma Rose at her nursing home earlier this year, and she gave this photo to me. Well, actually, I just took it from her room, but I'm pretty sure she isn't ever going to notice, if you know what I mean. That's Sybilla at eight and me at seven. We're practically *identical*." She examines the two photos proudly.

Ryan keeps talking in circles about how thrilling it was to get to know her biomom, the great times they had together, how alike they turned out to be, repeating anecdotes until it occurs to Jonathan that Ryan might be stoned. The light in the room grows darker as Olive and Jonathan sit there, stupefied, unwilling to break the spell. "Yeah, and then a month went by when she didn't get in touch with me, and I didn't know what was going on. Like, was she mad at me or something? But she'd told me not to call or email *her* because, well . . ." She gives the two of them a significant look. "But eventually I went online, and even though Sybilla wasn't on Facebook I looked you two up—I'd done that a few times already, just out of curiosity, right?—and that's when I came across the video." She turns to Jonathan. "The one of you talking at her memorial. It was a nice speech. That's how I found out she died." She twists away then, looking at the wall, so that he can't see her face. Her voice goes tiny and soft: "And . . . yeah. That sucked. I found her just in time to lose her again."

He studies the poor girl, pitying her—how awful to learn about your birth mother's death on Facebook. The futon is shaking and he looks over to see tears on Olive's face, her body heaving with silent sobs. She grips his arm. "Mom's really gone," she gasps. Her damp eyes search his. "Isn't she? She's dead. For real this time."

Jonathan nods. The release in this sudden clarity washes over him, relief and exhaustion leaving him limp. He reaches over and puts an arm around his daughter; she lets him pull her into his embrace. He feels his own eyes well up in concert with his daughter's, and reproaches himself for having poisoned the memory of his dead wife with so much resentment and recrimination. Billie was no saint, but who is? She was flawed like any human. Yes, he has every right to be angry about the lies and the infidelity, but it isn't fair for him to make that the whole story. She wasn't good *or* bad, he decides: Life is more complicated than that, there are endless shades of gray that comprise a human being. Billie *was* a loving mom, a thoughtful wife, she brought magic and joy into their lives. Why not remember her for those things rather than staying bitter about her failings?

Besides, isn't this ultimately how he'd prefer to remember their life together, too? The choice is his, and this is what he is going to choose: a loving family, an often happy marriage, the woman he fell in love with. He had all those things, he felt those feelings. It's a truth, it's *his* truth; and if he's learned anything by this point, it's that truth can be subjective.

When he looks up, he sees that Ryan is looking at Olive with a strange stricken expression, as if it has finally occurred to her that Olive might be grieving, too. "You OK?" she asks awkwardly. "Here, look, I'll get you a tissue." She hurls herself out of the chair and pads into the other room, socks flapping. A fan goes on in the bathroom; he can hear her blowing her nose.

Olive leans her head on Jonathan's shoulder, snuffling softly, swiping at her nose with the sleeve of her sweatshirt. After a moment, she sits upright. "Dad," she says. "I get it now."

"Get what?"

She looks at him with an expression of wonder that makes him nervous. "Don't you see? *This* is what I was supposed to look for all along. Not for Mom. For my sister. That's what Mom was telling me when I saw her in my visions. She wanted us to find Ryan. *She led us here*. She wanted us to know about Ryan because she didn't get the chance to tell us before she died."

He nods thoughtfully, as if this makes perfect sense; because what else is he going to do? He might as well let Olive have this one if it makes her feel better.

By the time Ryan returns to the room, holding out a bedraggled tissue packet, Olive has stopped crying. "You should come stay with us in Berkeley sometime," she tells Ryan. "We should get to know each other."

"Really?" Ryan stops mid-stride; the hand holding the tissue packet falters. "Um, wow. That's nice of you. You know, Sybilla told me she wasn't sure how you guys would react to my existence. That you might be kind of pissed. When she died—I wanted to come pay my respects but I was afraid to just show up. . . ."

Olive stands up, ignoring the tissue packet in Ryan's hand. Instead, she lunges forward across the coffee table and wraps her arms around her sister. From his vantage point on the futon, Jonathan can see the look that crosses Ryan's face: It's one of confusion, even mild panic, as if strangers have just intruded on her favorite fantasy and are insisting on a whole new ending.

"I'm sure this is what Mom would have wanted," Olive says, her voice muffled in Ryan's shoulder. "For all of us to be together. Right, Dad?"

There are moments when you look at your child and suddenly see a stranger there whom you never saw before, someone destined for things you can't even imagine. And you think: *How did they become this person?* Were they molded by you or by the world around them or were they always going to be this way? As Jonathan looks at Olive, he glimpses a woman who has the possibility of being a better person than either he or Billie proved to be. Maybe she won't remain this woman forever; he knows that life might someday drain this out of her. But in this moment, he cannot imagine being more proud of the person she promises to be.

"Of course," he says, willing it into truth. "We'd love to have you."

Olive turns to smile at him, releasing a startled Ryan from her embrace. Olive's cheeks are still mottled from crying and her eyes are rimmed with pink, but Jonathan notices only the new focus in her expression. It's as if she's finally stopped trying to see something that's behind him and is looking straight at him for the first time in months, maybe all year. Her smile is an invitation: *We did this together.*

It takes all the self-control he can muster not to drop to his knees right there and weep with relief.

WHERE THE MOUNTAIN MEETS THE SKY

My Life with Billie Flanagan

———

BY JONATHAN FLANAGAN

I used to believe there was some innate truth about Billie that I might discover by writing about her, like mounting a butterfly on a board and assigning it a classification and a taxonomy, fixing it forever in place. I conveniently forgot that you can't really do that with a person.

After Billie died, I spent a long time idealizing her. That's what you do when someone's gone. You remember only the best parts of them. You reassemble your memories to forget all their flaws, all the fights you had, the things about them that you really kind of hated. It makes your grief feel more powerful to forget how human they were and how human you were with them. Maybe it even assuages your guilt to forget all the dysfunctional parts of your relationship and all the pointless, petty grievances you held against them.

I think Billie wanted me to idealize her, too, which is why she kept the most unpleasant parts of herself hidden. She couldn't bear to be seen as less than perfect.

But all these months on, I know that if there's any truth to be found about my wife, it's that she contained multitudes. The Billie that I met on the bus; the Billie that blew up dams in Oregon; the Billie that devoted herself to our daughter; the Billie that hid the existence of the child she gave away: These were all the same woman, just viewed from a different tilt of the mirror.

I chose this woman. I didn't *want* to be with someone who was easy to pin down: I loved her because she was the challenge that felt right for me.

On the morning that Billie went off hiking in Desolation Wilderness, I woke up before dawn and saw her standing silhouetted in the doorway of our bedroom, already wearing her hiking gear. She was holding a cup of coffee, just watching me.

I pushed myself upright, squinting in the darkness. "What time is it?"

"Early. Sorry, I didn't mean to wake you." She came closer and sat down on the edge of the bed, handing me the coffee. "I'm leaving in a minute."

I've always wondered if I had a premonition that morning, because suddenly I was wide awake and feeling an urge to push back against her. She was leaving us again, and I was tired of it. "Don't go," I said, reaching out to pull her toward me. She smelled like sunscreen and bananas, a whiff of laundry detergent and ancient sweat from the bandanna tied around her neck.

She resisted me, teasing: "Why not?"

"Because. We need you here."

"No you don't," she laughed. "I left two casseroles in the fridge, and anyway, you always order in pizza when I'm gone."

"That's not what I meant."

She was silent. Her eyes glittered in the reflection from the hallway light. "So what *did* you mean?"

I thought about this. Our relationship had been tumultuous for a while; maybe we were starting to heal, but maybe wounds were festering under the Band-Aids we'd slapped on top. Was I willing to peel them back and take a look? Would I still love her if I did?

"I *want* you here," I finally clarified.

"Ah. That's something completely different." She smiled faintly and sat there for a long time. I couldn't read her face in the dark. Then she leaned in to give me a kiss before pulling away and standing up. "I'm pretty sure you're going to be fine without me."

Only now, after all this time, is it starting to feel possible that she was right.

You could say that I know more about Billie today than I did on that morning when she slid off our bed and picked up her backpack; or maybe I know her less. My portrait of her has expanded, grown blurry in places, sharper in others, diluted by the details everyone else keeps adding to the picture. But she will always be the woman I loved. She will always be the love that I lost.

19

JONATHAN SITS ON THE back porch with his laptop, soaking up the last lingering rays of a rare February sunset as he labors over the final pages of *Where the Mountain Meets the Sky*. The prime spot where Billie's easel once stood now houses a double-wide lounge chair that Olive and Jonathan dragged home from the Alameda flea market a few weeks back. The easel itself has been exiled to the garage, along with the painting that will never be finished: out of sight but not entirely forgotten.

The new draft of *Where the Mountain Meets the Sky* is a better book than the one he threw away last fall, Jonathan thinks as he reads it through one last time: more honest, even if he has still glossed over the ugliest aspects of their last years together. He's added in the existence of Ryan, but chose not to mention Billie's infidelity with Sean. Written about some of their more painful fights; removed the angrier passages that made his editor wince. A year from now, as the memoir creeps its way up the *New York Times* bestseller list, he'll be able to read the reviews—"Flanagan frames his marriage as an antimythic love story, one that reveals how even true love is inextricably intertwined with both doubt and loss"—without a twinge of guilt about what he left out. By that point, his memories of the month when he thought that his wife might have faked her own death will have faded.

For now, though, he closes the file and composes a quick email: *Jeff, take a look through the final MS. And tell my editor thanks for giving this a second chance. I think he'll be pleased with the results.*

He hits Send just as the sun vanishes over the fence, and carries his computer into the dining room, where Olive is hunched over her trigonometry textbook, a pencil anchored between her teeth. Recently, she has taken to doing her homework downstairs, near where Jonathan has been feverishly revising his book: a transition that happened without comment and yet has not gone unappreciated by Jonathan. Maybe a different parent would be alarmed by a father and child sitting side by side and staring at separate screens, the silence broken only by the rattling of their keyboards; Jonathan knows that this particular quiet is not a divide but a bond, one that doesn't need words to fill in the space.

This, doing their work together, is just one of the new routines that have slowly developed over the last few months since they found Ryan—fresh patterns naturally evolving now that they've both accepted the fact that their family is *two* rather than *two and one that's gone*. They've started cooking dinner together, and going to the movies on Friday nights. Ryan has even driven up to visit them twice, but despite the best intentions of all involved, it's not so easy to turn a stranger into a family member, especially one who shows up stoned for dinner and talks primarily about herself.

Another thing that's changing too fast: With Olive's senior year in sight, the mailman has begun carpeting their foyer daily with a fresh layer of college catalogs. Jonathan collects these and leaves them in a stack on the entry table, where they are mostly going ignored. Olive is far more interested in a different set of brochures: "International Service Abroad Programme," "Global Routes for Good," "Gap Year in the Galápagos." She has started leaving these in strategic places where he'll see them. Photographs of tan, shiny college-age kids digging latrines or replanting rain forests or standing among groups of smiling indigenous children while holding a lemur. Lots of endangered tortoises, no textbooks.

A gap year: Jonathan is trying to be OK with it. The Ivy-minded counselors at Claremont Prep would have tried to talk her out of it, but Berkeley High—where Olive has been enrolled since November—has a much more liberal attitude about potential futures. There are days when he imagines how painful it's going to be to put her on a plane—likely to land in some village halfway around the globe, a place with no decent hospitals or reliable Internet service—but this is the price of parenthood. Really, he's pleased that she's found something to call her own. He was afraid that the events of the last year might have drained some of the idealism out of her, but instead, she's doubled down. Sudanese famine victims, Guatemalan children, Darwinian finches: Olive is out to rescue them all. Maybe she even will.

"I just sent off the book to my agent," he says now as he sits down next to Olive at the dining room table. "Feel like celebrating?"

Olive looks up, the gnawed pencil drooping wetly from her mouth. "Crack open the champagne?"

"More like let's walk up to Ici's for a cone after dinner."

She nibbles thoughtfully on the pencil. "So. When can I read it?"

"Whenever you're ready." He hesitates. "You sure you want to? It might not be so easy to take."

"*Nothing* this year has been easy to take, Dad." Her sober eyes latch on to his.

He nods and looks down at her homework as he blinks away the sudden emotion washing over him. "What is this, trig? Need any help?"

"What do you know about ambiguous triangles?"

"Nothing."

"Jesus, Dad. You're useless." She smiles at him. "Forget it. I'm hungry, anyway. Let's make dinner."

He follows her into the kitchen and begins emptying the refrigerator onto the counter. Olive has recently decided to upgrade to veganism, which has necessitated a whole new culinary regime that Jonathan is unwilling to tackle on his own. The new negotiated deal requires Olive to provide the recipes, Jonathan to provide the ingredients, and the cooking to be embarked upon jointly. Tonight it's quinoa-kale-tofu stir-fry, a rather curdy mess that Olive determinedly pokes at with a spatula and Jonathan, more skeptical, lashes heavily with flavor-obscuring soy sauce. Their bodies ricochet off each other as they bump around the stove in the fading evening light, still unpracticed at their kitchen pas de deux.

Olive spins around to prod at the tofu and manages to collide with her father, sending a spray of soy sauce across both of their fronts.

Jonathan looks with mock dismay at his dripping arm. "That's a foul," he says. "Two-point penalty." He leans over and pretends to wipe his arm clean on his daughter's shirt.

She pulls away, laughing. "Hey, now I have to change. I was going to wear this tonight."

"Hot date?" He raises an eyebrow.

She blushes as Jonathan grabs a sponge and wipes at her cuff, making the mess even worse. "I have to do laundry anyway," he says. "I'll throw it in."

The laundry doesn't actually need to be done, which is a point of pride for Jonathan: He has finally eked out a conquest over the state of their house. The fridge is stocked; the toilet paper rolls are full; the property tax bills have been paid early. The bananas in the bowl on the counter are perfectly ripe, not even a black spot.

This has been accomplished, in part, by the hiring of a weekly housekeeper, Jonathan's very first splurge when the life insurance check finally arrived in mid-December. The rest of that money—minus the significant chunk that went to pay off the bills and Marcus's loan—is sitting in a bank account until he figures out what to do with it. Billie's death certificate itself is stored in the fireproof lockbox in his bedroom, although now that they have the document in hand, it feels far less significant than it felt when they didn't.

Billie's death certificate, it turns out, looks just like her birth certificate. After it arrived in the mail, Jonathan paired the twinned documents in a folder, the two of them marking the beginning and the end of Billie's life, the meager space between them representing everything she'd actually lived. He sat staring at the two pieces of paper for a long time, feeling something melancholy leak out of him, and then he slipped the folder in a manila envelope.

I forgive you, Billie, he thought; and even if angels didn't then sing down from above, bestowing peace and serenity upon him, it still felt pretty good.

The only real fallout from the last few months has been his breakup with Harmony. Jonathan did this shortly after meeting Ryan in Santa Cruz, in an uncomfortable conversation that went south surprisingly fast. "I'm still not ready for a committed relationship, and I *know* Olive isn't ready for me to be in one," he told her gently as they sat at his kitchen table that day. "Frankly, I'm not even sure that you and I got together for the right reasons, considering all the tangled history we have. Being with you—well, it just feels too much like I'm living in the past."

He'd expected Harmony to be rightfully hurt but also understanding and forgiving, centered about it all. But the pink flush drained from Harmony's face, as if the plug had been yanked from a bathtub. "You're kidding," she said flatly. "It's *still* all about Billie? Even now?"

"I wouldn't put it that way—" he began.

"*Fuck* her," she interrupted. She dropped her hands to the table as she sat bolt upright, her eyes bright with anger. "I spent so much time this last year protecting you from her crap, do you know that? Keeping my mouth shut about everything I knew about her because it wasn't *fair* to you, it would just *hurt* you when you were already hurting. Waiting for you to figure it all out for yourself, what Billie was really like. But you haven't, have you? Despite it all. You still have Billie up on this pedestal, just, like, *worshipping* her."

She jumped up then and walked into his office. He could hear her rummaging around in the desk. When she came back, she had a piece of paper in her hands that she thrust at him. He unfolded it, smoothing out the creases—it looked like it had been crumpled once—and read the first line: *Hi Sybilla, My name is Ryan Ratliff and I'm the daughter you gave away twenty-one years ago.*

He looked up. "I already know about Ryan," he said. "*You* knew?"

Something flashed in Harmony's eyes, something self-righteous and smug. "Of course I knew. I knew Billie was pregnant before *she* did. I went out to visit them in that cabin in the woods and found Billie bent over a toilet, throwing her guts up. She was in denial, but I knew immediately what was going on." She shook her head. "You're forgetting, I was her *best friend*." She said this emphatically, apparently not seeing the irony. And then her voice abruptly went flat: "Who do you think told Sidney last year that he had a kid he didn't know about? *She* sure wasn't going to."

Jonathan clutched Ryan's letter in stiff fingers. "But how'd you get this letter? Why was it in my desk?"

"I was here with her the day it arrived." She pointed to the chair across from her, as if Billie were sitting in it. "We were sitting here drinking wine and chatting while she opened her mail, and all of a sudden she went white as a sheet. I watched her crumple up the letter in her hand and throw it in the trash. When she left the room, I dug it out and saved it. For her sake, you know? Just in case she changed her mind." Harmony turned away from the disbelief in his face. "I put it in the back of your desk drawer a while ago, after she died, thinking that you'd find it there eventually. You deserved to know, but I didn't want to be the one to tell you myself. Because I knew you'd shoot the messenger." Her hands curled into helpless fists on the table. "But don't you see? Billie always got away with everything. She just did anything she wanted, didn't give a damn how it affected anyone else. She thought she was so much better than everyone else. Even when she was your best friend, it felt like she was always looking at you and judging, waiting for you to disappoint her so she could have a reason to turn on you. Over *twenty-five years* she pulled that on me, and like the masochist I am, I just kept coming back for more."

"She's *dead*," he said, growing defensive, not liking this side of Harmony at all. "What's the point in tearing her apart like this?"

She stared at him and then closed her eyes, inhaling deeply. "God, look at this, Billie is gone, and she's still undermining my Zen," she said. Her struggle to realign herself was visible on her face; and then she seemed to give up. She opened her eyes and twisted her lips up in a dark little smile. "You know what? I always wondered if the whole hiking accident thing was a sham. If she just walked off into the sunset in order to avoid dealing with her own messes. Just . . . disappeared and left us all behind as a big 'Screw you.'"

He couldn't stop himself from laughing—the irony was too rich—and when he did, Harmony glared at him. She stood up. "Call me when you come around," she said, and slammed the door on the way out.

But he hasn't called her. He doesn't think he will. Not that he's idealizing Billie so much anymore, but because there no longer seems to be a hole in his life that needs to be filled. Maybe it will gape open again once Olive leaves for destinations unknown, but for now the shape of his life feels whole.

Tonight especially, life feels markedly normal in a way he never would have imagined just a few months earlier. The quinoa is steaming on the stove, and the stir-fry has been loaded onto a platter and transferred to the dinner table, ominously congealing. They are just sitting down for dinner when the doorbell rings. Jonathan and Olive look at each other.

"Expecting someone?" Jonathan asks.

"No," Olive says, getting up.

When Olive flings the front door open, she is stopped cold. Natalie stands there in her post-badminton sweats, her curly hair wet from the locker room. Olive hasn't seen her friend (former friend?) in months—not since the day she bailed out of Claremont before first period, never to return—and it feels as if Natalie has just surfaced out of a time capsule, weirdly unchanged. And yet her friend's hair is a fraction shorter, she's wearing an unfamiliar pair of vintage Bakelite earrings, she's lost a little weight. Looking at Natalie, Olive experiences a sudden melancholy as she realizes there are all these moments with Natalie that she's already missed and will never get back.

Natalie is holding Olive's science fair project of a wind turbine, freckled with dust from its prolonged stay in the Claremont Girls display case. She thrusts the model toward Olive. "They were changing out the display. I thought you might want it."

Olive takes it and stares down at the cardboard model, finding it easier to examine its fading green paint and peeling electrical tape than to meet Natalie's eyes. "You could have trashed it. I honestly don't care."

"Oh," Natalie says, but she doesn't reach to take it back. There's an awkward silence that Olive doesn't feel compelled to try to fill. She checks herself—waiting to be overwhelmed by anger or longing or love—but she mostly feels scraped empty, as if the drag of time has cleared out any excess emotion.

Natalie tucks a damp curl behind her ear, smoothing it nervously into place. "So," she says. "How's Berkeley High?"

Olive shrugs. "I like it," she says. "I'm at the top of my class for a change."

"That's *great*." Natalie says this with a little too much emphasis. "And people are being nice to you? Because I've heard the students there can be really, well, judgey."

"They aren't nearly as bad as the girls at Claremont." The words bite so sharply that Natalie flinches. "Look, we need to talk about how you *outed* me. Totally unacceptable."

"No, you're right. I'm sorry." Natalie fixes her gaze on her UGGs. "I should have kept my mouth shut. But in my defense, I thought I was doing you a favor by telling Dominique. Sometimes it's not *so* bad to have a label, right? So you can find your people, you know, *solidarity;* and a common vocabulary to talk about your oppression? We talked about that in gender studies last month."

"I'm not feeling particularly oppressed," Olive observes. "And I'm also not interested in anyone's labels."

"Oh." Natalie looks at her for a long time, a funny expression on her face. "I heard through the grapevine that you've got a girlfriend now."

Olive feels herself blushing and puts a hand up to cover her cheek. "I don't know if I'd say girlfriend, exactly." She's still getting used to this, being *out,* her gayness just another normal facet of life. She imagined that transferring to a new high school mid-way through junior year would mean she'd been granted a blank slate; a chance for reinvention. But the funny thing was how little she felt like she'd changed—as if there really always was something innately *Olive,* something that she hadn't been able to pinpoint before. (She's still not entirely sure she could, and yet it's there.) The most marked differences were that she walked into her first Berkeley High Gay-Straight Alliance meeting without feeling like a fraud; that she met the eyes of a pretty girl with smooth coffee skin, her name tag reading ALEXIA, and felt a familiar flush; and instead of pushing the feeling away, she leaned right into it. Lesbian, bisexual, straight: The words weren't the important part. The only important part was that she could see what she wanted now.

She sometimes thinks back to the moment when Ryan opened the door that day in Santa Cruz, the disappointment she felt when she realized that she'd come to a dead end. That the path to her mother hadn't actually led to her mother after all. That there were no answers to be found there, at least not the kind of answers she'd been expecting. And then the dawning understanding as she sat there next to her father and listened to Ryan talk: *Your mother is gone, and it is all up to you now. You can't count on anyone else to show you who you are and how everything fits together.*

Three months later, she's finally starting to feel OK with this. She understands now that no matter how hard you try to see yourself—through someone else's eyes or from right inside your own brain—it's impossible to really assemble all the pieces and understand them clearly as one thing. In the same way that you can never get a true grasp on the entirety of the universe, regardless of your position inside it. Life is messy like that, she supposes.

She told her father about Alexia right after Christmas. "I'm glad you told me," he said, and hugged her. "Whatever you are is fine by me, as long as you're happy." It occurred to her that this *was* the right answer, and the one she might never have been given by her mother.

There are still days when she violently misses Billie, when she feels like there are things that she'll never understand, and she wishes her visions would come back so she could at least *try* to talk all this out with her mom. But she hasn't taken Depakote since November, and she's seen nothing at all. The doctor says the bruise on her brain healed, although Olive prefers to believe that once she saw what she needed to see, once the interconnection of everything was revealed and they met Ryan, an invisible circuit shut itself off. Every once in a while, she'll still get that *feeling*—that Billie is lingering somewhere just offscreen, waiting for her cue to speak—but for now, her mother has vanished. The only person Olive can feel in her head is herself; although she's aware that her mom will always be there somewhere, tangled up inside her.

Right now, on her front doorstep, Natalie is looking like she's about to cry. "Claremont sucks without you," she says. "Ming is mean, and Tracy isn't exactly firing on all cylinders. I miss you."

Olive takes this in with a pang of satisfaction, realizing how much power she holds in the moment. It's a curious sensation that she's not entirely sure she enjoys. "Me, too," she says shyly. It's almost like her friend on her porch is a stranger, and they're starting all over again. "Maybe we can hang out sometime. You, me, and Alexia."

"Really? That'd be great." Natalie grins, and her mouth lights up with a gleaming new set of braces.

From inside, Olive can hear her father calling that dinner is getting cold. Out here, the crickets are starting to chirp. The night is clear and cold, a half-moon pressing down on them from above, stars visible over the pale glow of the urban grid. The porch light behind Olive casts her shadow out toward the street, as if illuminating a path forward. She senses her life expanding, on the verge of dividing into two, into three, into a hundred divergent directions. Any one of them a choice that might preclude any other; any one a possible dead end. How will she ever know if she went the right way? How will she know who she might have been if she chose a different route?

But that's something to worry about tomorrow. Right now there's only one clear place that she wants to be.

"I gotta go, my dad's waiting for me," she tells her friend. Then she turns back toward her house, where her father waits in the dining room, the table set for two. "OK, I'm coming!"

EPILOGUE

IT'S MID-MORNING WHEN SHE stops at the lookout where the two trails fork. The view over Desolation Valley is spectacular here—the icy blue lakes set into the forest below, the blinding snowcapped peaks above, the barren fields of granite casting ancient fingers toward the sky. Billie stands there, the sweat pooling between her breasts, and allows herself to cool down for just a minute.

Although the ground beneath her boots is soft from the week's rains, the mountains up ahead are already frosted with snow. The air up here is thin and cold, and her lungs burn with each breath. She doesn't mind it. Nor does it bother her that the pack on her shoulders is particularly heavy, that even with the padding, it's biting into her lumbar so deeply that she already has a bruise across the tops of her hips. She knows how to lean into pain; it's just another challenge to conquer, proof that you're alive.

She unclips her canteen and drinks from it while she consults her map. There: The trail dead-ends at the waterfall, about 1.5 miles ahead. Beyond it, miles of wilderness leading north toward the pleasure boats and casinos of South Lake Tahoe.

A pair of hikers appear over the horizon, coming down the trail toward her. The first people she's encountered all day—it's late in the season to be out here—and she's pleased to see them. She lifts a hand in greeting and waits for them to approach. They are half her age, at least, probably post-college, the girl's high-pitched voice slashing through the silence as they pick their way down the mountain. Billie can hear empty beer bottles clanking in the boy's backpack with each step he takes.

When they get within earshot, she points to her map. "How far ahead is the waterfall?" she calls.

The girl smiles, self-consciously tucking stray blond hairs into her ponytail. "Two miles, maybe three? I'm bad with distances. What do you think, Matt?" She turns eagerly to the boyfriend for validation. He shrugs. The girl looks Billie up and down and furrows her brow. "It's a *really* tough hike."

"Oh, I can handle it," Billie says breezily, and smiles at the girl, thinking, *I'm probably in better shape than you are, kiddo*. "Anyone else up there?"

"Nope," the boyfriend says, absorbed with kicking the mud off his new-looking hiking boots. His face is as thick and florid as Play-Doh. *Beer for breakfast, fat by forty,* Billie thinks.

The girl persists. "There's ice up at the pass. I almost bit it twice on the rocks. Are you out here by yourself?"

"Yes," Billie says, her smile slipping.

"There's no cell reception out there, you know," the girl warns her.

"Well, I wasn't planning on texting anyone anyway." Billie blinks as she remembers the way her cellphone skittered down the side of the cliff when it slipped out of her hands the previous evening: nearly soundless against the all-consuming void of the wilderness. She peered over the edge of the rocks for a long time, finally spotting the shattered glass glittering in the sun, before continuing on. "But don't worry about me. I like hiking alone. It gives your thoughts the room they deserve, don't you think? That's why I come out here. Nice and quiet."

The boyfriend finally glances up to meet Billie's eyes with a flash of recognition. "Quiet, huh? Lucky you."

The girl swats her boyfriend's arm with the back of her hand, absentmindedly, as if this is something they do a dozen times a day. "I *totally* get it," she says. "Anyway. The hike is worth it. The falls are moving fast right now. It's stunning."

Billie murmurs enthusiastically and then watches them go, wondering what kind of an impression she made on them. The girl will remember her, though the boy was already erasing her from his brain before he turned away, just like he clearly plans to erase his girlfriend from his life as soon as they get to the bottom of the mountain. She laughs to herself: *Empty-headed children.*

She waits until they have disappeared down the

trail before lifting her pack and settling it back on her hips; then she turns and picks her way up the rocky path toward the summit.

She'd almost forgotten how glorious it is to be solitary like this, self-reliant, off the grid. How long has it been? Nearly twenty-five years since Oregon; but back then she wasn't alone so much, there were always sleeping bags on the floor, too many unwashed bodies living in too close proximity. Maybe those years of backpacking the world after Oregon went bad. She can still summon that feeling of exhilaration: the stale bun on the empty train carriage, the solo trek down dusty roads toward a town that didn't even merit a paragraph in the guidebooks, the possibility of reinvention and dominion.

Since Olive and Jonathan, she's barely been solitary at all. That's not to say that she's never alone in Berkeley—in fact, she has been *too much* alone recently, with Jonathan working those outrageous hours and Olive evasive, behaving as if the two of them are magnets that have unexpectedly had their polarities reversed—but that is not a solitude of her own choosing, not a solitude into which you can expand. No, *that* is a solitude that smacks of rejection, of abandonment.

There have been too many times in the last few years when Billie has found herself standing at the kitchen sink looking out at the twilight, just waiting for something to happen, feeling the emptiness around her like a suffocating blanket. Aware that the undiluted adulation of husband and child in which she'd once basked—the unexpected flowers, the hand-scrawled notes ("You are the best mommy

EVER!")—was slowly vanishing. Invisible, scraped raw with frustration, she'd stand there and remind herself: She chose to be here. She could have done anything she wanted—been an activist, an artist, someone who did big things—and she selected *this* for herself. Selected *this*, conquered *this*, and did *this* outstandingly well.

And yet she felt herself in danger of losing jurisdiction over her own life. She wasn't entirely sure that *this* wasn't starting to conquer *her*.

Just this last spring, at a routine doctor visit, her gynecologist casually asked her if she'd noticed any early signs of menopause. "You're at the age," the doctor said, handing her a pamphlet. "You need to pay attention." Menopause! The very thought made her dizzy.

After he left the room, she stood there for a long time, examining herself in the reflective metal of the industrial cabinets. With his words echoing in her head, those years of self-assured low maintenance—a beauty routine consisting of moisturizer and a flick of mascara, the confidence that she needed nothing more than a fit body and a sharp mind—now seemed like a rifle shot across the bow of an incoming battleship. She was going to get old. Things were starting to end for her rather than begin. As she stared at her warped reflection, she glimpsed a crone standing at the kitchen sink, a cooling cup of tea in her hand, as Death barreled down on her.

No. She spread her palm over her face and blocked out the reflection.

On her way out of the doctor's office, she impulsively grabbed a handful of complimentary condoms from the jar by the door. Let them fester in her purse, until she ran into Sean at the Elmwood Café a few days later, and he gave her that steady up-and-down look he always gave her—his face twitchy but handsome, his breath hot and meaty in her face. And then, instead of stepping away and putting him in his place, as she usually did, she stepped straight toward him. Thinking, *Fuck you, crone*. Thinking, *I refuse to let go of myself*. Thinking (of course) of Harmony and her perpetual youthful naïveté, her unwavering faith that the people she loved would always love her back in the way she deserved.

This is what the world is really like, Harmony, she thought as Sean put his hand on her knee in the front seat of his vintage Mercedes. *You have to take and take until the moment when no one wants to give to you anymore; and at that moment you will know that you are finished. But until that point, you never, ever relinquish control.*

Sean wasn't really worth her time, sexually speaking—she'd forgotten how lackluster and formal those sorts of casual encounters could be, and she found herself having to fantasize about Jonathan in order to enjoy it at all—but that wasn't the point of the exercise. She slipped out of Sean's bed that day exhilarated and renewed, reassured that life wasn't all over for her just yet. She could still be a locus of attraction and intrigue, the world circling dizzily around her. She retrieved her bra off the floor while Sean snored; and then she thought better of it and left it there. For Harmony's sake: She needed to know what kind of person she was choosing to waste her energies on. Billie was willing to martyr herself upon that berm; she was that kind of good friend.

There is snow by the side of the trail by the time she reaches the mountain pass. Billie breathes heavily, the air too sparse to really fill her lungs. She's rising toward the tree line now, her feet moving from the soft dirt of the forest to the granite of the peaks. The tread of her beloved old hiking boots has worn too thin, and she struggles to get traction on the slick rock. There's a new pair of boots at the bottom of her backpack, but she's not yet ready to let go of the old ones, which feel like slippers on her feet. She picks each step carefully, aware of the dangers of losing her footing.

She slows down to maneuver her way over an icy stretch of the trail and hears the thunder of the waterfall ahead. It's not far at all now. Her stomach is churning itself in a sickly knot; she realizes that she hasn't eaten a thing since the bagel that she devoured at dawn this morning while breaking down her camp. She's weak, a little shaky from low blood sugar.

A few minutes later, she comes around an outcropping, and there it is: a river of water crashing down the side of the mountain, a misty horse's tail dropping almost a thousand feet down a vertical wash of granite. The air here is so thick with the droplets thrown up by the falls that when she touches her face, her hand comes away wet. She can see jagged slicks of ice in the shady spots under the overhanging boulders.

The trail has deposited her about twenty yards

below the crest of the falls. She peers down the mountain to where the water vanishes into a ravine below, and then begins picking her way up the slippery path toward the top.

There, she clambers from rock to rock until she finds a flat area overlooking the rapids and digs into her backpack for a granola bar and some dried mango. The river here is wide and fast, clogged with boulders and tree limbs that didn't quite make it over the falls. She sits there for a long time, watching the water cascade over the side of the mountain, letting the bracing Sierra air clear out the cobwebs in her brain.

All year long, she believed that the shift in her perspective had been triggered the moment when she'd climbed in bed with Sean. But from up here, from this loftier vantage point, she can see that everything actually started changing when Sidney unexpectedly showed up in the Bay Area.

She never imagined that Sidney would get out of jail and *track her down*, for God's sake. For years, she believed that she'd disappeared herself so completely that this part of her past would never catch up to her. Who would look at Billie Flanagan, Berkeley supermom, and see Sparrow the ecoterror turncoat? Well, Harmony, of course: She knew Billie in all her adult iterations, which made her dear but also dangerous, which was why Billie kept her close—letting Harmony be her *best friend* and *confidante*, keeper of her secrets—even if she often couldn't bear Harmony's neediness. Otherwise, the only people who knew anything real about that part of her history were the pair of buffoons who were safely locked up in prison and the loony bin.

It's not that she felt she'd done the wrong thing up there in Oregon. Not at all: She'd merely done what any rational person would do. The initial righteous thrill of blowing up that dam had turned so quickly, with Sidney on his heroin-fueled high and Vincent cresting the far edge of sanity. She'd always known that what they were doing required total rigor—that's why she had dispatched Harmony back to U of O early on, before she could screw things up in that timorous way of hers: Harmony never did have the steeliness necessary for decisive action. But then Sidney and Vincent had grown reckless and sloppy, too, and Billie was stuck in a cabin with them in the middle of nowhere—no TV, no telephone, not even a radio—listening to their increasingly ludicrous plans. Wild mustangs? A *ski* resort? They even started talking about kidnapping a BLM officer, for chrissake. She'd created a monster.

And then, to make everything worse, she got pregnant. She was so distracted by the looming disaster of Sidney that she hadn't even put two and two together until Harmony showed up unannounced at the cabin (grocery bags in her arms, *Just checking on you guys!*, but clearly hoping to be invited into the inner sanctum). When Harmony pointed out what should have been obvious—Billie wasn't just sick, she had *morning sickness*—Billie was horrified: How was she going to find an abortion clinic in the middle of the Cascades? Harmony, proving herself truly useful, had returned a week later with a basket full of pennyroyal and tansy tea, but the abortifacients only made Billie sicker. By then it was too late to deal with the problem any other way. Soon Sidney was going to notice her tiny swelling belly, and knowing him, he'd want to keep their kid.

So now she was stuck having a baby; and stuck with two unreliable clowns who were inevitably going to get caught doing *something* illegal. It was growing quite clear: They were going to take her down with them. If Billie wasn't the one to go to the police, *she* would be the one in jail someday, permanently tethered to the father of this child she didn't want. She wasn't about to take that risk, so yes, she opted for self-preservation: made the call, took their money, and fled. She cleaned herself up before going to the police, smiled, flirted, cried, and the cops applauded her for "being so brave" and "doing the right thing." Sidney, bless his heart, had the integrity not to implicate her, just like she'd known he would. Vincent—well, he was nuts, who would listen to him? In no time at all, she'd shed Elizabeth Smith and Sparrow and disappeared back into Sybilla Thrace, a temporary way station on the way to bigger and better things.

You could say that this was a betrayal—Sidney certainly did when he finally found out what had happened—but really, if Sidney hadn't gone to jail and sobered up, he'd probably be dead by now. And Vincent *needed* to be hospitalized. So really, she did them both a favor.

She was shocked when she first saw Sidney last winter. He had become such a small person, a shadow of the magnetic rebel with whom she had fled the toxic backwater that was Meacham so many years ago. Working as a furniture mover, tending his houseplants in an apartment that smelled like cat piss. When he called her up out of the blue last January, wanting to talk about "old times," she figured he just wanted money. And she *did* owe him that, so she happily starting throwing him a few hundred bucks here and there, figuring a little generosity was a good strategy: She needed him grateful and quiet.

Maybe that would have been the end of it if she hadn't slept with Sean. And if Harmony, in a surprising little burst of vindictiveness, hadn't then gone and told Sidney everything: about Billie's betrayal back in Oregon; and worse, about the existence of the baby.

All those years and Billie had never been particularly interested in meeting the daughter she gave away. Not even when her mother hunted her down years earlier and said she'd received a letter through the adoption agency, written by a girl named Ryan. At the time Billie saw this for what it was—Rose's only ammunition, her pathetic end-of-life attempt to reel her daughter back in—and hung up on her mother. After all, she'd put the baby out of her mind the minute she pushed her out of her body: Even then she knew there was no point in sabotaging her future for the sake of a child who would inevitably be better off without her. So when Ryan's letter arrived in the mail, Billie threw it away.

But now, thanks to Sidney, the membrane between her past and her present had been pierced, and everything was threatening to pour through: the events she had long ago put behind her, the personas she had discarded. When Sidney started demanding that she put him in touch with "his daughter"—or else he'd tell Jonathan and Olive all about her ignoble history, "and how are they going to feel about you after *that*?"—she sensed that things were spinning out of her control.

She wasn't used to feeling powerless. She didn't like the sensation at all.

Maybe she should have told Jonathan the full truth about her history when she first met him, but she was worried that it would drive him away. It was as if she'd conjured him up out of nowhere, that day on the J Church, just when she needed him: The Oregon money was long gone, she was exhausted and alone, and he was ready to scoop her up and take care of her. No one had ever done that for her before, at least not someone so admirable and kind and *good*. She'd surprised herself by falling in love with him, and she wasn't going to risk all that by giving him a reason to dislike her. So she gave him half her life story, just enough to hew to the truth but leaving out the most unflattering details. What would she gain by doing anything different?

Still, she probably should have told Jonathan everything *then;* because she knew if it came out *now,* the situation was going to be far, far worse.

Already, her life in Berkeley felt like it was tearing apart at the seams. She and Jonathan had been growing more and more distant lately; the ambitious, passionate boy who'd thrillingly proposed to her after just six weeks had been siphoned away into a passive workaholic. She'd cheated on him, for chrissake, something she'd never felt compelled to do; and he, in turn, was starting to look at her with something alarming in the set of his mouth, something that looked almost like distaste. How long before Jonathan started demanding *couples counseling* and *date night* and all the other life preservers thrown to desperate, sad marriages on their way toward divorce? The thought made her queasy.

And then, most critically of all, there was Olive. Her beautiful daughter, her reassurance every time Billie looked at her life and questioned what she'd done with it: because she'd accomplished *Olive*. All these years she'd prided herself that her relationship with her daughter was not typical; that even when Olive hit puberty, there would surely be no screaming fights, no surly withdrawal, no withholding of love. She was wrong. Olive had been steadily pulling away ever since they enrolled her in Claremont; and Billie's latest attempt to reestablish their bond—that mother-daughter Muir Trail hike in September—had only made things worse. Olive had behaved like a petulant child, they'd fought, and when Billie had tried to smooth things over, she'd felt her daughter recoil from a hug. As if repulsed by her very touch.

She knew, at that moment, that this was the beginning of the end: that soon, if not already, Olive would be complaining about her to friends. That Billie would be repainted as the harpy mother, the unbearable millstone around her daughter's neck, and she would lose her grip on Olive entirely. Maybe she'd get her daughter back at some point in Olive's twenties. Maybe she'd never get her back at all.

It didn't seem fair: that you could have love, and then that love could fizzle, curdle, ossify into something less wonderful than what it once was. And then you were stuck, because ultimately, love is a kind of trap. Once you find it, you can't deviate from that commitment without everyone getting hurt. You can't just leave. Instead, *need* wins out over *freedom;* and everyone stands around feeling wounded and bitter, letting inertia take over.

She knew this because she *did* try to leave once, a few years back, when the claustrophobia and dissatisfaction first started creeping in. There had been a fight with Olive and Jonathan—the two of them ganging up on her for some idiotic reason, something about a sleepover with Natalie—and she found herself packing a bag, not quite sure where she was going but knowing she couldn't spend one more moment *there*. She scribbled an apologetic note—*I love you, I'm sorry, don't worry about me*—and then drove right past the Berkeley Bowl, past the Trader Joe's down the road, straight down University, and east onto Highway 80. By the following morning, she'd made it all the way to Utah, with no intention of coming back.

But then, about the time she saw the Wasatch Range in the distance, she started imagining Olive's and Jonathan's faces when they realized that she'd left them. Olive, crying until she retched, the way she used to as a baby. Jonathan, drowning in self-blame. Billie couldn't bear to be the cause of that pain. It began to dawn on her that they would eventually come to hate her, that *everyone* would hate her: She would forever be the Bad Mother, the mom who abandoned her family.

So she pulled off the road a half hour outside Salt

Lake City and reluctantly turned her car back west. By the time she rolled back into the driveway, she'd half convinced herself that the whole episode had never happened. That everything was just hunky-dory. She stepped back into the house and smiled at her beloved husband, went to give her darling daughter a kiss, warmed herself on the fire of their delighted relief. Then tried to pretend that she hadn't just walked right back into a box of her own making.

And yet here she is, four years later, opening the lid of the box again.

The sun is directly overhead now, marking midday. Time to move. She stands up and tucks the snack wrapper into her backpack; tosses a tough piece of dried mango into the river below. It lands on the edge of a current and swirls in pointless circles before getting caught up in the rapids. It teeters perilously on the brink of the waterfall and then, just like that, it's gone. So easily disappeared.

She stands up and stretches, peering across the rapids to the other side. The woods there are denser than they are on this side of the river; they climb toward the adjacent summit in a beckoning way. She shades her eyes and looks up: The next mountaintop over must have an incredible view of Lake Tahoe. There is no path that she can see, just a slight opening in the trees through which a deer or a slender woman would fit. On her map, the trail dead-ends right at the waterfall, but Billie can see that there's much of interest on the other side. Probably no one has hiked through there in years, everyone always so sensibly sticking to the marked routes.

She shoulders her backpack and reties the laces of her boots nice and tight. Then she jumps from the boulder where she's been sitting and lands, heavily, on a flat rock right on the edge of the water. There's a dead log lodged in the rapids a few feet ahead, and she coils herself up like a spring and jumps again, landing with a jolt that she can feel in her knees. The log sinks a bit in the water but holds under her weight. The backpack bites into her hips, and she tightens the straps to keep it square against her body. She can't afford to lose her balance.

She leapfrogs like this most of the way across the river, from rock to rock, the raging water sloshing across the top of her boots until her socks grow sodden and clammy around her toes. She feels almost as graceful as she was when she was twenty years old and scaling old-growth redwoods with her bare hands. *I still got it*, she thinks.

And then, when she's still too far out from the other bank of the river, she gets stuck. The next cluster of boulders is at least five feet away, a daunting distance, with a lacy crust of ice across the top. She turns in a circle, assessing her options, but there's no other way across. Downstream, the waterfall is so loud that it's drowning out the buzz of the adrenaline in her head.

She gathers herself and leaps.

Her left foot misses the rock entirely, plunging her left leg into the freezing water right up to her thigh. The other foot hits the patch of ice and slides sideways, fruitlessly scrambling to gain purchase with the worn treads of her boots. She flings herself forward in the hope that the weight of the backpack will pin her in place against the boulder. Her hands scrabble at the granite, seeking a handhold, the skin tearing off her fingertips. The rapids greedily suck at her, doing their best to pry her loose. *Christ.*

And then, just as she's starting to panic that she's going to get pulled into the water and tumbled over the falls, her right boot lodges in a fissure in the rock. Panting, she carefully bellies upward until she's above the waterline again. She reaches down and rinses her bleeding hand in the river and then sticks a finger in her mouth. The taste puckers her tongue: sweat and blood and mud.

The rest of the way across is simple, and in just minutes she's on the other side. She turns to look back at her route across the river—from over here, it looks like an impossible crossing—and then she walks into the woods.

The forest is thick and dark and loud with buzzing insects. She walks just inside the trees, parallel to the water's edge, knocking away dead brush to make a path for herself. After a few minutes, she emerges onto a sunny overhang, overlooking the waterfall but hidden by the trees from the trail on the other side. She peels off her boots and cargo pants and lays them out to dry.

She lies back on a sun-warmed rock in her underwear and closes her eyes.

. . . The funny thing is that once Sidney planted the notion in her head, she found that she *did* want to meet the child after all. With her marriage stagnating, Olive pulling away—the overall sense of a crisis building to a head—*Ryan* was a thread that she couldn't leave hanging. Maybe she was moti-

vated initially by the need to find her daughter before Sidney did—to make sure he didn't poison the
well before she arrived and turn the girl against
her—but when she walked into that grungy little
Santa Cruz diner and saw *herself* sitting there . . .
well, something inside her just lit up.

It was a fascinating exercise, to see how much of
herself was present in the girl whom she'd had no
hand in raising. There was Ryan's startling appearance, of course, but also a streak of familiar selfregard and an instinct for self-preservation. And
maybe Ryan was more frivolous than Billie ever was,
spoiled by her parents' money and a lack of
ambition—she smoked far too much pot for her
own good, that was clear—but she obviously appreciated the buzz of a life lived on the edge. In so many
ways, Ryan was more like Billie than Olive had
proved to be. Floating on a surfboard in the ocean
alongside Ryan, Billie felt as if she might slip out of
this skin and into her younger clone's and try on a
new life. A picture began to grow in her mind, options opening themselves to her like a flower in
bloom.

Living a double life, sneaking around behind her
family's back: It made her feel oddly alive, as if she
were once again firmly at the helm of her life.
Enough that she could bear, for a while, the way her
world in Berkeley was continuing to come apart at
the seams. She knew there was a clock ticking somewhere in the background: Sidney couldn't be deterred forever, and Billie's demurrals—*The agency
records were lost, I'm trying to find her*—were only
going to last so long. Meanwhile, Harmony was still

in the wings, licking her wounds at her meditation retreat or wherever she was, waiting to blow everything up. Billie had begun preparing, just in case. And yet she hoped she might be able to go on like this in perpetuity.

But then Harmony resurfaced and, in another surprise twist, threw herself at Jonathan. Which shouldn't have been such a shock: Billie had always suspected Harmony had a crush on him, but it was nothing to worry about, really, Jonathan was such a straight arrow. What she couldn't believe was that he *told* her about the kiss. And yet wasn't that also so Jonathan, always so sweetly concerned about doing the *right thing*? *We don't lie to each other,* he said, *we don't have that kind of marriage,* clearly unaware that they actually *did*. It would be funny if it weren't so phenomenally complicated, so indicative of how terribly tenuous everything had become.

That was when Billie knew it was time to take her family to the butterfly beach.

Fate. Funny, she never really liked the notion that some force other than her own could be allowed to steer her life. And yet it was kind of exciting, wasn't it? To know that her path might go in one of two directions and she was leaving it to the toss of a coin?

That morning at the beach, Billie watched Ryan emerge from the ocean with her surfboard under her arm—just as Billie had known that she would. She watched Ryan towel herself off, flirt with a preening group of boys, utterly oblivious to the family sitting at the far end of the cove. Billie's pulse started firing so rapidly that she was sure Jonathan must be able to feel it through her shirt. She had to lean forward so that she wasn't pressed against his legs anymore: She couldn't bear the feeling of his skin against her own.

She watched, and waited.

If Ryan looked up and noticed her mother sitting at the far side of the beach, and came over to her, Billie's world as she knew it would be blown apart. She would be forced to come clean to Olive and Jonathan and face the consequences: divorce, quite possibly. Estrangement from her daughter (daughters?). Or maybe—though less likely—the four of them would somehow come together as a blended family, with Billie at the center of it all.

If Ryan *didn't* see her, though, Billie would take it as a sign that she'd been given leave to put all this behind her once and for all. That her work here was done, and her freedom had been granted. Because why else would she get off so easy?

Less than a football field divided Olive from Ryan, both of her daughters lingering on the edge of the sea. One engrossed in seashells; the other flaunting her abs to a bunch of strangers. Neither even glanced in the other's direction. And then Ryan shouldered her surfboard and began sauntering toward the parking lot, so self-involved that she failed to look more than three feet in front of her. In a matter of a minute, Ryan was gone.

And that was it. It was done. Billie's pulse slowed, her breath came back. It had been decided for her, and she was back in control.

On the far side of the river, the light is shifting, growing darker. Billie opens her eyes and blinks, stands up. Her pants are still damp, but they are dry enough to drag over her legs. Overhead, a scrim of clouds has moved in to cover the sun, and she realizes she's shivering from the chill in the air. She'll need to start hiking soon in order to make enough distance before setting up camp for the night.

She picks up one of her sodden hiking boots and straps it to the outside of her backpack with a bungee cord. Picks up the other and holds it in her hand, hesitating.

. . . Thinking of the way Jonathan looked at her in the dark yesterday morning. *I* want *you here,* he said, so sincerely; and she almost had a change of heart, until she saw in his eyes all the work that would have to be done, everything that was already lost.

. . . Thinking of Olive, who hadn't even stirred when Billie slipped into her bed just a few hours before. She'd lain there by her daughter's side, watching her sleep, waiting for her to wake up and start talking: *Tell me what's in your heart today.* But Olive just lay there softly breathing, an innocent lost in her inscrutable dreams. Where did her generous heart come from, this daughter of hers? Because there in the dark, Billie understood that she could not locate that goodness inside herself; knew that she was instead scraping away at Olive's with her own sharpened edges.

For two hours Billie had lain there, unable to drag herself away. Her heart ached, unexpectedly pierced with guilt. And then, just as the birds began to stir in the garden outside, an unexpected moment of clarity: *Sometimes you have to make bad choices in order to protect the people you love from yourself. Olive needs to find herself, and yet I've been trying to turn her into me. I'm not a perfect mom, but I'm good enough to know I have to save my daughter from that. Motherhood demands sacrifice, in so many forms.* She pressed her palm against her daughter's soft cheek, as light as a sparrow, and then climbed from under the covers.

"You're going to be just fine," she says out loud now, though she's not sure whom she's talking to: her husband, her child, herself? Maybe all three. She pats the zippered pocket of the backpack just to confirm that the folded wad of cash is there, six months' worth of withdrawals in hundred-dollar bills. Underneath that, she can feel the corners of the Danish passport that Calvin Lim purchased for her off the Darknet a few weeks back, her own photo and the signature *Alina Pedersen*. Then she walks over to the precipice, just a few feet from where the waterfall plummets into a seemingly bottomless void.

She lifts the hiking boot and throws it as far as she can.

Leave, and they'll hate you. Die, and they'll love you forever.

ACKNOWLEDGMENTS

FIRST, THANKS TO MY AGENT, Susan Golomb, for your indefatigable work on my behalf. I can't imagine where I'd be without you as my champion.

Julie Grau's discerning eye and inspired vision shaped this book into what it is. It's been a pleasure to once again work with you and everyone else at Spiegel & Grau and Random House, including Laura Van der Veer, Cindy Spiegel, Maria Braeckel, Sharon Propson, Avideh Bashirrad, Andrea DeWerd, Leigh Marchant, and Jess Bonet. Thanks also to Gretchen Koss, quick on the draw and sharp as a tack.

I am indebted to those who gave me feedback, from the first stumbling pages to the very last words—including Lisa Hamilton Daly, Meredith Bagby, Suzanne Rico, Annabelle Gurwitch, Hadley Rierson, and Laura Millersmith. And above all, un-ending gratitude to the enduring Hive—Benj Hewitt,

Colette Sandstedt, Greg Harrison. I cannot tell you how much it means to me that I can always count on you for a smart read when I'm the most stuck.

The best writing experiences I've had while working on this book were with my writing retreat partners, whose talent and companionship were equal to that of the most exclusive artist colony: Carina Chocano, Keshni Kashyap, and Dawn MacKeen.

I couldn't have finished this book if it weren't for Suite 8 and all the writers there, who provided me with an endless well of inspiration and chocolate—including Erica Rothschild, Jillian Lauren, Marian Belgray, Tim Kirkman, Josh Zetumer, and many of the writers I've already mentioned.

Thanks to my Silver Lake (and beyond) friends, who keep me sane; and to my family—Pam, Dick, and Jodi—for a lifetime of encouragement.

This book is dedicated to my children, Auden and Theo, whose arrival in the world may have slowed down my writing, but who also inspired me to become a more thoughtful novelist.

And last but not least, thanks again to my husband, Greg, whose support and belief in me were what brought this book to life. You nourish my creativity and fill me with love. I couldn't have found a better partner in life.

WATCH ME DISAPPEAR

JANELLE BROWN

A READER'S GUIDE

QUESTIONS AND TOPICS FOR DISCUSSION

1. "Love is blind," the saying goes. Discuss the ways that love blinds the characters in the novel: Jonathan, Olive, Harmony, and Billie herself. Have you ever been in a situation where love blinded you to a truth that in retrospect was glaringly obvious?

2. Is it natural for a mother to want to leave her family sometimes, even if most don't act on it? How would the story be different if Jonathan had been the one to disappear?

3. How do you think the author meant to portray Jonathan? Did his relationship with Harmony change the way you saw him?

4. Do you believe there was genuine love in Billie and Jonathan's marriage? To what extent is some degree of secrecy a normal, even necessary, part of a marriage?

5. Olive felt that she was receiving psychic messages from her missing mother. Do you think this really was something paranormal? Part of a mother-daughter bond? A symptom of her epileptic attacks? Have you ever felt some kind of unexplained communication with a parent or child or someone else you love? If so, did you experience it on your own—as a dream or an experience of heightened intuition—or with the help of a psychic medium, like the Sharon Parkins character in the novel?

6. How does Olive's coming out fit into the novel's larger theme of searching for one's true identity? Discuss the ways other characters have sought to discover—or change—their personas.

7. Throughout the novel, you get to see Billie through different perspectives—those of her daughter, her husband, her friends, and more. After finishing the novel, did you feel that you knew who Billie really was, or did you still find her to be a mystery?

8. Is Billie a classic femme fatale? Why or why not? Is she a feminist character?

9. Do you think Billie's actions were the result of freedom of choice or of destiny?

10. As you read, there are many clues that suggest different possible endings for Billie. Were you surprised by the ending? If you were, how did you think it would end, and why?

Also by *New York Times* bestselling author

JANELLE BROWN

Two wildly different women—one a grifter, the other an heiress—are brought together by the scam of a lifetime.

Turn the page for a sneak peek . . .

1.

THE NIGHTCLUB IS A temple, devoted to the sacred worship of indulgence. Inside these walls there is no judgment: You'll find no populists, no protestors, no spoilsports who might ruin the fun. (The velvet ropes out front stand sentry against all *that*.) Instead, there are girls in fur and designer silk, swanning and preening like exotic birds, and men with diamonds in their teeth. There are fireworks erupting from bottles of thousand-dollar vodka. There is marble and leather and brass that is polished until it gleams like gold.

The DJ drops a bass beat. The dancers cheer. They lift their phones toward the sky and vamp and click, because if this is a church then social media is their scripture; and that tiny screen is how they deify themselves.

Here they are: the one percent. The young and

ultra-rich. Billionaire babies, millionaire millennials, fabu-grammers. "Influencers." They have it all and they want the whole world to know. *Pretty things, so many pretty things in the world; and we get them all,* says their every Instagram photo. *Covet this life, for it is the best life, and we are #blessed.*

Out there, in the middle of it all, is a woman. She's dancing with abandon in a spot where the light hits her just *so* and glimmers on her skin. A faint sheen of sweat dampens her face; her glossy dark hair whips around her face as she swivels her body to the grinding beat. The waitresses headed to the bottle-service tables have to maneuver around her, the fizzing sparklers on their trays in danger of setting the woman's hair alight. Just another L.A. party girl, looking for a good time.

Look close, though, and you can see that her half-closed eyes are sharp and alert, dark with watching. She is watching one person in particular, a man at a table a few feet away.

The man is drunk. He lounges in a booth with a group of male friends—gelled hair, leather jackets, Gucci sunglasses at night; twentysomethings who shout over the music in broken English and baldly leer at the women who careen past. Occasionally, this man will plunge his face to the table to do a line of cocaine, narrowly missing the flotilla of empty glasses that litter its surface. When a Jay-Z song comes on, the man climbs up on the seat of his banquette and shakes up a giant bottle of champagne—a rare large-format bottle of Cristal—and then sprays it over the heads of the crowd. Girls shriek as $50,000 worth of bubbly ruins their dresses and drips to the floor, making them slip in their heels. The man laughs so hard he nearly falls down.

A waitress lugs over a replacement bottle of champagne, and as she sets it on the table the man slips his hand right up under her skirt as if he's purchased her along with the bottle. The waitress blanches, afraid to push him off lest she lose what promises to be a sizable tip: her rent for the month, at the very least. Her eyes rise helplessly to meet those of the dark-haired woman who is still dancing a few feet away. And this is when the woman makes her move.

She dances toward the man and then—oops!— she trips and falls right into him, dislodging his hand from the waitress's crotch. The waitress, grateful, flees. The man swears in Russian, until his eyes focus enough to register the windfall that has just landed in his lap. Because the woman is pretty—as all the women here must be in order to get past the bouncers—dark-featured and slight, maybe a hint of Spanish or Latina? Not the sexiest girl in the club, not the most ostentatious, but she's well dressed, her skirt suggestively short. Most important: She doesn't blink as the man swiftly shifts his attention to her; doesn't react at all to the possessive hand on her thigh, the sour breath in her ear.

Instead, she sits with him and his friends, letting him pour her champagne, sipping it slowly even as the man puts back another half-dozen drinks. Women come and go from the table; she stays. Smiling and flirting, waiting for the moment when the men are all distracted by the arrival of a tabloid-friendly basketball star a few tables over; and then she swiftly and silently tips the contents of a clear vial of liquid into the man's drink.

A few minutes pass as he finishes his drink. He pushes back from the table, working to upright himself. This is when she leans in and kisses him, closing her eyes to push away her revulsion as his tongue—a thick, chalky slug—probes hers. His friends goggle and jeer obscenities in Russian. When she can't take it anymore, she pulls back and whispers something in his ear, then stands, tugging at his hand. Within a few minutes they are on their way out of the club, where a valet jumps to attention and conjures up a banana-yellow Bugatti.

But the man is feeling odd now, on the verge of collapse; it's the champagne or the cocaine, he's not sure which, but he finds he can't object when the woman tugs the keys from his hand and slips behind the wheel herself. Before he passes out in the passenger seat, he manages to give her an address in the Hollywood Hills.

The woman carefully maneuvers the Bugatti up through the streets of West Hollywood, past the illuminated billboards selling sunglasses and calfskin purses, the buildings with fifty-foot-tall ads hawking Emmy-nominated TV series. She turns up the quieter winding roads that lead to Mulholland, white-knuckling it the whole time. The man snores beside her and rubs irritably at his crotch. When they finally get to the gate of his house, she reaches over and gives his cheek a hard pinch, startling him awake so that he can give her the code for entry.

The gate draws back to reveal a modernist behemoth, with walls entirely of glass, an enormous translucent birdcage hovering over the city.

It takes some effort to coax the man out of the passenger seat, and the woman has to prop him upright as they walk to the door. She notes the security camera and steps out of its range, then notes the numbers that the man punches into the door's keyless entry. When it opens, the pair is greeted by the shrieking of a burglar alarm. The man fumbles with the alarm keypad and the woman studies this, too.

Inside, the house is cold as a museum, and just as inviting. The man's interior decorator has clearly been given the mandate of "more is more" and emptied the contents of a Sotheby's catalog into these rooms. Everything is rendered in leather and gold and glass, with furniture the size of small cars positioned under crystal chandeliers and art clogging every wall. The woman's heels clack on marble floors polished to a mirror gleam. Through the windows, the lights of Los Angeles shimmer and pulse: the lives of the common people below on display as this man floats here in the sky, safely above it all.

The man is slipping back into oblivion as the woman half drags him through the cavernous home in search of his bedroom. She finds it up a set of stairs, a frigid white mausoleum with zebra skin on the floors and chinchilla on the pillows, overlooking an illuminated pool that glows like an alien beacon in the night. She maneuvers him to the bed, dropping him onto its rumpled sheets just moments before he rolls over and vomits. She leaps back so that the mess doesn't splash her sandals, and regards the man coolly.

Once he's passed out again, she slips into the bathroom and frantically scrubs her tongue with toothpaste. She can't get his taste out of her mouth. She shudders, studies herself in the mirror, breathes deeply.

Back in the bedroom, she tiptoes around the vomit puddle on the floor, pokes the man with a tentative finger. He doesn't respond. He's pissed the bed.

That's when her real work begins. First, to the man's walk-in closet, with its floor-to-ceiling displays of Japanese jeans and limited-edition sneakers; a rainbow of silk button-downs in ice cream colors; fine-weave suits still in their garment bags. The woman zeroes in on a glass-topped display table in the center of the room, under which an array of diamond-encrusted watches gleam. She pulls a phone out of her purse and snaps a photo.

She leaves the closet and goes back into the living room, making a careful inventory as she goes: furniture, paintings, objets d'art. There's a side table with a clutch of silver-framed photos, and she picks one up to examine it, curious. It's a shot of the man standing with his arm flung over the shoulders of a much older man whose pink baby lips are twisted up in a moist grin, his wobbly folds of flesh tucked defensively back into his chin. The older man looks like a smug titan of industry, which is exactly what he is: Mikael Petrov, the Russian potash oligarch and occasional sidekick to the current dictator. The inebriated man in the other room: his son, Alexi, aka "Alex" to his friends, the fellow Russian rich kids with whom he pals around the planet. The mansion full of art and antiques: a time-honored means of laundering less-than-clean money.

The woman circles the house, noting items that

she recognizes from Alexi's social media feed. There's a pair of Gio Ponti armchairs from the 1960s, probably worth $35,000, and a rosewood Ruhlmann dining set that would go for well into the six figures. A vintage Italian end table worth $62,000—she knows this for sure because she looked it up after spotting it on Alex's Instagram (where it was stacked with Roberto Cavalli shopping bags and captioned with the hashtag #ballershopping). Because Alexi—like his friends, like the other people in the club, like every child of privilege between the ages of thirteen and thirty-three—documents his every move online, and she has been paying close attention.

She spins, takes stock, listens to the room. She has learned, over the years, how houses have character of their own; their own emotional palette that can be discerned in quiet moments. The way they stir and settle, tick and groan, the echoes that give away the secrets they contain. In its shimmery silence this house speaks to her of the coldness of life inside it. It is a house that is indifferent to suffering, that cares only about gleam and polish and the surface of things. It is a house that is empty even when it is full.

The woman takes a moment she shouldn't, absorbing all the beautiful works that Alexi owns; noting paintings by Christopher Wool, Brice Marden, Elizabeth Peyton. She lingers in front of a Richard Prince painting of a nurse in a bloodstained surgical mask, being gripped from behind by a shadowy figure. The nurse's dark eyes gaze watchfully out of the frame, biding their time.

The woman is out of time, herself: It's nearly

three A.M. She does a last pass of the rooms, peering up into the corners, looking for the telling gleam of interior video cameras, but sees nothing: too dangerous for a party boy like Alexi to keep footage of his own misdeeds. Finally, she slips out of the house and walks barefoot down to Mulholland Drive, heels in hand, and calls a taxi. The adrenaline is wearing off, fatigue setting in.

The taxi drives east, to a part of town where the houses aren't hidden behind gates and the meridians are filled with weeds rather than manicured grass. By the time her taxi deposits her at a bougainvillea-covered bungalow in Echo Park, she is nearly asleep.

Her house is dark and silent. She changes clothes and creeps into her bed, too tired to rinse off the film of sweat and smoke that clings to her skin.

There is a man already there, sheets wrapped around his bare torso. He wakes instantly when she climbs into bed, props himself up on an elbow, and studies her in the dark.

"I saw you kissing him. Should I be jealous?" His voice is lightly accented, thick with sleep.

She can still taste the other man on her mouth. "God, no."

He reaches across her and flicks on the lamp so that he can examine her more closely. He runs his eyes across her face, looking for invisible bruises. "You had me worried. Those Russians don't joke around."

She blinks in the light as her boyfriend runs his palm across her cheek. "I'm fine," she says, and all the bravado finally runs out of her so that she's shaking, her whole body quivering from stress (but also, it's true, with giddiness, with the high of it all). "I drove him home, in his Bugatti. Lachlan, I got inside. I got everything."

Lachlan's face lights up. "Fair play! My clever girl." He pulls the woman to him and kisses her hard, his stubble scraping her chin, his hands reaching under her pajama top.

The woman reaches back for him, sliding her hands up across the smooth skin of his back, feeling the clench of his muscles under her palm. And as she lets herself sink into that twilight state between arousal and exhaustion, a kind of waking dream in which the past and present and future come together into a timeless blur, she thinks of the glass house on Mulholland. She thinks of the Richard Prince painting, of the bloodied nurse watching over the frigid rooms below, silent guardian against the night. Trapped in her glass prison, waiting.

As for Alexi? In the morning, he will wake up in a dried puddle of his own urine, wishing he could detach his head from his body. He will text his friends, who will tell him he left with a hot brunette, but he will remember nothing. He will wonder first whether he managed to fuck the woman before he passed out, and whether it counts if he doesn't remember it; and then, somewhat idly, he will wonder who the woman was. No one will be able to tell him.

I could tell him, though, because that woman— she is me.